HOME FRONT

A NOVEL

BY

ELAINE ULNESS SWENSON

HOMEFRONT

Author - Elaine Ulness Swenson
Publisher - McCleery & Sons Publishing

International Standard Book Number: 1-931916-06-3
Printed in the United States of America

ACKNOWLEDGMENT

I *would like to thank Arnold and Gerda Jordheim for allowing me to interview them for this novel. Gerda grew up in Germany during the war and the experiences of Eva, a character in this book, reflect many of the horrifying things that Gerda herself endured and lived through. Arnold and Gerda met in Germany when he was in the service, as did Eva, and Allan, another character in this story.*

Other books by Elaine Swenson:
First the Dream
Bonanza Belle

Dedicated to the generation of Americans who served their country during World War II——those who wore their country's uniform and those who supported the war effort on the home front.

CHAPTER 1

May, 1942

Carrie thought she heard the telephone ringing. She quickly put the last clothespin on the pair of George's overalls that she had been hanging on the line and made a dash for the house. Two more rings. *Would she make it in time?* She just couldn't miss the call that she had been waiting for all day.

Her son-in-law, Stan, had phoned early that morning to announce that Livvie had started labor and that he would be taking her into Fargo to the hospital.

That had been what? About eight hours ago now?

"Hello!" Carrie said, out of breath, grabbing the receiver as she slumped down onto a nearby chair.

"Carrie! This is Stan. Guess what! The baby came about an hour ago. She's perfect and Livvie is doing just fine!"

"Oh, it's a girl, then! How wonderful!" Carrie felt relief fill her body and soul.

"Yes, and she is so beautiful!" Stan exclaimed excitedly. "When can you come and see her?"

"Oh, soon, I hope. Just as soon as we can." Carrie rose from the chair and peered out the kitchen window. "I can't wait to tell George. Give our best to Livvie. Oh, and congratulations, Stan, to both of you."

"I have to call my folks now," announced Stan, "so I'll talk to you later. Goodbye."

"Goodbye." Carrie fumbled, trying to return the receiver to its hook. She ran out the back door in search of her husband.

"Oh, George," she shouted, as she spotted him walking from the machine shed on his way to the barn.

He quickened his steps when he saw his wife running towards him. "Have you had news?" he called.

"Yes! Stan just called and the baby is here! It's a girl and everyone is fine!" Carrie stopped to catch her breath before she could go on.

"That's wonderful," George said, as he put his arm around his wife's shoulders. "I've been thinking about Livvie all day."

"Me, too," agreed Carrie. "I hardly dared to leave the house but don't you suppose the call came when I was out hanging up the clothes!"

The couple walked back to the house together. "I'll get you a cup of coffee," said Carrie.

George cleaned himself up at the washbasin and took a chair by the table. Carrie filled a cup and sat down opposite him. They looked at each other and smiled— smiles of relief that it was all over.

"When can we make a trip to Fargo to see them?" asked Carrie.

"Well, what is today? Friday? Perhaps we should wait until Sunday and go in right after church."

"I guess I can wait that long," laughed Carrie. "Oh, I have so many phone calls to make!" She jumped up and went for the telephone.

"That will take you until Sunday to get off the phone," joked George.

"I'll call over to Freddie's first." Looking at the clock, she remarked, "I don't suppose that he's home from the bank yet but Lenora will be home, I'm sure." After being connected by the operator, she waited impatiently for someone to answer.

"Oh, Lenora, I've got great news," she told her daughter-in-law. "Stan just called and the baby came this afternoon and she and Livvie are just fine."

"She?" asked Lenora.

"Yes, it's a girl!"

"Well, that's wonderful! How big was she and what did they name her?"

"You know, I didn't even find out all that. Stan was in a hurry to call his folks. I suspect he'll call again tomorrow, even if it is long distance."

"I'm sure you'll be driving into Fargo soon, then, to see them," remarked Lenora.

"George says we'll wait until Sunday afternoon."

"Do you think you can wait that long?" laughed Lenora. "It sounds like you're pretty excited."

"Oh, I am!" exclaimed Carrie. "Is that little Larry I hear crying in the background?"

"Yes, he just woke from his nap when the phone rang. I couldn't decide if I should run for the phone or the baby!"

"Well, I'll let you go. I have more people to call but I wanted you and Freddie to be the first to know," stated Carrie. "And what is Sandra busy with?"

"She took a nap, too, this afternoon, believe it or not, and is still sleeping. At three years of age, she's getting to that point where she won't nap every day. Maybe every other day or so."

"We haven't seen the kids for almost a week now. Maybe we'll drive into town real soon for a little visit."

"You do that," answered Lenora, "And I'll tell Freddie about the new baby as soon as he steps in the door."

On Sunday, after church, George and Carrie headed into Fargo. Carrie had packed sandwiches and a thermos of coffee so they ate while driving.

"Well, everyone at church was excited about the news today, weren't they?" George remarked to his wife.

"Yes, and I'm glad that Stan called last night with more information. I sure like the name they picked out. Cheryl May. Cheryl May Murphy. That has a nice sound to it."

"Yes, I think so, too," responded George. "Our three grandchildren all have such modern sounding names, don't you think? Sandra Kay, Lawrence and now Cheryl May."

"I think they made good choices," agreed Carrie.

Carrie sat back in the seat and sighed. "It's nice to have something to think about besides the war for awhile, isn't it?"

Since the Japanese had bombed Pearl Harbor about five months earlier, their lives had not been the same.

"I hope none of our family has to go into the service," said Carrie. "There's Freddie, Stan, Stan's brothers and a couple of my sister's grandsons from near Spring Grove that would be about that age, too." She was counting them off on her fingers.

They drove in silence for awhile, each reflecting on what the war might mean for them.

"Why don't you pour me a little more of that coffee," suggested George, "and I'll take one more sandwich."

As they continued north from Kindred a few miles, they drove by the turn that would lead to Stan and Livvie's place. The young couple had recently moved onto the old bonanza farm site where Carrie and her brother had come to so many years ago—back in 1908— to work for the Daud family. Carrie had helped in the kitchen, feeding the many hired men when the farming operation there was at its peak. Her brother, Amund, worked as a repairman for the farm.

Carrie turned and craned her neck in the direction of the farm. "It's kind of too bad that that big barn burned down. It was quite a landmark. It looks so bare there now with so many of the buildings gone."

"Well, if it hadn't burned, Stan would have had to tear it down and what a job that would have been. It was way too big for his needs."

"I wonder if they'll ever get around to tearing down the big house like they plan to do," wondered Carrie.

Stan and his father had purchased the quarter of the former Daud farm that happened to have the buildings on it. The young couple was living in the smaller house, which had been the home of the foreman. The so-called "big house" had been the residence of the Daud family and it also had held the big kitchen and dining hall where the men were fed. Stan and Livvie planned to tear it down and build a new house for themselves someday.

"With a war on now, it's likely that that job will have to wait for awhile," remarked George.

"Isn't it funny to think of Livvie as having a baby of her own now? It seems like such a short time ago that we got her," reflected Carrie.

"It's almost twenty years ago now, isn't it?"

Livvie had come to Carrie and George in a strange way. One day, a woman had come to their back door and said that she understood that they were wanting a baby. She told them that she knew of a young girl who was in the family way and needed to find someone to adopt her baby after it was born. It turned out to be this woman's niece and she was just trying to help in this unfortunate situation.

George and Carrie were skeptical at first, but after some agonizing, they decided that they would accept this baby when it came. A few months later, they were the parents of a beautiful baby girl and had never regretted their decision.

Carrie leaned her head back and before long, she was dozing a little and dreaming about the past.

Carrie had been married before, to a man named Fred Shutz, whom she had met while she lived and worked on the Daud farm. They had lived in

Davenport for a few years before Fred was killed while fighting a fire. Their baby boy, Joey, had died a few years before that, of diphtheria. Carrie was left with another son, Freddie.

She later met George Johnson and they were married and she moved with him onto the Johnson farm south of Kindred. After several years, they realized that Carrie wasn't able to have any more children, so when Livvie, whose real name was Olivia Oline, named after her newly acquired grandmothers, came to them, they felt blessed indeed.

"Well, here's the hospital," announced George. "I think you were dozing a little there, weren't you?"

They parked their car and entered St. Luke's Hospital and asked for the room of Mrs. Stan Murphy.

When they stepped off the elevator, they saw Stan in the hallway, looking into the nursery window.

"There she is!" said the new father, with a big grin on his face. He was pointing to a tiny bundle in one of the bassinets.

George slapped him on the back good naturedly. "Congratulations there, new papa!"

"Yes, you certainly have our congratulations, Stan," added Carrie. "I'll bet you both are very excited."

"I believe she's the cutest baby in the nursery, don't you think? One of the biggest, too, I guess."

"She certainly was a good-sized one, wasn't she?" agreed Carrie. "Nine pounds and four ounces."

Livvie says that that's why she was so uncomfortable for the last month or so. Here, let's go on down and see the new mama. She's been waiting for you."

They followed him down the long hallway to the very last room. Stan let his in-laws enter the room first.

"Oh!" squealed Livvie in delight. "You finally made it. I've been expecting you for sometime now."

Livvie shifted in the bed to get more comfortable and to sit up higher. "Have you seen her yet?"

"Oh, yes, and she's just beautiful!" exclaimed Carrie, as she approached the bed and gave her daughter a hug.

"You did a good job there," said George, chuckling.

"I'm feeling ever so much better today," she said, "so I'm glad you didn't come yesterday."

Just then, Stan's parents, Joe and Min Murphy, appeared in the doorway.

"Oh!" exclaimed his mother. "You beat us here." She gave her son and daughter-in-law congratulatory hugs. The Murphys and the Johnsons exchanged handshakes, pleased with the birth of their shared grandchild.

"It's exciting to be grandparents now, isn't it?" Carrie said to the Murphys.

"Oh, my, yes, it certainly is, that's for sure," agreed Min.

Mrs. Murphy turned to Stan and said, "Well, you better take us down to the nursery and show us the new baby."

"We saw her when we first came off the elevator. Stan was standing there looking at her," remarked George.

"He just can't get enough of that," laughed Livvie.

When the Murphys and Stan left the room, Carrie came over and took a chair close to her daughter.

"We like the name you picked out, Livvie."

I kind of named her after my two mothers," Livvie said softly. " 'Cheryl' for you and 'May' for Merrie."

Merrie, or Meridith, was the name of Livvie's real mother. When Livvie was about sixteen, she was told that she was adopted and shortly after, she was introduced to her real mother. Merrie's parents didn't know yet that their daughter had been reunited with the baby that she had been forced to give up years ago. Merrie's father was a very stern and unforgiving man and it was felt that it was better that he didn't know.

"Oh, Livvie, that was a nice thing to do," Carrie said, feeling a lump forming in her throat.

"Stan called Merrie yesterday and she said that she will try to get up here soon to see me."

"Well, of course, she's excited about being a grandmother, too, I'm sure," said Carrie.

Merrie had married eventually and was living about twenty miles west of the Johnsons', in the next county. She and her husband, Sam, had two children. A boy of ten, and a girl, a couple years younger. As far as the two children were concerned, Livvie was just a friend of the family.

The Murphys and Stan returned, and a few minutes later, Stan's older brother, Marty, came into the room.

"That sure is one cute baby out there," he said grinning. He clapped his brother on the back.

"How did you know which one was ours?" asked Stan.

"Well, now, I just sort of sweet-talked a pretty little nurse into showing me my new niece."

"You always did have a way with the girls," laughed his father.

After awhile, the men all left the room and went and sat in the family lounge to talk about farming and the war.

Carrie and Min talked about babies and the news around Kindred with Livvie. Soon a nurse entered the room and announced that she would be bringing the baby for a feeding so the company would have to leave, she said.

"How long do you think you'll be here?" Stan's mother asked Livvie.

"They tell me it will be about ten days or so before I can go home."

"We'll try and get up here next weekend again, dear," said Carrie.

"Goodbye," Livvie said to the two older women. "You better stop by the nursery and take another peek at the baby."

"We'll surely do that," said Mrs. Murphy.

The two couples left the hospital and walked to their cars.

"Joe says he's glad he bought a new car last year," George nodded at the Murphys' new Ford. "They might be hard to come by now, with a war on."

"I hope ours will last us awhile longer," stated Carrie as she got in on the passenger side.

"Well, with a brother-in-law for a mechanic, I think we can keep this thing going for a few years yet."

Carrie's brother, Amund, ran a service station in Davenport and had come to their aid many a time, fixing trucks and cars for them, to make them last "just one more year."

The country had just been coming out of the Great Depression and people were becoming optimistic and buying once again but now things would be on hold for awhile.

"What did the men have to say about the war?" Carrie asked. "Do they think it will last a long time?"

"No one knows that for sure, but I think it will be going on for sometime yet."

They rode many miles in silence. Carrie was deep in thought.

How would their lives change in the next few years?

A few days later, Carrie walked slowly down their driveway, reading a letter she'd just retrieved from their mailbox. It was from her family in Spring Grove. It was in her sister-in-law's handwriting, as usual. Carrie skimmed the pages, trying to detect if there was any bad news. She would read it more thoroughly when she got back to the house.

Carrie's father had passed away about five months earlier. In fact, it was just a few days after the incident at Pearl Harbor. Carrie wasn't able to travel to Spring Grove for the funeral as there was just too much snow. Even train travel was unpredictable at that time. She hadn't been back to see her family for several years and she often revealed to George that she felt very guilty about that.

"Well, just get yourself on the train and go, Carrie," he would tell her, but it seemed the older she got, the harder it was for her to make the trip.

Finally reaching the house, Carrie was relieved to get in out of the heat. She went to the refrigerator for some cold water and poured herself a glass and sat by the table as she opened the letter again.

She had read it twice through when she heard George coming in the back door. "We got a letter from my family today," she called to him.

He washed his hands and when he saw that his wife was drinking a glass of cold water, he fetched himself some, too, and savoring its coolness, drank it all in one gulp.

"Whew, is sure is hot for just being the end of May, isn't it?" He wiped his forehead with his sleeve.

"I found out just how warm it was when I walked to the mailbox!"

"Is everything all right in Spring Grove, then?"

"Mattie's squeezed a lot of news in these four pages," said Carrie. "Ma is doing pretty good. Olaf and Mattie want her to come live with them but she wants to stay in her house, even if it's lonely there without Pa. Maybe when winter comes they can talk her into a move."

Carrie read some paragraphs aloud to her husband and they discussed the contents. Mattie had saved some bad news for last. Olaf and Mattie's grandson, Spencer, who just turned twenty, had been drafted into the army and would be leaving home soon.

"So it's starting," Carrie said. "The first of our family members to go off to war. Who will be next?"

George didn't answer, but his biggest fear was that their son, Freddie, would have to go. Or Livvie's husband, Stan.

"I guess we don't have any control over that. We'll just have to take it as it comes," he told his wife, sounding braver than he felt.

CHAPTER 2

"Livvie's coming home tomorrow," announced Stan excitedly, over the phone.

"Oh, that's great," exclaimed Carrie. "We'll drive over to see her and the baby as soon as we can."

After hanging up, Carrie related the good news to George. "When do you suppose we should drive over there? Early in the evening?"

"I guess we could do that. I'll hurry through the chores."

"I should cook up some chicken soup to bring along. And maybe bake a cake or...." Carrie's voice trailed off as she began thinking of different things she could do to help her daughter get through the next few days.

"She'll be pretty tired for awhile, I'm sure," she told her husband, who had his nose in the newspaper again.

"They sure are urging everyone to buy those Defense Bonds," he said, looking up at Carrie. "I suppose we better start buying some, too. I'll stop by the post office tomorrow, I think."

"Freddie said that he has been getting his at the bank there and a lot of people have been coming in and asking about them."

George laid down the local newspaper and picked up the Fargo Forum. Carrie went into the kitchen to start the fixin's for the soup that she would make the next day.

It wasn't long before she heard George let out a whoop from the parlor.

"What's the matter with you?" she called to him.

"Come here and listen to this," he answered.

Wiping her hands on her apron, she came into the room and sat down on the sofa, waiting expectantly.

"I was afraid this was going to happen," George stated. "The government is forbidding sales of rubber tires and tubes now. It's all needed for the war effort. Here's a list of how we're supposed to get the maximum out of our tires so that they will last longer.

"First of all," he continued, "we're to cut down on our speed and only go 40 mph rather than 60. Then we're supposed to 'avoid short stops and quick starts. Keep tires inflated to proper pressure. Keep brakes evenly balanced, and change wheel positions every 5000 miles.'"

"Well," Carrie said, after digesting this information, "I guess we'll have to do all that, then."

"Yah, I guess we have no choice. It will keep me busy, what with a car and two trucks to keep up."

The next evening Carrie and George motored up to the farm that Stan and Livvie lived on to see the new mother and baby.

"My, the wheat is coming up nicely, isn't it," commented Carrie, looking at the fields along the Kindred Highway.

"Yah, it looks nice all over, I'm told. Let's hope for a good year again."

Before going up to Livvie's, they made a stop at the Davenport cemetery. It would be Memorial Day the next day and Carrie wanted to place some flowers on the graves there.

They parked next to several other cars with the same idea. George helped her carry one of the containers. They placed them to the side of the tombstones until they could cut away some of the tall grass and tidy up the area. Then they put the flowers in front of the stone for Carrie's first husband, Fred Shutz, and one next to her infant son's.

Looking at her little Joey's white headstone, Carrie felt the ache of emptiness that never seemed to go away, even after all these years. She brushed the tears from her eyes and started back to the car.

She was silent for quite sometime, until they turned into Livvie's driveway.

"Oh, I can hardly wait to hold that baby!" she exclaimed, ready to jump out of the vehicle as soon as it stopped. George carried the kettle of soup and Carrie managed the cake pan and a container of cookies.

Stan greeted them at the back door before they could knock.

"Come in, come in," he called to them. "What have you got there?" he asked, nodding at the gifts they bore.

"Oh, just some food to help Livvie out for a few days," Carrie said, as she unloaded the items on Livvie's counter. "I'll put this soup in the refrigerator."

Carrie hurried into the living room, where Livvie sat holding the baby.

"Oh, may I hold her right away?" asked Carrie.

"Of course," laughed Livvie, handing her precious bundle to her mother.

Tears pricked Carries eyes as she felt the warm, solid weight of a new baby in her arms once again. "Oh, she is so beautiful," she exclaimed. She hugged the infant up to her cheek and felt its sweet breath tickle her face.

George joined his wife on the sofa and together they gazed at their new grandchild. The baby opened her eyes and stared at them for many moments before screwing up her face. She let out a loud wail.

"I thought that would happen pretty soon," said Livvie, getting up to take her daughter in her arms. "It's time to feed her again. She sure eats often."

"Well, she's a big baby and it takes a lot to keep her going," Carrie remarked.

Stan came and sat with the new grandparents while Livvie went into the other room to change and feed the baby.

"My folks are planning to stop by, too, this evening."

George and Stan talked about the crops, especially how good everyone's wheat was looking.

"I wish we'd planted more of it this year," Stan said. "Maybe the prices will improve, too, now."

"Well, don't count your chickens before they're hatched, my boy," cautioned George. "I've seen too many good-looking crops turn out badly for some reason or another. Too much rain, not enough rain, hail, diseases and such." George shook his head, remembering many past crops.

Before they could get on the subject of the war, they heard the Murphy's car drive into the yard.

They all exchanged pleasantries while Stan went to get everyone something cold to drink. Soon Livvie emerged from the bedroom with little Cheryl.

"Here, you better let Min hold her for awhile, now. I've already had the privilege," laughed Carrie.

"Oh, Joe and I both are so excited to have a girl in the family, finally, after raising four boys," exclaimed Min, as she took the baby from Livvie.

Stan returned with a tray full of sweating glasses of nectar.

"This really hits the spot," said Joe, as he took a big swallow.

"Is this some of that Watkins stuff, Livvie?" asked Carrie.

"Yes. It's the cherry flavor, I believe." She looked at her husband for confirmation. He nodded.

"The Watkins man was just here yesterday. Glad I happened to be in the yard. We needed several things. Livvie had made a list at the hospital."

"Well, I had nothing else to do there all that time," she laughed.

"If it's this hot already, can you imagine what the summer will be like?" George remarked.

"Maybe it will be as hot as the summer of '36. I'll never forget that one!" added Joe.

"The boys will be coming over after awhile," Min said to Livvie. "Marty had to finish up some chore and then they all had to get cleaned up. Joe and I were ready so we decided to hurry over here."

"Yah, she couldn't wait to get her hands on that baby girl!" teased her husband.

The old Murphy pickup soon made its presence known as it rattled up to the house and the three occupants tumbled out. They were laughing and teasing each other about something as they came bounding into the house.

Marty, the oldest, was followed by Ronnie and last came young Allan, who was only eleven. Ronnie was two years younger than Stan.

"Who's going to hold the baby first?" asked Livvie.

"We were just trying to decide that on the way over here, now, weren't we boys?" Marty looked at the other two. They both burst out laughing.

"Oh, you boys," scolded their mother mildy.

"Ronnie won the honor," Allan piped up.

"OK, Ronnie, here you go." Livvie placed the baby into the arms of its uncle.

"How do I hold her?" he asked. "I haven't held a baby since Allan was born."

"Yah, and you told me you dropped me on my head so you better watch out with her," Allan said.

"He never dropped you on your head, Allan," his mother said, as she gave Ronnie a stern look.

"Good thing you had a girl, Stan," laughed Joe. "These boys are hard to handle."

After a pleasant evening of visiting, Livvie insisted that everyone have some cake before they left.

"I see you brought a cake, too," Carrie said to Min.

"We can each have two pieces, then," Allan chimed in.

"It's good that we didn't bring the same kind," said Min. "I tried out a new recipe yesterday. I've never made a sour cream filling like this before."

"Is that the recipe that was in the Kindred Tribune awhile back?"

"I believe it is," answered Min, as she licked some of the filling off her fingers as she cut into the cake.

They all sat around the big, round table and Carrie put two plates of cake, and another plate of cookies in the center. Coffee and more nectar were passed around.

There was much talking, laughing and joshing, until George looked at the clock and declared that it was time they headed for home. Everyone agreed and the dirty dishes were quickly washed up by the two older women.

They all peeked in on the sleeping baby and said their goodbyes.

"I suppose we'll have to think twice now about making unnecessary trips with our cars," Joe remarked to George as they all made their way to their vehicles.

"We'll probably have to be conserving on gas, too," George added.

"Yah, well, good night then, all of you," called Carrie to the Murphy family, as she got into the car.

"We sure have a pleasant time when we're with the Murphys, don't we," remarked George, as they turned onto the highway and headed south.

"It's so good that we all get along so well, I think," agreed Carrie.

"Not like some families I've heard about," George said.

It was another hot day in June and Carrie had fixed a cold supper. As George helped himself to a large helping of potato salad, he asked Carrie, "How was your Ladies Aid meeting today?"

"Oh, we had a good talk on Norway and how we can be helping those poor people. They've really been suffering since the Germans took over their country. It's been over two years now."

"So who was your guest speaker?" asked George.

"She was a lady from Fargo who is very active in the Sons of Norway and she has been going around to various organizations, asking for donations. We're going to have a clothing drive this next month. Blankets are needed, too."

"How will the goods get over there?"

"We'll be sending our boxes to Minneapolis and then they'll be shipped to Norway."

"I only hope the ship gets through. Many boats have been sunk."

"This lady, her name is Mrs. Berg, said that many people from northern Norway were homeless because their homes had been burned and they fled with only the clothes on their backs." Carrie rose to get more coffee for George.

George looked at the clock on the wall. "We better hurry if we're going to make it to the meeting on time."

There was to be a township meeting that evening for the purpose of organizing a Civil Defense Board. All residents of Barrie Township were requested to be there.

Carrie hurried through the dishes and changed her dress and away they went.

"I talked to Chris this morning," said George as they left the driveway, "and he said one of his boys, Clemens, I believe, was planning to go to Washington to work for the government as a stenographer. He had mailed in an application form only about two weeks ago and already he'd heard from them. They're badly needed, I guess. The salary isn't bad, either," George went on. "It starts at $1440."

"You don't say," remarked Carrie. "So he'll be going to Washington soon."

They drove to the Barrie school where the meeting was to be held and parked alongside a long row of cars. They hurried into the building.

After a lengthy meeting, some of the ladies served coffee and doughnuts to the group. George had been elected to serve on the board so he and several other men stayed late to discuss further details.

George was quiet on the short drive home. He felt burdened with the added responsibilities of serving on such a board. Carrie wished that he hadn't been nominated, but, also proud of her husband because he was usually sought after to serve on numerous committees. *They know a good man when they see one.*

"Your board will be busy, it sounds like," she interrupted the silence as they neared their house.

George sighed. "Yes, I guess so." The Township Defense Board needed to prepare for any emergencies that could occur when the country was at war. "I suppose I'll be involved in lots of meetings in the near future."

When the couple prepared for bed that evening, Carrie said. "Let's go to see a show tomorrow night. There's a comedy playing. Abbott and Costello."

Movies were shown occasionally in the Kindred Auditorium.

"Well," George said slowly, "I guess we could do that."

"Maybe Freddie and Lenora would like to go along. If they can get a sitter, that is."

The next morning, bright and early, Livvie called to tell her folks that Stan's brother, Marty, had received his draft notice.

"Joe and Min are pretty upset," Livvie told Carrie.

"Well, I would guess so," stated Carrie. "Oh, I worry so that Freddie will have to go," she confessed.

"I worry about Stan, too," said Livvie.

After the two finished their short conversation, Carrie went out to search for her husband. George didn't like to hear the news his wife brought to him. It was hitting too close to home.

"When does he have to leave?"

"I didn't ask but it sounded like it would be soon."

"Maybe we should drive over to the Murphys' this evening," suggested George.

"Yah, maybe we'd better."

So, instead of going to a movie that evening, George and Carrie drove up to the Murphy farm to share in the anxiety of their friends.

When they drove into the yard, there were several other cars parked helter skelter, some by the house and some by the barn.

"I see Livvie and Stan are here, too," remarked Carrie, as she got out of the vehicle.

About five or six men were seated on the porch and they all greeted the Johnsons. Carrie proceeded on into the house while George looked for a place to sit. One of the younger men got up and offered his seat.

Carrie found the women all seated around in the living room. Min stood up as she saw Carrie come in.

"Oh, Carrie. How good to see you," she said, as she came forward and the two women embraced.

"Oh, Min, how terrible for you. To think that Marty has to go and fight those Germans!"

"I know," said Min, wiping her eyes. "I guess I knew that this was a possibility, but when it actually comes, you're never ready."

Marty came into the house and walked into the living room just then.

"Hey, did somebody die or something? You all look like you're at a wake!"

Min looked embarrassed and said she'd go and start the coffee. Marty sat down and visited with the ladies. Livvie was there and Min's sister-in-law, Magda, and a few other neighbors.

"Ma's taking this pretty hard," Marty remarked in a hushed tone.

"Well, she should, Martin," said Magda. "Who knows what will happen to you!"

"Nothing's going to happen to me, Aunt Maggie," answered Marty with conviction in his voice. "Most of us don't really want to go, but we have to do our duty when our country calls."

Just then little Cheryl began crying in the other room and both Livvie and Carrie jumped up.

"I'll get her, Mom. You stay here."

Marty rose and went out to the porch to join the men again. His younger brother, Ronnie, and his friend Kenny had just come in the yard. The neighbor girl, Rosie, was with them.

"Here come the Fearsome Threesome," joked Marty. To the men, he said, "If you see one, you see the other two. They're always together these days."

Maggie's husband, Art, said, "Yah, I see those three driving by my place many times a day."

"Hey!" Marty called to the three. "Why don't we get a game of softball going? Anybody here want to play?"

"I do," said younger brother Allan, jumping to his feet. Stan rose, too, and several of the younger men.

It was a beautiful June evening with still plenty of daylight left.

"It's sure nice that the mosquitoes haven't showed themselves yet," remarked Joe.

"Yah, you can say that again," agreed Art. "Those pesky gnats finally wore themselves out, thank goodness."

"Your wheat still looking good, George?" asked Joe.

"The best it's looked in several years. Even better than last year."

"Yah, ours too," said Joe. "Hope we can bring it to harvest without anything happening to it." All the men nodded their heads in silent agreement.

"You'll be a little short-handed without Marty to help now, won't you?"

remarked one of the neighbors.

"When does he have to leave?" asked George.

"He has to report to Fort Snelling in Minneapolis next Tuesday."

"That soon!" exclaimed George.

"There's a train-load going from Fargo," said Joe.

The men were silent for awhile again.

"Yah, Min is pretty upset about the whole thing," Joe added, shaking his head. "I tell her that with four sons, it's pretty likely that some of them will have to go. She doesn't like to hear that."

They could hear shouts from the young people playing ball nearby. The birds were chirping as they settled down for the night. The sounds of dishes being clinked together in the kitchen reached their ears. *All normal, everyday sounds,* mused George. *But how long will things be normal anymore, with the country's young men going off to war?*

Min came to the screen door and asked the men if they'd like to come in for some coffee. "Or should I bring it out to you?" she asked.

"Oh, we can come in," said Joe, rising, and the others followed suit.

They joined the ladies round the big, kitchen table. Besides coffee, there was cake, cookies and doughnuts.

"Oh, my, so much food!" remarked George.

"Well, when Min gets worked up over something, she goes into a baking frenzy," laughed Joe.

"I'm just the opposite," said Luella, a neighbor lady. "I can't do a thing when I get upset."

"That's for sure," agreed her husband. Everyone laughed good- naturedly.

Little Cheryl let out a gurgle, as if in agreement, and everyone laughed again.

As the food and coffee were passed around for the second time, George said, "We better leave enough for that ball team out there. They'll be mighty hungry."

"As I said, there's plenty of food," chuckled Joe, looking at his wife mischievously. She swatted him on the shoulder.

They could hear the young people coming towards the house.

"Well, men," said Joe, rising, "let's go into the living room for a bit so they can sit here and have some lunch."

All the men got up and followed Joe out of the room. Clean cups and glasses were set on the table.

"I better refill those plates of cake and cookies, too," said Min, hurrying into the pantry.

The young people were in high spirits from their ball game. They didn't want to think about later, when they would have to say goodbye to their friend. They devoured the baked goods with a fervor.

Marty, especially, was in rare form. He told one funny story after another. The room was engulfed with laughter.

"Hey, hold down that noise in the kitchen there," laughed Joe, from the living room. "We can't hear ourselves talk out here."

"You'll have to come back and join us then," suggested Stan.

Things finally quieted down in the kitchen a bit. Marty suggested a game of cards. Some of the neighbors decided it was time to leave. The remaining men in the living room were in a serious discussion about the war. They were talking about the recent battle at Midway. This had been a very decisive victory for the Allies.

"We really stopped those Japs!" exclaimed Joe.

"Yah, hopefully that will keep them away from Hawaii now."

"And our own West Coast," added Art.

Joe looked into the kitchen at his son, Marty, sitting around the table with his friends, playing cards and having fun, like young people should. Joe felt a tug at his heart. *How much time does he have left to be young and carefree?*

It was close to midnight when the gathering finally broke up. Everyone hugged Marty and wished him lots of luck and hurried out before the tears started flowing.

Carrie looked back at the house when they were backing out of the driveway. She saw Min and Joe standing on either side of Marty in the doorway, waving at everyone. Marty had his arms around his parents.

I'll never forget that picture, Carrie thought to herself.

CHAPTER 3

George sat by the kitchen table, reading the paper which he had just picked up from their mailbox. Carrie came down the stairs, huffing and puffing.

"Oh, good, George, you're home. I have a heavy box for you to carry down for me later. Do you want some coffee?"

"Maybe a cold drink instead," he answered, and Carrie went to the refrigerator and got the pitcher of nectar out and also some ice cubes.

"I was digging in the closets upstairs and found some things for the clothing drive for Norway."

"You certainly picked a hot time to be up there, rummaging around," George remarked.

"Well, I know, but our Ladies Aid meeting is tomorrow already and I just haven't had the time to do it before this." She set a plate of sliced banana bread before her husband and sat down herself.

"I found a skirt and blouse that I can't fit into anymore but they're still good so I'm going to give those. I also found a sweater that I haven't worn for several years. I was thinking," she went on, "don't you have a sweater that you got for Christmas a few years ago that you don't wear?"

After a few moments she said, "George? Are you listening to me?"

"Oh, sorry, dear, but I'm reading about the rationing books that we'll be getting now. It says we have to fill out a form for each member of the family and then go to our local school and register for them."

"Oh, my," sighed Carrie. "What all is going to be rationed?"

"Well, it will be mainly sugar for now. I'm sure more items will be added as time goes on."

"Lenora told me that she heard at the store yesterday that chlorine bleach will no longer be available. Why would that be, I wonder?"

"I guess it's needed for some product for the war effort," George told her.

George moved the newspaper out of the way and discovered the rest of the mail that he had brought in.

"Oh, here's a postcard from Livvie that came today." He handed it to his wife and she eagerly began to read it.

After a few moments she said, "Livvie says that they don't think they can go with us on the Fourth of July over to Horace. She thinks it's just too hot to take the baby. Cheryl's been a little fussy the last few days. It's probably the heat."

"Well, we'll go alone then, unless Freddie and Lenora would like to go. Might as well fill up the car while we're at it. No use taking two cars if we're going to the same place."

"I'll give them a call this evening and see if they have any plans. The kids would enjoy it. There's going to be a parade."

"Did Livvie say anything about Marty? I wonder how his trip to Fort Snelling turned out."

"No, she didn't say anything about him."

As it turned out, George and Carrie ended up going over to Horace by themselves for the Fourth of July celebration. They ran into Carrie's brother, Amund and his wife, Edith, who lived over in Davenport. Joe and Min Murphy were there, too, so they all had a pleasant time together. After the parade, chicken dinner, band concert and speaker, a Ladies Aid auction was held. By the time that they headed on home it was suppertime and they were very hot and tired.

"This would have been too long and hot of a day for the kids," Carrie said, as she rolled down her window to get some breeze.

"Joe said that Marty will be going to Texas for his army training."

"Yes, Min said he'll be going to a place called Mineral Wells. Ever heard of it?"

"Joe said it's near Fort Worth," answered George.

"It's a shame he didn't even get to come home first. They just shipped them all off on a bus the next day."

"Well, in a way, maybe it's best that way."

Carrie didn't agree but kept her tongue. She wondered how she'd react if Freddie or Stan had to go that fast.

"Do you think Freddie or Stan will be drafted?" she asked her husband, voicing her deepest fear.

George had been asked this question many, many times over the past few months and he always had the same answer. "I certainly hope not. We'll just have to wait and see."

"They're married with children. Maybe they won't have to go," Carrie said, hopefully.

George didn't think that fact would matter one bit if Uncle Sam decided to draft them, but he didn't say this to his wife.

About a week later, on a fine Sunday afternoon, Carrie was in her garden, admiring all her vegetables when she heard a car drive into the yard. She went around to the front of the house and was surprised to see that it was Stan and Livvie. She hurried in their direction.

"Well, hello there!" she called to them as they got out of their car. "What a nice surprise."

Carrie took a sleeping baby from Livvie's arms and led the way to the house. Stan spied George over by the barn so he headed there.

"We decided to go for a drive and ended up here!" exclaimed Livvie.

"I was hoping someone would stop by this afternoon." Carrie carefully laid Cheryl on the bed in the downstairs bedroom and returned to the living room. "Sundays get so long sometimes," she went on. "We had early church this morning. How about you?"

"We went to church over at St. John's this morning and they had early services, too," said Livvie.

"Have you and Stan decided which church to join yet?"

"We don't know yet. Davenport is closer, but I know that Stan's folks would like us to join St. John's. Their family has belonged there for many years."

"Well, distance is going to make a difference now with everyone trying to cut down on their driving. George says he wouldn't be surprised but that they'll start rationing gasoline, too, pretty soon."

"I suppose we shouldn't have gone for a drive today but I wanted to talk to you. Guess who came to see me yesterday?"

"Who?" asked Carrie.

"My....real mother, Merrie!"

"Really? Well, I suppose she wanted to see Cheryl again."

"She came to tell me that her father died on Thursday. My grandfather."

"Oh, no!" said Carrie.

"The funeral is tomorrow. Do you think I should go?" asked Livvie.

"Oh, I don't think that would be a good idea, Livvie."

"That's what Merrie said, too. He didn't know about me and neither does Merrie's mother."

"It would be quite a shock to her, so soon after her husband's death," commented Carrie.

"Merrie said that she is going to tell her mother after awhile and then she'll bring her over to meet me."

"Oh, how does she think that will go, then?" asked Carrie.

"She thinks that after the initial shock, her mother will be happy for Merrie because she knows how hard it was for her to give me up. But her father insisted and he always got his way, I guess. Merrie said that her mother always had to do as her husband said."

They could hear Cheryl beginning to fret from the other room, so Livvie jumped up to go and get her. She returned with the baby cuddled in her arms and sat down on the sofa.

"Oh, Mom, imagine what it would be like to have to give up one's baby!"

"I'm sure it's the hardest thing a mother ever has to do." Carrie said, thoughtfully. "At least your mother hadn't the time to get really attached to you. She probably only saw you once and then you were whisked away."

George and Stan came in the house and joined the ladies. After a short while, Carrie went to the kitchen to start the coffee. Later they all sat around the kitchen table and enjoyed some fresh cake.

"I suppose I shouldn't have baked anything yesterday, with the sugar being rationed and all, but I can't get out of the habit of baking a cake for Sunday," laughed Carrie.

"I know," agreed Livvie. "This will take some getting used to for all of us. Just like us, driving over here today. We probably shouldn't have done that either."

"Yah, I wonder how long this war will go on," commented George. "Stan, have you heard from your brother lately?"

"Well, he's still in Texas, going through basic training. He says it's hotter than blazes down there!"

"I'm sure it is," said George. "It's nice that the weather has cooled off here now, though. I suppose you're getting ready for harvest up around your way pretty soon."

"Probably not for a week or so," answered Stan.

"Yah, here, too," said George. "It will be a little later than usual, I guess, what with the wet spring we had."

"Well, that 6 inches of snow in April sure set us back a bit," said Stan.

"Things are looking good, though, so I guess we can't complain."

Carrie looked out the kitchen window to see another car come into the driveway.

"Oh, it's Freddie and Lenora, I'll bet," she said, excitedly.

George rose to have a look. "Yep, that's who it is, all right."

"Oh, good!" exclaimed Livvie. "We haven't seen them in quite sometime."

Livvie handed Cheryl to Stan and hurried out the back door to greet her brother and his family.

"Hi there, big brother! Long time, no see!" she called to them.

Freddie was carrying Larry, and little Sandra was tagging along after him. Lenora was getting the diaper bag out of the backseat of the car.

Livvie swooped down and picked up Sandra. "My, what a big girl you are getting to be!"

"I'm three now!" Sandra said, holding up as many fingers.

Livvie turned to have a closer look at Larry. "My, he looks more like you every time I see him!" she said to her brother.

Carrie held the screen door open for everyone. She took Larry from his Daddy's arms and gave him a hug until he squealed in delight.

"Grandma, we brought you something!" Sandra said, hopping up and down in her excitement.

"Oh, now what could that be?" Carrie asked.

Lenora handed Sandra a large envelope and told her to give it to her grandma.

"Well, I wonder what's in here," commented Carrie, as she sat down by the table and opened the flap on the back. Sandra was right there to help. Carrie shook out the contents and there were two large pictures. One was of Sandra and one was of the two children together.

"Oh, aren't these beautiful!" exclaimed Carrie. "Look here, George."

"We had those taken last month by that photographer that came to the Evingson's Store," said Freddie. "Didn't they turn out good?"

"They sure did," said George. He picked up his granddaughter and said, "You look just like Shirley Temple there, with your hair in those ringlets."

"Who is Shirley Temple?" asked the little girl.

"Don't you know who she is? She was in many movies a few years back," explained George. "But then, I guess you wouldn't have seen any of those, would you?"

"I'll have to get some nice frames for these and put them on the piano," said Carrie, still admiring the pictures of her grandchildren.

"How about us men folk take a little drive and look at the crops?" suggested George. Freddie and Stan agreed that would be a good idea so they left and got into Freddie's car.

The ladies and children settled down in the living room for awhile. Cheryl fell asleep and was put back on the bed.

"Why don't we go out and have a look at my garden? You should see all the vegetables I have this year!" exclaimed Carrie. "Enough for the whole township!"

"I didn't have much room in our small yard in town for one, but I did my best to plant a 'victory garden,'" remarked Lenora, as they went out the back door. Sandra and Larry followed, excited for an adventure outside.

The idea behind the victory garden concept was that 'more gardens mean more food at home,' thus saving needed tin and transportation facilities that could thus be used for the troops. Every township had a garden committee and everyone was encouraged to take part in this effort on the home front.

"Well, I couldn't plant a garden this year because of my pregnancy," stated Livvie, "but Stan's mother planted a huge one, even bigger than yours, Mom. I'll go and help her with the canning whenever I can."

"Lenora, you can always come and get stuff from here when you need it," Carrie told her daughter-in-law. "We can't possibly eat all this!"

"I'll help you with the canning, then," said Lenora.

"It was certainly too hot for the peas this year. I didn't get too much out of them. The beans look good, though, and the beets. Oh, my! I'll have enough beets for many a jar of pickles, I tell you!"

"Will you have enough jars for all of this canning you'll need to do?" asked Livvie.

"That will be the next thing," remarked Carrie. "I suppose there'll be a shortage of those, too."

"It looks like you got carried away when you planted the cucumbers, Mom!" teased Livvie. "And the tomatoes! Just how are you going to take care of all this stuff?"

They all had a good laugh over Carrie's plentiful garden, and she admitted that maybe next year she wouldn't plant quite so much.

"Maybe you can bring some of these vegetables into the stores in town and they will sell them for you," suggested Lenora.

"Oh, no. I'll just give some away to people that didn't get a garden planted this year. For instance, that new family by town there, she was sickly all spring so I'm sure they could use some produce."

They saw Freddie's car return to the yard so Carrie said that she would go in and get things started for supper. "You can all stay, can't you?"

Livvie and Lenora agreed that they could stay and said they'd be right in to help her.

"No, no," said Carrie. "You stay out here with the kids for awhile. It's so nice out this afternoon. Such a welcome change from all that heat we had earlier."

As Carrie fussed about in the kitchen, fixing a simple supper for her family, she could hear the sounds of laughter from the front yard. The men were playing catch with the children so she left her food preparations for a few minutes to sit on the step and watch.

Larry, who had just turned one, would tumble on the uneven ground every time he reached for the ball. He'd get up and try again and the same thing would happen. Finally, he got fed up and he stomped his little foot in the grass and said, "I done!" Everyone laughed some more.

"Well, come on in everyone, and we'll have a bite to eat," said Carrie.

"I bet it will be more that a bite!" teased Stan.

"Yah, Ma never has anything for us to eat when we come," joked Freddie.

"We had ham for dinner so I just fixed some ham sandwiches," answered Carrie.

They all got settled around the dining-room table while Livvie went to fetch the baby from the bedroom. When things quieted down, everyone folded their hands and George led the table prayer.

Carrie brought in the big platter of sandwiches, a plate of deviled eggs, a bowl of cold pork and beans, another bowl of red Jello, a plate of cake, and one of cookies.

"Well, this should fill us up, don't you think, Stan?" remarked Freddie after a few minutes.

Stan, who had just polished off his second sandwich, said, "Oh, I don't know. I may go home hungry. There isn't much here."

They all laughed and Carrie looked a little chagrined. "Well, I guess there is plenty here, after all. If I had known you were coming, I would have made more, though."

That brought even more laughter from those around the table. George looked at the clock on the wall and said, "I guess it's almost time for Roosevelt to be on."

That prompted everyone to push back from the table. "We'll just clear everything off and then I'll wash the dishes later," said Carrie. "We don't want to miss the program."

A few minutes later, the family members all had found places to sit in the living room, near the radio. The familiar theme music for the "Fireside Chats" was soon heard and even the children quieted down to play with toys on the floor.

President Roosevelt commented briefly on the progress of the Allies but then spent the rest of the time telling the American people to keep up the good work back home and to not lose heart.

The children began to get restless and when the program was over, Livvie announced that it was time for them to pack up and head for home. Lenora agreed that they needed to go, too.

"We must help you with those dishes first, though, Mom," said Livvie.

"Oh, no. There aren't that many. Don't worry about those."

It took about a half an hour before everyone had said their goodbyes, and were in their cars and headed out the driveway.

"Oh, now wasn't that a fun afternoon," stated Carrie, as she watched them leave the yard.

"It sure was. It's been awhile since we've all been together."

"I'd better get started on these dishes," said Carrie, as she put a large teakettle on the stove to heat up.

"I'll help you," said George. "Just call me when you're ready for me." He went into the living room and picked up the Sunday paper.

"Oh, George," called Carrie, "look up the obituary page and see if the write-up of Livvie's grandfather is in there."

George looked at her blankly as she stood in the doorway. "Oh, I forgot to tell you that Livvie said that Merrie had been by to see her yesterday and told her that her father had died."

George flipped through the paper and found the right section. "Let's see, what was his name again?"

"Ah, Pete. Pete Munseth."

After scanning the page, George said, "Yes, here it is. Peter J. Munseth."

Carrie came and leaned over his shoulder as they both read the notice.

"It says he just had the one daughter, Meridith," remarked Carrie. After she finished reading, Carrie sat down beside her husband.

"Just imagine, having only the one child and then practically disowning her just because she got in the 'family way' and wasn't married. And then making her give up her child." Carrie shook her head. "He probably died a very lonely and bitter old man."

"Yah, it really was a shame for him the way it turned out. He missed out on knowing our Livvie."

The teakettle whistled from the kitchen so Carrie jumped up. "We can maybe get the dishes done before Jack Benny comes on."

CHAPTER 4

"I need to be at your mother's early tomorrow," Livvie told Stan as they were getting ready for bed one evening. "We're going to do some canning. I'll be there all day, I suppose."

"I hope Cheryl won't be fussy for you," remarked Stan.

"Well, she isn't teething or anything right now so I think she'll be pretty good." Livvie pulled back the covers and got into bed. "Aunt Maggie is going to be there, too, to help us."

"Oh, that will make for an interesting day," Stan joked.

The next morning, Stan helped Livvie get everything packed up in the car. He carried a big box of glass canning jars and placed them in the back seat. "I'll be over there in a little while so I'll carry that box into the house for you. Don't you try and carry it," he told his wife.

"See you later," Livvie called to Stan from the open car window. "It sure is going to be a hot day today," she said, thinking aloud, as she drove off. "Not a good day to can but I guess it has to get done."

A short while later she drove into her in-law's yard and parked close to the house. Joe was just coming out of the house so he stopped by the car to see if Livvie needed any help.

"You can carry that box of jars and I guess I can manage the rest," Livvie told him.

"Min will sure appreciate your help, and Maggie is coming over, too, I hear."

"Yes, we'll have a real canning bee over here today," laughed Livvie.

Min met them at the door and held it open, trying to shoo the pesky flies away at the same time.

"Here, I'll take Cheryl. It looks like you have a load there," Min said.

"Well, I brought jars, lids, and some sugar and vinegar. And then I have all the things the baby will need for the day, too."

"You really didn't need to come and help, Livvie," said Min. "You're busy enough with Cheryl here."

"Oh, I wouldn't dream of not helping you. I can't expect that you're going to just give us all those vegetables, already canned and ready."

They heard a step on the porch. "Yoohoo," called Maggie, as she let herself in. She too had an armful of canning supplies.

"I'm sure going to have plenty of help today, I can see," said Min.

"Let's get started then," suggested Maggie. "I was thinking we should have come earlier. It's going to be so hot by this afternoon."

"Yes, that's what I hear," replied Livvie. "It already feels pretty sticky."

"I had Allan go out early this morning and pick the beans so there's some in here for us to start with," Min said, pointing to the sink. "He's out there now picking some more and then he'll start on the beets."

"I told you that you planted too much this year, Min," scolded Maggie.

"Well, we were supposed to plant a big garden, you know."

"I planted the same as I always do. There's only three of us at our house to eat it all anyway," Maggie retorted.

"Yes, well, let's get going here," said Min. "One of you can start snipping the beans and I'll get the jars ready. The water is about to boil now I see." She put the empty jars into the canner.

"I told the men to forget about morning coffee today as we'd be too busy," said Min. "And they're just getting cold sandwiches for dinner."

"Well, I made a macaroni salad for Art and Grandpa to eat," Maggie told them.

Stan came into the house then. "I see you got help with the box of jars."

"Yes, your Dad helped me," said Livvie.

"Well, Stanley," said Maggie, "how are things way over on your place?"

"Just fine, Aunt Maggie."

"And how many cows do you have to milk now?" she queried.

"We have thirteen," he answered, edging closer to the back door as if to make his escape.

"I don't see why you wanted to have cows over there when your Dad has plenty here to milk."

"I just like cows, Aunt Maggie. See you ladies later," he said, grabbing a cookie from the counter and fleeing.

"I hear you have quite a few chickens over there, too, Olivia."

Maggie had a habit of calling everyone by their given name. No nicknames for her. Her nephews got away with calling her Maggie instead of Magda, though.

"Yes, we both like chickens, Aunt Maggie," replied Livvie patiently. She was snipping the beans as fast as she could to keep up with her husband's aunt. She didn't want to be called a slacker. "We sell the eggs in town and that really helps with the groceries, you know."

"Are those jars ready yet, Minerva?" she asked her sister-in-law. "We have enough beans ready to fill the first batch, I think."

"It won't be long now," Min answered.

By the time the men came in to eat at noon, there were many jars of green beans cooling on the counter.

"Here, you guys can sit at this end of the table and I'll get the food out for you." Min hustled to the refrigerator and came back with sandwiches and salad. "Ronnie, you get the milk, please."

They all sat down, even the women, and had a quick dinner.

"How soon do you think it will be before you start cutting the wheat, then?" asked Maggie.

"I think it could be any day now," said her brother, Joe. "How about Art? Has he started yet?"

"He's thinking tomorrow. That piece on the ridge is always ready earlier than the rest."

"Yes, I think the forty acres we have on the old Bemer place will be ready first. That's on a ridge, too."

"You'll be a little short-handed without Martin, won't you?" asked Maggie.

"Yah, but I guess we'll get along," answered Joe.

"I keep thinking we should be getting a letter from him soon again," said Min. "It's been over two weeks now."

The men left the house and the women quickly cleared off the table and got started on the beets.

"Allan sure must have picked every last beet out there!" exclaimed Maggie. "There's enough here to feed the U.S. Army!"

"My mother planted so much this year, too," laughed Livvie. "She got a little carried away. I should go and help her, too, but I guess Lenora is going to go there on Saturday and help."

"So, Olivia," started Maggie, "what do you hear from your—ah—your real mother? I hear her father passed away a few weeks ago."

"Yes, he did," answered Livvie slowly. "I never knew him, of course."

"Will you get to meet your grandmother now that he's gone? I hear that he was an old tyrant, if ever there was one."

Before Livvie could answer, Min stepped in. "Now Maggie, who has been telling you all these things?"

"Oh, I've just heard some people talking."

"Yes, Aunt Maggie, I guess he wasn't a very nice man," said Livvie, "but I hope to meet my grandmother soon and hope that she is eager to meet me."

"Well, I don't suppose she's too anxious to meet her illegitimate granddaughter!"

"Why, Maggie!" Min said angrily. "That's uncalled for. How can you say such a thing about our dear Livvie!" Livvie had never heard her mother-in-law raise her voice before.

"Well, I mean, it must have been quite a shock for her, to hear after all these years about a child that she would rather forget."

Livvie felt tears start to prick her eyes. She left the room and went to check on Cheryl, who had been put to sleep on the sofa nearby.

"That will be enough, Maggie," Min said slowly but firmly. "Can't you see you've upset the poor girl?"

"Well, I never!" said Maggie. "I was just taking an interest in her life, Minerva."

"Here, help me with these hot jars," said Min. "Careful now."

Livvie came back into the room and resumed her job of cutting the beets into chunks to fit the jars.

The women worked silently, side by side, for quite sometime. Allan came running into the house. "Here's the letter you've been waiting for, Mom," he said, handing her a thick, white envelope. "The mailman saw me in the yard and drove right in and handed me the mail."

"Well, old Pete knows how I wait for a letter everyday!" Min stated. She wiped her hands on a towel before touching the letter.

"Oh, my goodness, and it's such a thick one!" she said as she slit the envelope open eagerly. She walked out into the living room to read it by herself first.

After some minutes passed, Min came back into the kitchen and read the letter aloud. Joe and Ronnie had come into the house, too, by then. The men washed up by the basin while listening to what Marty had to say. The letter was indeed a long one.

"Marty really knows how to write letters, doesn't he?" said Joe.

"Just like when he talks," piped up Allan. "When he gets started telling something, he doesn't know when to quit."

"I guess everything is going OK for him, then," stated Maggie.

"It appears so," answered Min. "Except for the heat, he actually seems to be enjoying it down there in Texas."

"Just wait until he gets over to Europe," Maggie put in. "He maybe won't enjoy that so much."

No one said a word to this foolish statement of Maggie's. Joe rose from the table to go and get a drink of cool water from the refrigerator.

"Maggie," he said evenly, "we don't know yet if he'll be sent overseas so let's not even mention it, all right?"

"Well," she answered defensively, "you people should be preparing yourselves for the worst, you know."

Livvie stole a glance at her mother-in-law and could see that she was visibly upset.

"Maybe we should get back to the task at hand," suggested Livvie as she went to have a peek at the jars in the canner.

"Yes, let's do just that," said Min, rising from the table with a sigh.

Sometime later, the baby began to fret from the other room and Livvie went to pick her up. "Oh, she's so sweaty. I think I'll take her outside for awhile. I'll try to find some shade and a breeze."

"Go ahead," said Min. "We'll soon be finishing up here anyway. Another canner full and we'll call it quits."

Livvie and Cheryl found some shade on the north side of the house and sat down on the grass. Livvie leaned up against a tree. Oh, was she ever tired. And so hot!

After awhile, Allan came out with a cold glass of lemonade for her.

"Oh, thank you, Allan. How nice of you." She pressed the cold, sweaty glass against her cheek before tasting its sweet contents. She saw Stan and his father walking toward the house. Perhaps they were hot and thirsty, too.

Joe was wiping his face with his hankie as he neared Livvie and Cheryl.

"The thermometer by the back door there says ninety degrees!" he stated.

Stan sat down on the grass beside Cheryl and she reached out to him.

"It's almost too hot to pick you up," he said playfully to the child.

"I had to take her out here for awhile," said Livvie. "When she woke up she was just wringing wet."

"Allan, why don't you get two more glasses of that cold stuff for us," suggested Joe to his son.

"OK. Do you want anything to eat with it?"

"No, just something to drink. It's too hot to eat anything."

"Are you almost done canning?" asked Stan.

"We should soon finish up," answered Livvie. "If Maggie could just keep from saying things that upset everybody, we'd be OK."

"Well, that's my sister for you," said Joe, shaking his head.

"Now maybe you understand why we always called her Magpie when we were kids," chuckled Stan. "She likes to come in and stir things up and then she leaves."

Livvie laughed knowingly. "Now I understand. I've seen her in action."

After downing their cold drinks, the men reluctantly got up and headed back to work. Livvie and Cheryl returned to the hot kitchen.

"Oh, there you are," remarked Maggie. "I thought you had headed for home."

Livvie just looked at her but said nothing. She laid Cheryl on a blanket on the floor in the living room. She removed the baby's clothes and put only a clean diaper on her.

"Cheryl sure has been good today, hasn't she?" remarked Min.

"Yes, I guess she knew we were very busy," said Livvie.

"Well, the last jars are in the canner so I guess I can handle things myself here now," said Min. "If you two need to get on home, just go ahead."

"I guess I'll do that," agreed Maggie. She gathered up her things and was soon ready to leave. "Don't pick such a hot day to can next time, Minerva," she said, as she headed for the door. She turned around and had a last look at the baby.

"I see that Cheryl has found her thumb to suck. You really must put a stop to that right away, Olivia. It will ruin her teeth when they come in. Put some red pepper on her fingers and that will cure her." With that, the woman left, and not a moment too soon.

Livvie saw her mother-in-law plunk herself down on a kitchen chair and put her head in her hands. When Livvie got closer, she could see tears in Min's eyes. Livvie didn't know what to say.

"Oh, that woman! Some days she just really gets to me," Min said, as she wiped her eyes with her apron. "I really hated it when she started in on you, Livvie."

"Oh, don't worry about that too much, Min. Stan has always warned me about her so I won't take it too personally."

"I usually don't let her upset me like this. I've gotten so used to her ways after all these years. I guess today it's just the heat and me being tired and all, and then when she started in on you...."

"Think nothing of it, Min. Let's just try and forget about it."

"You know, she's really not such a bad person. If I ever need help, she's right there and she always defends the family to other people. If I'm ever sick, she's the first one here to help. When I had my babies, she was over here right away and helped me for a couple weeks afterwards." Min stood and went over to the canner to check things. She started taking out the jars and carefully placed them on a towel.

"I think she's not a very happy person," Min went on. "It seems like it makes her feel good to criticize other people."

"Maybe she feels bad that she never had any children of her own," volunteered Livvie.

"Well, that may be true," said Min. "I know she and Art really wanted a family but it just wasn't to be, I guess. She's so good with Grandpa, too, never complaining that he has to live with them."

"Does she realize how she upsets you?" asked Livvie.

"Actually I don't think she does. Tomorrow she'll drop by and it will be as if she'd never said those things. Like I said, she really has some good points if one can overlook certain things."

"It's taken a lot of patience on your part then, hasn't it, all these years?" Livvie said.

"I have to pray about it real often. That God will let me forgive her. It would be too easy to hold a grudge and I just can't do that. She really loves our family, you know, and has always taken such an interest in the boys."

"Yes, I suppose it would have been easy for her to be a little jealous of you, having so many children and her having none."

"I've thought of that," said Min, "but that doesn't seem to be a problem."

Stan came in the house just then. "Are you ready to leave for home, Livvie?"

"Just about. I'll gather up my things."

"When these jars have completely cooled, we'll box them up and bring some over to your house in the next day or so," offered Min.

"Oh, well, I don't need so very many. You should keep the most as you have the most mouths to feed over here. And Maggie will be getting some, too."

"I only have room for so many down in the fruit cellar so I'll bring enough over to last you through the year," said Min. "Until next year's garden," she laughed.

"Well, thank you, Min, for everything," said Livvie, holding Cheryl and waiting for Stan to give her a hand.

"I need to thank you for helping me today!" exclaimed Min. "Oh, say, why don't you take some of this cold meat for your supper tonight. And some of this salad. There's so much left."

"It was all so good but I think it was too hot to eat much," answered Livvie. "Thank you very much. It will be nice to have something quick to fix tonight."

Min walked with Livvie and Cheryl out to the car. Stan had put her things in the back seat and was heading for his pickup.

"I'll see you at home in a little bit," he called to her.

Min gave Livvie and the baby a hug and opened the car door for them. Livvie laid Cheryl on the front seat and closed the door.

"Whew! It sure is hot in here. I should have looked for a shadier spot," she said.

"Goodbye now, my dear," said Min.

"Goodbye," called Livvie as she backed up the car.

Livvie stopped at the end of her own driveway to pick up the mail from their mailbox. She noticed a letter to her and upon closer scrutiny, she saw that it was mailed from Leonard but it had no return address on it.

Maybe it's from Merrie. It looks like her writing. She hurried into the house with her things and laid Cheryl down in her crib. She sat down by the kitchen table and slit the envelope open with a knife.

It was from her real mother. As she read on, Merrie told her that she would be bringing her mother with her on Friday and would stop by and see Livvie.

When Stan came home about a half-hour later, Livvie greeted him with the information that she would soon be meeting her grandmother Munseth.

"Really? Is she coming here?"

"Yes, on Friday," answered Livvie. "I'm a little nervous about it, just how she will like me and everything."

"She'll like you just fine, dear. Don't worry about that!"

By Friday afternoon, Livvie had worked herself into quite a nervous state. She had called her mother, Carrie, and asked her to come but Carrie didn't think that would be a good idea.

"This should be a day just for you and Merrie and Mrs. Munseth. It will be better for everyone, I think."

Livvie watched as Merrie's car came slowly into the yard.

Perhaps Merrie is a little apprehensive about this, too. She saw an older woman get out on the passenger side. Merrie came around to offer her arm for support. The two made their way slowly to the house. Livvie waited until she heard a soft knock on the door. She took a deep breath and opened it.

"Hello, Merrie," she greeted her mother. She smiled at the woman who was her grandmother. She received a weak little smile in return.

"Come in, come in," she coaxed.

"Livvie, I'd like you to met your grandmother, Ethyl."

Livvie extended her hand to the woman. "How do you do, ah....Grandmother."

Mrs. Munseth took Livvie's small hand in hers and tears came to her eyes.

"Nice to meet you, child," she said in an almost inaudible voice.

"Let's go into the living room and have a seat," said Livvie. The two women followed her.

"Is the baby sleeping?" asked Merrie.

"Yes, she fell asleep shortly after dinner so she should be waking soon."

"I hope so," said Merrie. "We'll want to see her."

An awkward silence ensued. "Can I get you both something to drink? Some coffee, perhaps?" asked Livvie.

"That would be nice," said Merrie. Mrs. Munseth just nodded in the affirmative.

Livvie was relieved to be able to go into the kitchen for a few minutes alone. She poured the coffee into two nice, china cups and fixed a small plate of cookies.

"Here, I'll help you carry those," offered Merrie, coming up behind Livvie. Livvie turned and looked into her mother's eyes. Merrie gave Livvie a hug and said, "Now don't be nervous. It will be just fine."

The women enjoyed their coffee and some small talk and then they heard the baby start to fuss from the next room. Livvie hurried and went in to pick her up.

"Here she is!" she exclaimed proudly, as she came back into the room.

Mrs. Munseth's eyes seemed to brighten at the sight of the small child. Merrie stood to take the baby from its mother's arms.

"Oh, just look at you. You have surely grown since I last saw you," she cooed to Cheryl. Then she turned and placed the baby into the arms of her own mother.

Mrs. Munseth reacted stiffly at first but then relaxed and drew the child close to her. "Oh, she is so beautiful."

The rest of the afternoon went pretty well, Livvie related to her husband later.

"I can't tell for sure what she really thought of me," said Livvie. "She was a woman of few words. She really seemed to enjoy Cheryl, though."

"Well, who wouldn't, she's such a darling," said Stan, as he held his daughter proudly.

"After I get her to bed for the night," stated Livve, "I'm going to sit down and write a postcard to Mom. She's going to be wondering how this day went."

"And what exactly are you going to tell her?" Stan quizzed his wife.

After a pause, Livvie answered, "I'll tell her that I have a new grandmother, at long last."

CHAPTER 5

Because of the hot, dry weather, the harvest progressed quickly, both at the Murphy farm and at the Johnsons', south of Kindred. George was pleased with his yields and also with the price of wheat. It had gone up from last year. For the durum he got almost $1.00 per bushel.

"How much did you get for your barley here?" asked Stan.

"Seventy cents a bushel at the Kindred Elevator. How much did you get in Horace?" George asked his son-in-law.

"The same," he answered. "It looks like you got less rain this morning than we did."

"We got about a quarter of an inch. Not much, but every bit is welcome."

"Yah, it was getting pretty dry," Stan said. "We got almost a half an inch. That should help the ground plow up easier."

It was early on a Saturday evening and Stan and Livvie had stopped by to see George and Carrie before they went into town to do their weekly shopping.

"We could have gone to Davenport to get our groceries but Livvie wanted some things from Larsen's that she'd seen in an ad."

"Well, that was nice you came here," said George. "Then we get to see you a little bit. We've been so busy with harvest we haven't seen much of anybody lately."

"Livvie was thinking that maybe we could leave Cheryl here while we shop."

"Oh, I'm sure Carrie would love that."

The men walked to the house and went in the back door. Carrie and Livvie were talking in the living room.

"Oh, there you guys are," said Carrie. "I was just telling Livvie that if she and Stan want to stay and take in a movie after they get their shopping done, that would be all right with us."

"Of course," said George. "Then we get to have Cheryl a little longer."

Stan looked at Livvie. "Well, we'll see when we get our errands done," he said.

Carrie and George enjoyed the novelty of having the baby all to themselves. She soon fell asleep, however, so that put an end to their fun. Carrie sat and held the sleeping child, just because it felt so good to hold her, even though she could have put her down on the bed.

"Isn't she just about the sweetest thing?" Carrie said to her husband.

"That she is," he answered, looking up over his newspaper.

"I wonder if the kids will stay for the movie. I hope they do. They need some fun once in awhile."

"Yah, Stan has been working awfully hard lately," commented George.

"I imagine they really miss Marty. They sure could have used him during harvest."

Carrie's arms were finally getting tired, so she placed the baby on the sofa next to her. The baby squirmed a little but settled back down almost immediately.

"If she sleeps all evening, she'll be awake most of the night."

George put down his newspaper and went to turn on the radio. "It must soon be time for the Lux Radio Theater."

Carrie picked up her needlework and they listened to the program in companionable silence. Before long, they heard a car door slamming and then another. Carrie got up and went to look out the kitchen window.

"It's Livvie and Stan already," she called to her husband.

When her daughter and husband came in the back door, Carrie called to them and said, "You came back too early!"

"Why, what have you two been up to? Keeping the baby awake all this time so you can play with her?" laughed Stan.

"Oh, no, she fell asleep about a half an hour after you left," said George.

"You decided not to go to the movie, I take it," said Carrie. Before they could answer, she indicated that they should sit down at the kitchen table.

"Well, we almost did, but then we ran into Freddie and Lenora. We had a good visit with them and then it was too late," said Stan.

"They had some bad news to tell us," said Livvie.

Carrie's heart took a leap and she hardly dared to ask. "What is it?"

"Lenora's future brother-in-law got his draft notice today."

"You mean Lucy's fiance, Jack Gilbertson?" asked George. Lucy was Lenora's twin sister.

"Oh, my," commented Carrie. "Weren't they planning to get married soon, too?"

"At Christmas time, but now they don't know what they'll do. I guess just wait and see how it goes after he's been for his physical and all."

Carrie was quiet as she started to fix coffee and put out a plate of doughnuts.

"Where did you see Freddie and Lenora?" she finally asked.

"Oh, we thought we'd go in and check out the newly-remodeled Thompson's Cafe. They were having their Grand Opening today, you know."

"Yah, George was in there this afternoon, but I had too many things going here to get away. How was it?"

"Oh, it's really nice!" exclaimed Stan. "On the outside, it's a dark green plate glass on the bottom and a light cream on the top. There's also some brick siding, too. They've added some living quarters in the back."

"I thought it looked really nice," said George. "I was in town for parts this afternoon and dropped in for free coffee and doughnuts. Weren't they having some entertainment there this evening?"

"Yes, the Lane Sisters of WDAY were there so we got to hear them," said Livvie. "That's where we ran into Freddie and Lenora. They were sitting in a booth with Lucy and Jack."

"What did they do with the kids?" asked Carrie.

"Susie came over to sit with them," answered Livvie. Susie was Lenora's younger sister.

"Is this Susie's last year of high school now?" asked Carrie.

"Yes, I think she'll graduate next spring."

Carrie poured each one a cup of coffee. "Here, George, you're getting doughnuts again. It seems I make doughnuts more than cookies, now, what with the sugar rationing. They take less sugar."

"I was going to make a cake today," commented Livvie, "but then I stopped to think, too, that it would be better to make something else instead. The cake plus the frosting takes too much sugar."

"What did you make then?" Carrie asked her daughter.

"Oh, I just made a gingerbread cake and scrimped a little on the sugar. We'll put applesauce on top when we have it tomorrow."

"Did you read that they may be putting a ration on gasoline, too, now?" said George.

"I figured it would come to that," replied Stan. "They have been urging us all to use it sparingly. How will that go for farm use, I wonder?"

"I don't know," answered George thoughtfully.

Carrie put the coffeepot in the middle of the table and sat down.

"I understand there is a real teacher shortage nationwide this fall," she said.

"Yah, I heard that, too," said Livvie, "but I think that Kindred and Davenport were able to get the teachers they needed."

"For this year, maybe, but what about the next year?" asked Carrie.

"Do you think this war will last that long?" Livvie wondered.

The baby began to make waking sounds so Livvie went to pick her up.

"Well, we should be going, Stan, don't you think?"

"Yah, we have early church tomorrow."

"We have late church in Gol tomorrow, with a dinner," said Carrie. We will have a guest pastor, though, as Pastor Turmo will want to go over to Norman where his brother, U.A. Turmo will be installed."

"Isn't that a coincidence that two brothers have churches in the same community," commented Stan.

"Yes, but it's kind of nice, I would think. They'll have family nearby."

"Oh, Stan, did you hear what happened in town last night?" George asked his son-in-law. "Some tires were stolen from the Farmer's Union. Some guys broke into the rear of the building. Then they took Bennie Stenberg's car and drove that until one of his tires went flat, over by Ted Perhus' place."

"Did they catch 'em?"

"No, the car with the fourteen stolen tires in it was found in the morning but no sign of the thieves. They must have taken off on foot."

"How did they get that many tires into a car?"

"Well, the back seat was full and also the trunk," explained George.

Livvie finished packing up the baby's things and was ready to go.

"Did you get what you wanted at the Larsen's Store, then?" asked Carrie.

"Yes, they had bags of chocolate chips on sale for two for twenty-five cents. Ever since that recipe came out in the paper a couple years ago, that is Stan's favorite."

"I had George pick me up some this afternoon when he went in. I don't suppose I should be making cookies too often now, though."

"It's going to be hard for awhile, changing the way we do our baking, isn't it?" said Livvie.

"Well, let's hope this war is soon over and things can get back to normal."

The next afternoon, George and Carrie took a drive into town and they stopped to see Freddie and Lenora.

"I had a feeling you two would stop by this afternoon," said Lenora, as she greeted them at the door. "Freddie is taking a nap but I'm sure he'll soon wake up. He didn't sleep very good last night." She lowered her voice and went on. "I suppose Livvie and Stan told you about my sister's fiance getting drafted."

"Yes, they told us they had run into you last night," said Carrie.

Lenora led them into the kitchen as Freddie was lying on the sofa in the living room.

"The kids are both sleeping, too, so I was just sitting and relaxing a bit."

"Here, have a chair and I'll start the coffee," Lenora said. "The smell of that should wake up Freddie!"

"Oh, let him sleep," said Carrie.

"I think he was really bothered about Jack getting his notice in the mail yesterday. He's wondering if he's next."

"I worry about that myself, Lenora, and I'm sure you do, too."

"Yes, I do, but I try not to dwell on it. I really don't know what I'd do if he had to go, what with two small children to care for and all."

"Well, I pray many times a day that he won't have to go," sighed Carrie, "but I suppose every mother does the same."

"Why do we have to have wars, anyway!" said Lenora fiercely.

"That's a good question," said George. "I guess as long as we have Hitlers in the world, there will be fighting. It seems he wants to conquer the whole world."

"Then there's the Japs!" exclaimed Lenora. "It seems they want the whole world, too. I just don't understand it."

"Hey, what's all the noise in here?" said Freddie, in good humor, as he stood in the doorway. "I must have dozed off for a few minutes."

"Oh, you've been sleeping pretty good for over an hour now," said his wife.

Freddie plopped down on a kitchen chair. "Glad you dropped by," he said to his parents. "I suppose you heard about Jack being drafted."

Carrie figured that this subject was weighing heavily on her son's mind.

"Yes, Livvie and Stan told us last night after they had run into you in town."

Freddie ran his hand through his thick, brown hair in a nervous gesture.

"Every day you wonder who will be next."

George and Carrie spent a couple hours at Freddie's, played with the children when they woke up from their naps, and then decided it was time to go home and do the evening chores. George drove down the main street so Carrie could see the new cafe.

"My, that does look nice, doesn't it?" she said. "The last time I was in town, they didn't have that green siding on yet."

"We'll have to go and eat there sometime," George said.

"Yes, that would be fun," Carrie agreed. Eating out wasn't something they did very often so it was a real treat to do it occasionally.

They drove up and down a few of the other streets in town and then headed for home. Carrie was silent until they pulled into their driveway.

"I thought Freddie looked very tired and....and....worried, didn't you think?" she asked.

"I guess he did."

"Oh, I hope....I hope...." Carrie looked over at her husband. "Well, you know what I hope."

George nodded his head without answering. The words had been said many times between them.

CHAPTER 6

Summer seemed to want to linger over the Red River Valley but, by late October, it seemed that winter was in a hurry to take its place. The fall plowing had been completed and the gardens had been cleaned up in preparation for the first hard frost. Just a few pumpkins and squash remained in the Murphys' garden.

"Livvie, do you want any more squash? You can take as many as you want," said Min.

"No, I don't think I need any more. I guess we canned enough to last through the winter and then some," laughed Livvie.

"Yah, I guess we maybe did get a bit carried away," her mother-in-law confessed. "Are you coming over to Grandpa's birthday party tomorrow?"

"Oh, yes," said Livvie. "We wouldn't miss it."

"Why don't you call and tell your folks to come for it, too? Magda mentioned that Grandpa would like to have them come."

"Oh, really? I can sure call them and see," replied Livvie. "Did Magda say if I could bring something for the lunch?"

"Oh, no. You know Magda. She wants to do everything herself so I just let her have her way," chuckled Min.

"I suppose it's better that way," agreed Livvie. "Well, we'll see you tomorrow afternoon, then. I need to run into Davenport and get a little gift for Grandpa. Do you suppose he could use some socks or hankies or something like that?"

"I'm sure he can always use socks. He also loves chocolate covered cherries if they have any of those on hand."

"I called and talked to my mother today," Livvie mentioned to her husband at the supper table that evening. "Your Aunt Maggie said that your grandpa wants them to come to his party. I guess he took quite a liking to them ever since our wedding!"

"Oh, really? Are they coming, then?"

"Mom said they probably would."

"Did she say if Freddie and Lenora have heard from Jack since he got down to Fort Leonard Wood?"

"Lucy had heard from him the other day. He said that basic training is really tough and it had still been pretty hot there in Missouri."

Stan just shook his head and was quiet during the remainder of the meal. He and Freddie and many other young men like him all worried that they'd be the next to be called up.

Stan and Livvie were the last to arrive at Art and Magda's the next afternoon for the birthday party. Carrie and George were already there.

"Sorry we're so late," apologized Livvie as she handed the baby to her mother so she could remove her coat. "Stan had a problem with one of the cows. He had to call the vet and he's going to come tomorrow if things aren't better."

Besides close family and George and Carrie, a few neighbors were also there. Kenny, Ronnie's best friend, and Kenny's father, Jake, were there and Rosie and her parents. These were all the closest neighbors.

As Livvie walked into the living room, a card table had already been set up and Grandpa Ivar was sitting there playing a game of cards with Ronnie, Kenny and Rosie.

"What are you playing?" asked Stan.

"Rook," answered Rosie. "Do you want to take my place? I don't think your grandpa likes me for a partner. I didn't play his trump back when I should have," she laughed.

"Sure, I'll take your place if you really don't want to play any longer," said Stan, who loved to play cards as much as his grandpa.

"If you decide to play Whist, count me in," said Rosie, as she headed off to the kitchen where most of the women were.

George pulled his chair closer so he could watch the game. "So, Ivar, how old are you today, then?"

Grandpa paused in his shuffling to answer. "I was 69 years old yesterday. I think I'll stay 69 for the next few years," he chuckled.

"Well, that's not so old, you know," consoled George.

"You're just a young 'un yet," he said to George.

"Well, I'm only 10 years younger than you!"

"Is that so?" Ivar said, as he studied his cards.

Allan, who was only eleven, and thought everyone over 30 was old, said, "I can't imagine ever getting as old as you guys!"

His older brother, Ronnie, shot him a dirty look but his grandpa only laughed.

"You'll get there sooner than you think, my boy."

"Isn't that the truth," agreed George.

A loud eruption of laughter came from the kitchen.

"Those women can cackle louder than a bunch of hens!" snorted Ivar.

Magda soon came into the living room and announced that lunch was ready. "You'd better finish up that hand and then come into the dining room. The table is all set with the food."

Art had added all the leaves to the big table so it could seat over a dozen people comfortably. Magda was the only one who didn't sit down. When everyone else was seated, they sang the table prayer and then someone started "Happy Birthday."

Ivar looked at everyone and beamed. He was truly enjoying his special day.

"Boy, when Madga said lunch, she really should have said banquet. Look at all this food!" remarked Kenny's father, Jake.

"Well, I shouldn't have eaten dinner I can see!" said Rosie's father, Adolph.

Everyone laughed and agreed. Magda passed the food with pride. There was first a plate of ham sandwiches, then egg salad sandwiches, then beans, a macaroni salad, a Jello salad with fruit and whipped cream on it, then a plate of doughnuts. She reminded everyone to save room for the birthday cake.

"How do you expect us to have room for that?" laughed George.

After the merriment subsided, the subject moved to the usual topic—the war.

"Do you hear anything from Norway, Ivar, about how things are going there after the Germans took over?" asked Jake.

"Well, we haven't gotten a letter now for almost a year. Any news I get about how things are over there I read in the Decorah Posten. Do you get that paper?"

"No, not anymore. Not after Pa died."

"They manage to get a little information from the Red Cross and also from the British," Ivar explained. "It sounds like things aren't too good."

"Yah, that Quisling fellow, a real traitor he is," remarked Art.

"After the King and his cabinet fled to London, he set himself up as the head of the Norwegian government. He's a damn Nazi, that's what he is!" snorted Jake. "He's collaborating with those Germans."

"I hear that some of the royal family is here in the United States," remarked Magda."

"Yes, I've heard rumors that the Roosevelt family is sheltering them," said Myrtle.

"My, my, I wonder how all this is going to end," wondered Carrie.

"Did you know that that Sampson boy was with the US Marines when they landed on Guadalcanal?" mentioned Jake. "His parents are plenty worried about him. I just talked to Mrs. Sampson in the store yesterday."

"What do you hear from Marty, Joe?" asked George.

"Well, he's still safely down in Texas. I'm glad as long as he can stay in the States." Joe looked over at his wife. She wore a worried frown.

"Maybe we should talk of more pleasant things," said Magda. "After all, this is supposed to be a party!"

Try as they might, the conversation always seemed to be connected with the war in some way.

"I read where we're supposed to be saving even rags and burlap, too, now, besides paper and scrap metal," said Adolph.

"Yah, I guess we can't throw a thing away anymore."

"Hjalmer Rustad has volunteered to take care of the waste paper collection down there in Kindred," said George, "and I understand we're to haul all our scrap metal to town someplace, too."

"What are they going to make out of the paper?" asked Allan.

"They'll use it for making cartons and packing boxes," explained his Uncle Art.

"They're really pushing this scrap metal drive," said George. "They're giving away prizes to the one who brings in the most."

"What kind of prizes?" asked Allan.

"Oh, boxes of groceries, oil, wine, things like that," answered George.

"I read where the Red Cross is calling for more nurses for the Army and Navy. North Dakota needs to fill its quota of 193 in just a short while," said Rosie's mother. "I sure wouldn't want my daughter to have to go overseas and tend to all those wounded soldiers!" She looked pointedly at her daughter.

Rosie would be graduating from high school in the spring, and she worried about what the impetuous girl might do.

"Did you hear about that Rockstad boy from the Walcott area who was on the USS Lexington when it sank?" asked Art.

"Yah, wasn't he in the water for about two hours before he was rescued?"

"I guess he's home on leave now."

"Boy, that was a close call."

"I heard that the area Luther Leagues put on a nice send-off party for some of the boys a few weeks ago," said Min.

"Yes, Jack Gilbertson was one of them and Glen Erickson and about three others," said Carrie. "I heard that Orville Perhus was drafted, too."

Ivar looked thoughtfully around the table at his three grandsons, Stan, Ronnie and young Allan. And there was Kenny, too.

Would one of these be next? When his gaze fell on Stan, their eyes met, each understanding the other. Wanting to change the subject, Ivar said, "Where's my birthday cake? I'm still hungry!" Everyone laughed at this.

Magda brought in two cakes, one an angel food cake with white frosting and the other one chocolate.

"Where did you get the sugar to make all that cake?" asked Livvie.

"Oh, Min and my good neighbor Myrtle, gave me some of their ration stamps for this special occasion."

Magda struggled to light the candles on both cakes and then had Ivar blow them out.

"Make a wish, now, Grandpa," said Allan.

Ivar looked soberly around and was thoughtful for awhile and then he blew all the candles out with just one puff.

"It'll take only one year for your wish to come true, Grandpa!" cried Allan.

"I hope you're right about that, son," said Ivar. "I hope you're right."

"Grandpa, tell us again about how you changed our name on the boat coming over here from Norway," encouraged Stan. He knew his wife hadn't heard this story before.

"Yah, well, as some of you know, our name should have been Mjolsness and not Murphy."

"Really?" said Livvie. "Stan, you never told me that before!" She looked at her husband and he just shrugged.

"Well, anyway," continued Ivar, "it was back in 1903 when I came over here. It was in May of that year and on the boat I met a man who had been to America but had gone back to Norway to visit family and now he was returning to America on the same boat as I was on. We got to talking several times and he said he wanted to give me a little advice. He said that I should change my name because those Americans wouldn't be able to pronounce or spell such a name as Mjolsness. I asked him what would be a good name to change it to then and he said, 'how about Murphy, that's the name I changed mine to.' "

"What was his name before Murphy?" interrupted Allan.

"You know, I'm not even sure what it was," said Ivar. "Only that it was something hard to say and write. Anyway, I figured it wouldn't hurt to change my name. In Norway they do it all the time. So, that is how you got to be Murphys."

"In high school, kids would ask me if I was Irish," laughed Ronnie, "so I'd have to explain the situation."

"What made you come to America, Grandpa Murphy?" asked Livvie.

"To find a better life, I guess. It was hard times in Norway and we couldn't all make a living on my father's farm," Ivar explained, stroking his beard thoughtfully.

Ivar Murphy was a big, tall man with very large hands. He could sometimes look very gruff, but he had a smile that came easily and reached his eyes. Oftentimes, though, those eyes held a sad expression, thought Livvie. Perhaps there could be some deep-down sadness in his life, she often thought.

Livvie decided to press on. "What family did you leave behind in Norway?"

Ivar hesitated awhile before answering. "My parents and a sister and a brother. My parents are long dead now." He started to push himself away from the table. "It doesn't look like we're going to get any more to eat so maybe we should get a game of Hearts going."

The women began scurrying around, clearing up all the food and dishes. Allan ran and got the cards while the other men got up to stretch a bit.

"Maybe one quick game and then I'll have to get home for evening chores," said Stan.

"Me, too," seconded Adolph.

Allan, anxious to start the game, began shuffling the deck. "Can I deal?" he asked.

"If you want to," replied his grandpa.

All the men and boys plus Rosie sat down again around the big table and the game began. It ended up to be three games before some of the men decided it was time to quit and get to their milking.

Stan stuck his head in the kitchen and announced to Livvie, "It's time go, Mrs. Mjolsness." Everyone laughed at his use of their 'real' name.

Ivar thanked the departing guests for coming.

On the way home, Livvie said to her husband, "It seems like your grandpa has something in his past that he is sad about. Do you know of anything?"

"No, I've never heard of anything. Maybe he just had a hard life in the old country, like so many of them did."

"Well, he sure didn't want to talk about it, did he?"

"That was a long time ago, Livvie."

Livvie was thoughtful the rest of the way home.

CHAPTER 7

One beautiful Saturday in November, Stan and Livvie were over at his parent's farm, helping butcher chickens. Livvie wanted no part of the bloody work, so she took care of things in the kitchen. She cooked coffee and made dinner for all the workers. Art and Maggie were helping, as well as Kenny, so there was a good-sized crew.

They all came in the house at noon for dinner. Min had put a large roast in the oven so Livvie just had to make the potatoes and vegetables. She had brought a couple of pies from home to add to the bountiful fare.

Everyone ate heartily, as the fresh air and physical work of the morning had stirred up a good appetite in each of them. After the meal, they lingered over their pie and coffee, not really wanting to get back to the grisly job.

"Well, we better make hay while the sun shines," suggested Art. "In fact, it looks like it's clouding up a bit outside. Maybe we'll see some snow yet."

About mid-afternoon, his prediction came true. It first started raining but that quickly turned to snow. The butchering job was about finished and the helpers left for their homes.

"I'll go home and do the chores and come back for you and Cheryl," said Stan. Livvie was planning to stay for awhile and use her mother-in-law's sewing machine to finish a dress she was working on.

"Well, maybe I should go home with you in case it gets worse outside," Livvie said to Stan.

"Oh, I think the snow is already letting up so there shouldn't be any problem with me getting back."

"We'll wait supper for you, then," his mother said.

Livvie sewed the rest of the afternoon while Min watched Cheryl and started supper.

"I hope I can get a sewing machine of my own someday," commented Livvie.

"Well, maybe after this war is over," answered Min.

All of a sudden they heard a loud, rushing noise, like a freight train, and they both looked up, startled. It was like some large force had hit the northwest side of their house.

Min went to the window and looked out. "Mercy, you should just look out here. It's snowing so hard I can't see a thing!"

The back door swung open and in tumbled Allan and Ronnie.

"Wow!" Allan said, excitedly. "We were on our way to the house and just like that, this wall of snow is coming toward us."

"Where's your father?" asked Min.

"He's still out in the barn. He said he'd finish up with the chores."

"We cleaned the separator and Dad said he'd bring in the milk," said Ronnie, as he washed up at the washbasin.

"Where's Stan?" asked Allan.

"He went home to do our chores and then he was planning to come back and get me," said Livvie, "but I wonder if he'll make it now." Concern filled her voice.

"Well, I hope he hasn't started out yet and has the sense to stay put," said his mother.

"Maybe I should call him," volunteered Livvie.

"Maybe you'd better. Tell him to stay home. You can stay here tonight if it doesn't get better before dark."

Joe came in the house and brushed off snow from his overalls. "Did Stan go home?"

"Yah, he did and he's planning to come back and get Livvie and the baby but we were just saying that we should call him and tell him to stay home."

"I hope he hasn't started out yet. It's really bad out there," said Joe.

Livvie went to the phone and dialed Central. She gave the operator their number and waited while it rang and rang. No answer.

"Oh, no, I wonder if that means he's started out."

"Well, maybe he's still in the barn, Livvie," Joe said kindly. "We can try later, or maybe he'll call here so we won't worry about him."

Joe sat down to read the paper and the boys started a card game on the kitchen table. Livvie turned back to her sewing. She couldn't concentrate very well on her task but she needed to keep her hands busy. Anyway, she was very close to finishing the project.

"Have you ever seen a storm hit so fast?" asked Min, conversationally.

"Oh, yes, a couple of times, I guess," answered Joe. "Don't you remember that time we were over at your folks' place that one Christmas and we all had to stay overnight? I remember it hit just as fast as this one. It took everyone by surprise. Several people were caught out in it, too."

"Yah, I guess I remember that now. Didn't that Olson boy start walking and freeze his feet?"

"Yah, he lost several toes and he always walked funny after that."

"There, I'm finished!" announced Livvie, holding up the dress proudly. "I just have the hem left to do by hand."

"My, that looks very nice, Livvie. That blue is such a good color for you, too," said Min.

"You're getting to be quite a little seamstress, there," said Joe, looking up over his paper.

"Livvie will have to get a machine of her own sometime," remarked Min.

"Well, I'm sure she would make good use of one," said Joe. "Maybe after the war."

"That's what I told her."

"Everything is 'after the war' is seems," said Allan.

"If you boys could move your game now, I'll set the table for supper," said their mother.

"What are we having? I'm starved!" asked Allan.

"Again?" asked Ronnie. "You ate like a horse for dinner!"

"Well, I love roast beef, and anyway, I worked hard all morning so I was really hungry."

"We're just having roast beef sandwiches and some leftover soup from yesterday," Min told them.

"Should I try calling Stan again?" Livvie asked hopefully.

"Why don't you, dear," said Min.

This time Stan answered on the first ring. "I just came in from the barn," he told Livvie. "It really is nasty out. I don't know if I'll try to get over there just yet. We'll wait and see."

So the rest of the family sat down to eat their supper. Baby Cheryl was propped up in the high chair with pillows and seemed to be happy to join the family around the table. Livvie fed her some vegetables that she picked out of the soup and mashed up for the little one.

The wind continued to howl outside but the Murphys' kitchen was cozy and warm. Livvie was glad knowing that Stan was home and not out on the road.

After the dishes were done, Allan asked if anyone would like to play a game with him. He loved games of all kinds.

"Maybe later, son," said his Dad. "I think I'll take a little nap and read some more of the paper."

"I'll play Parcheesi with you, twerp," said Ronnie.

"Don't call me that, you jerk!"

"Now boys, don't call each other names," their mother reminded them from the living room.

Livvie set the baby on a blanket on the floor and set some toys near her. Then she took up her dress and started doing the hand hemming.

Min sat in the rocker and read awhile. As the time passed, they could hear that the wind was letting up and it got quieter and quieter.

When Joe got up from the sofa, he thought he'd go and take a look out the back door.

"Why, it's pretty calm now," he said. "Just a little bit of snow still falling."

"I wonder if Stan will start out now, then," wondered Livvie.

"Maybe you should call him and tell him to just wait until morning. I'd hate to have him out now after dark. You never know what the roads will be like," said Min.

So Livvie called Stan and suggested that he not come for them until the next day.

"Stan said that he would wait until morning, after he's done the chores," Livvie said after hanging up.

After Livvie got Cheryl put down to sleep for the night, everyone gathered around the kitchen table. Allan wanted everyone to play Hearts with him.

"I'll make up a batch of popcorn," offered Min, "and you guys start playing."

"Boy, this is going to be a fun evening!" exclaimed Allan.

As they were playing, the lights in the room blinked a couple times.

"Oh, no!" exclaimed Min, "Are we going to lose our electricity?"

"Well, that was some pretty heavy, wet snow so maybe the lines are all coated," suggested Joe.

Min served the popcorn and some Root Beer which she had brought up from the basement.

As they were eating their snack, the lights blinked a couple of times again.

"I think I better get the candles ready. Joe, you get the kerosene lamps from the pantry just in case."

Soon they had candles, matches and the lamps ready, within easy reach, if need be.

Allan dealt out another hand. All of a sudden they heard some stomping on the back porch.

"Oh, no, did Stan come after all?" wondered Min.

A loud, almost desperate knocking sounded on the door. Joe jumped up and went to see who was there.

When he opened the door, he was almost knocked over by a big man holding a child.

"Help me!" said the man. "Help me!"

Everyone jumped up and came to join Joe at the door. Without words, Joe reached out and took the child from the man's arms.

"The mother!" he panted. "The mother is still in her car. I need help to bring her in. The snow is so deep I had to walk all the way."

"Where is the car?" asked Joe, already slipping into his warmest jacket.

"It's about a quarter mile east of here, by that coulee."

"You stay here and warm up and rest. Ronnie, you come with me."

"Do you think we could make it with the pick up?" asked Ronnie, looking at the man.

"I don't know for sure. The snow is pretty deep."

"Maybe we should hitch up the sleigh to old Dolly," said Joe. "Min, get some blankets ready for us to take along. Send Allan out with them. C'mon, Ronnie, let's go."

In about fifteen minutes the horse and sleigh were ready and the two men started off down the road. They could soon see why the man had a hard time walking, especially carrying a child.

Meanwhile, in the house, the women had the child lying on the sofa, all covered up with warm blankets. The man removed his outer clothes and sat by the oil-stove in the living room.

"How old is the girl?" Min asked the man.

"I don't know. I just happened upon them as I was trying to drive down this road to get to my home."

"And where do you live?" asked Min. She had never seen this man before.

"Over by Leonard. I had been to Fargo and waited out the worst of the storm in Horace and then thought I'd try and get home when it looked like it had cleared up. I figured my wife would be worried sick."

"Yes, I'm sure she is. Perhaps you can call her from here."

"Well, we don't have a telephone," he said slowly. "Maybe I could call the neighbors and they could get word to her."

The child was whimpering and asking for her mother. "Mama, Mama," she cried.

"That's all right, little girl," said Min, soothingly. "The men went to get your Mama and she'll be here soon."

As Min laid her hand upon the child's forehead, she found it to be very hot. "Why, this child is burning up with fever!"

She went to the kitchen to fetch a cool, wet rag. She returned and laid it upon the little girl's forehead.

"The mother mentioned that the little girl was sick and she wanted me to get her to safety. We could see your yard light from where their car had gone off the road. I couldn't get around them with my pickup so I had to walk. It didn't look as far away as it really was though," said the man, still trying to catch his breath.

He looked really worn out, thought Min. She guessed him to be about in his fifties and rather overweight. "What's your name?" Min asked the man.

"John. John Peterson."

"I bet you could go for a nice, hot cup of coffee," said Min. She went to the kitchen and put the pot on the burner.

"It will be ready in just a few minutes, Mr. Peterson," she said, as she returned to the living room and sat down by the child once again.

Despite all the blankets, the girl was shivering now. Min ran upstairs to get another quilt. She warmed it by the stove and laid it on top of all the other blankets.

As Min was pouring a cup of coffee for Mr. Peterson, she heard some footsteps on the back porch. She went to the door and Joe and Ronnie were helping a woman up the steps. Min held the door open for them.

After the woman got herself unbundled, Min exclaimed, "Why, its Mrs. Bolstad, isn't it?"

"Yes, that's me," the woman answered through chattering teeth.

"Oh, my! Here, let me get you by the stove and warm you up."

The men took off their outerwear and left their wet boots by the door.

"You weren't dressed very warm, were you?" Min said to Mrs. Bolstad. "And this is your little girl, then. I didn't recognize her."

Min sent Livvie upstairs to get a heavy sweater for the woman and some slippers. "Here, let's get those wet shoes off, too."

The woman sat down by the child and caressed her gently. "Oh, Shirley, how are you doing, you poor thing?"

"I think she has a fever so I put that rag on her forehead for awhile. Should I give her some aspirin?"

"Oh, yes, maybe that would be good. Just a half of one, perhaps."

Min went to the pantry and found the aspirin bottle. She carefully split one in half and crushed it and put it in a glass of cool water. She gave it to the mother to give to her child.

"I'll get coffee for everyone," Min said, and Livvie jumped up to go and help her mother-in-law.

Mrs. Bolstad asked if she could use the telephone to call her boys, who were home alone.

"Of course," answered Joe. "It's right there on the wall."

"I suppose it would be long distance from here?"

"I think you're on the same line as we are."

A little later, as the adults were seated around the kitchen table, Joe asked Mrs. Bolstad how she happened to be out on such a night as this.

"Well, you know what a beautiful November day this started out to be," she began. I decided to take Shirley and drive over to my sister's. She lives over by Horace. We always take this road as a kind of short cut. We were busy making lefse together and were so surprised to see the storm come up so quickly. I told Shirley that we better hurry and head on home before it got worse. My two boys were home alone on the farm so I was anxious to get home to them."

Mrs. Bolstad took a big swallow of coffee and continued. "When we were in the car, Shirley started complaining that she didn't feel good. She said her throat was sore and she felt so hot. I guess I was driving too fast, anxious to get home, and I started to slip off the road back there. I couldn't get myself out, so we just had to sit there, hoping someone would come along. Then that terrible wall of snow just hit us and we couldn't see a thing for quite awhile.

"We were getting so cold," she continued, almost sobbing by this time. "I just prayed and prayed. I didn't know what else to do. Then it stopped snowing some and we could see your light over here but I couldn't possibly walk and carry Shirley, too."

"It's a good thing you came along, Mr. Peterson," said Joe.

"Yah, I guess there was a reason for me to be out on the road just then. I had been to Fargo and got as far as Horace and had to stop there. I went into the bar and there were a lot of fellows waiting it out. I had a couple beers to pass the time so excuse me if I smell of booze, ma'am," he said to Min sheepishly.

"I think after all that fresh air on your walk over here, there's no smell left!" laughed Min.

"I often take this road, too, because I live straight west of here. About ten miles, maybe. I live northwest of Leonard."

"How old is your family, Mrs. Bolstad?" asked Joe.

"First of all, please call me Dorothy. You probably know that my husband died about three years ago now."

"Yes, we were awfully sorry to hear that. He was a good man."

"My boys, Johnny and Bobby, are twelve and ten. Johnny tries so hard to be the man of the family. They were sure relieved to hear from me and know that we are safe. My little girl, Shirley will be six next month."

"It must be hard for you to manage a farm by yourself," said Min. "I'm surprised you didn't move into town after your husband died."

"Well, I rent out my acreage to my neighbors. My boys wanted to stay on the farm. We have a few cows and chickens and they take care of them. It helps us get by."

"So, Mr. Peterson, what is it you do over by Leonard?" asked Joe.

"I work for a rancher over there. Don Schultz. Heard of him?"

"I think I might have," answered Joe.

"Yep, I've been with him for almost 20 years now. Been a farm hand all my life. Used to work on some of the big bonanza farms around here. Worked on the Powers ranch for awhile."

Livvie tensed up at hearing this. "Did you ever work with any Canadians?" she asked, almost timidly.

"Oh, I remember a few. They'd come down during the busy months. I worked with all kinds of men, from all over. All nationalities, too. We'd see some pretty good fights sometimes between some of them. The Russians didn't like the Germans and the Norwegians didn't like the Swedes and the Irish didn't like anybody! I had to break up many a fight, I tell you! The trouble makers didn't last long. They were paid and told to hit the road."

It was decided earlier that the unexpected guests would stay the night as the condition of the roads was questionable in the dark. Mr. Peterson had let his wife know of his whereabouts by calling the neighbors.

"Well, perhaps we should get a place for all of you to sleep," suggested Min.

"Mr. Peterson, you can have Marty's room upstairs and, Dorothy, you and Shirley can have Allan's room."

"Oh, I don't want to put anybody on the floor!" said Dorothy.

"We have plenty of beds," laughed Min. "Allan can sleep with Ronnie. Livvie and the baby will have Stan's old room. We'll manage just fine."

When everyone had left the kitchen except Mr. Peterson, Livvie came back to him and worked up the courage to ask him a question. "Do you remember a Canadian by the name of..of..Alphonse Kastet?"

"Well, I'll have to think on that for awhile, miss. My memory isn't what it used to be." With this, he headed upstairs to find his room.

Livvie sat down on the sofa for awhile. Shirley had been carried up the stairs by Joe and was being settled down with her mother.

Livvie's real father was a man by the name of Alphonse Kastet. He was a Canadian who had worked on various farms and ranches in the area. Livvie's real mother, Merrie, had finally told her the name of her real father just a few years back.

Wouldn't it be something if this Mr. Peterson would remember him, thought Livvie. Of course, Livvie's adopted mother, Carrie, remembered the man all too well, from when she worked on the Daud farm, but she didn't like talking about him, for some reason.

The next morning, Stan arrived as the women were preparing breakfast for everyone. Livvie was happy to see him and he answered questions about the road situation.

"I didn't have too much trouble, but I'm glad I waited until daylight to come back over here," he said.

"Do you think Mr. Peterson will have trouble getting home?" asked Joe.

"Oh, I don't think so, but if he waits awhile longer, maybe they'll get the roads cleared off somewhat."

Little Shirley was still feeling pretty sick. "I was up with her several times during the night," said her mother. "I gave her water and some more aspirin."

"Has her fever gone down any, do you think?" asked Livvie.

"It maybe has, a little. I'm anxious to get her home."

Joe looked at his boys. "Well, we'll go and try and get your car out and bring it to the yard and then we'll see."

"Shall we carry Shirley back downstairs and lay her on the sofa again?" suggested Min. "Then we should try and get a little food down her."

"I'll carry her down for you," volunteered Mr. Peterson. "Then I'll go out and help the men with the car."

After the child was settled in the living room, Min brought her some orange juice and a little oatmeal, which she had thinned down with extra milk. Mrs. Bolstad did her best to get some of the nourishing food into her daughter.

Before long, Joe and Mr. Peterson came back into the house. "Well, we got your car out in no time at all," Joe told Mrs. Bolstad. "I don't think you should try and get home until sometime this afternoon, though."

She looked anxious but she knew that Joe was probably right.

"Do you think we should call the doctor and have him look at Shirley before you go?" suggested Min.

"Oh, I think it's just tonsillitis again. I looked down her throat this morning and her tonsils look really red. She's had this before. She'll probably need to have them taken out sooner or later."

By late morning, Mr. Peterson announced that he thought he'd better be hitting the road. He'd been pacing the kitchen for quite sometime.

"Oh, can't you stay for dinner? I'm making a big pot of vegetable dumpling soup," said Min.

"Oh, thank you very much, Mrs. Murphy, but I'm kind of anxious to be on my way. I can't thank you enough for your hospitality, though."

He went into the living room to check on the little girl. "I hope your daughter will be just fine very soon, Mrs. Bolstad," he said. "I'm going to be leaving now."

"Oh, Mr. Peterson, how can I ever thank you!" exclaimed Dorothy. "You know, I had been sitting in that ditch for quite awhile, praying and praying for someone to come along. And then I saw your headlights and I knew my prayers had been answered."

Mr. Peterson sat down on a chair and looked at Mrs. Bolstad thoughtfully. "You know, when I was in that bar in Horace, my common sense told me that I should just stay put until morning, like a lot of the guys were going to do, but something else told me to get on the road. Evidently your prayers were working on me."

"Well, I hate to think what would have happened if we'd had to sit in that cold car all night. Especially with Shirley sick and all."

Mr. Peterson rose and Dorothy impulsively jumped up, too, and gave him a big hug. "Thank you again," she said.

To hide his embarrassment, he leaned toward the child and took her hand and gave it a little squeeze. "You get well now, little miss."

Back in the kitchen, he said to Livvie, "You know, this morning I remembered that fellow you were asking about. There was a young Canadian that we called Alphie. I think his name was something like Kastet, or whatever you said."

Livvie's heart leaped. "Do you remember anything about him?"

"Well, he was a good worker, a good card player. Rather a ladies man, I'd say. Good looking son-of-a-gun. The hired girls all went crazy over him. He left as soon as the harvest was over. Never saw him again."

Livvie was digesting all this and didn't know what to say.

"Why are you asking about him?"

"Well, ah....ah....my mother used to work on the Daud farm and he was working there. She ah....mentioned him....several times."

"Oh, I see," was all he said. He walked towards the door. "Well, I'll be going, then. Thanks again everybody. I'll stop by the barn and say goodbye to the fellows."

"Keep in touch, Mr. Peterson," said Min. "Hope you get home OK."

Later that afternoon, Joe told Mrs. Bolstad that they would try and get her home, too. "I'll drive you and Shirley in your car and the boys will take the pickup. They can drive ahead of us and make a path, if need be."

The sick child was wrapped up warmly and taken out to the car.

"Goodbye, Dorothy," said Min, after giving the woman a warm embrace. "Do give me a call when you get home, won't you?"

"Thank you ever so much, Minerva. I don't know how I'll ever repay you."

"Think nothing of it. You'd have done the same for me, I'm sure."

Shortly after that, the two vehicles left the yard. The telephone rang and it was Mrs. Bolstad's oldest son. He was wondering when his mother was coming home.

"They're on their way. It shouldn't be long now," Min assured him.

CHAPTER 8

George came home from Kindred one morning full of news. "I stopped at Trom's Station and got the low-down on everything," he told Carrie, shaking his head. "It's pretty final now. Gas rationing will become official next week."

"Oh, no!" exclaimed Carrie. "Well, I guess we knew this was coming, didn't we?"

"I filled out a form at the station this morning. We'll be receiving a basic 'A' ration book to use for the gas we buy. Another thing I heard today," he said, as he poured himself a cup of coffee, "each car owner is asked to keep his best five tires and give or sell the rest to the government."

"Oh, my," said Carrie, "what next?"

"That's not all," said George. "I haven't read today's paper yet, of course, but there is something in there about farm trucks. We'll now need a Certificate of War Necessity to operate them. These certificates will govern the maximum mileage they may be operated on minimum loads and things like that. We won't be able to get gas, tires or parts for them without these certificates."

"Things are certainly getting complicated, aren't they?" sighed Carrie, as she finished ironing the last shirt in the basket and put it on a hanger.

"It seems that every time I go to town, I hear more bad news." George reached for another doughnut and Carrie raised an eyebrow at him. "Oh, I guess I don't need another one, do I?" he laughed. He got up and put on his coat again and went outside.

Carrie, tired from her morning of ironing, sat down with a cup of coffee herself. She took a doughnut and dunked it in her coffee and sighed. *Yah, all these things that are either rationed or in short supply. We can't buy rubber-soled shoes now without a ration stamp and even then, they are hard to come by. We're supposed to cut down on meat consumption. That will be rationed next, I suppose. And then, of course, there's the sugar. It's really hard to have to watch that so closely.*

She sighed again and slowly got up to tackle her next job. "Oh, well," she said aloud. "We should count our blessings. We have no one from the family fighting in the front yet."

The next afternoon George brought in the mail that had just been delivered. "Here's a postcard from Livvie," he said, tossing the mail on the kitchen table.

Carrie excitedly picked up the card and turned it over. She hadn't talked to Livvie for almost a week now. Too bad it was long distance to call her, she thought for the hundredth time.

She scanned the card quickly and then went back to read it over again. "Livvie had some good news," she said to George. "Stan's brother, Marty, thinks that he can get some leave at Christmas time. How wonderful!" she exclaimed.

George sat down at the table and opened the Kindred Tribune. He read for awhile and then started chuckling. "It didn't take old Clem long to make a comment on the gas rationing. He says 'we'll walk and not squawk.' "

"He sure has a way with words, doesn't he?" Carrie laughed.

"He also says here that whiskey and other strong drinks will not be made for the rest of the war, but he says, 'not to worry, the distillers have a five-year supply!' "

"Well, it's good he brings a little humor into reading the newspapers. There's so much bad news nowadays," remarked Carrie.

"Here, listen to this," George said to his wife. "Postmaster Alf Ringen has saved string for many years and he's formed a ball 71 inches in circumference!"

"Seventy one inches!" exclaimed Carrie. She stretched her arms out to try and get an idea what that big of a ball would look like.

"He placed it on the postal scale and it weighed in at 49 1/2 pounds! It'll be on display in the post office for the next two weeks."

"We'll have to go in and see it, then, sometime," suggested Carrie.

"Yah, I have to see it to believe it. It doesn't say just how long he's been saving string but he must have started many years ago."

"Are you going into town this afternoon?" Carrie asked her husband.

"Yah, I've got the truck loaded up with all that scrap iron. I'll drop it off at the collection site."

"I've got the tin cans all cleaned and flattened so you can bring them in, too," said Carrie. "When I was talking to Beatrice a little while ago, she mentioned that she'd heard that now we're supposed to be saving old silk hosiery, too. What do you suppose they can do with those?"

"I read that in the paper just yesterday," George replied. "They can use those old stockings to make powder bags for firing shells."

"Oh, my! They do think of everything, don't they?"

"They want scrap rubber, too, I heard, so I found some laying around here and there. I threw that in the truck, too." George grabbed his jacket and cap.

"Well, I'll be heading for town, then. Anything you need?"

"No, I'll be going in myself one of these next days."

Thanksgiving that year was cold and snowy. Carrie and George had all their children and grandchildren around their table—Freddie and Lenora, with Sandra and Larry, and Livvie and Stan with baby Cheryl.

"That was a wonderful dinner," Stan told his mother-in-law.

"You'd never know there was rationing going on today, would you?" said Freddie.

"Well, I've scrimped a little these last two weeks so we'd have enough sugar and coffee and things for a fine meal. In fact, the pumpkin pie you just ate took the last of my sugar!" said Carrie.

"I suppose we get our new ration books next week, though," said Lenora.

"Yah, then I'll have to be careful so I have enough for a little Christmas baking."

"Lenora, I hear that your sister's fellow may get to come home for Christmas. Is that true?" asked Carrie.

"Well, he hinted at it strongly in his last letter. He'll find out the first of next week. He says if he gets to come home for at least a few days, he thinks they should hurry and get married while he's here."

"Oh, my!" exclaimed Carrie. "That would be some real excitement in your folks' house, then, wouldn't it?"

"Well, Lucy says she's already been making some plans, just in case. She says she'll just wear a nice suit instead of the wedding dress that she was planning on getting. My mother tells her to just hold tight and wait and see for sure before she plans too much."

Carrie passed the coffeepot around again but she had no takers.

"Did you read where the US Government is planning to make alcohol from wheat now?" asked Stan.

"Yah, they expect to use eight to twelve million bushels of government-owned wheat during the first three months of 1943," commented George.

"What will it be used for?" asked Livvie.

"They'll use it to make industrial alcohol for war use," explained George.

"So, do you suppose we should be raising more wheat next year, then?" asked Stan.

"Probably would be a good idea. I read where they're encouraging us to grow flaxseed, and to raise more hogs and beef cattle," George remarked.

"And more chickens for more eggs, too," added Stan.

Carrie rose and started clearing the table. The men and kids headed for the living room and Lenora and Livvie stayed to help Carrie.

"Did you go into the Evingson's Store and sign the big Christmas cards that they're going to send to the servicemen?" Lenora asked Carrie.

"I did that a couple weeks ago. That was really nice," said Carrie. "I also brought in some used books to the school that I found around here. They're going to send them to the soldiers and sailors, too."

"There'll be many households around the country this Christmas that'll be missing a loved one who's gone off to war," stated Carrie, reflectively. "A father, brother, husband." She looked at both Lenora and Livvie. "I hope we don't get any bad news here before Christmas."

Lenora picked up a clean dishtowel and started wiping the plates that Livvie had just washed. "I know Freddie worries constantly about getting called up but he tries to hide it from me."

"Stan, too," Livvie said in a hushed tone. "He's been worrying lately that his brother, Ronnie, might do something stupid like enlist. He hears him and Kenny talking about it sometimes."

"Oh, do you think they'd really do that?" asked Carrie.

"Ronnie has had a real restlessness about him lately. He doesn't seem to know what to do with himself," revealed Livvie. "Stan's father has suggested to Ronnie that maybe he should go on to college. He's real smart, you know, but he doesn't seem to take to that idea very much."

"Well, we're living in such an uncertain time. I'm sure it's hard for all the young men, not knowing what's going to happen to them and to the country," said Carrie.

Livvie finished washing so she took another dishtowel and began helping Lenora wipe. Carrie was kept busy putting food and dishes away.

Finally they were able to hang up their towels and their aprons and join the men in the living room.

"In the bank yesterday," began Freddie, "I heard some guys talking about a unique fund-raising idea. They might start up a couple of basketball teams. They'd get some of the old timers who used to play on the high school teams to play."

"Who would that be, then? Did they mention any names?" asked George.

"Oh, it would be maybe Nate Thompson, Rudy Lykken, Ivan Rustad, Oscar Erickson, Johannes Rogne and some of those guys."

"How about Ted Lee?"

"Yah, him, too. And Olander Olson."

"Well, that would be quite a good thing. Lots of people would come to see those guys in action. Who would they play?"

"They'd form two teams and play each other," said Freddie.

A baby's cry was heard from the bedroom. "I was thinking that it was about time for her to wake up. She's been sleeping for three hours!" said Livvie.

"She'll be up all night now then, after such a good nap," commented Carrie.

Sandra and Larry were happy to have the baby awake so they'd have someone to play with. They were getting bored with each other.

"Let's get a game of Whist going, shall we?" suggested George. "Who wants to play with us men?"

"I'll play!" answered Lenora. "That is, if someone will watch the kids," she added.

"Oh, I'll watch them," said Carrie. "You go on and play with the fellows."

As Stan was shuffling the cards, he said, "I read where they won't be making license plates for the year 1943 because of war restrictions. Did you hear that?"

"Yes, I guess we'll just be getting a sticker to put on our window," said Freddie.

After George looked at the hand that he'd just been dealt, he said, "Play 'em out, Lenora. I've got a barn-burner hand here!"

"Oh, is that right?" she laughed. "Then it looks like Freddie and I have our work cut out for us."

The card playing went on the rest of the afternoon. Carrie made some turkey sandwiches and served them with a Jello salad for a light supper and then the guests departed. Stan had to get home to his milking and Freddie and Lenora were anxious to get their kids home to bed.

"This was a good Thanksgiving Day, wasn't it?" Carrie remarked to her husband as they relaxed on the sofa later. "I wonder what next Thanksgiving will be like? Do you think we'll still be at war?"

George shook his head slowly. "I don't know. I sure hope not."

Neither one expressed their real fear that always lingered near the surface.

One day in early December, Carrie got a phone call from Lenora. "Oh, I'm so excited," she exclaimed. "I just got a call from Lucy. She got a letter from Jack today and he's coming home for Christmas! And they're going to get married for sure!"

"Oh, my goodness!" was all Carrie could say.

"He gets here on the 23rd. The wedding will be just a small family affair in the church on Christmas Eve afternoon."

"How long can he stay?" asked Carrie.

"He has to leave again on the 27th."

"Your mother sure will be busy then, won't she? Is there something I can do to help her?"

"She'd like to make the wedding cake but doesn't know if she'll have enough sugar. I told her that if some of her friends could give up just one fourth of a cup each, then that would be enough. She doesn't want to ask anybody because she feels everyone will need to use all their rations for Christmas baking."

"I could give up maybe a half cup," volunteered Carrie.

"Oh, are you sure you could give that much?" asked Lenora.

"Oh, yes, you tell her that I'll give her that much. I'll drop it by her house or send it to town with George someday soon."

"That will be just great," Lenora said. "Have you heard from Livvie? Is Marty going to get to come home for Christmas?"

"I got a card from her just yesterday and she said that he is coming home for sure, too, but I don't know exactly what day. He can only stay about five days, too, I think."

"Well, it will be a happy, exciting Christmas for many of us then," remarked Lenora, before hanging up.

That evening, Carrie was looking at the Larsen's Store ad in the Kindred Tribune. "Just look at all these nice toys they're advertising," she said to George. "Here's a set of play dishes and a little stove. That would be cute for Sandra. I wonder if Larry would be too young for this farm set."

"Probably," remarked George. "Wait a year or two for that. How about some building blocks or something?"

"Yes, they've got those, too, here. They've also got a soldier set and a tank war game. It's too bad that Christmas toys have to be about war, don't you think?"

George didn't answer. He was absorbed in the Fargo Forum. "It says here that the government is going to need five million pounds of turkey to feed Christmas dinner to the servicemen!"

"You don't say!" exclaimed Carrie. After thinking about that for awhile she said, "Boy, that's a lot of turkey!"

Carrie put down the paper and stretched a bit. "Beatrice was telling me today that they aren't going to put the Christmas tree up on Main Street until the week of Christmas. It's to conserve on electricity, I guess."

"Yah, I heard that too, today, when I was in town," said George.

"When shall we get our tree?" Carrie asked.

"Oh, in another week, I suppose."

George laid the paper aside and stretched. "Tomorrow it will be a year since the attack on Pearl Harbor."

"Why, yes, it will be. December 7th. Well, I hope that by next year at this time the war will be over and all our servicemen will be back home safe and sound."

On Christmas Eve, Carrie and George were invited up to the Murphys'. Freddie and Lenora were tied up with her sister's wedding and the family celebration following the ceremony.

"This will be the first Christmas Eve that we haven't had both our children home," sighed Carrie, as they were driving up north to the Murphy farm.

"Well, we'll have them all at our house tomorrow," George consoled her.

"Yah, at least they aren't overseas or anything like that," she answered.

The Murphy house was bustling and full of people, it seemed. Livvie and Magda were helping Min in the kitchen. Joe was trying to find enough chairs to go around the big dining-room table. He even sent Allan upstairs to get the bench from Min's dressing table.

"We can put two small people on that," he commented.

Marty came up from the basement with a small stool. He gave Carrie a big hug and George slapped him on the back.

"Well, Marty, how's it going? How was that basic training that they put you through?"

"I survived it and here I am!" he laughed.

George finished putting all their gifts under the Murphys' tree. "I don't think there's room for one more package!" he exclaimed.

Min announced that the meal was ready and that everyone should find a place to sit around the table. Cheryl was placed in the high chair and it was squeezed in between her parents.

When everyone was seated, Joe looked around at the table. "Pa, would you like to say the table prayer for us in Norwegian?"

Ivar hesitated for sometime before answering. There were tears in his eyes as he looked at his big family. "Yah, I can do that."

Everyone bowed their heads and even Cheryl became quiet. Those who knew the prayer followed along.

"I Jesu Navn gaar vi til bord, at spise, drikke paa dit Ord, dig Gud til aere, os til gavn, saa far vi mat i Jesu Navn. Amen."

When he was finished, Joe stated that he would say a prayer, too. "Thank you, our Heavenly Father," he began, "as we celebrate your Son's birth, for all our blessings which you have bestowed on us. Thank you for sending our son, Marty, home to us for this short time. Keep him safe wherever he may go. Keep all our servicemen safe and bless them this Christmas season. Bless this food that we are about to receive, that we may use it and all your blessings to your glory. Amen."

Min and Livvie went to the kitchen and brought back big platters and bowls of lutefisk, mashed potatoes, gravy, melted butter, lefse, corn, pickles, and buns.

"Hey, quit passing so much food, so I can start eating!" laughed Marty.

"Bet I can eat more lutefisk that you," Ronnie challenged Marty.

"Oh, we'll see about that! I need more food now to keep up all these muscles I've built up during training."

"Well, I built up more, too, doing all your work for you after you left," joked Ronnie.

The joking and bantering lasted throughout the meal. Pumpkin pie was passed around for dessert and the coffee cups were refilled.

The men groaned with full stomachs as they pushed their chairs back but everyone seemed reluctant to leave the table and the feeling of goodwill that was present in the room.

Finally, Min started picking up the dirty dishes and that was the sign for the rest of the women to help clear the table. Marty helped, too, saying that he'd had plenty of practice with doing dishes in the army.

"Martin, I can't imagine you with an apron on and washing dishes," chuckled Magda.

"Why, Aunt Maggie, I look really good in an apron," he laughed, and he folded the dishtowel in a triangle and put it around his waist.

He stayed in the kitchen and helped the women while the remaining males in the family headed for other rooms in the house.

It took almost an hour before the kitchen was declared cleaned up by Min.

"She's the sergeant around here, you know," remarked Marty, and everyone laughed knowingly.

Everyone found places to sit in the living room, either on the floor or the sofa or chairs.

"Livvie, maybe you could play us some Christmas music on the old organ," suggested Joe.

"Well, I'll try, but I haven't played it much."

She played some of the simpler songs that she knew by heart and the rest sang along. Then Joe took up the big family Bible and turned to Luke to read the Christmas Gospel. Everyone listened attentively.

Carrie was studying Marty's expression. He looked sad, not like the usual jolly character that he was. *Perhaps he's worried about where he'll be going now when he goes back to the base.*

Now it was time to pass out the gifts to everyone. This job fell on Allan, as he was the youngest. Carrie tried to watch everyone else as they opened something but it soon became impossible so she just opened her own gifts and tried to keep them in a neat pile. There was wrapping paper and string and ribbon lying all over the floor.

Joe went and found a big box and put all the paper in it and put it outside on the porch. Cheryl had been having fun playing with all the wrappings. Now, however, she turned to her toys that she had received. Marty was right down on the floor with her, showing her the spinning top that he had bought for her.

After much laughing and visiting, Min announced that they needed to have some Christmas goodies and coffee. She and Livvie filled big serving plates with Norwegian treats. There was krumkake, berliner kranser, julekake and rosettes.

"I'll have to apologize for not having as many baked things as I usually do," said Min, "Magda brought some of this. And Livvie and Carrie brought the pies that we had for supper."

Everyone was gathered around the dining-room table again. They enjoyed the rich, buttery treats.

"Mmmm, these just melt in my mouth," commented Marty, as he took his second cookie.

"I love these krumkake," said Ronnie, trying to eat one without making too much of a mess out of the fragile, cone-shaped delicacy.

"It's sure different this year from last year, isn't it?" stated Magda. "I bet Min and I baked almost twenty different things for the holidays then."

"Yes, so many things are different this year from last year," stated Stan reflectively.

"So, Marty, where do you think you will go after you get back?" asked George.

Everyone at the table was quiet. Marty hesitated a few moments before answering. "Well," he said slowly, "I really am not sure. I'll find out as soon as I get back there."

"I just hope you can stay in the States as long as possible. Maybe the war will be over in a few short months," said his mother.

Marty met his father's gaze. "Maybe it will be, Mom. Maybe it will be."

"Hey, pass those cookies around again," Ronnie said, wanting to change the subject.

It was almost eleven o'clock when George suggested that it was time for them to go home. Art and Magda agreed. There was a flurry of activity with everyone gathering up their gifts and finding their wraps.

"Well, mange tusen takk," Carrie said to Min and Joe. "It was sure nice of you to invite us to join you all for Christmas Eve."

"You folks have a good time tomorrow with your family," Min told Carrie.

Carrie gave Marty a big hug. "I wish you the best," she said.

George shook Marty's hand and said, "Good luck to you, son."

"Will we see you before New Year's?" Joe asked the Murphys.

"Maybe at the dance on the 28th?" said Carrie.

"Oh, yes, we'll probably go to that. The Music Masters are playing and we really like them."

"I think we're going, too," said Magda.

"Well, we'll see you all then," called back George from the porch. Carrie waved. "We'll see you tomorrow, Livvie."

CHAPTER 9

January of 1943 proved to be a very cold and snowy month. Roads were blocked time after time. George had to park their car out by the mail box a couple of times as their driveway filled in so when it blew from the north.

"I'm going to get to that basketball game tomorrow night if I have to walk," he'd declared.

As it turned out, he walked up to the end of their driveway and caught a ride with a neighbor who was also determined to go. Carrie stayed home, deciding it was too cold to walk all that way. She was catching up on some of her reading and needlework, waiting for George to return.

This basketball game had been long anticipated in the community. Besides being a fundraiser for the war effort, the publicity of the event between these two teams, named the Fats and the Leans, had reached far and wide.

"How did they come up with such funny names?" Carrie had asked George.

"I think Clem pinned these names on them when he wrote about them in his column," he'd told her. Clem Clemenson was the editor of the Kindred Tribune and he wrote a column titled Klem's Komments.

Carrie turned the radio on. The programs would be good tonight. First there was the "Amos 'n' Andy" show and then "Fibber McGee and Molly." Carrie stitched on her dishtowels while she listened, laughing out loud many a time.

When those two programs were over, she went to the kitchen to make herself a cup of coffee. The phone rang and she answered it on the first ring. It was Beatrice. She said Carl had gone to the game, too, and had taken Donnie and James with him. She had just gotten Elaine, their 18-month old daughter, to sleep and thought she'd call her friend for a chat.

Carl and Beatrice Ulness were good friends of the Johnson family. George's parents and Carl's parents had been friends for many years. And Carrie was actually a cousin of Carl's father. She and her brother, Amund, had discovered this when they had first come to North Dakota back in '08. The elder Mr. Ulness had died many years ago and Carl's mother, Lena, had moved off the place where the family had grown up. She now lived with several of her children, spending a few months at a time with each.

Carl and Beatrice lived in Kindred and had three children. Carrie and Beatrice spent quite a bit of time on the telephone with each other.

"Yah, George went to the game, too," Carrie told her. "I guess almost everyone who can make it is at the game tonight."

"Except you and me!" laughed Beatrice.

"So Carl is feeling pretty good now, then?" asked Carrie. He had been laid up with scarlet fever a few months before and the whole family had been quarantined for several weeks.

"Yes, he's feeling good now. That was really a tough time," Beatrice said. "I'm sure glad it's over."

The two women talked for almost half an hour, being somewhat careful about what and who they talked about as they knew that someone was probably rubbernecking on the line, as usual.

"Well, I hear Carl and the boys coming in the back door now so I better hang up," said Beatrice.

"Well, George should be along soon, too, then," remarked Carrie.

About a half an hour later, Carrie heard George come in. He soon joined her in the living room and began telling her all about the big game.

"Lots of people there. You should have come, Carrie," he said.

"Well, which team won, then?" she asked him as he got settled in his favorite chair.

"The Fats won 27 to 25. Boy, it was close all the way! Nate was the high-point man for the Leans. He had six field goals and three free throws. Rudy Lykken had four field goals for the Fats. It was tied up at the third quarter. Ted Lee broke the tie with a long shot and the crowd went wild!"

Carrie laughed at his enthusiasm. "It sounds like you had a great time. I'm glad that you could get there. Were there many from the country that made it?"

"Oh, yes, quite a few. Some had to do some shoveling to get there, I'm sure."

"Well, it took in lots of money, then, for the cause," said Carrie.

"I heard tonight that there's going to be a card party at the end of the month to raise money for infantile paralysis in honor of President Roosevelt's birthday."

"Well, I hope I can make it to that," Carrie said. "I'm kind of getting cabin fever."

"Yah, we'll try and go to that."

"I talked to Beatrice for a long time on the phone tonight," Carrie said. "We were talking about the Victory War Bond auction to be held in February. It'll be held around Valentine's Day. Our Homemakers is going to make about twenty Valentine corsages and put them on the auction. What do you think about that idea?"

"Sounds good to me," George answered, somewhat absently. He already had his nose deep in the paper.

"Do you want some coffee?"

"Yah, that would taste good. I'm still rather cold from that long walk."

Carrie brought him a cup of coffee and a doughnut. "I listened to some good programs on the radio while you were gone and then Beatrice called so the evening went pretty fast."

"It says here," said George, reading the paper again, "that North Dakota raised five million dollars by its citizens purchasing Series E War Bonds. That amount will provide forty-three fighting aircraft."

"Isn't that something. That's a lot of money for such a small state to raise, isn't it?"

"Well, we certainly do our part for the war effort," remarked George.

"We have to remember tomorrow night at 10 p.m. is the state-wide test blackout that Governor Moses advised. It will last 20 minutes."

"So, we'll just turn everything off and go to bed," said Carrie.

"Yah, we could do that."

February third brought another winter storm. Roads were blocked and George didn't get out for three days. Carrie called up to Livvie and Stan to see how they were doing, and was glad to hear that they were home safe and sound.

One evening the phone rang and it was the call that Carrie had been dreading for over a year now.

"Hi, Ma," said Freddie. Something in his voice made Carrie's heart skip a beat. "Well, I finally received a letter from Uncle Sam today."

"Oh, no!" was all Carrie could say. She found a chair and sat down hard. George looked her way and knew instinctively that it was Freddie and what he had to say.

"I'll be making the trip to Minneapolis next week. It sounds like several other guys from here got their notices, too." He sounded dejected but resigned. It had been expected.

When Carrie found her voice, she asked, "How is Lenora taking it?"

"She's pretty broken up about it. She's been crying all afternoon. The kids are wondering what's going on."

"Well, I'll keep praying for you, as I always have, son," Carrie told him, almost sobbing out the words. "That's all I can do."

After the call, Carrie couldn't settle down to anything. She paced back and forth between the kitchen and the living room, where George was reading.

George looked at the clock and rose to turn on the radio. "Edward R. Murrow will be on in a few minutes," he said. Carrie sat down on the sofa beside him to listen.

As Mr. Murrow was reporting on the war, they could hear what sounded like bombing in the background. "Ladies and Gentlemen, that is London being bombed in the background," he told his listeners.

"Oh, I can't bear to listen!" exclaimed Carrie. She got up and went upstairs. She lay down on the bed, fully clothed.

For the next couple days, Carrie couldn't control her nervousness and couldn't concentrate on anything.

"You need to get a grip on things, Carrie," George told her one evening, after watching his wife pace back and forth.

"I know. I know," was all she could say. She fled to their bedroom once again and undressed. Slowly she dropped to her knees beside the bed. She poured out her heart to her Heavenly Father, knowing she should have done this before.

She asked Him to help her accept whatever came and not to be so anxious about everything. She opened the Bible and read some passages of scripture that she thought would be helpful. She started with some of the Psalms and found them helpful, especially the 77th and the 88th that the Psalmist David wrote when he was in deep despair. She ended with the beloved 23rd Psalm.

By the time she had finished, she felt like a heavy load had been lifted from her shoulders.

Later, when George came upstairs, he found a different woman than the one he'd seen for the past few days.

"I finally turned everything over to God and now I'm at peace with whatever happens," she told him. She read to him some of the scriptures that had so comforted her.

Freddie left for Minneapolis on a snowy February day. Lenora's younger sister, Susie, came to stay with her and the children for a few days. Carrie called her several times and told her about turning over her worries and anxieties to God and how it had helped her.

"Lenora seems to be doing pretty good now, I think," Carrie told George one evening.

"She's a strong young woman. She'll be alright," said George. "Have you talked with the Murphys since Marty found out that he's being sent overseas?"

"No, but Livvie said Min is pretty upset. When I talked to Livvie today, she said that he'll most likely be sent to Italy or France. He leaves next week, I guess."

"How about Lenora's new brother-in-law, Jack Gilbertson?" asked George. "Has he gotten his marching orders yet?"

"I haven't heard anything about him."

At the end of the week, Carrie answered a phone call and it was Freddie again.

"Hi, Ma," he almost shouted. "Well, I'm home again," he said, and Carrie wondered what he would tell her next. She wasn't prepared for what she heard.

"Well, it looks like Uncle Sam doesn't want me after all!" he exclaimed.

"What do you mean?" she asked, relief spreading over her.

"I didn't pass my physical," Freddie related.

"Why is that?" she asked, concern in her voice.

"They tell me I have a heart murmur."

"A heart murmur!" Carrie exclaimed.

"Yes, that's what they found," Freddie said. "They said I had probably had it since I was a child. I was maybe even born with it."

Carrie didn't know what to say.

"I told them I had never had any problems and they said that could very well be, but they said that I would maybe have problems during the grueling boot camp and they didn't want me dropping dead on them!"

"Oh, Freddie, don't joke about it," Carrie reprimanded him mildly.

"I'm not joking about it, Ma, but that is the reason they don't want me in the army."

Carrie let out the breath she had been holding. "Well, I'm so glad you don't have to be drafted, Freddie. You just don't know how relieved I am."

"Well, me too," Freddie said. "And same with Lenora. We decided we'd deal with this other thing when something comes up."

"What did the doctors say you could expect, then?"

"They asked if I got tired easily or if I felt any discomfort when I did something real exerting and I answered no to both of those questions. They said that maybe I wouldn't have any problems at all or at least not for a long time yet."

"That's a relief, then," Carrie said.

Freddie went on to tell her that his brother-in-law, Jack, was being sent overseas soon. Lucy was very worried about where he'd have to go.

After hanging up from talking to her son, Carrie went into the living room and sat down with a sigh. George looked up from his paper.

"Who was that?" he asked, almost dreading her answer.

"Well, I guess it's a matter of both good news and bad news," she began. "That was Freddie. He won't be getting drafted, and that is the good news." George had a relieved look on his face. "But the doctors at Fort Snelling found out that he has a heart murmur."

"How serious is it?" George wondered.

"Well, they say he may not have any problems with it, at least not for quite sometime. They told him that he may have had this since he was a child."

"How could something like that happen?"

"I don't know. He may even have been born with it, they said."

George digested this information for awhile. Carrie tried to interest herself in the newspaper. She sighed again.

"I am really relieved, though, that he won't have to go off to war and risk the chance of possibly never coming back again," Carrie told him. "And like Freddie said, they're going to deal with this heart condition when the time comes."

"Yah, that's all we can do, I guess," agreed George.

That night in bed, Carrie thanked the Lord for answering her prayer to keep Freddie safe from the war. She also asked God to keep him healthy and able to lead a normal life.

When George joined his wife in their bed, he admitted how worried he himself had been for many months that Freddie would get drafted.

"Now there's Stan to worry about," he said.

"We're not going to worry any more, remember? We're going to put it all into God's hands."

"That sounds so simple, Carrie," he said, "but it's hard to actually do it."

"I know, George," she said softly. "I know. Let's just keep praying about it."

CHAPTER 10

"You did what?" shouted Stan at his brother, Ronnie.

"I told you. Kenny and I enlisted in the Navy today," Ronnie answered defensively.

Stan had his brother pinned up against the barn wall. He was furious at him. "You stupid fool! Why did you do something like that?" Stan finally let go of his grip on his younger brother. He continued staring at him, waiting for an answer.

"Well, it was just a matter of time before we got drafted anyway," Ronnie started to explain. "There was a whole bunch of us from this area who enlisted this morning."

"Does Dad know yet?"

"How could he? I just got home. I'll tell him tonight."

"With Marty gone, we're already shorthanded around here. What if I get drafted soon? What will Dad do then?" Stan was still fuming.

The Murphys had just taken on 120 more acres the previous year and it would be hard to put the crop in and get it harvested without everyone's help. Joe had counted on the fact that he had four sons. Now two would be gone and maybe one more. That just left Allan, who was only eleven.

"Dad's going to kill you when you tell him!" With that, Stan spun on his heels and went to his pickup and headed for home.

That evening around the supper table, Min noticed that Ronnie was awfully quiet and preoccupied. More than usual, she thought. He hadn't been himself lately.

While she was clearing up the dishes, Ronnie cleared his throat and said, "Dad, Mom, I have something to tell you."

Min's heart started beating fast in her chest. She felt she knew what was coming.

Ronnie dropped the bombshell. "I enlisted in the Navy today."

Allan was the only one who could find words. "You're going to be a sailor?"

Ronnie nodded and looked at his Dad, waiting for a reaction. Joe finally recovered and said, "I was hoping you wouldn't do something like that, son." He shook his head back and forth.

Min sat back down by the table. "Oh, Ronnie, I don't want you to go off to war, too. It's bad enough having Marty gone. We don't even know where he is right now. Now we'll have to worry about you, too." She put her head in her hands and began to cry.

"Ah, Mom, don't cry," Ronnie said gently. He got up and stood beside her chair and rested her head against his chest. "I knew it was only a matter of time before I got drafted. I've felt so restless all winter, wondering what's gong to happen. It's hard to plan a future when things are so uncertain. I'd like to go to college, but not with this war and the draft hanging over my head."

Joe rose, too, and went to his son. "I understand your feelings, Ronnie, and I'm proud of you for wanting to serve your country. It's just that I was so hoping you wouldn't have to go. I was thinking that maybe you and Stan could apply for a farm deferment. I'm really going to be shorthanded this spring."

"I know, Dad," said Ronnie. "And I know this isn't a good time for me to be going but all the other guys were going to do it today so I didn't want to be left behind."

"Oh, Ronnie!" exclaimed his mother. "I don't know how I'm going to cope with this."

Joe helped his wife off the chair and led her into the living room. They sat down together on the sofa. Ronnie followed them. "You're going to get through this just fine, Min," Joe said gently, handing her his hankie. "Let's not expect the worst. We'll just take one day at a time."

"What if Stan gets drafted soon?" asked Min through her tears.

Joe was silent for a time. "I'll talk to him tomorrow. Maybe he should make a visit to the draft board."

"How soon would you be leaving, Ronnie?" asked his mother.

"In about a week, they told us."

"Oh, that soon?" Min said.

"Well, the sooner the better," said Ronnie. "Then I don't have to sit around and think about it."

Min looked at her third-born son.

Why, he's frightened. She was scared for him and proud of him at the same time.

Word soon spread throughout the communities of Kindred and Davenport of the ten young men who had enlisted in the Navy and who would soon be leaving home.

Stan and his father visited the draft board and they were waiting to hear if Stan's application for a farm deferment would come through.

The weekend before the young men were to leave, there was a big farewell party at the town hall in Kindred. There was music, dancing, back-slapping and wishes for good luck as the boys received a whopping send off.

The morning of Ronnie's departure, the whole family was gathered on the porch. Magda and Art had come to say goodbye. Kenny and his father drove in the yard.

"Now, Ronald, you write to us regularly," said Magda, who had begun to sob at the sight of her nephew picking up his bag and preparing to leave. Kenny's father was going to give them a ride into Fargo, where the new enlistees would all board the train that would take them to Idaho for their basic training.

"I will, Aunt Maggie," Ronnie replied. He set his jaw firmly so no one would see it quivering. His mother threw her arms around him and then he broke down in sobs that he could hold back no longer.

"You take care, now, son," she said, "and I'll be praying for you every day." She couldn't get any more words out.

Joe gave Ronnie a big hug and wordlessly walked him to the car. Stan followed and when they reached the car, he said to Ronnie, "Well, take care of yourself, little brother." He sought and held Ronnie's gaze. What he couldn't say in words, his look revealed——"I'm sorry for what I said to you," and "Come back alive!" The two brothers shook hands and nodded in mutual understanding.

The family watched as the car left the yard and disappeared out of sight by the coulee. No one was able to speak for awhile. They just stood there. Finally young Allan broke the silence.

"Well, now I have two brothers in the service," he announced.

Stan's farm deferment came through to the relief of everyone.

"He's like a different person now," Livvie wrote to her mother. "He doesn't have that hanging over his head."

It was actually a one-year deferment and then it would have to be re-evaluated. But that was good enough for Stan.

"Why, the war will probably be over with by then," he stated, with more confidence than he really felt.

"Did you read where North Dakota topped the nation again in War Bond sales for last month?" Joe said, as the family sat around the table after supper one evening. "That's on a quota basis, of course. We purchased 156 percent of our quota."

"That's really good," remarked Min.

Stan had stayed for supper and Livvie and Cheryl had come over, too. Joe and Stan needed to fill out some forms together. All farmers were to file a Farm Plan, showing their intended seedings of war crops and feed crops.

"We're urged to increase crop production," remarked Joe. "Every possible foot of ground must, if possible, be planted. The question is, are we going to have the fuel, machinery and parts to do that?"

"And the labor to help with the harvest in the fall?" added Stan.

"I'm sure glad that you're going to be here, Stan," his father said, for about the tenth time that day.

"You and me both," agreed Stan, with a sigh. This got both men to thinking about how Ronnie and Marty were doing.

"I wonder if Marty has reached his destination yet," said Joe.

"It's been quite sometime since his last letter," said Min. "We'll probably hear from Ronnie soon, though. He must be in Idaho by now and settled in."

The women got up to do the dishes and the men finished their paperwork.

Stan was in a hurry to get home and do his evening chores. Livvie went to gather up the baby and her things.

"Did you read about the Navy SeeBees?" asked Joe.

"No, what's that?" asked Stan.

"It's a special campaign to recruit men age 38 up to 50 for truck drivers, construction workers, electricians and things like that, for the war effort," explained Joe. "Even bulldozer operators and plumbers!"

"Really?" said Stan. "I wonder if they'll get many to volunteer."

"Oh, I would suppose so. Some men might find that kind of exciting. The Forum mentioned that a couple guys from Fargo had already signed up."

"We're ready," announced Livvie, holding a sleepy Cheryl in her arms.

As the war continued, things kept tightening up on the home front. Rationing began for coffee, meat, butter, cheese, fats and oils. Everyone was urged to buy twice as many war bonds as before. Thirteen billion dollars needed to be raised in four weeks through sales of government securities. This was the "acid test" for the American people. "They give their lives, you lend your money!" was the motto.

There were problems of a local nature, too. George was called to come to the aid of some neighbors, the Engens, where volunteers hastily erected a dam across the coulee. They hoped to prevent water from running west onto farm land which, if flooded, emptied slowly and would delay spring planting.

The flooding that spring had been the most severe since 1897. George's land was not affected but many of his neighbors had been hard hit. Planting of the much-needed crops would be delayed in the Red River Valley.

The families of servicemen kept a daily vigil by their mailboxes. Livvie reported that Ronnie and Kenny were still in Idaho and Marty had finally been heard from. His parents had received a V-mail letter from him just recently. He couldn't tell them exactly where he was, but they gathered he was in North Africa.

Lenora reported that Jack Gilbertson was now in Louisiana. He complained of the heat and the many snakes there, she had said.

Every newspaper one picked up was full of war news. The last German troops in Stalingrad had finally surrendered. German troops were, however, occupying all of France by now. President Roosevelt and Prime Minister Churchill held a meeting at Casablanca, Morocco. They announced that the Allies would accept nothing less than unconditional surrender from the Axis nations. In early May, the last organized Axis army force in Africa surrendered.

"Oh, I wish we would hear more from Marty," wailed Min, after reading about the goings on in Africa. "Everything has to be so secret. He can't even talk about what he's really doing."

Grandpa Murphy had heard, through the Swedish Red Cross, some news of his family in Norway. They were safe, they said, but severe shortages were being felt now and things in general were not good. The German presence was everywhere.

Life went on in small-town America, however. The high schools graduated their young people that spring. Rosie Olson, friend of Ronnie and Kenny, was one of them, and so was Susie Stevenson, Lenora's younger sister.

"Rosie needed a pair of hosiery for her graduation," related Livvie to her mother, "so I gave her my ration stamp. I figured she needed them more that I did. I'll get along."

"That was nice of you," Carrie had told her daughter. "What does Rosie plan to do after graduation?"

"I don't know," said Livvie. "Probably get a job some place around here."

It wasn't long before Livvie was proven wrong. Three days after graduation, Rosie announced to her parents that she had gone and joined the WAVES. Her parents were very upset, but Rosie was adamant about her decision.

"I want to do something for my country, too," she told them. "Just like Ronnie and Kenny."

"But you're a girl!" they said. "What can you do?"

"They've been asking for women volunteers to help in the war effort," Rosie tried to explain. "There's many things we can do."

The WAVES, Women Accepted for Volunteer Emergency Service, was a name used for female members of the US Navy. Young women were wanted, the newspapers stated, to "free up" the navy men to "punch Japs instead of typewriters" and to "take dictators instead of dictation."

Susie's parents were no less distraught about their daughter's plans. Susie and a girlfriend were planning to go and work in a defense plant. Susie's friend, Carol, had a cousin who lived in St. Louis, Missouri, where the Curtiss-Wright Aircraft plant was located. Women were desperately wanted to fill positions vacated by drafted servicemen. The cousin was already employed at the plant and suggested that Carol come down and apply for a job.

"Bring a friend," she had suggested. Carol didn't have to talk very hard to convince Susie to accompany her. Many young women were at odds with themselves in this wartime situation, just like the young men. They wanted and needed to feel that they were doing something for their country.

A few days after graduation, Livvie and Stan were hosting a birthday party for Cheryl, who was now one year old. Freddie and Lenora and the kids rode up with George and Carrie.

The talk was all about these young women who were leaving traditional roles and going on to find meaning and adventure, and possibly danger, in their lives.

"I just don't understand these young girls nowadays," spouted Magda.

"Things aren't like they used to be, Aunt Maggie," said Stan. "Things are changing so fast that when this war is over, none of us will be quite the same."

"Oh, don't say that, Stan," said his mother. "I want things to be just as they were."

"There's always change, in every generation, but I think it's changing very fast now because of the conditions we're put under," said Carrie, thoughtfully.

Cheryl started to cry when her piece of cake fell on the floor.

"Oh, look what you've done," lamented Livvie. The piece of cake had fallen from the highchair, frosting first. Livvie cleaned up the mess and gave her daughter another piece. Cheryl grinned and proceeded to push a big piece into her mouth, getting frosting almost from ear to ear. The grownups laughed at her antics.

Soon the men drifted towards the living room and the talk turned to the war, farming, and subjects of local interest.

"I guess that the 'Jeep Drive' at the school last month did quite well," remarked Freddie. "They took in $1300 the very first day! Their goal was to sell enough war bonds and stamps to buy five jeeps for the war effort."

"Did you ever hear how much they actually took in?" asked Joe.

"No, but I suppose something will be in the Tribune soon," said Freddie.

"I suppose you hear a lot of news, working at the bank there," commented Art.

"Yes, I guess I do. I hear talk about where the boys from here are. Everyone's so anxious to share what little news they get," said Freddie. "Today, some guys were talking about Larry Blumer."

"And who is that?" asked Art.

"Don't you know his parents?" asked George. "They run the creamery in town. Used to live by Walcott."

"Larry graduated from high school here about five or six years ago," Freddie said.

"Isn't he in the Army Air Corps?"

"Yah, and he just won his 'wings' down in Arizona. He's been training on those P-38's. They're one of the latest model pursuit planes. They go up to 25,000 feet and fly about 400 mph."

The men shook their heads, pondering this information.

"I suppose he'll soon be sent overseas, then, to pursue those Germans," said Joe.

"Well, he's out in California, now, at Oxnard, for more training, I heard today," said Freddie.

"We heard from Ronnie yesterday. He's still in Idaho, of course. We're sure waiting to hear from Marty again," said Joe.

"Lenora talked to her sister, Lucy, today, and she had just heard from Jack. He's still in Louisiana. He said that some of the men from there are being sent over to India," remarked Freddie.

"India!" exclaimed Stan. "Boy, this war is involving the whole world, isn't it? I wonder what our guys are doing over there?"

"So, George," said Art, wanting to change the subject, "what is your forecast for the crops this year?"

"Well, now, it's too early to predict anything, but with such a wet spring and late planting, I don't expect much."

"Yah, and it keeps on raining. We need sunshine and dry conditions."

Memorial Day, 1943, produced just that. It was a pleasant, warm day. Pastor Turmo gave the address at the Kindred Lutheran Church that morning. Because of the gas rationing, the trip to the various cemeteries in the community was not made, but after the program, the whole audience walked or drove to the cemetery in town for the Legion memorial service.

The next day Carrie was able to finish planting her garden. True to her word, she did cut down on the number of rows she planted. The newspaper had assured the home gardeners that jar lids would be available for their home canning this year. People were also encouraged to turn in their pop bottles to the stores and they would eventually be turned into glass jars for home canning.

In the afternoon, after cleaning herself up, she drove into town for the Pie Social put on by the American Legion Auxiliary. Proceeds were for the purchase of war bonds. She stopped by to see Lenora and the kids for awhile and then bought her groceries for the week.

That evening, George suggested that they go into Kindred to hear a speaker at the Town Hall who would be talking about Norway under Nazi rule. It was sponsored by the local Sons of Norway organization. Joe and Min were there, bringing with them Joe's father, Ivar. He was very interested in what was going on in his home country and to his family who still lived there. The speaker, a Lt. Land, gave a vivid story of conditions there and told of the atrocities that were being committed.

"I wonder how he knows all that," remarked Min to Carrie afterwards.

"I suppose he got his information from the British. The exiled Norwegian government, you know, is in England and they manage to get information in and out of Norway."

"The Norwegian Resistance seems to be very active," said Joe.

"I'm glad to hear that our men are doing something to fight back," Ivar remarked.

"Well, we Norwegians are a stubborn lot," commented Joe. "We don't want to let those Germans push us around."

CHAPTER 11

The first week in June was full of important events for the Johnson family. Carrie and Livvie both had birthdays that week and it was also George and Carrie's wedding anniversary on June 5. In fact, it was their 25th wedding anniversary, so there was to be a big Silver Wedding celebration at the church the following Sunday, put on by a committee of friends of the couple.

Carrie couldn't seem to put her heart into getting prepared for this event, what with the war going on and everything. She decided that she would wear one of her older "best" dresses and wouldn't fuss about getting anything new.

Livvie had other ideas, however. She absolutely insisted that her parents get some new clothes for the occasion. So, about two weeks before the event, Carrie and George went to Fargo with Freddie one Saturday morning. Freddie had to go in anyway on business so he said they could ride with him.

"Where shall I drop you off?" Freddie asked, as they neared Broadway.

"Well, I think I'll start at the Herbst Store," said Carrie. "I usually have the best luck there."

"I'll be back in about two hours so I'll meet you out front, then."

Carrie and a reluctant George entered the big store and proceeded to the dress department first. After about a quarter of an hour, Carrie had several selections with her in the dressing room. She decided on a nice pale blue one with some lace and covered buttons.

"You don't think it looks too dressy, do you, George?" she asked, as she carried the dress to the counter. "I want to be able to wear it for Sunday services for sometime to come and not feel over dressed."

"No, I don't think it's that fancy. It will do just fine. You looked real nice in it."

"Well, that didn't take too long, did it?" Carrie said, as they went to the front of the store. "We have some time left. Why don't we look for a suit for you here?"

They checked out the suit department but George thought they were too expensive and didn't see anything he particularly liked.

"I still don't think that I need a new suit, Carrie," he protested.

"Yes, you do, George. You've been wearing that old gray one every Sunday for the last ten years. I wanted you to get a new one when Livvie got married, remember?"

"Oh, all right then," he conceded. "But let's go over to Penney's and see what they've got."

The couple crossed the street to the J.C. Penney Store and sought out the men's department. A salesman was right there to assist them.

"Don't even look at the gray ones, George," Carrie said. "You need to get a different color this time. Here, how about this nice blue one?" She took one off the rack and held it up.

"Well, that looks like a nice one," George said.

"Here, let me get you measured up," volunteered the salesman.

Before the hour was up, George had himself a new suit and they left the store just in time to see Freddie standing in front of Herbst's, waiting for them.

"Here we are," called Carrie to her son.

"I can see that you had some luck," said Freddie, looking at their packages.

"Yah, we're all set now," said George. Little did he know that their shopping had just begun.

"Well, it's noon so why don't we go over to the Red Apple and have some dinner," suggested Freddie. "In fact, I parked right in front of there with that in mind."

They walked down the block and Freddie put their packages in the trunk of his car. They got into the cafe just before the noon rush. They ordered the day's special which was roast beef, mashed potatoes and gravy.

"So, tell me what you bought," said Freddie.

"Oh, I found a really nice dress," said Carrie, excitedly. "It's a pretty blue and it has some lace and some large covered buttons down the front. It's not too fussy, though. I didn't want that!"

"Well, good," said Freddie. "I'm glad you didn't have to run to every store in town to find one."

"Me, too!" agreed George dryly.

"So, Dad, did you get something new, too?"

"Yah, your mother made me buy a new suit. We found it at Penney's."

"He looks real nice in it, too," said Carrie. "It fit him to a tee. Even the sleeves. All I have to do is hem the pants about an inch. They would have done that but we wouldn't have had time to come back for them so I said I could do that much."

Their meal came quickly and they occupied themselves with eating and watching all the people.

"I can't believe all these people eating out on a Saturday," remarked Carrie. "It is kind of fun, though, for a change," she conceded.

"So what did you do all this time, Freddie?" asked his father.

"I had to meet with the bank's lawyer on a certain matter and I had to wait for him for quite awhile. I just got done, now, when I met you."

"You know," admitted Carrie, "now that I think about it, I really should have some new shoes to go with this dress."

"Well, we have plenty of time left," said Freddie. "Why don't you try and find some?"

"What will you guys do, then?"

"Well, Dad, do you need anything else? Did you get a new shirt and tie to go with your new suit?"

"I tried to get him to buy a new tie but he wouldn't hear of it," complained Carrie.

"Dad, you really need a new tie. You've been wearing that same old gray and blue one for many years now. We give you new ones for Christmas but you don't wear them."

"Well, I like my old one," George said, defensively.

"Dad, while Ma is looking for shoes, I'll take you back to Penney's and we'll find a tie to go with the new suit. I insist."

"You know, George, while we're at it, you really should get some new dress shoes, too. You really can't put on that new suit and then wear those old shoes."

"My shoes will be just fine with a coat of polish on them," he insisted.

"No, Dad. Ma is right. We'll look for some shoes, too."

"You two are ganging up on me. Anyway, don't we need our ration stamps for new shoes?"

"I have our books in my purse here," said Carrie. "I'll send one along with you and Freddie."

"I guess I know when I'm beaten," chuckled George. He grabbed for the check before Freddie could get his hands on it. "I'll get this, Freddie. You drove."

"OK, Dad," laughed Freddie. "I guess I know when I'm beaten, too."

When they left the store, Carrie said, "I'll run over to Johnson's Shoes and see if I can find anything. Then I'll go to Dotty Dunn's to see about a hat."

"Let's meet in front of Herbst's again," suggested Freddie. "There's a place to sit there."

Carrie had good luck finding shoes and a hat and then she happened to think that maybe she should have new jewelry for the new dress. She walked way down to Moody's, at the south end of Broadway and there she found just what she needed. She was standing by the counter, waiting for her change. The salesgirl put her money into a little cup and sent it up, via a pulley system, to the office in the balcony and then the change was sent back down to the customer.

Standing there, Carrie realized just how tired she was and how much her feet hurt! Her numerous packages and hat and shoe boxes were getting heavy. Well, she was finished now and could go and meet the men.

"Sorry it took me so long," apologized Carrie, as she rushed up to the two men who had been sitting on the bench in front of the store for quite sometime.

"That's all right, Ma, as long as you got what you needed."

"Oh, I did all right," she admitted. "I'll tell you all about it in the car. We better get going, I suppose."

"I was thinking we should have a cup of coffee before we head for home," suggested Freddie. "We can go to the Red Apple again. Here, let me carry some of those packages."

While sitting in the cafe once again, sipping their coffee, Carrie related the details of her shopping spree. "I found just the shoes I needed right away. Then I remembered that perhaps I should have a new girdle and some new under things, you know, a slip and some hosiery. I used another ration stamp for the hose."

"Well, we got Dad all decked out, too," said Freddie. "We picked out a nice tie and a white shirt and then I talked him into a new pair of black shoes."

"Oh, that's good," said Carrie, happily. "You have better persuasive powers than I do! What made me so late was that I decided that maybe I needed some new jewelry for that new dress. I had to go to several stores for that."

"One thing sure leads to another, doesn't it!" said George. "At first we were going to just wear what we had. No fussing. Now we've spent I don't know how many dollars and all for just one occasion!"

"Well, George," said Carrie, "these are things we will wear for the next ten years. And I guess we really did need some new things. We haven't bought anything for ourselves for a long time."

"No, you two are pretty conservative," said Freddie. "You don't have to feel guilty for spending a little on yourself for a change."

Carrie took a taste of the rhubarb pie that George thought he needed to go along with his coffee.

"Oh, that tastes really tart. I guess they were scrimping on the sugar."

On the way home, Freddie noticed that his parents were dozing off and on after their big shopping trip. He chuckled to himself about all the things they had bought.

Livvie will be glad to hear that they had done so well.

The day of the big occasion started out somewhat drizzly but by late morning, the sun was out and it was turning out to be a fine day. George and Carrie had gone to church in the morning, came home and had a light dinner and rested a bit and then put on their new finery.

As Carrie stood in front of the long mirror, George was looking at her. "My, you look as beautiful as the day I married you," he told her.

Carrie, who just recently turned 52 years old, was still an attractive woman. She still stood tall and slender. Her blond hair was only now starting to show some streaks of gray. She had been to Marie's Beauty Shop in town the day before so her hair looked very nice and she had spent a little more time than usual on applying her make-up.

She turned to George and as she was straightening his new tie, she said, "Well, you look pretty handsome yourself, you know."

They both turned and looked at themselves in the mirror. "We do look pretty good, don't we?" laughed George. "Thanks to you and that shopping trip you dragged me on."

"Livvie can't wait to see us all dressed up, she told me. She never had time to come and see my new dress."

"And don't forget, my new suit!" chuckled George.

"Well, we better get going, then."

They arrived at Gol Church early and the committee was still fussing with the tables and decorations. The church seemed to be filled with peonies and lilacs.

"Oh, who brought all these lovely-smelling flowers?" Carrie asked no one in particular.

"Well, I saw Cordia come in with a big armful right after church this morning," said Beatrice. "I didn't think there were any lilacs left this late."

The honored couple was presented with a corsage and a boutonniere to wear. "My, you have such a pretty dress, Carrie," said Marie, one of their friends on the planning committee. George winked at his wife and they smiled at each other.

"And you look pretty dapper yourself there, George," remarked Nelius, Marie's husband.

The program began and the upstairs of the church was packed. There was a musical selection by the Erickson sisters and Pastor Turmo gave a few remarks. A humorous reading was given and then one of the husbands got up and told some funny stories about the couple. Then Carrie and George were presented with some fine gifts. The committee gave the couple a silver service set. Various other silver items were also given. Freddie and Livvie gave their parents an oblong silver serving tray with their name and date engraved on it.

George and Carrie stood up before the congregation and thanked all the people who came and the committee for putting on such an enjoyable occasion. Then a delicious lunch was served downstairs in the church parlors.

"You'd never know there was rationing going on, would you?" joked George, as he looked at all the food being served.

Friends and family came from far and wide. There was a lot of visiting to do so it was late afternoon before the last ones left.

On the way home, Carrie remarked, "I can't believe all the people who came today. I didn't know we had so many friends! And it was so good to see your mother there."

George's sister, Caroline, who lived over by Wyndmere, brought their mother, Olivia, over for the event.

"It looks like she is having a harder time walking now. It was hard for her to get down those stairs to the basement," George said.

"Well, she is getting up there in age now, you know."

"We really need to go and see her more often, I guess."

"I only wish some of my family could have come from Spring Grove," Carrie mentioned. Carrie's brother, Olaf and his wife had planned to come and bring Carrie's mother but then a postcard came a few days earlier saying that they wouldn't be able to come after all. Carrie's mother had caught a bad chest cold and was not feeling up to the trip.

"Yah, that's too bad that your family couldn't come," agreed George. "We'll have to take a drive over there this summer sometime."

"Your mother sure enjoyed seeing Freddie and Livvie and their families," remarked Carrie.

A they entered the house, Carrie kicked off her new shoes and said," Oh, I really am so tired! I'm going to go up and change my clothes and then rest a bit."

They piled their gifts and many cards on the dining-room table. "We'll take care of them later," said Carrie.

George also changed his clothes and went out to start the evening chores.

Because of the war, the usual big celebrations held during the summer were cancelled or scaled back. Davenport's big Farmers' Day, usually held every June, became simply a community picnic this year, and the Fourth of July events in various small towns were not as big either. There were none of the usual parades or carnivals, and very few dances.

Lenora reported that her sister, Susie, was now down in Missouri and she and her friend had found employment at the aircraft plant there. Jack was still in the States and Marty was believed to be in North Africa. His infrequent V-mail letters were few and far between and didn't bear much news. Rosie Olson was now in Florida, training for her duties as a WAVE.

The Italian dictator, Mussolini, fell from power and was imprisoned by his own government. It was later learned that a daring band of German paratroopers rescued him. It was rumored that he had set up a puppet government in Northern Italy.

Names such as Mussolini, Hitler, Hirohito and Tojo stirred fear in the hearts of Americans and their Allies. Americans on the home front were asked to continue to support the war effort financially, as well as in the production of food for the nation and goods to be used by the servicemen.

Farm families had received a Certificate of Farm War Service for their efforts in crop production for the year 1942 and they were now urged to produce even more in 1943.

"Our production in this area will be down from last year," predicted George, " because of the weather conditions."

"Well, that can't be helped. At least you tried hard enough," consoled Carrie.

In early August, Livvie was invited to her grandmother's birthday party at the home of her real mother, Merrie. Livvie drove over for the afternoon, taking Cheryl with her. As she drove in the yard, there were several cars already there. Livvie's grandmother, Ethyl, seemed happy to see her and greeted her more warmly than usual.

When Livvie was in the kitchen with Merrie, she remarked, "It seems that your mother is really enjoying this party. I've never seen her so talkative before."

"Mother has really come out of her shell. When my father was alive, it seemed like she was always walking on eggshells, even when he wasn't around," Merrie sighed. "Now she's more relaxed and is really enjoying herself. She gets together with her friends often, for coffee parties and church events."

"She seemed to really be glad to see me today," said Livvie. "Perhaps she's no longer ashamed of me."

"Oh, Livvie!" cried Merrie. "She was never ashamed of you. Maybe of me, for what I did, but never of you."

Merrie's aunt, Julia, the one who had arranged for Merrie to give her baby to Carrie and George, came into the kitchen.

"We need more coffee," she announced, carrying the empty pot.

"I was just going to bring some out. And Livvie, you can bring the birthday cake," said Merrie.

After the ladies finished their cake and coffee, Ethyl opened her cards. Then, when she had everyone's attention, thanking them for coming, she said that she had something important to tell them.

"My dear friends, I want to share something with you. Perhaps you have wondered who Livvie is and why she's here today. I told you she was a family friend, but she is more than that. She is my granddaughter."

Ethyl paused here to let this information sink in. With Merrie being her only daughter, the ladies soon concluded what this meant. They looked at Merrie, who had a very surprised look on her face. She hadn't known that her mother was going to reveal the family secret.

"You see," Ethyl went on, "about twenty years ago, Merrie had a baby girl and because of the circumstances, my husband decided that she would have to give her up. Well, my dear sister-in-law, Julia, arranged for an adoption and always knew where the child had gone. She didn't go very far away. Only over by Kindred. Well, anyway, I just got to meet her this last year and I'm proud to introduce her and her little girl, my great granddaughter, to you today."

Ethyl held her head high, and dared anyone to think any less of her daughter for what happened so long ago.

"The details of how this happened aren't important and I hope that you will not discuss it with anyone else at this time, but I wanted you, as my dearest friends, to know the rest of my family." She looked lovingly toward Merrie and Livvie.

Merrie was in tears and Livvie felt a lump in her throat. It had taken great courage for Ethyl to make this secret known. Merrie didn't know what to say and Livvie was very uncomfortable with all eyes on her.

The guests were uncomfortable, too, with this revelation. They didn't know how to respond. Ethyl waited for someone to speak. Finally, a woman named Lily found her tongue.

"Well, Livvie, I am pleased to meet you. Your....ah....grandmother is a dear friend of mine and has been for many years. I feel bad that she never was able to share her secret with anyone before."

"I'm pleased to meet you, too, Livvie," said another woman.

And so it went, around the table, as all the women, in turn, accepted Livvie with love and friendship. Their words also included Merrie, and as the ladies rose to begin to take their leave, one woman embraced her.

"Merrie," she said kindly, "you have a beautiful daughter. And granddaughter," she added.

When all the guests had left, including Ethyl, who rode over with Julia, Livvie and Merrie just looked at each other and then fell into each other's arms.

Merrie wept tears of relief. Relief for all the years that she had to keep her secret hidden from the world. Livvie felt compassion for her mother as never before.

"Well," said Merrie, as she regained her composure, "that was certainly a surprise. I can't wait to talk to mother and find out what she has to say about this. She could have at least warned me."

"Yes, I was certainly shocked when she came with that," agreed Livvie.

"I guess it's all for the best, that it happened this way. I would have been very nervous if Mother had told me that she was going to do this."

Livvie helped Merrie clear off the table and offered to stay and help with the dishes. The two women worked side by side in silence for a time.

"I wish you would tell me more about my real father," said Livvie suddenly.

Merrie turned to her daughter and said, "Oh, Livvie, I don't know any more things to tell you about him." She took the dishtowel from Livvie's hand and led her to the kitchen table. "So what is it you really want to know?"

"Well," said Livvie slowly, "all I know is his name and that he was very handsome, a hard worker, a good card player, and that he was a ladies man. I guess I need to know more. I can't explain it, mother."

"To tell you the truth, Livvie, I really don't know much more that that. I only knew him for about three months. I was asked to help out on the farm where he was working. It was harvest time and when that was over, heÖheÖjust left."

"But didn't he love you? Didn't he tell you that he was going?"

Merrie turned her head and stared out the window. "No, Livvie, he never told me that he loved me. But I thought I loved him and I was so young and foolish that I guess I figured that was enough. That he would love me eventually. When he left without a word, I kept thinking he would be back soon. But I was wrong."

"If he had known about....about....your condition, do you think he would have stayed and done the right thing?"

"I have wondered about that many times, Livvie, but you know, I really don't think he would have been at all happy about the situation. He may have run off even if he'd known. I can't say why I think that, but I just have a feeling that he was not the kind of man who would have made things.... right."

"So, my father was probably not an honorable man, is that what you're saying?"

Merrie paused. "I guess so, Livvie. I'm sorry."

Livvie looked at the clock on the mantle. She stood and went into the living room and picked up her sleeping daughter. "I think I better go home now. It's getting late. Stan will wonder why I'm not home yet."

"Thank you for coming today, Livvie, and for helping me."

Livvie turned at the door. "Someday I'm going to find my real father."

CHAPTER 12

Carrie and George's trip to Spring Grove to see Carrie's family came sooner than expected. Carrie had received a call early one morning from her sister-in-law telling her that her mother had passed away. It was pneumonia, Mattie had said. Carrie called her brother, Amund, over in Davenport to tell him the news.

"The funeral will be the day after tomorrow," she told him.

"Well, we better go then, don't you think?" he'd said. "Can George get away?"

Harvest was just a few days away, but George decided he could take the time, so the two couples traveled together, combining their gas ration stamps. Amund had insisted on taking his car, as he thought it had the better tires.

They arrived at the farm of their brother, Olaf, late in the afternoon. His wife, Mattie, had a nice supper waiting for them. It grieved Carrie to see that her oldest brother had aged so. He was only seven years older than Carrie but he was walking with much difficulty. It was his arthritis, he told them.

At the funeral the next day, Carrie would get to see her other family members, but her sisters, Sylvia and Rosina, and their families arrived early and came out to the farm. Younger brother, Martin, farmed just a few miles away and had stopped by the night before. He lived in the old farmstead where Carrie had grown up.

Carrie and her sisters drove over to the old farm place to have a look around. "Look, there's the grove of cottonwood trees that we always played in," she exclaimed, as they drove into the yard.

As they walked around the house, she felt a pang of homesickness and a little guilt for not returning to see her family as often as she should have. Martin's wife had died two years ago, so he lived here alone, moving in after their father died and their mother had gone to live with Olaf and Mattie.

"I guess we'll try and sell this house," announced Martin. "It's too much for me to keep up alone. I'm going to look for something in town."

This was news to Carrie and she felt sad to think that her old home place would no longer be in the family. "I guess that's life," she sighed. *Things are always changing.*

Their small church was filled to overflowing, a tribute to how much their mother was loved and respected in the community. Following the service, a lunch was served in the basement by the Ladies Aid.

As Carrie was finishing her last sip of coffee, she noticed a somewhat familiar face talking with Olaf across the table from her. She stared at him and then he looked up and acknowledged her.

Oh, it's Ted Gunderson. Carrie's thoughts went back many years. He was a former beau of hers. In fact, he was the reason why she had left Spring Grove and gone to North Dakota with her brother. He had jilted her for another girl and Carrie had felt the need to get away.

He was coming towards her now and she rose from her chair. He extended his hand and mumbled his sympathies. She could only stare at him. He had changed so much. He was completely gray and he had a terrific paunch spilling out of his suit coat.

She thanked him for his condolences and he turned to leave. "Wait, Ted," she called to him. "How are you doing?" She no longer harbored any bad feelings towards him. She only felt concern now. He looked like he was ill or something.

"Oh, all right, I guess," he answered. Ted had been the pastor's son in town there, back when both of them were young, and he had led Carrie to believe that their relationship was going somewhere, and then, when he was away at college, Carrie found out that he was getting engaged to someone else. He married the woman and moved back to Spring Grove and took over the bank.

"Are you still at the bank?" Carrie queried.

"Yes. Yes I am," he answered. "And how are you doing, may I ask?"

"Just fine," she said. "George and I are still farming over in North Dakota." She nodded in her husband's direction as she said this.

"That's nice. I'm glad you're doing well. You look well. I guess I better be getting back to the bank. It was nice seeing you, Carrie."

"It was nice of you to come today, Ted." As he left, she went over and stood by her husband. She took a good look at him. *How nice he still looks. I'm glad things turned out as they did.*

That evening, Carrie's brothers and sisters were all over at Olaf and

Mattie's. They talked and reminisced long into the night. They talked about their parents and their childhood years. They talked about the war, the shortages, the lives that were being changed by it. Olaf and Mattie had a grandson in the front lines. They were very worried about him. Sylvia's granddaughter's fiance was in the navy somewhere in the Pacific. They all knew of someone who had been drafted and answered their country's call to service.

"Well, if Ma and Pa hadn't left good old Norway, we'd now be living under the Nazis," commented Olaf. He was just a baby when his parents had come over to this country back in 1885.

"Yah, things don't sound too good over there," said Martin, "from what we read in the Decorah Posten."

On a lighter note, Sylvia said to Carrie, "I see you had a conversation with Ted Gunderson this afternoon."

"Yah, wasn't that your old boyfriend?" teased Martin.

"I hadn't talked to him in over 30 years," said Carrie. "My, how he's changed! He looks so old and so....so....beaten."

"Well, I think his wife has done that to him," stated Olaf.

"You mean Birdie?" asked Rosina.

Carrie and her sisters looked at each other and chuckled. When they had heard many years ago that he was marrying a woman named Birdie, they all had had a good laugh at such a name as that.

"Yes, Birdie!" said Mattie. "She's something else, I tell you! She's one woman who's really hard on her man and it shows."

"Yes, I felt really sorry for him when I saw him today," said Carrie.

"Well, fellows," Olaf said to the men, "we're lucky we have such good wives. We still all look pretty good, don't we?" He laughed and the others joined him.

The subject finally got around to farming, which reminded George that they needed to leave early the next morning for home. Harvest was awaiting him. Mattie got up and went for the coffeepot but had no takers. Everyone had had enough coffee for one day.

After an early breakfast the next morning, the two couples said their goodbyes to the family.

"I'm so glad that we could make the trip," said Amund, as they were driving west. "It was good to see everyone again."

"Yes, it was," said Carrie. "I'd give anything if I could have seen mother just one more time, though."

"It is too bad that she couldn't have made it out for your silver wedding," said Edith.

"Martin seems to be doing OK, doesn't he?" mentioned George.

"He seems lonely, though," said Edith. "It's a shame that Eunice had to die at such a young age."

Martin was the youngest in the Amundson family, being only forty-seven. His wife had died two years earlier, of cancer.

"Yah, and it's too bad that his children don't live closer. They're scattered all over the state of Minnesota," said Olaf.

"I wonder if we'll ever be all together again," reflected Carrie.

"Well, let's hope it's under happier circumstances," said Amund.

Just one day after returning from the trip to Spring Grove, George plunged into harvest. He took out the swather and began to cut the wheat on his farm. Then he would go and cut what was ready on Ole's land. Ole was a close neighbor and they often helped each other with planting and harvest. Ole had had the foresight to buy a combine two years earlier so the two men had made an agreement. George would do the swathing and help haul grain for Ole and Ole, in turn, would run the combine on both farms.

Freddie would come out and help drive truck for the men and Ole had a grown son who lived nearby who also helped when needed. This year, with the severe shortage of young men to help with the harvest, the business places in town voluntarily closed at 5 p.m. so that the male employees could go out and help the farmers. Many farmers didn't have combines yet and still had to shock and then thresh. Old Clem of the Kindred Tribune nicknamed these helpers "emergency shockers".

Things were a little more hectic up on the Murphy farm. They didn't have a combine yet so they needed a lot of help. The US Government came to the rescue. A contingent of soldiers from a base in Sioux Falls came up to Cass County specifically to help area farmers with their harvest. They camped near Casselton and lived in tents there.

Carrie received a postcard from Livvie a few days after their harvest started. She said that Stan and Joe were running the binders and these soldiers did the shocking. They had five of them working on their particular farm. Grandpa Murphy, wanting to be of some help, volunteered to drive the truck up to Casselton every morning and pick up the soldiers. There were about a dozen of them who rode in the back of the truck. Ivar would drop off half of them on another farm nearby. In the evening he would reverse his route.

Joe Murphy and his brother-in-law neighbor, Art, worked together on their harvest so they shared machinery and labor.

"Yah, I sure wish I had bought a combine last year," Joe said often during the next few days. "I was planning to get one this year but now they're not available. Not even used ones."

Livvie and Magda took turns helping Min out with providing meals for all the men. On the days that Livvie wasn't over at her mother-in-law's, then she was busy baking for all the lunches that had to be made.

Freddie came out to his dad's farm one day after work with an interesting story. "I heard in the bank today," he began, "that Fred Hendrickson called Plath's Implement in Kindred and needed a part for his combine and he needed it now! Mr. Plath drove to Fargo, picked up the part, and then drove to Hector Airport where his private plane was stored and flew over the Hendrickson farm and dropped the part!"

The men got a chuckle out of that story. "Floyd will probably have to charge double for that part!" laughed George.

The weather remained dry and the yield was small so the harvest moved along quickly. After several weeks, the soldiers, who were with the 412th Aviation Squadron, took down their tents and returned to their base.

The war in Europe and the Pacific droned on. With the harvest over, George had time to read the newspapers and listen to the radio. The news wasn't always so good, but President Roosevelt praised the American people for doing their part and told them to keep the faith.

Freddie reported that his brother-in-law, Jack, had been sent to India. He was among a group of infantrymen sent over there to train the Chinese in their struggle against the Japanese.

The Murphys had received word from Ronnie that he and Kenny were in San Diego and awaiting further orders. He said that he thought they would soon be sent somewhere in the South Pacific.

"Oh, please let the war be over soon," Min prayed aloud, "before they have to go!"

There were movies occasionally in the Kindred Auditorium and the residents would flock to see them, not only for the entertainment, but because there was always a newsreel regarding the war. That's where the people could really see what was going on overseas.

Early in October, there was a show company called the Big Ole Show that came to town and presented some entertainment. First, though, there was a program telling the true facts about Nazism and the persecution of the Jews, followed by a stage show and a free dance.

George and Carrie attended but didn't stay for the dance. They went to the Thompson Cafe for lunch instead with Amund and Edith who had come over for the evening.

"Yah, after hearing all that terrible stuff about what they're doing to those poor Jews, I didn't feel much like dancing!" exclaimed George.

"That is really awful. I can hardly believe it, can you?" asked Amund "I thought we lived in a more civilized age."

The two couples were silent for sometime, each thinking about what they had just seen and heard.

Carrie broke the silence by asking Edith about their family. They had two grown children, Irene and Ken, and they both lived in Fargo. Irene was a hair dresser and Ken worked at Hanson's Auto Mechanics School as an instructor. He, too, was worried about the draft but had so far been lucky.

The men talked about the scrap metal drive. "How did you like Clem's comments about that?" asked Amund. "Slap the Jap—bring in your scrap!"

"Yah, that Clem, he sure comes up with some good ones," replied George.

"I've hauled almost all the scrap metal I can find around the garage there," said Amund.

"I'll have to go looking around in the woods," said George. "I think there's some really old stuff out there that I haven't taken yet."

"I hear that if you bring in your scale tickets for the metal to the Evingson's store, you can get in on certain sales," commented Edith.

"Yah, I guess you can get blankets, men's sweaters, apples, flour and stuff like that," said Carrie. "You could use a good sweater, George."

"Too bad they aren't giving away sugar!" exclaimed Edith, with a laugh. "Wouldn't that be a nice surprise!"

A week later, George announced one morning that he thought he'd go down to Wyndmere for the Richland County Corn Show.

"I'll stop in at Caroline's and see mother for awhile. Do you want to come along?"

"No, I've got Ladies Aid this afternoon and I hate to miss that. Beatrice and Ruby are serving today, you know."

George left, and that afternoon, on her way home from the church, Carrie stopped at their mailbox and picked up the mail. There was a letter from Livvie. She said that her in-laws had received a letter from Marty, finally. He was now in Italy and had had quite a rough time of it recently.

"You know, George," Carrie said to her husband that evening, "I think we should take a drive up to see Joe and Min soon."

"Yah, perhaps we should. From what I've been reading in the newspapers, there was some fierce fighting in Italy recently."

"Maybe on Sunday we could go," suggested Carrie. "We could stop by Livvie's, too."

Early on Sunday afternoon, George and Carrie drove up to Stan and Livvie's. When they came into the yard, it looked like no one was home. The car was gone and everything seemed quiet.

"Maybe you should run up to the door anyway," suggested George. "Just in case Stan has the car and Livvie is in the house."

Carrie rapped on the door and waited for several minutes and then came back to the car.

"No, I guess they're both gone. Perhaps they're over at Joe and Min's."

"That could be," said George, as he backed up the car and headed back to the road.

As they drove into the Murphys' yard, there was Stan and Livvie's car. As they walked up to the house, Joe appeared in the doorway and called to them.

"Well, what a nice surprise! We haven't seen you folks for quite a long time." He held the door open for them. "Come in, come in."

"Oh, hi, Mom!" said Livvie from the kitchen. "Did you stop at our place first?"

"Yah, we did, but then we thought maybe we'd find you over here."

"Have a seat by the table here," said Min. "I was just going to make coffee."

"Oh, my, we sure came at the right time," laughed George.

Everyone sat down and began getting caught up with each other's news. Carrie picked up little Cheryl, who seemed happy to see her other grandma. Min brought out a plate of cake and doughnuts and then sat down herself.

"The coffee will be ready in a few minutes," she said.

"Well, we wanted to come up and talk to you about Marty," George started. "Livvie said that you had heard from him recently."

"Yah, a long letter finally came a few days ago," answered Joe. He wore a worried look on his face when talking about his oldest son.

"It sounded like he was in the thick of things there in southern Italy," Joe went on. "He's with Gen. Clark's Fifth Army and they had just sailed up from North Africa to Salerno. The Germans threatened to push them back to the sea so there was some intense fighting going on. Then Clark's men joined up with some British and Canadian forces, I guess, and the Allies were able to hold their own."

"I was just reading about that in the paper last week," said George.

"Yah, George reads those newspapers from one end to the other, I tell you," commented Carrie.

"Well, I like to keep up with what's going on over there."

"I wonder how much longer this war is going to keep on," sighed Min, getting up to get the coffeepot. Everyone was silent for a few moments, each wondering the same thing.

"Well, have you heard from Ronnie, then, lately?" asked George.

"Oh, I suppose it's about two weeks ago that we got a letter from him," answered Joe. "He's pretty sure he'll be sent to the Pacific someplace."

Min came around with the coffee cups and put one down in front of each one. "Help yourself," she said, handing the pot to Carrie. "I also have a cold drink if you'd prefer that."

"No, coffee will be fine," said Carrie. "We try and cut back on the coffee drinking at home now so this will taste mighty good."

"I made this cake using white syrup instead of sugar and I guess it doesn't taste too bad," said Min.

"I think it's very good," said Livvie.

"I had to beat it longer than usual but it seems to work well for a substitute."

"So how did your harvest go, then, down by Kindred?" asked Joe.

"It went pretty well. It didn't take as long as usual as there was not much there to work with. How about up here?"

"Our wheat wasn't too bad up here but I've sure seen better years."

"How did it go with those soldiers helping you out?"

Joe laughed and shook his head. "Well, we had five or six at a time, not always the same ones. A few of them knew how to work but there were some that didn't know anything about the farm, I tell you. Most of them were from the east, originally. They were with some aviation squadron stationed down at Sioux Falls."

"Do you suppose they'll come back next year?" asked Livvie.

"Oh, don't say that!" exclaimed Min. "I'm hoping the war will be over before then!"

By the middle of November, the ground had frozen hard so that put an end to the fall plowing and general yard work. George had worked up Carrie's garden and it stood black and barren, waiting for next year's seeding.

"I talked to Beatrice this afternoon," Carrie related to George one evening. "She said she and Carl will be taking her folks to Fargo tomorrow to catch the train. They're going down to Indiana to spend the winter with their other daughter, Edna."

"Is that right?" George remarked, rather absently. After a pause, he said, "It says here that the ban on materials used to repair household appliances will be lifted." He pointed to the article that he was reading from the newspaper.

"And why is that?"

"Well, we're unable to buy new appliances so what are we supposed to do when they break down? This will also affect auto repair shops, blacksmiths, electricians, even radio repair shops, it says."

"That will be a good thing. Maybe we can get our kitchen radio fixed. I have missed listening to my afternoon programs while I work in the kitchen."

"Yah, I'll have to check with Joe Owen about getting that fixed now."

"Beatrice said that she heard that the Rustad Pioneer Museum will be open for three afternoons next week. We'll have to go and have a look," Carrie suggested. "It costs 25 cents for admission."

"Yah, I hear there's some pretty interesting things that people have donated."

George stuck his nose back in the newspaper. "I see the price of wheat is going up. It was $1.48 a bushel today. I think I'll haul some into the elevator tomorrow."

"Maybe I'll go along in with you," commented Carrie. "We could take in the grand opening of the Gambles Store. Let's see, what's the name of the new people who are going to be running it?"

"Hoganson, I believe," answered George.

"Yes, that's what it is. I want to check out that moonstone glassware they've got advertised. And they're selling rayon hosiery for 69 cents."

Christmas of 1943 approached and while Carrie and George enjoyed the holidays, especially with their three young grandchildren, it was somewhat subdued.

"Just think," exclaimed Carrie. "This is the third Christmas of the war. I never thought it would go on so long!"

"What's the next year going to bring, I wonder," said George.

"It can't possibly last until next Christmas, can it?"

CHAPTER 13

The spring of '44 brought optimism to the American people. Surely this would be the year that the war would come to an end. Some promising events were happening in Europe. In January, the Russians had broken the siege of Leningrad and pushed the Germans back. For five days in February, the Allied Air Forces, in overwhelming strength, had bombed German aircraft industries, and caused considerable damage to Hitler's famed Luftwaffe. General Henry Arnold, commanding general of the U.S. Army Air Forces, reported that "those five days changed the history of the air war."

However, in March, Germany swept into Hungary, seemingly as strong as ever. It was a sewsaw ride for the Americans on the home front. One day it seemed like the end was in sight, only to change the next day with news of Hitler's determination and strength.

One afternoon in March, Lenora paid an unexpected visit to Carrie.

"What a nice surprise!" exclaimed Carrie, as she welcomed her daughter-in-law and the two children.

"It seemed like a nice day to get out a bit," said Lenora, taking Larry's coat and mittens off. Sandra, of course, wanted to do hers by herself. She had recently had her fifth birthday and thought herself to be very grown up.

Carrie put the coffee on and found some toys for the children. She could tell that Lenora had something on her mind, but she waited patiently for the young woman to speak.

"Well, it's sure nice to see the sun today, isn't it?" she said, conversationally.

Lenora barely answered. "Carrie," she finally said, "you're probably wondering why I came out today." She paused and took a sip of her coffee. Setting the cup back down carefully, she continued. "I just don't know what to do. Freddie's been acting so 'down' lately, and I think I know what's bothering him but he won't talk about it."

Alarmed now, Carrie sat down opposite Lenora. "Go on," she said.

"Well, I think he's feeling guilty because so many young men have had to go into the service and he didn't have to go."

"Well, he had a medical reason not to be drafted!" exclaimed Carrie.

"Yes, of course, and at first he was so relieved that he didn't have to go, but I think that as time went by, he has started to feel guilty. People see him in the bank every day and wonder why such a young, healthy-looking man is doing a job that a woman could do."

"Oh, dear," said Carrie, shaking her head. "I can understand how this could happen. Are you sure this is how he's thinking? You said he won't talk about it."

"No, he won't say much, but he has told me enough so that I know this is what he is feeling. He comes home from work very depressed some days. I don't know what to do or say to him!" cried Lenora.

"You know, when we were all together for Sandra's birthday, I did notice that he was awfully quiet whenever the subject of the war came up."

"Yes, we can hardly even talk about it. It just makes things worse."

Carrie got up to refill their cups and sat down again. "Well, I don't really know what to tell you. His father—his real father, I mean— my first husband, Fred— He could get terribly moody sometimes. After our baby died, little Joey, he wasn't ever himself again." Carrie wiped at a tear beginning to form in the corner of her eye. "I couldn't talk to him about anything, it seemed. Then, of course, he was killed in that fire."

Lenora looked horrified. "Oh, I'm sorry!" Carrie exclaimed. "Why am I telling you all this? It won't make you feel any better. I don't mean that Freddie will get that bad. I just meant that I understand how you are feeling. It's a hopeless feeling, to not be able to help someone you love."

"Yes, I just can't seem to say the right things to make him feel differently."

"Can you think of someone who could talk to him? Perhaps your pastor? You have a new one there in Kindred Lutheran now, don't you? A Pastor Laaveg?"

"Yes, and he's very nice. Perhaps I could talk to him but I don't know if he could help Freddie."

Carrie and Lenora discussed the situation until the children became bored and started fussing.

"Well, I better go," said Lenora. "I want to get home before Freddie does. He'll be wondering why I came over here today."

"I guess the best thing that you and I can do for Freddie is to pray for him," stated Carrie, matter of factly.

"Yes, I will start doing that this very night," said Lenora.

"And I will, too, my dear." Carrie gave Lenora a warm hug and kissed the children goodbye.

Carrie was troubled the rest of the afternoon and when George came back from town, she hadn't even started supper. She jumped up as he came in.

"Oh, I hadn't realized how late is was getting! I guess we'll just have to have cream and bread for supper tonight. Is that all right?"

"Of course," he said. "Anything will do. I had coffee in the cafe late this afternoon with a couple of the fellows and I had several donuts so I'm not exactly starving!"

"Here, can you open this jar of chokecherry syrup for me?"

"Oh, this looks good," he said, opening the jar with care.

As they ate, Carrie told George everything about Lenora's visit. He looked troubled as he heard the details.

"Well, I don't know what we can do for him. Maybe I can stop in and have a talk with him sometime soon."

"Yah, why don't you do that. You better not tell him that Lenora told us about it, though. You'll have to think up something to say, to bring the subject out in the open."

George looked thoughtful as he got up from the supper table. He went into the living room and sat in his favorite chair and opened the newspaper. He had trouble concentrating on what he read.

"I have half a mind to go over and see him this very evening," he told Carrie as she joined him later.

"Oh, no, you better not do that. Wait until some afternoon when he gets done with work."

At bedtime, as Carrie had her evening devotions, she asked George to pray with her about their son. They both fell asleep thinking about him.

That same afternoon, Livvie had opened her door to find her real mother, Merrie, standing on the step.

"Oh, I sure didn't expect you today!" said Livvie. "Do come in. What a nice surprise."

"I was going to phone you but then I got busy and had an errand near Kindred and so thought I'd drive up here and see you for a little while. Is

Cheryl sleeping?"

Merrie came to see Livvie and her family about once a month or so. Often she would bring her mother or her two children.

"Yes, she just went down for her nap, but she doesn't sleep long anymore, it seems."

Livvie led the way into the living room and the two women sat on the sofa together. They had a good relationship and enjoyed each other's company.

They talked at length about their families, the war and the weather.

"You know, Livvie," confided Merrie, "each time that I go home after seeing you, I feel that I'm getting closer to healing the hurt of all those years when I didn't know where you were."

Livvie looked at her mother in surprise. She saw tears beginning to form in the older woman's eyes.

"My mother and I were just talking about this the other day," Merrie went on. "She feels the same way. She told me that she thought of you often, too, and wondered where you had been taken, that day, after you were born. She never asked her sister-in-law where she brought you. Can you imagine that?"

Livvie had no answer.

"She said that she could never bring up the subject in front of my father. He absolutely would not talk about that 'shameful incident.' She knew that I was hurting, though, but could do nothing to help me." Merrie dabbed at her eyes and Livvie, too, felt tears starting to roll down her own cheeks.

"Oh, Mother, I don't know how you endured it!" cried Livvie. "I couldn't even imagine giving up Cheryl!"

"Well, it was something I couldn't talk about to anyone, and so, I just had to get through each day some way. It helped after I got married but then when we had our first baby, the ache in my heart just seemed to get worse. I couldn't forget the baby that I was forced to give up."

The two women sat in silence for awhile. Then Merrie began again. "My mother says she feels guilty because she didn't take a firmer stand against my father. She would have let me keep the baby, she said, if she could have."

Cheryl's loud wailing from the other room brought mother and daughter up short.

"Oh, someone's not very happy, it sounds like," Merrie chuckled.

"She always wakes up from her nap like that. It's like she's mad that she fell asleep!"

"Here, let me surprise her," said Merrie, jumping up to go and get her granddaughter.

A startled Cheryl stopped crying and soon a grin spread over her face. She was always happy to see her grandmother. She was the same with her other two grandmothers.

Merrie stayed awhile longer to play with Cheryl but when she looked at the mantle clock, she declared that she better get home before the kids got home from school.

"Do you have to pick them up?" asked Livvie.

"No, this week they're riding home with the neighbor. We kind of take turns. When the weather's warmer, they can walk home, you know."

"Well, I'm sure glad you stopped by today," Livvie told Merrie.

"Yes, well, I hadn't seen you or Cheryl for over a month now."

Mother and daughter embraced and Livvie stood by the window, holding Cheryl, and watched as her mother drove out of the yard. She felt the tears coming again but hurried to busy herself with preparing supper.

"Why do I feel like crying?" she said aloud to her little daughter. Cheryl just looked at her with a wide-eyed expression. Livvie had to laugh at her.

When Stan came home a short while later, Livvie had a hot meal ready to put on the table. She told her husband about her mother's visit and about what she had said about getting over the hurt that she had felt all those years.

"It must have been tough," he said, helping himself to the potatoes. "Oh, by the way, my folks got a letter today from Ronnie. He's near some island in the Pacific now. His job is to service the navy's aircraft aboard ship. He likes that, he said. It keeps him busy and then the time goes fast."

"How long has he been there?" asked Livvie.

"I don't think he said, but he told about the trip over there. It was a long trip from San Diego and they ran into some pretty rough seas and he was so seasick that he said he wanted to die!"

"Did he say where Kenny is?"

"Well, I think they're still together, the way he talked. They wouldn't be too happy if they got split up."

"No, that would never do," laughed Livvie.

Livvie did up the dishes as Stan played awhile with Cheryl.

"Oh, I read in the Tribune today about a movie that's coming to Kindred this weekend. Maybe we could go," suggested Livvie.

"What's playing?"

"It's called 'Song of the Islands' and Betty Grable and Victor Mature are in it. It's even in Technicolor!"

"Well, that sounds like it might be good. Maybe we should go on Saturday night."

"We could probably leave Cheryl with my folks. They'd like that," said Livvie.

"Yah, we could do that."

"I'll drop Mom a postcard tomorrow and tell her we'll be coming. Did you know that postage is going up at the end of this month? It'll cost three whole cents now to mail a letter!"

On Saturday, Stan hurried through the chores so they could get an early start to Kindred. They arrived at the Johnson farm just as George and Carrie were finishing their supper.

"Do you have to hurry right off to the movie?" asked Carrie, as she was helping to get Cheryl's wraps off.

"I'd like to get a few things at Larsen's Store first," said Livvie.

"OK then, you'd better hurry," said Carrie. "We'll talk after you get back. We'll get along just fine with Cheryl. Go and have some fun now."

About three hours later, the young couple quietly let themselves in the back door. George was dozing in his chair and Carrie was just coming out of the bedroom.

"Oh, you're back already. I was just checking on Cheryl. She fell asleep about an hour ago now."

"Oh, Mom, that movie was so good!" exclaimed Livvie. "You and Dad have to go and see it."

"Well, maybe we can go tomorrow night," she said, glancing over at her husband. George nodded.

"Here, take off your coats and sit awhile so we can talk. Do you want some coffee or anything?"

"No, we're all right," said Stan, joining Livvie on the sofa.

"There was a good newsreel about the war before the main feature," said Livvie. "It makes you think about all the guys we know who are in the service."

"It had some footage about some action on an island in the Pacific. That's where my brother, Ronnie, is now, you know," stated Stan.

"Yes, Livvie mentioned that on her postcard the other day."

The four of them talked about the war for awhile longer. "Lenora's brother-in-law, Jack, is still in India. Lucy is so worried about him."

"Well, I would be, too," said Livvie.

"I heard today that Larry Blumer was sent over to England," said George. "He'll be flying on bombing missions, I suppose."

"That sure sounds dangerous," Stan said, shaking his head.

"I pray every night for all our boys to come home safely," said Carrie.

"Carrie, do they know about Freddie?" asked George.

"What about Freddie?" said Livvie, looking anxious.

"Well, Lenora stopped over here a few days ago and she's worried about him."

"Isn't he feeling well?" asked Stan.

"It isn't that, but he's so depressed sometimes, she said. He's feeling so guilty because he wasn't called up and so many others have been."

"Stan, did you feel like that, too?" George asked his son-in-law.

"Not really. Well, maybe a little at first, but now I realize how important it is to have a good workforce on the farms, to produce the food we need. What is it the newspaper calls us? 'Soldiers of the Soil—America's land army'."

"Yah, I don't know what your dad would have done without you. Farm laborers are hard to come by these days," said George.

"Maybe you could go and have a talk with Freddie sometime, Stan," suggested Carrie.

"I guess I could do that," he answered. He looked over at his wife. "Livvie, you have some news to tell your folks, don't you," he said, changing the subject.

Livvie blushed slightly and cleared her throat. "Well, it looks like Cheryl is going to have a little brother or sister in a few months."

"Oh, Livvie, that's wonderful!" cried Carrie.

"Is it, Mom?" Livvie asked. "I don't know! Look at how much turmoil the world is in right now. I don't think we should be bringing another baby into it." She was almost in tears now.

"Oh, don't feel that way, Livvie," said Carrie. "Things just have to get better soon. Why, maybe by the time the baby is here, this awful war will be over."

"But what if we don't win this war, Mom? What then? What if Hitler wins? What will this country be like then? Or if the Japs should win and take over the world? What will it be like here?" Livvie buried her face in her hands.

"Livvie's really been worried about these things lately," explained Stan.

"Well, maybe it's just her condition. Women sometimes get very emotional when they are going to have a baby," Carrie said, soothingly.

"You can't tell me that you never think these thoughts yourself, Mom. Dad?"

"Well, of course it does cross our minds sometimes but we just try and remain confident that the US and her Allies will prevail," replied George.

"I'm sorry," said Livvie. "I just get so worried sometimes. And then I think, what if Stan gets drafted after all?"

"Do you think you will get another deferment?" George asked Stan.

"I surely hope so. I have to go and see the county draft board next week again and see if I can get one for another year."

"Are you sure you don't want any coffee?" asked Carrie again.

"No, I think we better get started for home. It's getting late."

"So, when is the baby due, Livvie?" Carrie asked her daughter as she helped her on with her coat.

"About the last of August, I figure. I haven't been in to see the doctor yet. I'm going the end of next week."

"Well, have you been feeling all right?" asked her mother.

"Just a little sick some mornings, but not as bad as last time."

Stan appeared with a sleeping Cheryl. Carrie embraced Livvie at the door. "Everything will turn out all right now. Don't worry so much about the war and everything."

"I'll try not to but some days the news is so discouraging. This war should have been over a long time ago."

"I know, dear, but we just have to keep our spirits up for awhile longer. It can't go on forever!"

CHAPTER 14

Sometimes it seemed to everyone that the war would indeed last forever. It consumed almost every aspect of daily life for those on the home front. The latest thing now was to save waste paper. A shortage of paper had been declared last November and now everyone was encouraged to save "Bundles for Berlin." The newspaper stated—"save a bundle a week and save some boy's life."

A sixteen billion-dollar bond drive was to go into effect in June or July so the American citizens were to dig deep into their pockets again.

The railroads were short of laborers and were asking for men to be machinists, blacksmiths, car men, electricians or carpenters.

"It looks like one could certainly get a job if you needed to," commented George, as he resumed reading the paper.

It was early on a Sunday afternoon and the phone rang. It was Beatrice, telling about a big fire the night before.

"I just talked to my brother and he told me all about it." A fire had burned down the Pleasant Consolidated School and gymnasium.

"It burned to the ground," Beatrice said.

"Do they know what started it?" asked Carrie.

"No, I don't believe so. The building that was used for the gym was formerly the old Opera House in Walcott. I remember that so well," Beatrice went on. "It was moved out in the country by the Pleasant Township school back in about 1936."

"So where will the students finish out the year?"

"Well, the teacherage is still standing. And, of course, there's only about a week or so left now."

While Carrie was talking on the phone, George left for a meeting. A group of men in the neighborhood were getting together to talk about the proposed improvements to the Gol Road.

He returned home about two hours later and Carrie was in the garden, pulling weeds.

"How did your meeting go, then?" she asked.

"Well, all the farmers who live near this road are going to chip in and help improve it. It will be an all-weather road from highway 46 south to the Bakko corner."

"How much will that cost?"

"We figure if everyone pays in at least $200 each, then we will have enough."

"So, is that how much you pledged?"

"Yah, and so did almost everyone else. The work will begin as soon as possible. It will surely be nice to have a decent road over to the church and up to the highway."

"Yah, that's for sure."

Carrie related everything she had heard about the fire from Beatrice.

"They were talking about it at the meeting, too."

"Do you feel like going for a little drive? Maybe we can stop by Freddie's and see how they're doing."

On June 7, the newspapers and the radio were full of the big news of the invasion of France the previous day. D-Day, it was called. The Allies stormed the beaches of Normandy, and after suffering tremendous losses, they had, by nightfall, secured a firm hold.

This news buoyed everyone's spirits and the American people looked for the fighting to be over soon. However, less that a week later, the Germans sent the first flying bombs over London. This opened a new age in air warfare. The Germans called their new secret weapon the Vengeance bomb. The previous euphoria gave way to crushed hopes.

Two days after D-Day, the members of Gol congregation and the Kindred community gathered for the funeral of a young local man, a husband and father, who died suddenly of sleeping sickness. Thus their thoughts and emotions were directed away from the happenings across the sea and focused on a very personal loss for many of them.

Carrie and George attended the funeral, as did so many others. "Why did this have to happen to such a fine young man?" Carrie said to George afterwards on the way home. She shook her head in disbelief. "We sure don't know, do we, from day to day, who will be taken next."

They were both silent as they drove into their yard. "Freddie said he may stop by on his way home," George told Carrie.

They had just gotten changed into their everyday clothes when a car drove into the yard. It was Freddie. He strode up to the back door and let himself in after a little knock on the screen door.

"Hey, anybody home?"

Carrie came bustling into the kitchen. "Oh, we were just changing out of our good clothes. I didn't get a chance to talk to you at the church. I'm glad you stopped by."

"That sure was a big funeral, wasn't it?"

"Yah, one of the biggest for quite some time."

George came into the kitchen. "So, Freddie, you got the afternoon off to go to the funeral?"

"Yah, I don't have to go back. Thought I'd stop and chat with you awhile."

"Lenora didn't want to come with you?"

"She couldn't find anyone to sit with the kids. Everyone was going to the church."

"I suppose you had enough coffee there so I can't make you some."

"Oh, I've had plenty."

"Well, let's go sit in the living room, then," suggested Carrie.

George and Freddie followed her and each sat down. Carrie had a feeling that Freddie had something on his mind.

"I've been wanting to come out and talk to you for some time now. I know that you were worried about me awhile back. Lenora told me that she had talked to you because she didn't know what to do with me. I want to apologize for the way I acted."

Before either George or Carrie could say something, Freddie went on. "Our new pastor came over and we had some good talks. He put my head on straight again."

"I'm glad, Freddie," said George. "When I came and talked to you that one night, I didn't think that I had made much headway."

"And Stan made a special trip down to see me one night, too. What he said made sense and it got me turned around some. I saw what I was doing to Lenora and it was affecting the children, too."

"So, are you still having those guilty feelings?" asked Carrie.

"Oh, I can't say that I don't have them at all, but I need to get over that and start thinking more positive. We can't all be soldiers, but there are things

I can do here on the home front. I work at a bank and we sell war bonds and I can certainly help along those lines. I encourage people to buy more and I buy as many myself as I can afford."

"I'm happy that things are going better for you now, Freddie. I've prayed for you so much lately," Carrie told him.

"Well, I guess I better be going now," said Freddie, standing up. "We're going to Lenora's folks for supper tonight. Her sister, Susie, is home from Missouri for a few days."

"And what is it that she's doing down there again?" asked Carrie.

"She and her friend are both working in the Curtiss-Wright Aircraft plant. Susie is a riveter in an experimental lab. It's very top secret, she says. Maybe she can tell us more when she's home now."

"Any news from Lucy's husband?"

"No, not lately. Letters are slow to come through. No news is good news, I guess."

"I'm glad you stopped by," Carrie said to him as he was leaving. "My mind will be more at ease about you now."

George came home from town one day and was telling Carrie about the display in the electric shop window. Two servicemen, Phil Lund and Howard Hanson, had sent some souvenirs from Australia, New Guinea and the South Pacific.

"There were some actual parts of Japanese planes, some shell cases, Jap tree-climbing shoes, a Japanese prayer box and several other articles there," he told her.

"A few weeks ago, didn't they have some fox pups in the window? I wonder what they'll come up with next?"

"Well, it gets people in the store!" exclaimed George.

"Yah, it got you in there," laughed Carrie.

"I was there to pick up our radio," he said dryly.

"Oh, good. Now I can listen to my programs during the day when I'm working in here."

"I heard that there's going to be a drug store opening in town."

"Where?" asked Carrie.

"In the old Poole building. You know, where Jessie Rustad had her grocery store."

"Oh, you don't say. Who's going to run it?"

A family by the name of Haugen. They're coming from Fergus Falls. I guess they'll live upstairs, above the store."

"Well, that will be nice to have a drug store here, won't it?"

"Yah, I think that this Mr. Haugen is a pharmacist."

In late July, the newspapers reported the plot by German military leaders to assassinate Hitler. Someone had placed a time bomb under Hitler's table during a staff meeting. The bomb exploded but only injured Hitler.

"Too bad the bomb didn't do the job!" exclaimed George, after reading the account.

"I'm sure most everyone feels the same way," said Carrie. "I can't understand why someone doesn't do something to get rid of that madman!"

"He's probably got bodyguards aplenty. I'm sure he knows that there are many who would like to eliminate him."

After awhile Carrie said, "Let's go to the movies tomorrow tonight. Maybe it will get our minds off Hitler and this blame war." When George didn't answer, she went on. " 'Government Girl' with Olivia de Haviland is playing."

"Well, you know there will be a war newsreel before the main feature."

"Yes, I suppose there will be, but I'd like to go anyway."

"Well, we can go if you want. This will probably be our last night out until after harvest."

As harvest approached, there was a plea in the newspapers for shockers again. George wondered if he and his neighbor, Ole, could get along with just some part-time help. Freddie would come out as often as he could.

As it turned out, with neighbor helping neighbor, the crop was harvested in a couple week's time. The crop had been fair this year. A little bit better than last year. The price of wheat was down slightly so George was planning to store most of his. At least, as much as he had room for in his bins.

In the August 10th edition of the Kindred Tribune, there was an account of Lt. Larry Blumer's exciting bombing mission where he'd had to bail out of his burning plane. He'd landed about half a mile in "back of our own lines" and when he was asked what was the most exciting part of that mission, he'd answered, "the ride home!"

The same article also told about another time when he flew low to bomb an enemy train engine and it blew up but he had difficulty in coming out of the dive. He ran into telephone lines and came back to base with 180 feet of telephone wire wrapped around his wings.

"This Blumer kid is beginning to be something of a hometown hero!" exclaimed George, after reading the article.

"He sounds like a real daredevil," commented Carrie. "He better be careful. Maybe he won't be so lucky next time."

"We've been lucky around here. None of our hometown boys have been killed in the war so far. Hope it ends before anything tragic happens."

"You know, we haven't heard from Livvie in over a week," commented Carrie. "Maybe we should take a drive up there tomorrow. That baby is due real soon now."

In the early hours of the first day of September, Livvie woke her husband and urgently told him that it was "time to go." With those words, he woke up quickly and jumped out of bed.

"Do you mean it?" he asked excitedly, pulling on the first pair of pants he could find.

"Yes, I definitely know that the time has come. I've had some contractions for the last hour and they're getting a little closer together."

"Why didn't you wake me before?"

"I wanted you to get as much sleep as possible. It could be a long day. Remember how long it took Cheryl to make her appearance?"

"Well, it might be different this time. It usually goes faster the second time." He paused. "Doesn't it?"

"I don't know. Maybe we better get going. We have to drop Cheryl off at your folks' first. Why don't you give your mother a call and I'll get Cheryl and her things."

By four o'clock that afternoon, Livvie and Stan were the proud parents of a new baby daughter. She weighed in at exactly eight pounds.

"She looks a lot like Cheryl did," Stan told Carrie over the phone.

"Oh, I'm so glad it's all over! We'll be in to see them in a day or two."

George walked in the door just as Carrie hung up the phone.

"Oh, that was Stan. The baby came about an hour ago. It's another girl and everything's just fine!"

"Another girl. What did they name her?"

"He didn't say. I guess we'll find out when we go there to see them. I told him we'd come in the next day or so."

"Maybe we can go tomorrow. I need to tend to some business in Fargo one of these days."

The next day, George dropped Carrie off at the Penney's store in Fargo while he went to take care of his business.

"I'll be back in about a half hour."

"That should give me time enough to buy a little something for the baby."

Carrie picked out a little pink sweater with a cap and booties to match and also a little rattle. The store wrapped it for her in some pretty paper.

At the hospital, Carrie and George got a good look at their new granddaughter in the nursery window before they went to Livvie's room.

"Oh, she's such a cutie!" Carrie told the new mother.

"Yes, isn't she though!" beamed Livvie.

"I suppose Stan was hoping for a boy this time," commented George.

"Well, maybe he was," said Livvie, "but I guess I'm glad it's another girl. If it was a boy, maybe he'd have to go to war someday."

"Oh, Livvie, don't think that way. This war will be over soon and then there should never be another one."

"This is supposed to be the war that ends all wars," said George.

"Maybe you're right. Well, maybe Stan will get his little farmer next time!"

"You must be feeling pretty good to be thinking about a next time already," laughed Carrie.

"I do feel better this time than with Cheryl."

"Speaking of Cheryl, how is Stan's mother getting along with having her there day and night?"

"She's doing pretty good, I guess. Stan is there a lot. He stayed last night until she was sleeping."

"Oh, my goodness!" Carrie said suddenly. "We haven't even heard what you're going to name the new baby."

"We decided on Linda Louise."

"Oh, that's a nice name," Carrie said.

"How long will you be in here?" asked George.

"Well, they aren't keeping new mothers as long as they used to, because of needing space for wounded soldiers and such, so I could be out of here in a week."

"Well, that's nice. We probably won't come up again. We'll wait until you get home."

"When will Stan be coming again?" asked George.

"He'll maybe wait until Sunday now and then come once more to take me home. They have about a day or two left of harvest. They're helping Art now."

"Well, Min has her hands full then, with a little girl and making all those meals and everything," said Carrie.

"Magda has been helping her out so it's going all right, I guess."

"Well, we better be going. We'll take another peek at the baby—Linda Louise." Carrie gave her daughter a hug before leaving the room.

On the drive home, Carrie said to George, "We certainly have been blessed, haven't we? We have four beautiful, healthy grandchildren."

"Yah, we certainly have been blessed all right."

Larry Blumer, now a Captain, made the news again in the local papers. This latest incident told how he became a flying ace by downing five enemy aircraft in a matter of about fifteen minutes. Mr. Clemenson, editor of the Kindred Tribune, had a lengthy article describing the incident in detailed form.

George was reading parts of it aloud to Carrie one evening. "They've given Blumer the nickname of 'Scrappy' or 'Scrap Iron' because of the condition in which he brings back his planes." George chuckled at this and just shook his head. "You have to admire the guy."

"One of these times he's not going to be so lucky," said Carrie.

The very next week's edition of the Tribune had a very different story. One that the community hoped would never appear in their paper. One of the local servicemen had been killed. Pvt. Glenn Erickson had been killed in a plane crash in Scotland. He was the first one to die in the service of his country from this area. A memorial service was held in Kindred on September 10 and it was attended by the whole community.

Many parents of other servicemen were there and Carrie noted that they all had a scared look in their eyes. Would their loved one be the next one memorialized by a service such as this?

In early November, the 1944 presidential election was all the talk. Roosevelt, feeling that he shouldn't run for a fourth term, was nevertheless the Democratic candidate. The Republicans felt strongly that no man should be in office for 16 years and the Democrats countered with the slogan, "Don't change horses in mid-stream."

George, who usually voted Republican, had always liked Roosevelt and had voted for him the last two elections. Roosevelt won easily over his opponent, Thomas Dewey, the Governor of New York. Harry Truman, the senator from Missouri, became the new Vice President.

It was hard to get into the Christmas spirit when December rolled around. This would be the fourth Christmas of the war. The community was saddened by another local serviceman's death. David Hedland had been killed overseas and everyone wondered, "who will be next?"

In the middle of December, Hitler began a last-stand onslaught in the Ardennes Forest to attempt to halt the advancement of the Allied Forces deeper into Germany. This battle, which later became known as the Battle of the Bulge, because of the bulging shape of the battleground, lasted for more than a week. In fact, it was two days after Christmas that the Allies halted the German offensive there.

The Murphy family was very worried about Marty. He indicated in his last letter that his unit would be leaving Italy and Joe figured it was because they would be moving into France and then on to Germany. Joe followed the newspaper accounts of the Allied troops' movements very closely. At Christmastime, they had not heard from their son for about seven weeks.

On Christmas Day, George and Carrie had their whole family around their table. The high spirits of the young children helped to dispel the anxiety that the adults were feeling. Could this really be the fourth Christmas at war? Will next Christmas find the world at peace?

CHAPTER 15

January of 1945 began with optimism on the home front. The Allies were advancing into the heart of Germany and the Russian armies were rolling toward Berlin from the east. Everyone wondered, could this soon be the end of the war?

One day, Kenny's father, Jake came over to the Murphy farm. He had just received word from the Navy that Kenny had been injured. It had happened on board ship. There had been some kind of explosion.

"They told me his injuries weren't life-threatening but that he may lose the sight of one eye," Jake told them.

"Oh, that's just awful, Jake," said Joe. "I'm so sorry to hear that. Come into the house and we'll tell Min."

The men came in the back door and found Min in the kitchen. Jake related what he had heard about his son.

"Oh, when did you get this news?" she asked.

"I got a letter yesterday. I was wondering if you had heard from Ronnie. I believe they were still on the same ship together."

"Yes, I think they were," Joe said, sounding worried now.

"We haven't heard from Ronnie for several weeks now," said Min.

The three very worried parents sat at the kitchen table together, concerned about the safety of their sons.

"I guess no news is good news then," remarked Joe.

"Yes, I guess if he had been injured, we would have heard about it by now," said Min.

In February, the community heard some more disturbing news. The Amund Hertsgaard family of Kindred had received word that their son, Paul, was listed as missing in action from the army and that he had possibly been captured.

Min was becoming increasingly nervous and edgy. She worried so about her two sons. Would they both come back alive and in one piece? Joe himself looked like he had aged ten years, thought Livvie. He had lost weight and he wasn't his usual jolly self. The only time he seemed like his old self was when he was near his two little granddaughters. They were the joy of his life. He called the new baby his little "Lindy Lou." Cheryl liked to tag along after him and he would try and read to her whenever he could. Livvie often found him holding his granddaughter tightly, but looking pensively off in the distance.

"He's probably wondering what's going to happen to this old world and what kind of future it will hold for these little girls," Livvie mentioned to Stan one evening.

"I wonder that many times myself," Stan remarked. "But I think this war will be over soon. I think Hitler is at the end of his reign of terror."

"Oh, I certainly hope so!"

"I just hope Marty and Ronnie make it home."

Livvie couldn't answer for the lump in her throat. Stan looked so worried about his brothers.

Freddie and Lenora and the kids drove out to the Johnson farm one evening. Freddie had to tell his folks what had happened in town that morning. The "hometown hero" Larry Blumer, now Captain Blumer, had made an appearance in town in a plane and had buzzed Main Street and the school. He had flown so low, right above the tree tops, that everyone ran out of their homes and business places to see what was happening. All the school kids poured out the doors, too.

"Yah, Supt. Kvikstad lost all control of the students for awhile there!" exclaimed Freddie.

"Oh, my!" was all Carrie could say.

"What was he flying?" asked George.

"Well, I talked to some people later and they said he had "borrowed" a plane from Hector Airport, a P-63 Cobra fighter that was sitting on one end of the field. He told someone that he thought it would be fun to come home and buzz the old hometown!"

"Is he just home on leave?" asked George.

"I believe so. I suppose he'll have to get back and keep fighting those Germans!" said Freddie.

One day, early in May, George came home from town with some news.

"The Hertsgaard family has received word about their son," George told Carrie. "He'd been taken prisoner by the Germans but then he was rescued by the Allies. He's in a hospital in Belgium now."

"Oh, but I bet they are relieved!" exclaimed Carrie.

"Yah, you can say that again!" replied George. "He'd been injured pretty badly, I guess."

"Well, at least they know he's alive."

Two days later, as George was listening to the radio in the evening, the program was interrupted by a news flash. The President was dead! Franklin D. Roosevelt had died earlier in the day, the announcer told them. He had been at his cottage in Warm Springs, Georgia, for a rest. He had not been in the best of health since taking office earlier in the year.

"It has now been confirmed," the announcer went on, "that the President died of a cerebral hemorrhage."

"Oh, that is just terrible!" cried Carrie. "What will happen now?"

As if answering her question, the announcer said, "Vice President Harry Truman has been sworn in as the new President of these United States!"

"I wonder if Truman will be up to the challenge?" wondered George.

"And right in the middle of a war, too!"

The nation and its allies were stunned and saddened. They, too, wondered what would happen now. Servicemen mourned the death of their commander-in-chief. It was reported that soldier and sailor alike wept openly when they heard of it.

On May 1, German radio announced that Hitler had died while defending Berlin against Russian troops. However, Allied investigators later learned that Hitler committed suicide with his wife, Eva Braun, in Berlin on April 30.

On May 2, German forces in Italy surrendered and Berlin finally fell to the invading Russian armies. It seemed that the end was finally near.

On May 7, 1945, American radios were blasting the news that everyone had been waiting for. Germany had surrendered unconditionally.

"Oh, my goodness, I can hardly believe my ears!" cried Carrie.

"I can't either. It's the best news ever!" exclaimed George.

"Let's jump in the car and drive to town," suggested Carrie.

They did just that and found themselves in front of Freddie's house. He was home for his noon break from the bank. There were some neighbors talking excitedly in clusters. He invited them all into the house.

"Let's celebrate!" he said. "Lenora, let's find something for these good folks to drink, shall we?"

Lenora had the coffeepot on and Freddie looked for some bottles of Christmas wine. Carrie helped Lenora find extra glasses. With some drinking coffee and some drinking Mogen David, a toast was made.

"Here's to peace at long last!" said Freddie. The people were laughing and crying at the same time.

Up north at the Murphy farm, they heard the news around the noon hour, also. Min was listening to The Co-op Shoppers while she prepared dinner. The program was interrupted with the good news. She ran outside and hailed the men as they were just driving into the yard.

"The war's over! The war's over!" she called to them.

Joe, Stan and Min all hugged each other and jumped up and down.

"The boys will be coming home soon!" cried Min.

A car drove into the yard and it was Art, Magda and Grandpa Ivar. They tumbled out of the vehicle and were surrounded by the Murphys.

"I'm going to go and call Livvie and see if she's heard it!" announced Stan.

In every city, town and village across America, scenes like this were re-enacted. It had been a long time in coming.

The free world would celebrate May 8 as V-E Day—Victory in Europe Day. After more than five years, the European phase of World War II had ended.

CHAPTER 16

The war in Europe may have ended, but the war in the Pacific Theater was still playing out. U.S. troops had landed on the island of Okinawa and a fierce battle was desperately fought. This campaign, lasting into mid-June, proved to be the last major land battle of the war. Major casualties resulted on both sides.

The Murphys had heard from Marty shortly after V-E Day and he told them that he would be coming home the end of June.

"Oh, thank goodness!" cried Min. "I can't wait until he's home safely."

"But what about Ronnie?" Livvie asked her mother-in-law.

"I don't know." She wrung her hands worriedly. "We haven't heard from him for quite sometime now. That war in the Pacific is still going on. I wish those Japs would just give up!" she exclaimed.

But the Japanese would not give up. On July 26, heads of state of the United States, Great Britain, and China issued an ultimatum calling for unconditional surrender. Japan ignored the ultimatum, and so the United States decided to use the newly developed atomic bomb.

On August 6, the people of the United States heard on their radios that we had dropped the bomb on the Japanese city of Hiroshima. Three days later, we dropped another one on Nagasaki. Heavy civilian casualties resulted. The American people were stunned, as was the rest of the world.

"Surely this will make the Japs give up," said George, when they were up to Livvie's for little Linda's first birthday party. Joe and Min were there, too, as was Magda, Art and Grandpa Ivar.

"So, how is Marty doing since he got home?" George asked Joe.

"Well, OK, I guess. He's not quite himself yet, but he's mighty happy to have made it back in one piece, he told me."

Freddie, Lenora and their two children arrived for the party, also, and later on, Marty showed up, too. He was welcomed heartily by everyone.

There was much discussion about the use of the atomic bomb.

"What do you think, Marty, about dropping the bombs on Japan?" asked Art.

"I guess it was the necessary thing to do," he said, with conviction.

"Oh, but all those innocent civilians being killed, I don't know," said Magda.

"I think our government felt that we'd have many more casualties if the war went on. They were planning to invade Japan but then when the bomb became available, they decided to use that," Marty told them.

"I'm sure that was a difficult decision for Truman to make," exclaimed Carrie. "Imagine having to do that!"

"Yah, you can say that again," agreed Joe. "I wouldn't want to have to decide such a thing."

"So what do you hear from Ronnie? And his friend Kenny?" asked George.

"No word from Ronnie for several months now," replied Min, "but Jake heard from Kenny last week. He's out of the hospital now and will be coming home next week."

"How about his injuries?" asked Carrie.

"He didn't say."

"Well, I think the Japanese will be giving up soon," said Marty. "How can they not after what has just happened?"

The day after the birthday party, the news broke that Japan had indeed given up. On September 2, 1945, aboard the U.S.S. Missouri in Tokyo Bay, Japan officially surrendered. Army General Douglas MacArthur signed for the Allies. Three years, eight months, and 22 days after Japan bombed Pearl Harbor, World War II finally ended.

Christmas of 1945 was the happiest Christmas in several years for everyone. Rations had been lifted and things were starting to become plentiful. Christmas trees and lights were put up and the nation was enjoying peace at long last.

Carrie had her whole family for Christmas Eve and the four grandchildren lent a great deal of excitement to the holiday. Carrie had splurged on many gifts for every member of the family and didn't skimp on the goodies she had baked for the occasion.

"Just how many cookies did you actually bake?" Stan teased her.

She just shrugged, but Livvie said, "I think she told me she had made 22 different kinds!" Everyone laughed and helped themselves to more.

"I guess my mother made just as many as you did, Carrie," Stan confessed.

"Well, after several years of not having the sugar to bake with, it was good to make as much as I wanted to again," Carrie declared.

When the children settled down to playing with their toys quietly, the grown- ups gathered around the kitchen table.

"How is Marty getting along, Stan?" asked Carrie. "He sure doesn't seem his old self the few times we've seen him."

"No, he doesn't." Stan sounded worried. "Mom said that he's been having some bad nightmares lately. He wakes up screaming."

"Oh, no!" exclaimed Carrie. "I sure hope that that goes away soon. That must be awful!"

Stan just shook his head. "Ronnie seems to be adjusting well, though, to being home again."

"Maybe he didn't see the terrible things that Marty may have seen and experienced," suggested Livvie.

"Has he talked about the war?" asked George.

"Well, no, he hasn't," said Stan. "Whenever I ask him to tell me how it was over there, he just clams up."

"How about Ronnie's friend, Kenny? How is he doing?"

"He's going to be permanently blind in one eye. And he can't see very well out of the other one, either. I guess he's lucky he has some sight left, though."

"What's Ronnie going to do now that he's home?" asked Freddie.

"He's talking about going to some school and get some kind of training."

"What's he interested in?"

"Well, in the navy he worked on aircraft engines, you know, and he likes that type of work. Maybe he'll go to a mechanical school or something like that," said Stan. "The government will pay for his schooling under the GI Bill."

"Yah, he might as well take advantage of that. Do you think that Marty is interested in going on to school?"

"I think he'll stay on the farm. He was always more interested in farming than Ronnie was."

"It's getting late, Stan," said Livvie. "I think we should get the kids home."

Awhile later, as they were all going out the door, a sleepy Sandra looked at her grandma and asked, "Grandma, are you coming to my Christmas Tree program tomorrow night?"

Carrie stooped down to embrace her granddaughter, who was going on seven years old now. "We sure are! We wouldn't miss it."

"Larry, you have to wait another year before you are in the program, don't you?" Carrie asked her grandson. He nodded sleepily. "And then it will be Cheryl the year after that. My, how the time flies!"

"Thanks, Mom and Dad, for everything," called Freddie from the back step. "We'll see you tomorrow night then."

On New Year's Day, Freddie and Lenora hosted a big gathering of family and friends in their new home. They had just recently moved into a bigger house on Main Street. Besides George and Carrie, Livvie and Stan and the kids came, and the rest of the Murphy family, and Lenora's parents, her sister Susie, and Jack and Lucy. Ronnie Murphy's friends, Kenny and Rosie, were there, too.

"We couldn't have fit this many people into our old house!" exclaimed Freddie, as there were people situated in almost every room in the house. There were about eight around the dining-room table, playing a game of Hearts. Four men were in the kitchen engrossed in a serious game of Whist. Another four were seated around the folding card table put up in the living room. They were enjoying a game of Rook. The children were upstairs playing.

Late in the afternoon, Freddie called all of the guests to come into the dining room as he wanted to say some things. It took awhile for them all to gather together. Some were standing in the doorways and others were sitting on the floor and around the big table.

Lenora had passed around wine glasses for everyone. "Now we're going to have a toast," announced Freddie. "But first I have to make my speech." There was laughter at this and some good-natured groans.

"First of all, I want to say how happy we are that you all came today for this little house-warming party. It's good to have family and friends gathered around. Besides toasting in the New Year, I want to express our thanks and gratitude to you who served our country so well just recently." Here Freddie looked pointedly at Marty, Jack, Ronnie and Kenny, nodding at each of them. "And you, too, Rosie."

Freddie took a deep breath. "You don't know how we worried about each of you and prayed for your safety. We just want to welcome you all back." He choked up here and couldn't go on. Instead he raised his glass and everyone followed suit.

"Hear, hear!" said someone and they all tipped their glasses.

Lucy's husband, Jack, stood up and called for attention. "I'd like to say something, too. First of all, I can't tell you how wonderful it is to be home. There were times when we wondered if we would make it home at all. So many didn't." He stopped here for a moment, because of the lump forming in his throat. Marty covered his face with both his hands. Everyone waited politely.

"As I was saying, we're happy to be here. But I also want to thank all of you, back on the home front for all that you did to help win this war. We couldn't have done it without you—your support and hard work and sacrifice. You all endured shortages and many inconveniences, and the government was always asking you to dig deeper to come up with the money to buy more bonds that financed the war effort. We could just feel how you supported us all, isn't that so, fellows?" Here he looked at the Murphy brothers and Kenny.

"And you farmers, 'Soldiers of the Soil' you were called. Thank you for all the hard work you put in, without much help, and shortages of equipment and parts. We were aware of all this over there," Jack told them. "We read the newspapers from back home when we could get them. And also, all the letters from back here. They were always full of news and we thank you for them."

Thinking awhile, he continued. "And Susie, my young sister-in-law, who, by the way wants to be called 'Sue' now, and you, too, Rosie, we thank you and all the other young women who went to work in the factories or joined the WAVES and such. When I got home, I found out that Susie—I mean Sue—had been working on the big C-46 transport planes. That's the very planes we used for flying supplies 'over the hump,' as it was called, in the China-Burma-India theater where I was stationed. Maybe I was riding in a plane that my sister-in-law actually put the rivets in!" Everyone chuckled.

"Well, anyway, enough said." Here he raised his glass and the others followed.

"One more thing. Lucy and I just made the decision to move to St. Paul, Minnesota, where I will be going to work for my uncle and cousin. We'll be moving next week."

There were murmurs of surprise around the room. Freddie jumped up and told the group, "Lenora says that supper is now ready and you can all come and get your food at the kitchen table and we'll try and find a place for all of you to sit down someplace."

The table was laden with turkey, ham, scalloped potatoes, homemade buns, lefse, corn, and relishes of all sorts.

"There's cake for dessert later," announced Lenora. "I couldn't find room on the table for it!"

After the meal, Marty came to his father and told him that he would go home and do the evening chores. "Oh, I can do that," said Joe. "You stay here and have some fun."

"No, no, I'll go. You and Mom stay."

"Can you come back after you've finished?" asked Min. "We're having such a good time, I don't want you to miss out on it."

"Well, I'll see," he answered slowly.

Joe knew that his son would not be back. He could see that faraway look in his eye and knew he just wanted to get away and be alone.

"We'll have to go soon, too," announced Stan. "My cows are probably waiting for me right now!"

"Oh, I hate to leave. We're having too much fun," said Livvie.

"Well, we can wait a little while," her husband conceded.

Everyone seemed to gather in one room again and the story telling began. Jack had the best jokes. He said he was trying to find the nicest ones that he learned in the army—ones he could tell in mixed company.

"My, the children sure are quiet upstairs, aren't they?" mentioned Carrie.

"I think I know why," said Lenora. She got up and looked up at the ceiling in the other room. Sure enough, several pairs of eyes were looking down through the floor register, trying to see and hear the grownups. When they saw her, they dashed away.

"They've been spying on us," laughed Lenora, as she returned to the others.

The party eventually broke up, with some having to get home to their chores, George among them.

"That sure was a fun day, wasn't it?" Carrie said to her husband on the way home.

"Yah, a good way to start the New Year, I guess."

"I'm rather concerned about Marty. Did you notice how withdrawn he seemed at times today?"

George nodded. "Perhaps it will take some time for him to be his happy-go-lucky self again."

"I was surprised to hear that Lucy and Jack will be moving," said Carrie.

"Lenora will certainly miss her twin sister."

"Yah, I guess there will be many changes now. When a country goes through what we just went through, things will never be the same again," George said, philosophically.

"Oh, don't say that, George!" cried Carrie. "I want things to be just as they were before this blame war started."

George just chuckled. "My dear, you never want things to change, do you?"

"Well, only when they change for the good," she answered defensively.

"Maybe some of these changes will be for the better."

CHAPTER 17

The New Year started out with great optimism. The weather even cooperated. It was a mild winter. The farmers looked forward to the coming planting season.

"I'm going to get that new combine that I've been wanting!" exclaimed Joe Murphy.

The American factories were once again making things like refrigerators, machinery parts, and new automobiles. They no longer had to be making the tools for war—guns, ammunition, and tanks.

The many returning servicemen were going on with their lives, putting the past few years behind them. They were marrying, buying houses and cars, and some were going to college to finish their education.

"Ronnie has decided to go to that mechanical school in Fargo," Stan told Livvie one evening.

"Oh, good for him," she said. "When will he start?"

"He'll be starting this next week, I believe."

"Maybe he'll have my cousin for a teacher." When Stan gave her a blank stare, she continued, "You know, Ken Amundson, from Davenport. My uncle, Amund, is his father."

"Oh, yes, I remember now. I forgot that he taught there at that school."

"Your mother told me that Rosie is going into nurses training at St. Lukes. Is that right?"

"Yah, and I guess she's already started."

"How about Marty? Has he made any plans?"

Stan shook his head. "No, I don't think he's thinking about anything. He's been drinking quite a bit, Dad told me. He goes out three or four nights a week and comes back late and stumbles up the stairs to bed."

"That's too bad. I wonder how we could help him?" asked Livvie.

"I don't know. He won't talk about anything personal."

Several weeks later, Stan picked up the ringing phone. He glanced at the clock. It was half past midnight.

"Stan?" said the voice on the other end of the line. "This is Norm, at the bar in Davenport. Your brother is in here—has been all evening—and he's pretty drunk. I don't think he should drive home by himself. I thought maybe you could come and get him."

Stan sighed and answered, "Yah, I'll be right there. Thanks for letting me know, Norm."

"Who was that?" Livvie asked her husband when he returned to the bedroom.

"The bar in Davenport. Marty is there and he's not doing too good. I'm going to go and get him so he gets home safely."

"Oh, it's such a cold night for you to have to go out at this hour."

"Well, I sure don't want him to try and drive home. He'd probably go in the ditch and freeze to death," Stan told his wife as he hurried out the door.

When Stan entered the bar, he could see Marty sitting at a back table by himself. There were only two other patrons in the room. Norm, the bartender and owner, met Stan by the bar.

"He's had a lot to drink and he's been crying and shouting and then he mumbles to himself. I didn't know what to do with him."

"You did the right thing in calling me, Norm. Thank you." Stan made his way to the back of the room. Marty looked up.

"Well, if it isn't my little brother," he said, his speech slurred. "The one who didn't have to go and serve his country!"

Stan sucked in his breath but didn't say anything. Marty went on. "He got to stay at home, where it was safe, and help Daddy."

"Marty, you're terribly drunk. I'm going to help get you home."

Norm came to assist in getting Marty to his feet. "I'll help you get him into the car."

"Did he pay you for his drinks?" asked Stan.

"Yah, he's paid for all of them."

The two men held Marty under the shoulders while they attempted to get his jacket on. Marty was resisting their efforts until Stan said, "Marty, for Pete's sake, let's get this thing on. It's freezing outside!"

He quit resisting and they finally succeeded in their task. They propelled him toward the door. One of the other customers hurried to help them. They put him in the back seat of Stan's car.

"Hey, I want to take my own car home," Marty shouted at them.

"We'll come back for it in the morning," Stan told him evenly.

Norm went to Marty's car and took the keys out and handed them to Stan.

Stan headed the car for the Murphy farm. The pair rode in dead silence, Marty asleep and Stan madder than he had ever been.

He parked the car as close as he could to the back door. "Marty, wake up. We're home. I'll help get you into the house."

After a short while, as Stan stood holding the car's back door open, Marty stirred and got himself out and to a standing position.

"I feel sick," he told Stan. He staggered to the back of the car and threw up in the snow. Stan waited, not too patiently, seething all the while.

"OK, Marty, let's go," Stan said. "Let's get into the house."

Marty didn't put up any more resistance, but let himself be led, like a child, up the porch steps and into the house.

"Let's try to be quiet now," suggested Stan. "We don't want to wake everybody up."

"No, we musn't wake anybody up," Marty said, mockingly.

"Here, we'll just lay you down on the sofa. You can sleep here until morning." He knew it would be impossible to get Marty up the stairs in a reasonably quiet fashion.

Marty sat down hard on the sofa. He looked up at Stan. "Thank you, little brother. I suppose you feel noble now, getting me home safely and all."

Stan ignored his remark. "Here, you can use these afghans to cover yourself up with." He tried to get Marty to lay down.

"Hey, maybe I'm not ready to go to sleep yet," he shouted. "I don't want to sleep." He groaned and put his head in his hands. "I don't want to sleep."

Stan heard footsteps on the stairs. Their father appeared and looked down at the scene with sorrow in his eyes. He probably had seen this happen several times before, thought Stan, feeling pity for the older man.

Before his father could speak, Stan explained how he came to be bringing Marty home. Marty started to get up and he tripped over the coffee table.

"Where are you going, Marty?" asked Stan.

"I need to relieve myself," he said, saying his words slowly and carefully.

"We'll help you," his father said. "Here, let's just take him out the back door."

After they accomplished their mission, and returned to the living room, they found Min standing there, in her robe, and a concerned look on her face.

"Oh, sorry to wake you, Mom," said Stan.

"Well, hello, Mother, nice to see you," Marty said, trying to straighten himself up.

"Maybe you'd like some coffee, Marty," she suggested kindly.

"Yes, some coffee would be nice," he said.

They all went into the kitchen and sat around the table. Min put the coffee on to boil. Marty laid his head on the table. Stan and his father just looked at each other hopelessly. Joe sighed.

"How often has this been happening?" asked Stan.

"Oh, several times now lately. He goes to town two or three nights a week and comes home late and stumbles around."

Marty lifted his head and looked at his father and brother through bleary eyes. "So, you're talking about me, huh?"

"Marty, this excessive drinking has got to stop," warned Stan.

Marty started to rise. "Who are you to tell me I shouldn't drink? You don't know anything about why I drink." With this, he sat down again and began to sob.

Min came over to him and put a cup of coffee in front of her son. "Here, Marty, drink this coffee now."

He tried to take a sip from the cup but his hand shook so that it spilled on the table. Min got up and brought back a rag to wipe it up.

"Son, why don't you tell us why you are drinking so much," Joe said to him.

He was silent for awhile and then he suddenly said in a loud voice, "I'm trying to forget. Just trying to forget. And when I sleep, I wake up with the most awful nightmare."

"Tell us about your nightmare, Marty," his mother said softly.

"It's always the same," he started. "I see two men....climbing up on the roof of a church, dropping something in the chimney and then....boom! The two men are scrambling down....and women and children are running out the front door....some of them on fire!"

"Why do you think that you dream this dream over and over?" asked Joe.

Marty just put his face in his hands and cried.

"Marty, who are those two men on the roof?" his mother asked.

The sobbing young man looked up and met his mother's eyes. What she saw in them made her draw back.

"No! Oh, no, Marty," she cried.

"Yes, that was me up on that roof! I killed women and children! I KILLED THEM!" he shouted. Then he slumped in his chair and sobbed desperately.

Min stood up and went to him, putting her arms around him. He clung to her.

"Tell us what happened," said his father.

Marty's sobs subsided and he got control of himself. The others waited patiently.

"We were on patrol in a small town in Germany towards the end of the war. I was ordered to go up on that roof and drop a grenade down the chimney. Another soldier was with me." He paused for a few moments, thinking. "Then we scrambled down as fast as we could. Leo....the other guy....broke his leg when we hit the ground. I was trying to pull him away from the building. Then we heard the explosion. Windows blew out, glass flying all over." His gaze went above the heads of his parents and brother as he seemed to be in another world. A world that he wanted to forget.

"Son, you were ordered to go up there. What choice did you have? This was war!" his father said.

Marty just shook his head back and forth. "I know that, but I still feel so bad! Those were innocent people inside."

"Your commanding officers must have thought otherwise."

"Yes, they thought there were Nazi soldiers in there, holed up. They had been told that."

"Maybe they were in there, among the women and children."

"I don't know. All I know is that about a dozen innocent people were killed, because of me!"

"If it hadn't been you up there, it would have been someone else, Marty," said Stan.

"I know that, too, but I can't erase the memory of what I saw." Raising his voice, he said, "Sometimes I wish I had been killed over there. That would have been better than this!"

"Oh, Marty, you can't mean that!" cried his mother. "We were so worried about you all the time and so happy when you came home safely to us."

"Yes, I came home safely, but I'm living in a kind of hell. I don't want to go to sleep at night, because then I'll have that dream again."

No one knew what to say to him then.

"There were other things that I want to forget but can't." They waited for him to go on. "Sometimes, late at night, after we'd had a skirmish with the Germans, the officers would give us a lot of beer to drink and then send us out to pick up our dead comrades. They hoped we were drunk enough so that we wouldn't remember in the morning what we'd just seen!"

"Oh, for awful!" said Min, putting a hand over her mouth.

"The wounded had been picked up earlier by the medics but they left the dead ones until later. We called it....cadaver patrol."

Joe just shook his head from side to side and Stan, feeling sick, rose and started walking back and forth.

Min broke down and sobbed. "Oh, Marty, I'm so sorry that you had to go through such awful things."

The clock from the living room chimed and told them that it was now two o'clock. Marty finished his coffee and stood up.

"I'm sorry to keep you all up so late. I'm going to lay down on the sofa for awhile. You all go back to bed now."

He staggered slightly but made it into the next room. Min gathered up the empty cups and rinsed them out.

"Well, I guess I'll be going, then," said Stan. He put his jacket and gloves back on.

"Thank you, Stan, for bringing him home," said Joe. "I hope it doesn't happen again." Father and son just looked at each other.

Stan was upset all the way home. He was angry at his brother for going out and drinking so heavily, but he was also feeling great sympathy for him. *Imagine, having to cope with what happened to him.*

When he got into the house and up to the bedroom, he found that Livvie was awake and waiting for him.

"I've been worried about you. It took so long."

"Yah, I guess it did. After I got Marty home, we sat around and talked. Mom and Dad woke up. Marty told us some awful things that he experienced in Germany. He told us about the nightmare that always wakes him up."

Stan told Livvie all about it. When he was finished, he was sobbing. Livvie held him and tried to comfort him. "It must be so awful, knowing that what he was ordered to do caused the lives of innocent women and children."

Stan finally fell asleep, in his wife's arms. What he didn't tell her was how hurt he was when Marty talked about him not having to go into the service. That struck a nerve.

The next morning, Stan resolved that he would have to have it out with his older brother about the things that he had said. *I have to find out if he really feels that way about me.*

It was two days before the opportunity came for the two brothers to be alone. Stan was over at his Dad's place, in the barn. Marty came in, looking for a shovel.

"Stan, I want to say that I'm sorry for making you come way over to Davenport to get me the other night," Marty said. "It won't happen again."

Stan figured that this was a good time to ask his brother how he really felt about him. "Marty, you said some things to me that night and I need to know if you really meant them."

"I don't remember much about what I said. What was it?"

Stan paused. "Well, you made some sarcastic remarks about me not having to go into the service." He waited awhile for Marty to answer.

Marty leaned up against the stall. "Did I? Well, I didn't mean that. The fact is, when I was over there, I was really jealous of you, because you got to stay home. Where I wished to be."

Stan waited for him to go on. "I know that you were needed here on the farm and that all of you that stayed home were an important part of the war effort."

Stan still didn't say anything. "I'm sorry if I said things I shouldn't," said Marty.

"OK, I'll try and forget about it," said Stan. "Do you remember that you told us all about....the reason behind your....nightmare?" he said slowly.

"Yah, I remember that part. I was maybe sobering up some by then."

"I really feel bad for what you had to go through," Stan told him. "It helps me understand your need for drinking too much."

"Yah, well, I'm going to try and clean up my act. I've gone for two nights without the nightmare now so maybe it helped to tell someone about it."

"That could be. I hope so, Marty." Stan put his arm around his brother's shoulder.

"I'm glad you're home," he said simply.

"Yah, me too," and the two young men hugged awkwardly.

About two weeks later, Marty surprised everyone by announcing that he was planning to go to school.

"Go to school?" asked his mother, surprised.

"Yes, I'm going to start spring quarter at the AC." That was the North Dakota Agriculture College in Fargo.

"Oh, Marty," exclaimed his mother. "I'm glad for you but I thought that you wanted to farm."

"Well, I don't really know what I want to do, but I thought I may as well take advantage of the GI Bill and get educated. That's the least they can do for me after I put in my time," he added, somewhat sarcastically.

"This is really a surprise," Joe said. "I suppose you know that we could really use you now that spring planting is right around the corner."

"I know, Dad, but I want to try this. Maybe it will give me the incentive to straighten up and stay sober."

Joe, though disappointed in his son's decision, had to agree with him that maybe it would be a good thing for him at this point.

A couple days later, Marty packed up his things and moved into an apartment in Fargo, near the college.

"I wonder how it will go for him," Min said to her husband that evening.

"I don't know. We'll have to wait and see."

CHAPTER 18

Spring came early that year and, after the three previous wet springs, it was a welcome change. Stan and Joe got all the seeding done in record time, without Marty's help. Allan, who was now fifteen, was a big help when he wasn't in school.

One evening, Magda called over to the Murphys' to tell them that Grandpa Ivar wanted the whole family to gather at Magda and Art's the following evening. He had something to tell everyone, he told her.

"What could that be, do you think?" Livvie asked Stan when he told her about it. "Do you suppose he's sick or maybe dying and he wants to talk to us all?"

"I don't know," said Stan, "he seemed healthy as a horse just the other day when I saw him. I don't think it's that."

"What could it be, then?" persisted Livvie.

"Well, we'll just have to wait until tomorrow night."

The next day was a Saturday, and early in the evening, the Murphy family began to gather at Art and Madga's. Marty was already there when Stan and Livvie arrived and Ronnie, who wanted to be called Ron now, came shortly after. Joe, Min and Allan came hurrying in about the same time.

"You look like you've really been rushing, Minerva," said Magda to her sister-in-law.

"Joe and Allan came in kind of late for supper so I really had to hustle!" exclaimed Min.

"That's all right. We're all here now so we'll go into the living room. Grandpa is waiting for everyone."

Art was asking Ron if he liked the mechanics school. "Yes, I like it very much. I like doing that kind of work."

"Well, there'll be a great demand for it now, I'm thinking," said Art. "How about you, Marty? How's school going for you at the AC?"

Marty was rather evasive in his answer but said that there were sure a lot of pretty co-eds.

"That's just like you to notice that!" exclaimed Art.

"Well, everyone find a place to sit," suggested Magda. Min raised her eyebrows at her, as if to say, do you know what this is all about? Magda just shrugged.

Livvie found some toys for the little girls to play with.

Ivar, now center stage, cleared his throat and looked around the room. "I suppose you are all curious to know why I wanted to talk to you tonight. First I'll tell you that it has nothing to do with my health." He chuckled. "You probably thought I was ready to kick the bucket!"

Everyone squirmed at this. They had indeed all entertained this thought.

Ivar cleared his throat once again. "You all know how worried I was during the war about....my family in Norway. I've received several letters since the war ended now and they are all fine. I got a letter yesterday that I want to tell you about." He paused here and thought awhile.

"First I need to tell you something that I've never told anyone before. Something that happened in my past, before I came to this country. I came to America in 1903, and I was 23 at the time. What you don't know is that I was married before I came over here." He paused to let this sink in. Magda gasped audibly and looked at her brother, Joe.

"You were married before you married our mother?" she asked her father. She was standing now, visibly upset.

"Sit down, Magda, and I'll tell you all about it," Ivar said. "About a year before I came over here, I had married my childhood sweetheart. Her name was Magda."

"You named me after her?" Magda almost shouted.

Ivar ignored her question and went on with his story. "We were young and in love and we had made plans to go to America together. Then Magda found that she was going to have a baby. We thought, well, we'll have the baby and still be able to leave in the spring as planned. As it turned out, the baby came early and, in fact, there were two of them! Twins! A boy and a girl."

Ivar looked around at his family. They were absorbed in his story. Magda looked like she would explode, he thought, but he just continued.

"The babies were very little, especially the girl and she was kind of sickly. It was decided that I would go on to America, as we had already purchased tickets, and then I would either send for Magda and the babies later or I would go back for them. It was hard to leave them, but we thought that this was the best plan. How wrong we were!"

Ivar got out his hankie and wiped perspiration off his forehead. He sighed. "This is hard for me, telling you all this. And it's probably hard for you, too," he added, looking at Magda and Joe.

"After I had been in this country for about two months, I got a letter from my sister, Ingeborg. It was bad news, in that letter," he said, shaking his head back and forth. "She told me that my dear wife had died and also the little girl." Ivar's shoulders shook as he began to cry softly.

Livvie could feel the tears pricking her eyes and as she looked around, there were others, too, with the same problem. They all waited patiently for Ivar to continue.

"It was the flu, I guess. It hit our area hard that spring. Others died, too. The little boy, who we named Karl, made it through the illness and was now being taken care of by Ingeborg and her husband." Ivar blew his nose and wiped his eyes.

"I mourned terribly for them and I didn't tell anybody. I just couldn't share my grief. I wanted to try to endure it all alone. I know now that that was wrong. I couldn't even tell your mother," he said, looking at Magda and Joe.

"She didn't even know that you had been married before?" asked Magda.

"No. I knew that I should have told her at the very beginning, before we were even married, but I waited too long and then it got to be impossible to tell her."

"So she didn't even know that you had a child back in Norway!" said Joe.

"No, I couldn't tell her. My sister asked to adopt my little boy and I said that she could raise him. He took their name, which is Moe. So his name is Karl Moe. My son is now 44 years old."

"Pa, why did you decide to tell us about all this now?" asked Joe.

"Since the war ended, I've been getting letters from my son and my sister. He wants to come and see me. She told him about me when he was about 15 years old. He was planning to come here a few years ago, but then the war interrupted things."

"So when is he coming?" asked Min.

"He says he is coming in June. That's why I thought I better tell you the whole story long before he comes. Then you can get used to the idea by the time he arrives."

"Whew!" said Joe, rising from his chair. "This is a lot to digest. We have a brother, Magda."

Magda was speechless, for a change. She got up and left the room. She came back with an old shoebox. "There must be a picture of him in this box here. Your sister sent some pictures once in awhile."

"Yah, there should be some when he was younger. His confirmation picture was probably the last one I got, though."

"Didn't he ever get married?" asked Stan.

"No, he hasn't yet. He's been planning this trip to the US for many years now but it never seemed to work out. But now he's finally coming. He has his ticket, he says."

"Well, Grandpa, I bet you're pretty excited to see him!" exclaimed Allan.

"Oh, I am, for sure, for sure," he answered.

"Here it is," said Magda. "His confirmation picture."

Everyone gathered around to have a look. "He kind of looks like Allan here," said Art.

"He does, in a way, doesn't he?"

"He actually looks like his mother," Ivar said. "She was beautiful." His hand moved back and forth over the picture.

"Do you have any pictures of her?" asked Livvie.

"No, unfortunately, I don't."

"Does your sister have any pictures of her? Like your wedding picture?" asked Allan.

"We didn't take a wedding picture back then. We were too poor and were saving every penny to buy our tickets for America."

Magda just thought of something. "What if mother would have known that you named me after your first wife?"

Ivar shook his head. "She wanted to name you Alice, but I insisted that it had to be Magda."

"Did she wonder why you wanted that particular name?"

"I just told her that it had always been a name that I liked, so she finally gave in. She got to name Joe when he came along two years later."

The family had many more questions to ask Ivar and he answered them one by one. Magda served coffee and it was late before the gathering broke up.

"Well," said Livvie to Stan as they drove home. "The mystery is solved.

I never thought it would be something like that!"

"Me neither. It's funny that he never told anyone here in this country about his wife's death. How could he behave like nothing had happened?"

"Well, he said that he changed jobs right after he received word so that the men there wouldn't really have known him."

"I wonder if my grandmother ever suspected anything."

"Wouldn't she have read the letters from Norway?"

"Grandpa probably told his sister to refer to Karl as his nephew. Actually, though, I don't think that Grandma could read Norwegian. She could speak it some but not read it, if I remember correctly."

"What if she had still been living now and your Grandpa would have to tell her the story!"

"She would have been pretty mad at him!" Stan said. "She could get really upset and on her high horse, I remember!"

"Maybe that's who Magda takes after!"

"Oh, absolutely. She's just like her. I don't think that my grandmother was an easy person to live with."

"Maybe Ivar married her because he was so lonely and sad after what had happened to him."

"That could be," agreed Stan.

About a month after Marty had moved into Fargo to attend school, he came into the yard one afternoon and started unloading his car.

"What are you doing?" asked his mother. "Moving back home?"

"Yup, that is exactly what I am doing," he told her.

"Why, don't you like living in that apartment?"

"The apartment was just fine. It was school that I just couldn't take."

"You mean that you quit school? Already?"

"Yah, Mom, I quit school already." Marty sat down by the kitchen table. He looked defeated.

"How come?' she asked. She sat down opposite him.

"Well, I just couldn't concentrate on my studies. I'm just too restless yet. And all the other students are so much younger than I am."

"Oh, Marty," wailed Min.

"Mom, I'm almost 28 years old. Most of the guys in my class were eighteen or nineteen. Just kids! After what I've been through, I don't have anything in common with them."

Joe came in the house awhile later and Min told him about Marty quiting school.

"I was wondering how it would go," Joe said.

Marty came down from upstairs. By the look on his father's face, he knew that his mother had told him the whole story.

"Dad, before you say anything, I knew that I would never finish the whole quarter and I certainly would not pass so I decided to quit."

"So how long did you actually go to classes?" asked his father.

"Only about a week."

"Only one week!" exclaimed Min.

"I knew at the end of the first week that this just wasn't for me."

"So how come you're just coming home now? Were you afraid to tell us?"

"Well, yes, and I had paid rent for the whole month so I just decided to stay there."

"What did you do all day, then?" asked his mother.

Marty hung his head sheepishly. "Well, I slept late in the mornings and partied most of the night. I might as well tell you the truth."

"Oh, Marty! I was so hoping that this would be a good thing for you."

"Well, it wasn't but at least I gave it a try. I'm home now and I'll help you with the farming, Dad, if you'll let me stay here."

"Of course you can stay here. This is your home," said Min.

"Well, I haven't been the best son since I got home from Germany."

"You're still a member of this family and we love you. You're always welcome here."

"One good thing came out of this whole deal," said Marty. "I met a girl. Her name is Jean."

"Oh, really?" said Min.

"I met her at the Vet's Club. She was an army nurse and she was also over in Germany. She understands me. She's been through some horrible things, too."

Min got up and started making supper. "I hope that you aren't going to start that drinking again, Marty."

"I'll try to behave myself," Marty assured her.

In the weeks to come, Marty stayed away from the local bars, but he made several trips into Fargo each week. He'd stay out very late and some nights, he'd almost meet Joe, who was going out to do the milking early in the morning.

"Marty, you can't stay out all night and expect to do a good day's work the next day. Do try to get in earlier, won't you? Your mother worries about you terribly."

Marty hung his head but said nothing in his defense.

Meanwhile, Ron was doing well at the Hanson's Mechanical School. He would graduate at the end of summer. He came home on weekends to help his Dad. Rosie came home some weekends, too, from the nursing school. She would often catch a ride with Ron. On Saturday nights, they would go and pick up Kenny and the three old pals would go to dances or into town for a movie.

Kenny, in spite of his limited eyesight, was able to help his dad around the farm some. He wasn't allowed to operate any machinery, though.

"Kenny seems kind of down in the dumps lately, don't you think?" Ron asked Rosie after the three had been out.

"Well, he's sure not like he used to be, but I suppose when a person becomes almost blind, it changes you some."

"Well, this afternoon Grandpa's son arrives from Norway," Min told Marty and Allan at the breakfast table one day.

"That will be quite a reunion, I imagine."

"Yah, I bet Grandpa is a little nervous about now."

"Art and Magda will take him to the train station in Fargo. His son, Karl, will be coming by ship to New York, and then by train through Chicago."

"I bet Dad is excited to meet his new brother," said Marty.

"Well, I think he is. He's a little nervous about it, too."

"Are we all going over to Magda's this evening to meet him?" asked Marty.

"No, I think maybe just your father will go over there and then we'll all meet him tomorrow, a few at a time perhaps."

"That sounds like a good plan. He might be too overwhelmed if we all descended on him at once."

"Does he speak English?" asked Allan.

"Oh, yes, I think he does. I don't know how well, though," said Min.

The next afternoon, Magda and Art brought Karl over to the Murphy farm. Joe had gone over to meet him the night before. It had gone well, he told Min when he finally came home.

Min invited them all to come into the house after they had shown him around the farm.

"You have a very nice farm here. And so big!" Karl said to Min. "Our farms in Norway are very small. Nothing like this."

Karl was interested in everything and everybody. He was easy to converse with as he had a good handle on the English language.

"Where did you learn such good English?" Marty asked him.

"Well, my mother, Ingeborg, made me take all the English classes I possibly could. I guess she knew that someday I would be going to America to meet my father. She told me about him when I was about fifteen. That's when she sent me to high school and told me to learn English."

Ivar had stayed home to rest up after all the excitement. But Magda told Min that he and his son had stayed up well past midnight, talking.

"Well, Joe got home pretty late, too," Min said.

Next, Art and Magda drove Karl over to meet Stan and Livvie and to see their place. They told him about the bonanza farm that used to be there. He just couldn't grasp such a large operation.

"Yah, everything is so big in America," he said. "So big and so fast."

"So how long do you plan to stay, Karl?" asked Stan.

"Well, I don't know yet. As long as you all will let me," he laughed.

He had a nice laugh and was really a very pleasant fellow, Stan thought.

"Grandpa must be so pleased," Stan said to Livvie after their guests had gone.

"Yes, I'll bet he is. Karl seems like a very nice man."

In August, Ron finished his course at the mechanic school but didn't look for a job right away. He came home to help with the harvest. Joe, true to his word, had bought a new combine—an Allis Chalmers. He and Art used it together, and with the help of all the boys, harvest went pretty fast. The crop was fairly good and the prices were up some.

On September 1, Stan and Livvie had all the relatives over to help celebrate Linda's birthday. Marty brought out his new girlfriend, Jean, for everyone to meet for the first time. She was a cute gal, thought Livvie, with dark hair and flashing brown eyes. After the war, she resumed her career as a nurse and worked at St. John's Hospital in Fargo.

Jean and Rosie, who had also been invited to the get-together, had something in common as they talked about their work in the medical field. They were discussing the polio epidemic in Fargo over the past few months.

"It's official now," said Jean. "Fargo had a total of 90 polio cases this year."

"Really! That many?" asked Livvie. She had worried so about taking her little girls out in crowds, especially to Fargo, for fear that they would contract the dreaded disease.

"Yes," answered Jean. "Some were very light cases but I saw some pretty bad ones, too."

Rosie agreed. "Those iron lungs were really scary to see. I felt so sorry for the young children who had to be put in them."

When fall came, Karl was still there and he announced his intention of staying permanently. He had been a big help on the farm, helping both Art and Joe. He was, however, a carpenter by trade and he wanted to look for work for the winter.

"You could advertise in the Tribune," suggested Art. He did this and he had offers for several jobs the first week. It seemed that many people were busy building or remodeling after the war.

In October, Magda had a birthday party for Grandpa Ivar. Karl enjoyed getting in on his father's birthday for the first time. George and Carrie were pleased to be invited again.

"So tell us, Karl, what it was like in Norway during the occupation," said George, after a delicious late-afternoon meal.

Karl leaned back, lit his pipe and began. "Well, the Germans attacked us in the spring of 1940. This was quite a surprise to us all. By June, the whole country had given up to the Germans. King Haakon and the royal family fled, the King going to England. A German by the name of Terboven arrived in Oslo and he wielded absolute power. The Norwegians were to supply whatever it was capable of for the war machine—workers, material, food, paper and iron ore, fish, ports and bases.

"The Norwegian newspapers," he went on, "were told what to print. The year 1941 was especially bad. Arrests of pastors and teachers began. People were tortured and even executed for standing up for their beliefs. I had a teacher friend who was sent to prison because he would not pledge loyalty to the Nazi party. They finally let him out, as there was a shortage of teachers by this time, but they watched him very closely."

"What about the resistance movement that we read about?" asked George.

"I wasn't in it but some of my friends were and a couple of times, I carried information across to Sweden for them. One of my friends was killed in a sabotage attempt. He and several others were trying to destroy a munitions factory."

Karl sighed and said, "Yah, these were very bad times for our people, but I was proud of them, how they tried to stand up against the Nazis."

"Time for cake and coffee now," announced Magda, as she carried in a big, frosted layer cake. She had Ivar blow out the candles, as usual, and she cut a piece for everyone around the table.

"So, Martin, how come you don't have your girlfriend with you today, then?" asked Magda.

"She had to work at the hospital this weekend," he answered.

"Is it getting pretty serious between the two of you?" teased Art.

"Well, time will tell," laughed Marty.

"I hear Ron got a job at an auto repair shop in Moorhead," said George.

"Yah, he started there about a month ago now," replied Joe. "He found an apartment in the basement of a real nice family."

"How is your carpentry job coming along, Karl?" asked George.

"I've had several jobs right in Kindred and one in Davenport since I put my ad in the paper. Tomorrow I start a big job for a widow woman west of Kindred," he told them.

"Yah, he's going to remodel the house of that Mrs. Bolstad," said Joe. "Remember, she's the one who spent the night at our house after that November storm?"

"Oh, I know her," said Carrie. "Her name is Dorothy, I believe. Her husband died some years ago now, didn't he?"

"Yah, and she has two sons and a daughter," explained Joe. "The oldest boy is about sixteen or so and is quite the farmer. She used to rent all her land out, but now the family is going to try and farm it themselves next year."

"Well, all good things must come to an end!" exclaimed George, as he stood and said that they had better be getting home. "There's milking to do, you know."

The other men reluctantly got up, too, and the women helped carry the dishes into the kitchen.

"Thank you again, Magda, for a lovely time," said Carrie, as they were preparing to leave.

"Say, how do you like that new car of yours, George?" asked Art, before the Johnsons went out the door. "What kind did you end up with?"

"It's a '46 Chevy. Brand new off the floor. It's nice to have a good car again," George told him.

"I've been looking at the new Fords. I may have to get me one of those," said Art.

On the way home from the party, Livvie said to Stan, "It seems that your grandpa is really happy that his son is planning to stay here."

"And Karl is equally happy to be here with his father."

"It must be nice to finally meet a father that you never knew before," Livvie sighed.

Stan looked over at his wife. "Ah, Livvie, you're thinking about your own real father, aren't you?"

"Yes, and someday I'm going to meet him," she said with resolve.

CHAPTER 19

Livvie and Magda were helping Min one fall day with the apple harvest. They were peeling and slicing the apples, preparing them for canning. These canned apples would be used the rest of the winter for making pies and applesauce.

"You certainly had a good apple crop this year, Minerva," said Magda.

"It was a lot better than last year. Remember? I hardly had any apples at all."

"I always say I'm going to plant some apple trees," Magda said, "but then you usually get so many that I don't really need to have any."

"Well, there's plenty here for the whole county, I think!" exclaimed Livvie.

The three women had been at it since midmorning. It was now almost noon and soon time to stop and get dinner on the table.

"So, what do you think of Martin's girlfriend, then?" Magda asked Min.

Min answered carefully, "I don't know her very well but she seems nice enough."

"I noticed that she smokes," remarked Magda.

"Well, yes, and so does Marty," Min said. "He said that nearly all of the soldiers smoked while they were in the service. He said that cigarettes were in good supply and urged upon the men."

"It probably was a habit that they picked up to help calm their nerves," suggested Livvie, who was reaching for more apples to peel.

"And I suppose it was the same for the young women who served as nurses."

"Well, just the same, I don't like to see a woman smoking," huffed Magda.

"I don't either," conceded Min, "but I'm not going to judge them if they do."

After dinner, and when the men had left the house, Magda again brought up the subject of Jeannie, Marty's girl.

"I understand she works at St. John's Hospital."

"Yes, that's right," said Min.

"Well, that's a Catholic hospital. Did you ever think that she may be a Catholic?"

"I never gave that a thought, Magda."

"Well, maybe you'd better. You ask Martin next time he comes home."

Livvie looked at her mother-in-law to see her reaction to Magda's meddlesome comments. Min just ignored them and got busy with putting the apple slices into the hot jars.

At the end of the day, after Livvie and Magda had gone home and Min had the kitchen cleaned up, she sat down and began to think about what Magda had said. She decided that maybe she better ask Marty about his girlfriend before things got serious between them.

As it turned out, Min didn't get a chance to talk to Marty about her concerns until it was too late. He came home one weekend in November and told his parents that he and Jeannie were engaged.

"Engaged!" said Min. "You've only known her a short time."

"I know, but I wanted to give her a ring, so I bought one the other day and gave it to her last night."

"I have to ask you Marty, is she a Catholic?"

Marty hesitated for a few moments before he answered. "Why would you ask that, Mom?"

"Because she works at the Catholic hospital."

He took a deep breath. "Well, yes, she's Catholic, but what has that got to do with anything?"

Min's heart sank. "Well, do you really think it is wise to marry one? You know, your children would have to be raised Catholic and would you want that?"

"Mom, I haven't thought that far ahead yet. I just want to marry Jeannie, and I'm going to!" He got up and left the house. Min watched him as he walked to the barn. That's where he usually strode off to when he was upset. Min looked at her husband who was sitting at the kitchen table.

"I guess we might as well accept the fact that he's probably going to marry her, with or without our blessing," Joe said.

Min sat down hard and sighed. "I guess so. I sure wasn't expecting something like this to happen in our family."

"Well, the world is changing now, especially after what everyone just went through, with the war and all. The old rules maybe won't apply anymore." Joe got up and went outside, too.

The next evening, Joe and Min went over to Art and Magda's. Ivar and Karl were playing a game of two-handed rummy.

"Want to join us?" Ivar asked Joe, taking the deck and resuffling.

"You bet," said Joe, pulling out a chair for himself.

Min and Magda sat at the other end of the table and watched.

"I see Martin came home yesterday," remarked Magda. "Did he go back to Fargo already?"

"He left a little while ago. He had some news to tell us yesterday," said Min.

"And what was that?"

"He and Jeannie got engaged."

"Oh, my!" exclaimed Magda. "And did you ask him if she was Catholic?"

"Yes, I asked and yes, she is."

Magda sucked in her breath. "Oh, no! What are you going to do?"

"There's nothing we can do now. It's too late."

The men had stopped their playing and were listening to the conversation between the two women.

"We'll just accept it and make the best of the situation," said Joe evenly. "And I suggest you do, too, Magda," he told his sister.

She just huffed but didn't say anything for awhile.

"So, when are they getting married?" she asked, after she couldn't stand the silence any longer.

"Oh, I don't know. He didn't say. I hope they wait a good, long time."

To change the subject, Joe asked Karl about his carpentry job over at Mrs. Bolstad's.

"Well, it's coming along pretty good. She wanted the back porch replaced first thing so I'm almost done with that. Then I'll be working inside."

"What is she going to have done there?" asked Joe.

"She wants the wall between the kitchen and pantry removed and the kitchen made bigger. She'd also like some new cupboards."

"It sounds like you'll be busy over there for quite sometime."

"Yah, I kind of think Karl rather likes it over there, too," laughed Art. "He says that she's a good cook and feeds him so well."

"She makes forenoon lunch, a big dinner, and then afternoon lunch."

Karl patted his stomach. "My belt is getting too tight for me."

"Yah, he isn't very hungry when he comes home here for supper," said Magda.

"If I remember right," said Joe, "Mrs. Bolstad is a mighty handsome woman, too!"

Karl just blushed and looked down at his cards. The other men laughed.

Min's hope that Marty and his girlfriend would wait a long time before getting married didn't happen. Two days before Christmas, early on a Saturday evening, Marty and Jeannie stopped by the Murphy farm just as the family had finished supper.

The young couple was beaming and Marty announced that they had gotten married that afternoon. Min had to sit down, with the shock of it.

"You what?" she said.

"We got married today!" Marty repeated. He put his arm protectively around his new wife.

"What was the hurry, son?" asked Joe. "Why didn't you wait and have a wedding and we could all have been there?"

Marty and Jeannie sat down by the kitchen table after taking off their coats. Marty sighed. "Well, it's this way," he started. "Jeannie's parents were not happy at all that she was planning to marry me. They were upset, like you were, about her marrying outside her faith. So, we decided to just run off and get married and avoid all the fuss."

"Where did you get married?" asked Min, when she finally found her voice.

"We found a priest over in Moorhead who would marry us. We went there this afternoon. A friend of mine from the Vet's Club and Jeannie's sister stood up for us."

He took Jeannie's hand in his. "We wanted to come out and tell you, face to face. Now we're going to go and tell her folks."

"So, what are your plans? Where will you live?" asked Min, concern all over her face.

"Tonight we're going to stay at a hotel in Fargo and then next week we'll look for an apartment. I'm going to get a job in town someplace."

Joe stood up. "Well, then, I guess congratulations are in order." He shook his son's hand and gave his new daughter-in-law a hug. There was nothing for Min to do but do the same. She hugged both of them and wished them much happiness.

"This calls for a little celebration," said Joe. "I'll get the wine and you get the glasses, Mother."

The four of them plus Allan drank a toast to the new couple.

"Well, we better be heading back to Fargo to the Rilley's," declared Marty. "Wish us luck!"

After the excited couple left, Min sat down in the living room and sighed. "I don't like this one bit. Imagine, running off and getting married like that! What will people say?"

"Now, my dear," said Joe. "We just have to make the best of the situation. We'll just tell everyone and act like we're happy about it."

"That's not going to be easy," replied Min. She began to cry. The more she thought about it, the harder she cried. Allan had gone upstairs to his room. Joe sat beside her and tried to console her.

"And to think that he didn't even have one of his brothers stand up for him at his wedding!" Min started crying all over again.

"It's not the end of the world, you know. You've gained another daughter; let's try and be happy about it."

As Min blew her nose and wiped her eyes, she said, "You're always the calm and sensible one. You'll have to tell your sister. I don't want to even be around when you do it."

Joe just laughed. "You leave Magda to me."

Karl Moe and Dorothy Bolstad were beginning to become an "item" around the community. After Karl finished his carpentry job in the early spring at the Bolstad farm, he found himself going over there quite often anyway, just to see Dorothy.

"Karl, I understand that your car just automatically goes over to the Bolstad place now," teased Joe. Karl had bought himself a new car shortly after he made the decision to stay in the United States.

"Yah, I can't understand it!" he laughed.

"We're going to the Sons of Norway dance tomorrow night," Joe told him. "Are you and Dorothy going to be there?"

"I haven't asked her yet but I'll be seeing her tonight. She's invited me over for supper. It's her little girl's birthday."

"That little girl was pretty sick the night she and her mother spent the night here. How old is she now?"

"She's eleven now, I believe."

"So Johnny, the oldest, is going to try farming by himself this spring, I hear."

"Yah, he seems to think that he can do it. They'll have to rely on their neighbors a lot, using their machinery and all that. Dorothy has said that everyone's been so good to them. I guess her late husband was well thought of around here."

"Yes, I guess he was," replied Joe.

One Saturday in early April, Marty came by his old home for a visit. Min watched him drive into the yard. Instead of coming right up to the house, he walked over to a little building back in the trees and went inside. It was the little house that Stan and Livvie had lived in for a few months when they were first married. It had originally been used as a bunkhouse for hired men.

When he finally came into the house, Min had some coffee ready for him and a few slices of fresh banana bread.

"Oh, this tastes so good," he told his mother. "I don't get things like this very often."

"Doesn't Jeannie bake for you?" asked Min.

"No, she's not much of a cook, you know. Very seldom does she bake anything."

"How is it going with her folks now?" asked Min. "Have they warmed up to you some yet?"

"Well, I think they like me well enough but there's that religion thing. It really is a big deal to them. Jeannie has four sisters and brothers and they all have married Catholics so I guess they consider Jeannie the black sheep of the family."

"Do they come and visit you?"

"No, they haven't actually been to our apartment yet. We go over there every once in awhile. The rest of the family has accepted our situation, though, so we are with her sisters quite often."

Joe had come in and was washing up. "So, how is your job coming?" he asked his son. Marty was working in a food distribution warehouse in Fargo.

"Well, I'm not really very happy there. That's one reason I wanted to come out here today and talk to you."

Marty lit up a cigarette and Joe and Min waited until he blew out his first puff of smoke.

"What's on your mind, son?" asked Joe, taking a seat by the table and grabbing a slice of the bread.

"I don't like my job and I don't like living in the city so I was wondering if we could come out here and live in the little house back there and I'd help you farm." He took another drag on his Lucky Strike. "I was thinking I could maybe rent some land for myself someplace around here, too."

"Well, this is a surprise," said Joe, putting his coffee cup down.

"What does Jeannie think of this idea?" asked Min.

"Well, she's willing to give it a try. She knows I'm not happy there."

Joe was thoughtful for awhile. "There's your mother's uncle's land over by Kindred that might be available soon, but I don't know of anything right now. Most people are ready to start seeding by now."

"Do you have enough work for me to help with? Enough so that I could make a living off of it?" Marty asked.

"Well, Stan and I share everything down the middle now. Then there's Allan, who wants to help this summer, too. He plans to go on to college in the fall. We'd have to figure something out."

"Do you think that little house is in good enough shape to live in?" asked Min.

"I was just out there," replied Marty. "It could be fixed up some. Here, let's all go and have a look."

Joe and Min followed their son out to the building. There were just two rooms. When Stan and Livvie used it, they had a small kitchen in the one room and then a combination bedroom-living area in the other room.

"When would you want to move?" asked Joe.

"As soon as possible. I'll be done with my job at the end of next week."

"Doesn't Jeannie want to take a look at this before she agrees to move out here?"

"I'll bring her out tomorrow. She had to work today."

Before the month was out, Marty and his bride had moved out to the farm, settling into the little "honeymoon cottage" as Marty called it. Min had her reservations about how this was going to go, but she wisely kept silent. She asked Jeannie if she would like to help plant the big garden.

"I'll give it a try," the young woman said. "I've never done it before, though," she warned.

Marty was able to rent 80 acres from a man over by Horace, a few miles to the east of the Murphy farm. "I'll try and get more next year," he told his dad. Joe didn't say anything. He, too, was wondering how this arrangement was going to work.

Livvie, who had announced after the first of the year that she was going to have a baby, wasn't feeling well, so Stan took her into Fargo to see her doctor.

After checking her over, Dr. Hunter looked solemn as he told the young couple the bad news. "The baby has died in your womb, Mrs. Murphy."

"Oh, no!" Livvie exclaimed in disbelief. "Are you sure?"

"Yes, I'm very sure," he answered kindly.

"So what do we do now?" asked Stan.

"Well, you may have a spontaneous abortion on your own shortly. If not, we'll have to do a D & C procedure." The doctor got up from his chair. "You go home and wait and see what happens. Call me in a week or so." He patted Livvie gently on the arm and left the room.

Livvie burst into tears and Stan didn't know how to comfort his wife. He just held her until she stopped sobbing. They rode home in silence, not knowing what to say to each other.

Several days later, Livvie started having contractions and some bleeding. By the end of the day, it was all over with. She called the doctor's office to report what had happened.

"You get some bed rest and the bleeding should diminish after a few days," Dr. Hunter told her. "If not, be sure to call me again."

The bleeding gradually diminished by the end of a week. Livvie felt all right physically, but certainly not emotionally. She cried often and at the littlest thing. This went on for many weeks. Stan was beside himself, not knowing what to do.

One day he went into the house on his folk's place, when he knew that his mother would be in there alone. She was working in the kitchen, as usual. She looked up from her bowl of bread dough.

"What is it, Stan?" she could tell that something was bothering her second-born son.

"It's Livvie. I don't know what to do for her. She cries all the time and hardly has the ambition to get her housework done or take care of the girls." He sat down at the table and watched as his mother kneaded the dough.

"That often happens after a miscarriage," said Min. "Especially when Livvie was as far along as she was. She had become so attached to that unborn child by that time that it was really hard for her to lose it."

"What should I do? Take her to the doctor?" He looked so worried, Min thought.

"Give it a little more time, why don't you. One thing that you can do, though, is talk to her about the baby. Don't pretend that it didn't happen. What she wants from you now is for you to tell her how bad you feel about losing the baby, too."

Stan looked up at his mother. "I guess I had thought that if I didn't mention it at all, that would be better."

"Oh, no!" exclaimed Min. "That's the worst thing you could do."

"How do you know so much, Mom?" he asked, getting up from the chair.

"Well, I don't know if you remember, but I also had a miscarriage. It was between Ronnie and Allan."

"Oh, I guess I had forgotten that. I'm sorry."

"Well, I think I know how Livvie is feeling. You go home tonight and have a good long talk about this and see if that doesn't help."

"Thanks, Mom. I'll try that," Stan said as he headed for the door.

"I could go over and talk with her, too," suggested Min. "I'll go tomorrow. Tell her I'm coming."

The next day, Min drove over to Stan and Livvie's place. Livvie greeted her mother-in-law at the back door and tried to put on a cheerful face. Cheryl and Linda came running when they heard their grandmother's voice in the kitchen. She gave them each a hug and listened to their chatter.

"Would you like a cup of coffee?" asked Livvie.

"Oh, that would be nice, if you have some made."

Livvie poured two cups and set them on the table. "You girls go out and play for awhile now so Grandma and I can talk. When you come back, you can have some cookies."

The girls left reluctantly. "They've made a little tent over the clothesline and they like to play in there," Livvie said.

Livvie sat down opposite Min. "Stan said you'd be over today. He's been pretty worried about me, I guess. Last night we had a good talk."

"Yes, well, I told him some things. I've been through this same thing, too, you know. Maybe you didn't know. It was a couple years after Ronnie was born."

"I know that many people have miscarriages so people tell me that I should just get over it and that I can always have another one." Livvie was reaching for her hankie now.

Min patted her hand. "I know what you are feeling right now. You want to grieve for this particular child. You don't want to be told that it doesn't matter. That you can just have another one."

Livvie looked at the older woman sitting across from her. "Yes, that's exactly how I feel. Last night, Stan admitted that he also grieved for this child and that made me feel better, that we can share in this."

"When I lost my baby," Min told her, "I wondered if it was the little girl that I'd always wanted. I'll never know, of course, but I always think of it as being a girl."

"Maybe this one was our little boy, then," Livvie said, trying to smile through her tears.

"Maybe it was," said Min. "Maybe it was." The two women drank their coffee in silence for awhile.

"How long did this....feeling of loss....stay with you?" Livvie asked Min.

"Oh, I don't quite remember now, but I think it lasted for several months. What bothered me," she went on, "was the fact that none of my friends would talk about it. They acted like it had never happened."

"Yes, that is happening to me, too. I guess they feel that if they don't talk about it, I won't think about it and get so sad. What they don't realize is that that is all I can think about!"

"Yes, only the ones who have gone through it will understand," Min told her.

The girls came running into the house and were asking for cookies. They wanted to have a "nicnic" in their little tent, Linda told their Mom.

"OK. I'll make you some nectar, too, if you can wait for a few minutes."

"Oh, goodie! Nectar!" exclaimed Cheryl. "Make the grape."

After Livvie got the girls settled outside in their tent, she came back in and sat down again. Changing the subject that they'd been on, Livvie asked, "How are Jeannie and Marty getting along in their little house?"

"Oh, just fine, I guess. They didn't have much furniture. Their apartment in Fargo had been furnished. They've bought a new sofa bed and a chair."

"I should go over and pay Jeannie a little visit one of these days, I guess," said Livvie, "but I haven't felt like doing anything for sometime now."

"Things will get better soon now, Livvie, I'm sure," Min said. "Well, I better be going. I'm going to run into Davenport and get a few things at the store."

"Thanks for coming over, Min. It was good to have this talk."

The next morning, Livvie announced to Stan that she might take a drive down to Kindred in the afternoon. "I haven't been to see my Mom for quite sometime now. She'll enjoy seeing the girls."

"Yah, you do that," said Stan. "It will be good for you to get out some."

Livvie hadn't let her Mom know that she was coming so as she drove into the yard, she hoped that she'd find her home. The two girls jumped out of the car first and ran to the house. They knocked on the screen door and waited impatiently. By the time Livvie reached the back steps, her mother appeared at the door.

"Oh, what a wonderful surprise!" she exclaimed. "I was just thinking about you girls this morning. And how are you doing, Livvie?" She gave her daughter an extra warm embrace and then she stood back and looked at her.

"Well, I'm doing better now, Mom. I had some rough weeks there. Stan was getting worried about me. We've recently had some good talks and that has helped."

"Well, it's always tough to have a pregnancy end that way." Turning to the girls, she said, "I bet you two would like some ice cold lemonade."

"Oh, goodie!" said Linda.

"When you knocked, I was down in the basement, looking for a quart jar. I was going to bring something cold to drink out to George for his afternoon lunch."

"He'll appreciate that today, I'm sure," commented Livvie. "It turned really hot, didn't it?"

"Yes, June was so cool and July hasn't been much better so far. I was beginning to wonder when summer was going to begin!"

Livvie and the girls stayed in the kitchen while Carrie made up a lunch for George.

"We'll carry this jug of cold drink and some glasses and you can go out to the field with me. Here, girls, you can carry the cookie container. Livvie, you grab those glasses. We'll take the pickup."

They bounced along on the field road until they spotted George. He was cultivating a field of corn. A huge smile spread across his face when he saw all of them.

"Well, this is a great surprise!" he said, as they all tumbled out of the pickup cab. "All my favorite girls have come out to see me."

Carrie spread a blanket and a cloth out on the grass under a tree near the edge of the field. George and the little girls plunked themselves down on the ground.

"This is fun!" exclaimed Cheryl. "Having a picnic with Grandpa out in the field."

"Well, it sure made my day!" he said. "I believe this is the hottest day yet this summer." He took out his big blue hankie and wiped the sweat from his forehead and neck.

"How are Stan and the boys doing up there?" he asked Livvie.

"They've finished the cultivating, I think. Now they'll be getting ready for harvest soon."

Cheryl reached for her third cookie. "These are good, Grandma."

"They're called Aunt Sally's Cookies. I hadn't made them in oh, so long. That's what I did yesterday."

"I never think to make them," said Livvie.

"I'll send some home with you then."

"Stan and I are thinking that we may send Cheryl to first grade this fall," Livvie told her parents. "She's only five, but I think she is so ready for school. What do you think?"

"What school would she go to?"

"The Warren Township school along the Kindred Highway. The school just west of us has been closed for a few years now. One of the school board members stopped by last week to see if we had anyone old enough to start."

"Well, she is mature for her age," Carrie said. "And certainly bright enough."

"She is really ready to start learning things, I think," said Livvie.

"Is she excited about starting?" asked George.

"Oh, yes!" laughed Livvie. "She talks about it all the time. I'm surprised that she didn't tell you when she first got here."

"So, how is the Norwegian carpenter doing?" asked George.

"Karl, you mean? He's doing fine and is very busy. He's been helping Art farm again this summer."

"Is he still courtin' that Mrs. Bolstad?"

"Well, I guess he is. He talks about her all the time!"

"I think they'd make a very nice couple," said Carrie.

"You think everyone should be coupled up, Carrie," teased George.

"Well, just think how nice that would be for her to have a man around the house and help with the farm and the kids and everything," Carrie defended herself.

"I think it would be great if they would get married," agreed Livvie.

"Have they talked about it?"

"Not that I've heard."

The summer that was so long in coming lasted way into early October. In early September, Cheryl had started the first grade in the country school.

"So how do you like school, then?" Joe asked his granddaughter one Sunday after church. It was a beautiful morning and the people were enjoying visiting outside the church.

"I like it," Cheryl answered, "but I only have boys in my class. And they're all so dumb!"

"There's only four pupils in the first grade and the other three are boys," Livvie explained to him. Cheryl ran off to find someone her age to talk to.

One woman came up to Joe and said, "I hear that your Norwegian brother is going to be tying the knot soon."

"Yah, I guess that's right. That old love bug bit him hard, that's for sure!"

Karl had just announced to the family a few days earlier that he and Dorothy were planning to get married. The wedding was set for Thanksgiving weekend.

"It would sure be nice if my mother could come from Norway for the wedding," he had told Joe one day. "I think I'm going to write to her."

His mother, Ingeborg, who was actually Ivar's sister, had raised him since he was a baby after his real mother died.

"That would be nice if she could come," agreed Joe.

A letter arrived from Norway about a week before the wedding. Karl opened it excitedly. He read it quickly and then looked up.

"She's not coming," he told his father. "She doesn't feel up to such a long trip."

Ivar could tell that his son was very disappointed. "Well, Karl, maybe someday you can take your new bride over there for a visit."

Karl brightened at this suggestion. "That's right, I could do that. Dorothy would love that. Maybe in a few years, when the kids get older."

"Well, son, don't wait too long. Ingeborg isn't getting any younger, you know."

"That's true. I should have thought of taking Dorothy there now for our honeymoon. We'll need to save up some money, though, for that big trip."

The Saturday after Thanksgiving was a beautiful, crisp fall day. No snow had fallen as yet. The wedding of Karl Moe and Dorothy Bolstad took place in the afternoon at the West Prairie Lutheran Church west of Kindred. Only family and a few close friends were invited.

Karl had asked his brother Joe to be his best man and Dorothy had her sister stand up for her. Dorothy's daughter Shirley sang a song which caused many members of the congregation to shed a few tears.

Some friends and neighbors had volunteered to serve a light supper for the family after the ceremony in the church basement. Joe stood up and gave a memorable toast, telling how much it meant to him to have this new brother in his life.

Karl and Dorothy opened their wedding gifts in front of everyone and then the happy couple headed for Fargo where they would spend their first night together. They planned to take a short trip to Minneapolis and be back in a few days. The two boys were old enough to get along by themselves for awhile and Shirley went home with her aunt.

"That was a beautiful wedding," Min said to Joe on their way home. "And it seems that Dorothy's children really like their new stepfather."

"Yah, they sure do. Karl told me that when he proposed to Dorothy, she told him she wouldn't marry him unless her three children wholeheartedly accepted him."

"Well, Karl is a really likeable man and he will be a very loving and caring father to those kids, I think," said Min.

At Christmas time that year, Karl and Dorothy invited the whole Murphy clan over on Christmas Day. Dorothy had cooked a tremendous turkey and ham dinner with all the trimmings. Afterwards, the family members had played games and cards until quite late.

"That sure was fun, wasn't it?" Livvie said to Stan on the way home.

"Cheryl and Linda sure attached themselves to Shirley."

"I was very impressed with all three of Dorothy's kids," remarked Stan. Johnny will be graduating in the spring now, won't he?"

"I believe so," replied Livvie. "I suppose Karl will help him do the farming. That will sure be nice for him."

"I bet Art will really miss Karl's help over there. He was a good worker."

"I imagine Ivar will miss having his son under the same roof now."

"Well, I'm sure he will but he was really happy for him, finding such a nice woman to marry and all. And a ready-made family, too!"

"What if Karl had decided to go back to Norway? Things wouldn't have turned out so well for Ivar or for Karl either."

"I hope that Karl and Dorothy can take a trip over to Norway sometime," said Stan.

Livvie was thoughtful for several miles before speaking again. "You know, Stan, I've been thinking a lot lately about going and looking for my....real father. Would you help me?"

"What do you want to do?"

"Well, we could make a trip up to Canada and see if we can find him."

"Where would you even start looking?" Stan asked his wife.

"Merrie said that he came from a place called Moose Jaw and that he probably went back there to his family's farm."

"Well, you don't know that for sure. He could have gone anywhere." Stan sounded doubtful.

"I've been looking on the map," Livvie told him. "Moose Jaw is in Saskatchewan."

"Well, what would you do? Just appear out of nowhere and surprise him?"

"I don't know," Livvie said, thoughfully. "I don't know just how I should do it."

CHAPTER 20

The telephone rang in the Murphy's kitchen one winter afternoon. Min answered it and it was a call for Marty's wife, Jeannie.

"I'll have to run next door and get her. Hold on, please."

Min threw her coat on and ran hurriedly on the snowy path which led from their house to the little cottage. Marty hadn't had a telephone installed as yet so all their calls had to come through Joe and Min's telephone.

Min knocked on the door. She knocked again more loudly. When there was no answer, she opened the door slightly and called in. "Jeannie! There's a telephone call for you."

A few moments passed before she heard some rustling in the other room. Jeannie appeared and Min could see that she had been crying.

"It's a long-distance call so you need to hurry."

"Oh, thank you, Min. I'll be right there."

Min went back to the house and told the person on the other end that Jeannie would be there in a minute. Jeannie came into the house and talked for a short time.

When she hung up, she turned to Min and told her that it was her sister from Fargo who called. Without offering any more information, Jeannie returned to the little house.

A short while later, Min saw Marty through the kitchen window and she opened the back door and called to him. He came up to the house.

"Marty, have you got a few minutes to come in and talk?"

"What is it, Mom?" he asked, as he tried to shake the snow off his boots before entering the house.

"I just want to talk to you about some things. It seems I don't see much of you anymore."

Marty sat down at the kitchen table. Min sat down, too. "Is everything all right with Jeannie?" she began.

"Why do you ask?"

"Well, for one thing, I had to run over there a short while ago to fetch her for a phone call and I could see that she had been crying." Min waited for a possible explanation.

Marty paused for sometime and then heaved a big sigh. "Well, I may as well tell you. Jeannie is not very happy out here. She just can't adjust to living out here, 'in the middle of nowhere,' as she calls it. She cries a lot. I don't know what to do." Marty put his head in his hands. Min felt great compassion for her son. He was really hurting, she could tell.

"I suppose it does get lonely for her here," said Min.

"She's used to working in a busy hospital, you know," said Marty. "And here there's not enough to occupy her time, especially in the winter."

"I've asked her to come over many times and we could bake or sew or something together," Min declared.

"I know, Mom, but those just aren't things that she likes to do."

"Well, she needs to get out more, perhaps. Take her to the movies and to visit friends or something more often," Min suggested to her son.

"I don't know if any of that will help."

"How long has she felt like this?"

"Oh, for many months now," Marty answered.

Min got up to pour her son a cup of coffee. "I've been meaning to ask you, Marty. Do you still have those awful nightmares that you had when you first came home from the war?"

"Oh, not so often anymore. Maybe once or twice a month." He took a cookie to go with his coffee. "When they come, I have Jeannie to comfort me. Then I can go back to sleep. You know, Mom," he continued, "Jeannie has her own bad dreams. She wakes up in a cold sweat every so often. When she was overseas working in army hospitals, she had to work for awhile in the unit that did amputations. She still hears the men's screams and sees the severed limbs in the waste buckets."

Marty had tears in his eyes and Min reached over and took hold of his arm. "Oh, Marty, I feel so bad for both of you. You young people shouldn't have had to go through such horrible things!" Min wiped some tears from her own eyes.

After awhile Marty stood up and reached for his jacket. "I'd better get going, Mom. Jeannie and I, we have some problems but we need each other. No one else understands what we've gone through."

Min just nodded her head. When Marty was going out the door, she called after him. "Why don't the two of you come over for supper tonight and maybe we can all play some cards or something."

"I'll go over to the house and check if that's all right and let you know," he called, as he hurried down the path.

Jeannie's moods were a hard thing for Min to penetrate. She tried many things—she invited her daughter-in-law over for baking sprees, sewing bees, and invited her along to coffee parties. Jeannie participated, but only half-heartedly. Livvie tried, too, to do things with her and to interest her in various activities.

"Maybe when spring comes, things will get better for her," Livvie told Min.

"Well, I don't know; I sure hope so. Maybe she could get involved in gardening or planting flowers around her house or something."

Before spring could come, Livvie had talked Stan into taking her up to Canada on a mission to find her real father. Stan was rather reluctant, but he knew he would get no peace unless they at least tried.

During a spell of nice weather in early March, the two of them left for Canada.

The two girls stayed with Min and Joe. Livvie had asked Jeannie if she would help their mother-in-law out. Jeannie said she would and Livvie thought maybe this would be good for her sister-in-law.

Both Carrie and George and Joe and Min thought that Livvie and Stan would be just going on a wild-goose chase.

"How are they going to find a man up in that big country, anyway?" asked Joe.

"I don't know, but they do know where he came from, so they'll start there," said Min.

Stan and Livvie drove as far as Bowbells the first day and then made it up to Moose Jaw the next evening. They got a hotel room and the next morning they started making inquiries. They first asked the hotel clerk if he knew of any Kastets living in the area.

"Oh, yes, there's a few of them east of town."

"Do you know of an Alphonse Kastet?" Livvie asked, so nervous that she could barely get the name out.

He thought awhile. "Maybe you should go and ask at the post office," the clerk told her.

After being told there to look in the telephone book, Livvie wondered why she hadn't thought of that herself. She found two entries for an A. Kastet.

"Let's have breakfast first," suggested Stan, "and then maybe you could place a call or two."

Livvie could hardly eat a thing but forced down some coffee and toast. They went back to their hotel and asked if they could use their telephone. With trembling hands, Livvie dialed the first number. It turned out to be disconnected. Her heart sank. She dialed the other number. It was answered by a man.

"Is this the Alphonse Kastet residence?" she asked, with a quiver in her voice.

There was a long pause in the other end. "It might be," said the man. "Who are you and what do you want?"

Now Livvie was really nervous and could hardly find her voice or think of what to say. "I'm Olivia Murphy from North Dakota and I'm looking for a man by the name of Alphonse Kastet who worked on some farms in North Dakota some twenty years ago." There, she'd said it, now what would he answer, she wondered.

"Why do you want to know, ma'am?" he asked.

Livvie wasn't prepared for this question so she stammered out the first thing that came to her mind. "Well, do you know a woman by the name of Meridith Munseth? She went by the name of Merrie." When there was no answer, she babbled on. "She lived over by Leonard, and this Mr. Kastet worked on a big farm near there."

A long silence on the other end of the line again. "Well, why would you be looking for this man after all these years?" he asked.

Livvie was getting weak in the knees and wished that she could sit down. She took a deep breath and answered, "He may be my father." There was another long silence and then a click.

Livvie waited for sometime and then turned to Stan. "I think he just hung up on me." She was trying hard not to cry, but tears started streaming down her checks. Tears of frustration and humiliation. Stan came to her and took the receiver out of her hands.

"Hello! Hello!" He hung it up and turned to Livvie and took her in his arms. She sobbed with great heaves. He held her for a long time and just rubbed her back until she calmed down.

She finally composed herself and wiped her eyes. "Well, we came all this way to find out nothing!" She almost started crying again.

"Do you think that the man you talked to was Alphonse?"

"I have a feeling that it maybe was."

Stan thought for awhile and then went to search out the hotel clerk. He showed the man the telephone listing and asked him if he would know directions out to the man's place.

"Well," he said, scratching his head, "I think I know the family. You'd drive east until you get to the highway and then turn south. I think you'd go about six miles or so in that direction and the farm is somewhere over there. I'm not exactly sure. You could stop and ask. There's plenty of farm places in that area."

"Thank you," said Stan. He took Livvie's arm and led her to the car. "We'll take a little drive and try to find his place. At least we have to try one more thing before we give up and go home."

Livvie was silent all the way. Maybe this wasn't such a good idea, she was thinking to herself. Her stomach was tied up in knots and she almost felt sick.

"There was the Kastet name on that mailbox," Stan pointed out, "but not the right first name." He kept driving.

"Maybe I'll stop in at this next place and ask directions. He pulled into a farmyard and got out of the car. A woman was coming from the barn. She came over to the car.

"Do you know where we might find the farm of an Alphonse Kastet?"

Livvie could see her pointing further south and giving Stan some directions.

"It's just a little further on down the road," he told Livvie as he started up the car again.

Livvie placed a hand on his arm. "Wait!" she whispered. "I'm so nervous I can hardly think."

Stan took her hand and squeezed it. "You'll be all right, hon. Just take some deep breaths. We came up here to find him and we'll go and see if this is the right man."

Stan drove slowly into the next yard. The mailbox had read 'A. Kastet.' Livvie thought she was going to be sick. She grabbed her hankie to have it ready just in case.

Stan rolled down the window and looked around. A young man was working over by the barn. He saw the car and came toward it cautiously. Perhaps he noticed the North Dakota license plate, thought Stan.

"Can I help you?" he asked. He looked to be about fifteen or sixteen years old.

"We're looking for Alphonse Kastet," Stan told him. "Is he at home?"

"And who are you, might I ask? Are you selling something?"

"No, no, we're not selling anything." Stan tried to laugh. "We just want to talk to him."

"I'll go see if he's around," the boy said, and he started for the house.

Stan and Livvie looked at each other and each took a deep breath. They waited. After about ten minutes, the young boy came back to the car.

"He can't come out now. Maybe you can come back some other time," he told them.

"But we've driven all the way from North Dakota to see him," Stan started to tell him.

"He....ah....can't see you now." The boy looked down at his feet. "Actually, he said to tell you that he doesn't want to see you and not to come back here again."

"Well, all right," said Stan. "I guess we'll just have to go, then."

"Wait!" Livvie cried out. "I want to give him my name and address. In case he would ever want to talk to me."

"OK," mumbled the boy.

Livvie found a piece of paper and hurriedly scribbled her name and address on it. Stan passed it through the window. The boy glanced at it and put it in his pocket and headed back to the barn.

The drive back to North Dakota was pretty quiet. Stan could just feel how disappointed Livvie was. His heart ached for her.

"I'm sorry how it turned out, Livvie," he said to her after many silent miles.

She couldn't trust herself to answer, but Stan could see her mouth quivering.

When they reached home, Livvie asked Stan if he would go and pick up the girls by himself. He could tell his folks how it had turned out. Then she wouldn't have to face them and explain what happened, she thought.

The day after they returned, Carrie and George drove up to see Livvie. They were anxious to hear how the trip had turned out. Merrie, Livvie's real mother, had been there earlier that afternoon.

Livvie explained once again what had transpired. She was exhausted by the time they had left. She went to bed early that evening. She told Stan that she was ready to put this quest behind her and she would never mention it again. She also didn't want to discuss it with anyone else from now on.

Stan feared that his wife would fall into the same depression that had plagued her after the loss of their unborn child. As it turned out, Stan and Livvie would have something else to occupy their minds for quite sometime.

The day after they had returned from Canada, Joe had something to discuss with his son.

"I was going to tell you this last night, Stan, but you looked so down and preoccupied when you came for the girls that I left it until today."

Alarmed, Stan said, "What is it?"

"While you were gone, your mother's Uncle Ole came to see me. He was wondering if we would be interested in buying his farm."

"He wants to sell his farm?" Stan asked.

"Yah, he says he has to quit this year. His health isn't good and he wants to move to town, closer to his daughter. He really would like us to have it. He hasn't mentioned it to anyone else yet."

"How many acres is it?"

"There's three quarters in all. The two quarters around the farmstead and then he owns the quarter a half mile to the northeast."

"Well, what do you think? And how much does he want for it?" Stan asked his father.

"I'm telling you about this now because the other boys already know. I asked them all to be here this morning about nine o'clock and we'll discuss it. Ole would like an answer soon."

"Is Ron coming out from Fargo, too?"

"Yah, I called him the other day and he said he'd get the morning off and come."

Stan looked at his watch. "Just time to get the milking done then."

"I think Marty has already started."

A little after nine, Joe and his four sons were seated around the kitchen table with coffee cups in their hands. It was a Saturday so Allen was home from school. Min sat down with them.

"So, you all know what this is all about," Joe began. "We have to decide if we want to buy Ole's land or not. I talked to Ole again last night and he'd like to know by Monday. It's soon planting time so he needs to know one way or another."

Joe told them the price that Ole wanted for the sale of his land. Marty whistled and Stan looked thoughtful.

"Before you decide," Ron said, "I should tell you that I really don't ever plan to come back to the farm so you will have to decide things with that in mind. I like my job in town too well."

"Is that for sure, son?" asked Joe, seeming surprised at Ron's declaration. I thought that if there was more land, you'd maybe come back and farm someday."

"No, I've given it a lot of thought lately and I'm pretty sure that I'll stay with my mechanics job."

"Well, OK, then," Joe said. "How about you other boys? Any more surprises?"

Marty squirmed and cleared his throat. "Dad, I don't know for sure, but I feel I need to warn you. Jeannie and I may move back into Fargo soon. You know how she dislikes it out here. I guess being a farmer's wife is not for her."

"Well, it's not for everyone," conceded Joe, "but how about you, Marty? Could you be happy in town? What would you do the rest of your life if you didn't farm?"

"I don't know. I guess I'd have to try and find a job that I liked. Jeannie is anxious to get back to work at the hospital."

"Well, I had been thinking that if we bought this farm, maybe you and Jeannie would want to live on it. There's a nice, big house on it. Maybe she'd be happier if she wasn't cramped into such a little house like you are now."

"I don't think she'll change her mind."

"Maybe if you showed her the house," suggested Min.

Marty swallowed hard. "I have to tell you something, but don't ever let on that you know." He paused a moment before going on. "She said she'd leave me if I didn't....move back into Fargo with her." He almost broke down, telling his family this.

"Oh, no, Marty! You can't mean it!" exclaimed his mother.

"I'm afraid so."

"Maybe she was just bluffing," said Ron.

"I don't think so."

Joe got up and paced the kitchen floor. Min got up and got the coffeepot.

"That leaves just Stan and Allan and me," said Joe. "I'd been thinking that we really should accept Ole's offer. It's such good land. Most of it's on a ridge and he's always had good crops on it."

Joe sat down once again.

"Dad, I hate to remind you of this now, but I'd like to go to college next fall," Allan announced. "I like farming but I wouldn't be around much once I start school."

"Whew!" exclaimed Joe. "It seems like maybe we aren't supposed to buy this land, then. It would be too much for just Stan and I to farm."

"If that land is so good and you really want to buy it, maybe we could get rid of some other land that we have, that isn't quite as good," suggested Stan.

"Like what?" asked Marty.

"Well, for instance, the farm I'm living on. That isn't the best land in the world. Some of it's pretty low and in a wet year, we run into trouble."

"That's true," said Joe, thoughtfully.

"You mean we'd sell the bonanza farm land and buy Ole's land?" asked Allan.

"I don't know what we should do," conceded Joe. "Where would you live, then, Stan?"

"Well, I suppose we could move into Ole's house. It's a better house than the one we're living in now."

"But you had plans to tear down the big house there and build a new one," said Min, worry filling her voice at the sudden turn of events.

"We had planned to do that someday, but I'd been actually thinking lately that that would be a big undertaking and a great expense, too."

Joe was writing some figures on a piece of paper and showed it to the rest. "Let's see, if we sold that farm up there for this amount, then we could buy Ole's three quarters."

"If we got a full-time hired hand, maybe we could manage all the farming until Allen comes back to the farm," suggested Stan.

"If he goes off to school, he probably won't be happy to come back to farming," said Ron, looking at his youngest brother. Allan just shrugged.

"He's too young to know what he wants to do yet for sure," said his mother.

"Well, let's think about this until Sunday and then we have to decide," Joe told them. "Stan, why don't you take Livvie over to look at the house.

Ole said he'd be around and we're welcome to stop by."

Later that day, after supper, Stan took Livvie and the two girls out for a drive. They drove over to Ole's farm. Livvie had been very surprised when Stan came home with the news that they might be buying another farm.

"I don't want to move," whined Cheryl. "What would happen to all my kitties?"

Ole graciously showed them the whole house and then asked them to sit and visit a spell. He was a lonely old man, Livvie could see. His wife had died about two years ago and she could tell that the house had been lacking a woman's touch for quite sometime.

When they were driving out of the driveway, Stan turned to Livvie and asked her what she thought.

"Well," she answered slowly, "it is a pretty nice house and plenty big. Just needs a little paint and some fixin' here and there. What do you think?"

"If we decide to buy the farm, I guess I wouldn't mind moving here."

"Are you sure Marty and Jeannie wouldn't want to live here?"

Stan told her what Marty had confided to them that morning.

"She would actually leave him?" she almost shouted.

"He was pretty sure about it. It didn't sound like he would even bring her over here to have a look."

"I can hardly believe that."

That night in bed, Stan and Livvie discussed the pros and cons of moving from their present location.

"Are you sure you don't want to stay here and tear down the big house and rebuild?" Livvie asked her husband.

"I guess I wouldn't feel very badly if we moved. There's something about this farmstead that I never was too crazy about."

"How come you've never said anything before?"

"Well, I thought you really liked it here."

"Well, I guess I would like a place with more trees around it," said Livvie. "Maybe that's what you don't like about this place. It's so open out here."

"That could be," Stan said thoughtfully. He was thinking that if they moved further south, he'd be that much farther from his folks' place. "It wouldn't be quite so handy just to run over to my Dad's place," he told her.

"That's true," said Livvie. "I think that this won't be an easy decision to make and we have to decide so quickly. I think we better pray about it and leave it in God's hands."

CHAPTER 21

On Monday morning, Joe and Stan paid a visit to Ole Peterson. They told him that they had decided to buy his farm. He was very pleased with their decision.

"I really wanted you to have it," he told them. "I know that you are good farmers and will take good care of my land."

The next day, Joe sent off notices to several newspapers, advertising that he had some land for sale. They had decided to try and sell the farm that Stan now lived on.

"I hope we get some responses real soon," said Joe. "Spring planting isn't very far off."

Joe felt that this was a good time to be selling farmland and that they wouldn't have too much trouble finding a buyer. Farm prices were going up and it was a good time for farmers, ever since the war ended.

A week later, Joe received calls from two different parties in response to his ad.

"A guy from Durbin wants to come over and talk with us this afternoon," Joe told Stan.

By the next day, a deal was made and the new owner would soon be planting the next crop on the old bonanza farmland.

Things were happening quickly, and Stan and Joe were busy getting ready for a new planting season, getting the machinery ready and purchasing seed.

"When will we move?" Livvie asked Stan one evening.

"Well, Ole will be having an auction sale the end of June and then we can get in there and see what we need to do to the house before moving in."

"Oh, this will be kind of exciting, won't it?" said Livvie. "A lot of work, too, though."

"We may have to wait until after harvest to actually move, unless we can get everything ready over there before," Stan told her.

Joe said that he thought they should consider getting a full-time hired man now. Marty and Jeannie were going to be moving the end of April so Marty would no longer be helping.

He and Jeannie had found an apartment in Fargo and Jeannie got a job at the hospital where she used to work.

"So, Marty, what are you going to be doing when you move to Fargo?" Stan asked his older brother.

"I'm not sure yet, but Jeannie's brother, Ralph, works for an insurance company and he said that they need another man so I may apply for that."

"You'd be selling insurance?" asked Stan, incredulous.

"Well, that wouldn't be the worst thing in the world," answered Marty, defensively. "Ralph says there's good profit in it and I like to talk to people so he thinks I'd be good at it."

Stan had his doubts but didn't say anything further.

The Murphys were able to start planting the crops the first of April. Joe put Stan in charge of the new land near Kindred. Stan was excited to be putting in the crop there. The soil worked up so nicely, he told his father.

They had hired a man from over by Christine, Rudy Anderson, to help them do the farming. He was a small man, about 50 years old and had many years of farm work under his belt. He moved into the little house vacated by Marty and Jeannie. He seemed pleased as punch to have a little house to live in. He was used to bunkhouses or the upstairs bedroom of his employer, or even the hayloft for a summer job.

Rudy was a pleasant fellow and a good worker and the family took to him immediately. He was especially good with children and he adored Stan's little girls. They were calling him Uncle Rudy after only a short while.

In May, Allan graduated from high school. He wanted to go on to college in the fall. "Maybe I'll wait until winter quarter if you need me to help with the fall work," he told his father.

"I don't see why he feels the need to go to college if he's just planning to farm," grumbled Joe to his wife one evening, as the two were getting ready for bed.

"Well, now, don't discourage him," said Min. "If he wants to go to college, let him try it. Maybe he won't like it and that will be that."

The day that Marty and Jeannie moved, it was an unusually warm day for the end of April. Min brought cold glasses of nectar over to the little house. Stan and Joe were helping Marty load what little furniture the young couple had accumulated.

Jeannie and Min were alone in the house. "I'm sorry, Min, that it didn't work out for us out here. I want to thank you for always being so nice to me."

"Well, you're my daughter-in-law," answered Min.

"I'm sure you and Joe are disappointed that Marty isn't staying on the farm."

"I guess we are, in a way," Min admitted, "but I guess he has to do what he thinks is best for the both of you."

"And then there's Ron, who's planning to stay in Fargo, too," said Jeannie.

"Yes, I sure didn't think it would turn out this way, but, you know, the war came and changed many things," said Min sadly.

"Yes, I guess it did."

Marty interrupted them just then. "Hey, we're all loaded and ready, so let's be on our way."

Min hugged first her son, and then his wife. "I'll miss you both, you know. It won't seem the same without the two of you around." She wiped a tear beginning to form.

"I'll miss you too, Mom," said Marty. He hugged her extra long and she could tell that he really meant it. "I'll probably be home often."

Joe and Stan drove the pickup, and Marty and Jeannie were to follow in their car.

Min waved until they were out of sight.

The whole Murphy family attended the auction sale on Ole's farm the end of June. There was a very large crowd, some were buyers and some just neighbors coming to show support at such a time. Ole's two daughters had spent many hours getting things moved out of the house for the sale.

"Yah, I guess my wife and I accumulated a lot of things over the past fifty years!" he told everyone. "My girls have worked their fool heads off this past week!"

Livvie and Carrie were able to go into the now empty house and have a good look around. They checked each room carefully.

"As for the upstairs," Livvie told Stan later, "there are cracks in the ceilings in two of the bedrooms and they all will need painting, of course."

"It would be nice to put in a bathroom upstairs, too," said Stan.

"We'd have to take part of a bedroom, then, I suppose," Livvie said slowly.

"How about the downstairs?" asked Stan. "I only took a quick look at each room."

"Just a good coat of paint for now, except the kitchen," answered Livvie. "I'd really like some new cupboards. The pantry is kind of in bad shape, I noticed."

"Eventually we'll have to reshingle the roof and paint the outside," said Stan. "Maybe next year."

The month of July, Livvie, Carrie and Min spent many hours over at the new house, painting every room. Stan had asked Karl to come over and do the ceiling repair and to put in a bathroom. The biggest bedroom was chosen for this. The other half of that room Livvie would use as her sewing room. That still left three good-sized rooms upstairs.

The remodeling of the kitchen would have to wait until another year, Stan had told Livvie. She was disappointed but made the best of the situation. A coat of paint was put over the old cupboards to brighten them up a bit. She put colorful shelf paper on the shelves in the pantry and that would do for now, she'd told herself.

The harvest went smoothly. Ron came home on the weekends to help and so did Marty once or twice.

"So, Marty, how is the insurance business going so far?" Stan asked his brother when they were eating a meal brought out to the field by their mother one Saturday.

"Well, you know, it's kind of hard to get into it at first, but I actually like it. I think I'll do all right," he answered. "Jeannie's brother has been doing extremely well. He and his wife were able to buy a new house this year."

"Does Jeannie seem happier now that she's back in Fargo?" asked Min.

"Oh, yes, she certainly is happier. She's seeing more of her parents now, too."

"So they're finally accepting you now?" asked Min.

"Well, it isn't that they didn't like me before. It's just that they were so disappointed that Jeannie got married so quickly and to someone outside her faith," explained Marty.

"So what are you two doing about church, then?" asked Min.

"Jeannie goes to her church and I go occasionally to a Lutheran church close by."

"Well, you should try and go regularly," advised Min.

"It's not much fun going alone."

Min felt like saying that he should have thought of that before he married but she wisely held her tongue.

By the middle of August, harvest was completed and Stan and Livvie prepared to make the big move. They had lots of help. Karl and his two new stepsons came and Ron came out from Fargo to help, too. Carrie took care of the two girls to keep them out of the way and George brought his truck up to help load furniture. Min made food to feed the hungry workers.

After two days, everything was moved and put into place in their new home. Min and Carrie helped make up the beds, and Stan, Livvie and the girls slept there for the first time.

"It smells paint in here!" complained Cheryl, unable to get to sleep that first night.

Livvie got up and opened her daughter's window wider and told her to keep the door open. Each girl had her own room for the first time. Linda was afraid to sleep alone, so the next morning, Livvie found her snuggled up against her older sister.

In September, Cheryl would be going to school in Kindred. She was a little worried about going to such a big school, so Carrie suggested that Livvie take her over to Carl and Beatrice's and let her play with their daughter, Elaine, who would be in the same grade as Cheryl. They played together nicely and this seemed to help calm Cheryl's first-day-of-school anxiety.

Carrie and George enjoyed having Livvie and Stan living so much closer. They drove over there every once in awhile just for short visits. About a week after school started, when George and Carrie had driven over, George asked Cheryl how she liked her new school.

"It's so big! It's three stories high," she said of the big, brick building.

"And have you made lots of new friends?" Carrie asked.

"Oh, yes! There's so many girls in my class," Cheryl told them.

"And what are some of their names, then?" asked her grandpa.

She looked thoughtful as she answered slowly. "There's Elaine, Gloria, Carol, Carolyn, LaVonne, and two Sharons."

"Two Sharons!" exclaimed George, playfully. "My, my."

"What's your teacher's name?"

"It's Miss Rise and she's real pretty!"

"She really is enjoying school this year," said Livvie. "At least she has girls in her class."

"Is Stan's brother, Allan, going off to college soon?" asked George.

"No, he's going to wait until winter quarter," answered Livvie. "He's needed on the farm to help with all the fall plowing."

The fall turned out to be a wet one so the farm work took much longer than usual. In fact, it was almost Thanksgiving before the plows were finally put away.

On Thanksgiving Day, Min had a house full of family. Marty and Jeannie came out for the first time since their move, and Ron brought Rosie over for dinner, too.

"Where's Kenny?" joked Joe. One usually didn't see Ron and Rosie without their friend, Kenny, too.

"He's home with his father. His sister is home for a couple days," answered Ron.

"How's he doing now?" asked Marty, helping himself to another drumstick.

"It seems every time I see him, he's changed," said Ron.

"How so?" asked Jeannie.

"Well, he seems to be getting more and more....down in the dumps. He isn't interested in anything anymore, and it's like he's living in a....a shell," Ron tried to explain.

"That's too bad," commented Marty. "He was always such a fun person, so happy-go-lucky."

"Yah, I don't know what's going to become of him," said Ron. "I really worry about him. I think his dad does, too."

"You know, he's not supposed to drive, but a couple of times lately, I've seen him come by here real slow in his pickup," commented Joe.

"Yah, well, he could probably drive over here in his sleep!" said Marty dryly.

"Or else his pickup could almost drive over here by itself!" joked Allan.

"Ron and I are going to stop by and see him on our way back to Fargo tonight," said Rosie.

"He'll appreciate that, I'm sure," said Min.

The subject finally turned to politics. The presidential election earlier that month had been an interesting one. Truman, who was not expected to win a full term as president, ran a good campaign and beat Thomas Dewey.

"How about that Chicago newspaper that declared Dewey a winner!" exclaimed Marty. "Wasn't that something?"

"Yah, I'm sure they're still eating crow over that blunder," agreed Ron.

"I was hoping that Eisenhower would have run for president," said Joe, "I would have voted for him."

"He's been pretty well liked ever since the war," said Jeannie. "I think he could win if he runs next time."

"That could be," concurred Joe. "He doesn't seem to want to have anything to do with being a candidate, though."

Winter finally arrived early in December and with it came lots of snow. Livvie and Stan were over at George and Carrie's for Christmas Eve, and Livvie had an announcement to make.

"I have some good news for everyone," she said.

"You're going to have a baby," declared Freddie.

"How did you know?" asked Livvie, surprised.

"I didn't, but I'm a good guesser," laughed her brother.

"Yes, that's our good news!" she exclaimed.

Oh, Livvie, that's wonderful," cried Carrie, as she stood up to give her daughter a hug. "When is the blessed event to take place?"

"Mid-July," she replied. "Or maybe a little earlier."

"Maybe a Fourth of July baby!" exclaimed Lenora.

"Maybe," said Livvie, with a radiant smile.

"I hope everything goes all right this time," Carrie said to George later that evening, after everyone had left.

"Oh, I'm sure it will, my dear. I'm sure it will."

On New Years Eve, Ron had his own announcement to make. He had come out earlier that afternoon to spend the weekend at home, as New Year's Day fell on Sunday.

"As you probably have guessed," Ron began, "Rosie and I have become more than just good friends." He let that sink in before going on. When no one said anything, he told them, "I'm going to ask her to marry me."

"Really?" asked Min, a little flustered. "I guess I didn't realize that things were....that way with the two of you."

"How could you not see that, Mom?" asked Allan. "Even I knew what was going on."

"Well, I don't know, I guess I should have seen it coming."

"When are you going to pop the question?" asked Allan.

"Tonight," replied Ron. "We're going to that dance in Horace. I have the ring right here." He pulled out a little box from his pocket and opened it.

"Wow!" exclaimed Allan. "I bet that cost a pretty penny!"

"Well, I guess it did at that," laughed Ron, as he gave his younger brother a friendly punch on the shoulder.

"Maybe she'll say no," teased Allan.

"Not after she sees that ring!" laughed Ron. "I better get upstairs and start getting ready. This is an important night, you know. I'm going to wear my new sweater that Rosie gave me for Christmas." With that, he left the room and headed up the stairs, taking two at a time.

Min joined Joe at the kitchen table and the two looked at each other. Min smiled. "I guess he couldn't have done any better. Rosie's a wonderful girl."

"Did you ever think that she'd one day be your daughter-in-law?" asked Joe, taking the last sip of coffee from his cup.

"No, I didn't, really. She's been like a part of our family since she and Ron were babies. Almost like a sister."

"Well, she won't be like a sister any longer."

On New Year's Day morning, Min was up early. She knew, however, that she'd have to wait quite awhile before Ron got up.

"I'm anxious to hear how the proposal went last night," she told Joe.

"You don't think that she'd turn him down now, do you?"

"Oh, I'm sure not," she laughed.

"Well, for someone who didn't know what was going on under her very nose, you're pretty sure of yourself."

It was almost noon before Ron made his appearance downstairs.

"Finally!" exclaimed Allan. "We've been waiting for the big news. Did she turn you down?"

"Oh, no, little brother," laughed Ron. "She told me that she'd been actually waiting for me to ask her."

"I can't believe that," joked Allan.

When Ron came into the kitchen, Min turned and said, "I just heard what you told Allan. Congratulations to you!" She wiped her hands on a towel and came and gave her son a big hug.

Ron was beaming, and grinning from ear to ear. "Yep, I'm so happy I could just bust!"

"Tell us how you went about it," suggested Allan.

"Well, we were dancing and then I suggested we go out in the car for awhile to cool off. We were sitting there listening to the music from the hall and I took her hand and asked her if she'd like me to put a ring on that finger."

"You didn't!" said Allan. "How drippy!"

"She looked at me but didn't say anything at first. I pulled out the little box and her eyes got big as saucers. I took it and slipped it on her finger and it just fit."

"Hadn't she said anything yet?" asked Allan, almost sitting on the edge of his chair.

"She was speechless, for a change!" replied Ron, laughing. "Finally she looked at me and said, 'I take it that this is a proposal?' "

"I nodded and she shrieked and hugged me and said, yes, she'd marry me and why did it take so long for me to ask her!"

"Women!" said Allan, getting to his feet now and shaking his head. "Why would anyone be so excited to marry you?" he teased.

"Why, Allan!" his mother said. "I think Rosie is a very lucky girl to get a fine, young man like Ron."

"I'm just teasing, Mom."

"I'm going to bring her over here this afternoon for awhile before we go back to Fargo."

"Oh, good. Then I can congratulate her, too," said Min.

That afternoon, before Ron left to go and pick up Rosie, Min said to him, "I suppose you'll be stopping over at Kenny's, too, to share the good news with him."

Ron hesitated a brief moment before answering. "Yes, I guess we should do that."

Later in the afternoon, Magda, Art and Grandpa Ivar came over to visit Joe and Min. Min decided that she wouldn't say anything about the engagement, but she'd let Ron and Rosie tell the news themselves.

They were all playing cards at the kitchen table when the young couple came in the back door. "So, what are you playing?" asked Ron, nonchalantly, as they took off their wraps.

"We've got a good game of Rook going here," said Joe. "The men are beating the women something awful.

"Oh, that's not true!" exclaimed Magda. "Who won the first game?"

"That was just a practice game," laughed Joe.

Magda looked up at the young couple standing beside the table. "Well, Ronald, you look like a cat who's just swallowed a bird!"

Ron and Rosie started laughing and Min told Ron that he'd better tell his aunt the good news so she could be the first to hear it.

"Aunt Maggie," he started, "I have an important announcement to make. Rosie and I are engaged!"

"Well, it's about time, I must say," sputtered Maggie. "I had a feeling that this would be happening sometime."

"You did?" asked Min.

"Well, of course. Couldn't you see that the two of them were in love?" Everyone laughed at the blushing couple.

"Here, sit down and we'll get a game of Rummy going. Then we can all play," said Joe.

"Ivar and Allan," Joe called into the living room, "why don't you come in here and play with us?" The two had been playing Parcheesi.

While everyone was getting settled, Min said that she would get up and start supper.

"Did you stop by Kenny's and tell him?" asked Allan.

Ron and Rosie looked at each other. "Yah, we did," Ron said slowly.

"I imagine he was excited for you," stated Magda.

"Well, I don't know if he was or not," said Ron. "He didn't say much of anything. After talking with his father for awhile, we finally excused ourselves and left."

"That's kind of strange, isn't it?" asked Min, pausing in her task of buttering some buns.

"I guess it's not so strange, really. Kenny's not been himself for a long time now. His father is worried about him, he told me," related Joe.

After a couple games of Rummy, Min had supper ready to put on the table. Magda got up to help her.

"Oh, this looks mighty good!" exclaimed Art, as he watched plate after plate being set on the table. There were two kinds of sandwiches, two kinds of salads, a variety of pickles, a layer cake, and a plate of leftover Christmas goodies.

When the meal was over, Ron and Rosie excused themselves and said that they needed to get back to Fargo. Min hugged Rosie and said, "I'm so happy for you and Ron. I'll love having you in the family."

"Thank you, Min. Of course, I've always felt a part of this family, you know."

After they left, Magda said, "When those two were just young kids, I always thought that maybe this would happen."

"So, Allan, how is school going for you at the AC, then?" Ivar asked his grandson.

"Well, I've only been going for a few weeks now, but I think I'm going to like it a lot. I keep thinking, though, what a long road I have ahead of me to finish, especially if I don't attend every quarter."

"Time goes fast," Min reminded her son. "Before you know it, you'll be done."

"Yes, time surely does go fast, doesn't it?" mused Magda. "Can you believe that it's eight years now since Pearl Harbor? And over three years since the war ended."

"Well, today is the first day of 1949." Joe raised his coffee cup and said, "Happy New Year!" The others picked up their cups and glasses and joined him in a toast.

CHAPTER 22

"The roads are so muddy, I don't know how we're going to make it to church tomorrow for Easter Sunday services!" complained Min.

"Well, we'll get there somehow," Joe said calmly. "Is Ron coming out?"

"Yah, he said he'd be here this afternoon," Min answered. "I sure hope it doesn't rain anymore."

"I think it's over for now. It looked all clear in the west when I came in."

Min was busy preparing food for the next day. She was having the whole family for dinner. She had just finished putting the white frosting on a cake when Ron came in the yard.

"Oh, Ron's here now," she called to Joe.

"Boy, the roads are really slippery around here!" Ron said, as he came in the back door. "You got more rain then we did in Fargo, I believe."

"It kept on all of yesterday and into last night," Joe told him.

"Are Marty and Jeannie coming out tomorrow?" asked Ron, taking a lick of leftover frosting from the bowl.

"Yes, they'll be here and so will Stan's and Art and Magda, and Grandpa."

"Oh, good, I'll get to see everybody at one time. Then I can make my big announcement."

"And what's that?" Min asked, as she whirled around to face her son.

He laughed. "Oh, just that Rosie and I have set our wedding date."

"Well, you better tell me right now, young man, and not make me wait until tomorrow!" she said sternly.

He laughed again. "We're going to get married June 28th. Rosie graduates from nurses' training the first part of June, so we thought that would be a good time."

"Oh, how exciting!" exclaimed Min. "A wedding in the family to plan for!"

Easter Sunday turned out to be a nice, sunny day. The roads had dried up somewhat.

"Pastor Turmo certainly gave a wonderful sermon today, I thought," Min remarked to her family, as they were all seated around the big table. She was bringing the platter of ham to be passed around for the second time.

"This meal is so delicious!" exclaimed Jeannie. "I wonder if I'll ever learn to cook like you, Min."

Min looked at Marty, but neither one said anything.

"Kenny and his dad weren't in church today, were they?" asked Magda.

"Perhaps they went to visit Kenny's sister in Horace," remarked Art.

"No, I don't think so. I saw both their vehicles in the yard as we went by," Joe said.

Ron cleared his throat and clinked his glass for attention. "The wedding date has been set," he announced. "Mark June 28th on your calendars."

"Oh, wonderful!" said Magda.

"Hurrah!" shouted Allan.

"And where is Rosie, by the way?" asked Art.

"Her family was getting together at her grandmother's."

Min got up to get the dessert ready. "We have two kinds of pie," she announced. "Lemon meringue and apple."

"I'll want one of each, please," joked Marty. Jeannie nudged him in the ribs.

Magda got up and helped Min serve the pie and pass around the coffee.

"Livvie," Ron said, "we were wondering if Linda could be our flower girl."

"Oh, my! That would be fun, wouldn't it?" Livvie looked at her youngest daughter. Linda's eyes got big as saucers.

"What would I have to do?" she asked shyly.

"Just wear a pretty dress and carry a basket of flower petals down the aisle," Magda told her.

Cheryl was looking a little put out for not being asked. "And you, Cheryl," said Ron, "being you're too old to be a flower girl, we want you to pass out favors. Would you like to do that?"

She just shrugged and looked at her mother. "I'm sure she'll be glad to do that," Livvie told Ron.

After dinner, the women cleaned up the kitchen and the men went into the living room to visit. Grandpa Ivar was anxious to go home and take his usual nap, so Magda and Art soon left with him.

"We have to go, too, I guess," said Marty after awhile. "We may stop in at Jeannie's folks' for a bit.

Later in the afternoon, as Min was putting things away in the kitchen, she happened to glance out the window. There she saw Kenny's pickup parked at the end of the sidewalk. Upon looking more closely, she could see that the door was open and he was just sitting there.

Feeling a bit uneasy, she hurried into the living room and shook Joe awake.

"Kenny's out here in the yard. Maybe he wants to see Ron."

"Is he upstairs?" asked Joe.

"Yes, I think he went up there to take a nap, too."

"Ron?" she called up the stairway. "Are you awake? I think you have company."

Joe went to the window and took a look outside. Kenny was standing outside the cab now and Joe could see that he was holding something. It was a gun.

Ron came into the kitchen and poured himself a glass of water as he looked outside.

Joe turned to his son. "Why would Kenny be carrying a gun?"

"A gun?" Ron looked out the window once again.

"You're right. That looks like his hunting rifle. What in the world would he be hunting now?"

Ron grabbed his jacket and headed outside. Joe followed suit. Ron reached his friend and greeted him. Kenny didn't say anything at first.

"What are you hunting today, Kenny?" asked Ron. He knew that his friend shouldn't be hunting anything at all, being he couldn't see very well.

Kenny stepped right up to Ron, until the two were almost touching noses. "I'm hunting you, Ron!" he spit out. Then he shoved his gun into Ron's stomach and pushed him backwards.

"What the heck are you doing, Kenny?" Ron shouted at his friend.

Joe came over to see what was happening. He saw the gun pointed right into his son's stomach. "Kenny! What do you think you're doing?" He grabbed the gun and pointed it downward.

Kenny stepped back and almost stumbled. "I wanted to have a little talk with Ron here," he said in a menacing way. "I thought he was my friend, but friends don't steal another guy's girl."

"What are you talking about, Kenny?"

"I'm talking about Rosie!" he shouted. "My girl, Rosie. You're taking her away from me and I'm not going to stand for it." He raised his gun and pointed it at Ron once again.

"Now, Kenny," soothed Joe, "let's talk about this in a calm fashion. Put down that gun. It might accidentally go off, and you wouldn't want that, would you?"

"Maybe I would, Mr. Murphy." Kenny continued to point the gun at Ron.

"Kenny, listen to me," said Ron. "I'm not stealing your girl. Rosie is not your girl. Rosie was never your girl!"

"I've thought of her as my girl since we were little kids, Ron. Didn't you know that?" Kenny kept moving closer to Ron as he spoke.

Ron, feeling somewhat panicky now, suddenly grabbed the gun and got it away from Kenny. He threw it on the ground and Joe ran and picked it up. He checked to see if it was actually loaded. It was!

"How could you not see that Rosie was my girl, Ron? We were always together."

"Kenny, the three of us were always together, but only as good friends."

"I always thought that someday, she and I would get married. I was waiting for her to get done with her nurses' training. But, of course she probably wouldn't want a blind man like me." His shoulders started to shake and he began to sob.

"I've lost my sight, I've lost my girl, so what is there left for me now? Huh, Ron? What's left for me now that you took everything away from me?"

"How did I take everything away from you, Kenny? I didn't take your sight away. That was an accident."

"Yes, but you were always the golden boy, the handsome one, the one that nothing bad ever happened to. So I had to be the one who was injured. And you got the girl in the end, didn't you? You dirty bastard!" He started for Ron's throat, but Joe and Ron were able to subdue him. He was fighting mad, so he was hard to control.

Just then, a car came racing into the yard. Joe could see that it was Kenny's father, Jake. He jumped out of the car before it even came to a full stop.

"Kenny, what's going on here?" he barked at his son, as he saw both Joe and Ron holding onto him.

"He threatened Ron with a gun, Jake. He's accusing Ron of stealing his girl."

"Oh, for heaven's sake, Kenny, are you crazy?" ranted his father.

"Yah, I probably am!" Kenny started to sob again. His father took him into his arms and held him. They both were crying now. Jake raised his head and looked at Joe. "I'm sorry this had to happen. Ron, I'm so sorry."

Joe and Ron just stood there, not knowing what to say. Min came running outside. She stood surveying the scene and didn't say anything.

Jake finally got Kenny to get into the pickup and he shut the door, after taking the keys away from his son.

He shook his head. "I don't know what to say. I'm so sorry for what happened. Kenny needs help and I don't know what to do." He started to sob again. "My only son, and this had to happen to him. That accident he had on that ship. It took more than his eyesight. It took away the person he used to be."

"Jake, do you want help getting him home?" asked Joe, kindly.

"I suppose I could use some help. Maybe he'll settle down now, I don't know."

Jake opened the pickup door again and told Kenny to slide over. "I'll drive him home in this and maybe someone can bring my car home later."

"Yes, we'll do that, Jake," said Joe. "You get him home and settled."

They watched the pickup drive slowly out of the yard. Ron let out a deep breath and finally broke down himself. "I thought I was going to be shot right in the stomach! I figured it was all over for me."

The three walked slowly back to the house. Ron plunked down on a chair by the table without taking off his coat. "Look how my hands are shaking! I was really scared out there!"

"I'll bet you were!" exclaimed his mother. "I was scared just watching the three of you through the window. I figured I better call Jake."

"I'm glad you did, Mom. I don't know what we would have done with him."

"If Jake hadn't been home, my next thought was to call the sheriff."

"The sheriff?" said Ron.

"Well, he was threatening to shoot you, son," said Joe. "I guess actually we should be reporting this incident."

"This is my friend, Kenny, we're talking about."

"I know, but he wasn't in his right mind today, that's for sure," said Joe.

"Poor Kenny, I wonder what got into him," said Min.

"I don't know, but he definitely needs some medical help, that's for sure," remarked Ron.

"Well, let's get Jake's car back over there and then we can see how things are going," suggested Joe after awhile.

I'll get my suitcase and then I need to get over to Rosie's and pick her up and head back to Fargo."

"What will Rosie think when you tell her about this, I wonder?" Min asked her son.

He just shook his head. "She won't believe it, I know that!"

The next evening, as Joe and Min were finishing up their supper, the telephone rang. It was Jake. He talked to Joe for a few minutes. After hanging up, Joe told Min about the conversation.

"Well, Jake took Kenny into Fargo to the doctor this morning. They took him away to the Jamestown State Hospital."

"Oh, no!" Min gasped. "Not to Jamestown!"

"Yes. The doctor said that he was a very disturbed young man and needed to be put into treatment for awhile. Jake is pretty broken up about it."

"Well, I imagine he would be, but then something had to be done. Jake even said so himself."

"I'm going to call Ron and tell him," said Joe. "He wanted to know right away if we heard something."

"Here, I'll find his number for you." Min found her address book and Joe rang the operator.

Ron's landlady answered. "Ron's not home right now," she said. "I'll tell him to give you a call as soon as he gets home."

Joe related this news to Min.

"All right. I'll start the dishes," Min said, as she finished clearing the table. "Do you think you should go over and check on Jake? Maybe he needs someone to talk to."

"Maybe I should do that." Joe headed for his jacket and the back door.

Later that evening, after Joe returned home, the telephone rang. It was Ron, and Joe told him what had happened to his friend that day.

"Ron feels just terrible about all this," Joe told Min after hanging up. "He just hopes that this treatment works. He wants the old Kenny back again, he kept saying."

"That terrible war!" exclaimed Min. "It affected so many lives. There's

Kenny and his father. Ron and Rosie. And Marty. Marty will never be the same man he was before he went in either. If he hadn't had those terrible experiences over there, he probably wouldn't have...." Here Min stopped and let her voice trail off.

She didn't want to voice what she really felt. That perhaps Marty wouldn't have married in such haste if he hadn't gone through what he had during the war. She didn't want to say anything against her daughter-in-law, but she felt that he would have probably married someone else, someone more suited to him.

"The war's been over for four years now but we're still feeling the effects of it." She just shook her head slowly, back and forth.

"Yah, it changed a lot of things, that's for sure," agreed Joe. He was thoughtful for some time.

"Well, I guess I'll go up and get ready for bed," announced Min. "You coming?"

"Yah, I'll be up in a little while. I'll check the furnace first."

One morning, over at the Johnson farm, the Farmer's Union Oil truck came into the yard. George and Carrie were still eating their breakfast.

"Oh, that's Carl already. I called there yesterday and ordered some fuel oil."

"Well, tell him to come in for a cup of coffee when he gets ready," Carrie told her husband.

About a half an hour later, George and Carl came into the kitchen. "How about that coffee now, Carrie?" called George to his wife.

"Yah, I've got some ready. Hello, Carl," she said, indicating that he should have a chair by the kitchen table.

"I should take these boots off first," Carl told her.

"Oh, no. This floor needs washing anyway. You're all right."

The men sat down and Carrie came with three cups and the coffee pot. "So, how is Beatrice? And the kids?"

"They're just fine. Did you hear the big news?" Carl asked her.

"No, what?"

"We're going to buy the drug store in Kindred. Beatrice wants to operate that and I'll keep on at Farmer's Union."

"You don't say!" exclaimed Carrie. "What a surprise. I hadn't heard anything about that."

"Well, it just happened a few days ago. We'll take over next month. The Haugens were anxious to get out of the business, I guess. We thought it would be a good thing. Beatrice is real excited about it."

"So she'll be running the drug store," mused Carrie, trying to get used to the idea.

"We'll have to hire some help, I suppose," Carl told them. "Maybe eventually we'll move into the upstairs apartment."

"Oh, really? How much room is up there, then?" asked George.

"Only two bedrooms, a kitchen, living room and dining room. No bathroom."

"Well, I suppose you could make do with that, couldn't you?"

"Donnie will be a junior next year so he'll be gone in another two years," said Carl. "I guess we could make it work. We'll see."

When Carl left, Carrie could hardly wait to get to the phone and call some people. First she called over to Freddie's. Lenora answered. Carrie asked her if she had heard that the Ulnesses were going to be running the drug store.

"Why, yes, Freddie just came home with that news last night," Lenora told her.

Next Carrie called Livvie and told her about it. "Have you talked to Beatrice about it yet?" asked Livvie.

"No, but I may have to call her sometime today."

"Will you have time to come over and help me sew Linda's flower girl dress sometime soon?" Livvie asked her mother.

"I guess I could come tomorrow afternoon. Would that work for you?"

The next day, Carrie went over to Livvie's to help her sew. Livvie had picked up a pattern and some white dotted-Swiss fabric at Larsen's Store in Kindred. She also picked out material and a pattern for Cheryl.

"She wants a new dress, too," Livvie told her mother, "so I picked up this pretty pink."

"Yes, that is very pretty. It will make a cute dress."

"I cleared the dining-room table off and Stan put in the extra leaves at noon so we can use that to do our cutting."

Linda was excited when she saw them unfolding the white material for her dress.

The two women cut out both dresses and started sewing on the white one. Then Stan came home with Cheryl. He had picked her up after school.

"Do you want to stay and have supper with us?" Livvie asked her mother. "We could call and tell Dad to join us."

"Well, I don't know," said Carrie, slowly.

"I've got cold roast to make sandwiches and lots of soup left over from yesterday to warm up."

"I'll give your father a call and see what he thinks," said Carrie, heading for the telephone.

After she'd talked to her husband, she turned and said, "He says that he'll come."

"Oh, good, then we can keep on sewing. It will be good to get this project done. I've had the material for about a month now but never got around to it. I don't move very fast nowadays!" she laughed.

Livvie was in the seventh month of her pregnancy and everything seemed to be going fine.

"I was just thinking how very big I'll be by the time of the wedding. That will only be a couple weeks from my due date."

"You seem to be quite a bit bigger this time than you were with the girls," remarked Carrie.

"Perhaps it will be a big boy!" stated Livvie.

"Maybe it will be at that," agreed Carrie.

Joe and Min attended Rosie's graduation from nursing school in early June. It was an impressive ceremony, all those young women in their crisp, white uniforms. Rosie looked excited and happy.

Three weeks later, family, friends and other relatives gathered at the St. John's Church for Ron and Rosie's wedding. Little Linda took her job as flower girl very seriously, setting the rose petals down on the aisle cloth very deliberately.

"I only wish Kenny could have been here," Ron said to his mother after the ceremony. Kenny would have been Ron's best man for sure, but it was not to be. Allan filled that spot. Rosie's sister, Janet, was the maid of honor.

After a reception in the church basement, the happy couple went out to find that their car had been elaborately decorated with toilet paper and tin cans and such. Rice was thrown on them by the bystanders and Rosie threw her bouquet, which was caught by her sister.

On the way home from the church that night, Min said to Joe, "Well, now we have another exciting event to look forward to with the new baby coming in a couple weeks."

They didn't have to wait the full two weeks. On the Fourth of July, Livvie woke up with a backache that plagued her all that day. She was so uncomfortable and had been for the last month.

"This must be a very large baby," she told Stan.

That night as she lay in bed, she fought back tears. Tears from the frustration of this long wait. "I can't take it much longer, Lord," she prayed softly. Stan was asleep beside her.

A short while later, as she lay there still awake, she thought she felt a small contraction. She waited awhile longer and there was another one. "Oh, thank you, Lord!" she exclaimed. She lay there quietly so as not to awake her husband too soon.

Finally, as the clock said 5:30, and the contractions were getting a little stronger, she woke her husband. "Stan! Stan!" she shook him gently. "I think it's time."

"Time for what?" he asked groggily. "Time to get up?"

"Time for the baby, you sleepyhead!" she laughed.

"What?" Stan was in a standing position in an instant. He looked around for his pants. "So we need to go right now?" he asked.

"Well, I think we can wait awhile. You can have breakfast while I call Mom and get my suitcase packed."

"You hadn't packed your suitcase yet?" he asked.

"No, but it won't take me long. I know what I'm going to put in it. Why don't you start the coffee?" she suggested to her husband, as he headed for the stairs. "I don't feel like eating but I need a little coffee before we go."

She and Stan were ready and waiting when Carrie and George came in the yard. "Oh, good, they're here," said Stan, looking out the window.

"We'll just let the girls sleep," Livvie told her mother as she met her at the door.

"That's all right," said Carrie. "Well, good luck to you, then," she said as she hugged her daughter. Stan drove the car up to the end of the driveway and away they went.

CHAPTER 23

"It's a boy!" announced Stan excitedly over the telephone, as he called his parents to relate the good news to them.

"Oh, how wonderful!" exclaimed his mother. "And how is Livvie?"

"She's fine and very relieved that it's over. It was quite a hard labor. The baby was so big. He was over 10 pounds!"

"Oh, my! That is a good size," said Min. "What are you going to name him?"

"We think it will be Robert, but it's not for sure yet. Well, I better call Livvie's folks now. Talk to you later."

"Do you want me to call them for you?"

"Oh, no! I want to tell them myself."

"OK. And congratulations to both of you," Min told him before he hung up.

Carrie and George received the news with great excitement. They called Freddie and Lenora right away.

"Too bad it wasn't born a day earlier. It would have been a little firecracker!" joked Freddie.

"Well, if Livvie had had her way, it would have been born a couple weeks ago!"

The new baby, named Robert Stanley, came home a week after his birth and was baptized three weeks after that.

Stan and Livvie had joined Norman Lutheran Church shortly after their move. "We live just two miles from Norman, so we thought it made good sense to switch churches," Stan had told his parents. The pastor was the same, as he served those two churches plus one more to the west.

After the baptismal service, Livvie and Stan had their parents over for dinner, and also Pastor Turmo and his wife. Carrie and Min had helped prepare some of the food, as Livvie still tired easily.

"So, how do you like your new home?" Mrs. Turmo asked Livvie at the dinner table.

"Oh, I like it very much! The house, the yard. I love living here!"

In the afternoon, other members of the family dropped by. Ron and Rosie, Marty and Jeannie all came out from Fargo. Freddie and Lenora and their kids stopped by and Art and Magda came and brought the new baby's great-grandpa, Ivar. Even Rudy, the hired man, came over for awhile.

"How lucky you are, Livvie," remarked Jeannie, as she held the new baby. "You have three beautiful children. We've been trying to have a baby for quite some time now."

"Oh, I hope you have one soon, Jeannie," said Livvie. "It must be terrible wanting to have a baby so badly and it doesn't happen."

"Yes, it is really hard, especially for me."

"Doesn't Marty want one?"

"Oh, yes, he certainly does. And I think he'll make such a good daddy."

"Oh, I know he will. He's always been so good with our kids."

The men were gathered out on the front porch, enjoying the nice afternoon.

"Marty," said his Uncle Art, "tell us about the insurance business. How is it going for you?"

"It's going good now," he answered. "Very good, in fact. I like it and I've been able to pick up many new clients this past year."

"That's good. I'm glad you found something you like. Do you miss farming at all?"

Marty glanced into the kitchen to see if his wife was listening. "Well, I do miss it sometimes," he said softly. "I miss being out in the country, but I'm adjusting just fine to city life."

"I hear you have a nice house there in Fargo," said George.

"Yes, we like it. It has a nice, big backyard so I put in a garden this year. That's the farmer in me, I guess," he laughed.

"Ron, what do you hear about Kenny?" asked George. "Is he still in Jamestown?"

"Yes, he's still there. I talked to Jake the other night. He calls me once in awhile. He's pretty lonesome now without Kenny around."

"Has he been there to see him since he was committed?"

"He said he'd been there only once but was going again next week. They wouldn't let him come to visit for the first several weeks."

"No, I suppose not."

"As far as Kenny's actual condition, I just don't know," said Ron. "It will take some time, I guess."

"I thought maybe Karl and Dorothy would be here today," said Marty, changing the subject.

"We invited them, but they had a silver wedding in Leonard to go to today. They may stop over later," said Stan.

"I guess Karl plans to take Dorothy to Norway this fall," said Art. "That is, if the crops are good."

"How is it going with them? How much are Karl and his stepson farming now?" asked Ron.

"They're farming three quarters this year. All of the land that Dorothy's former husband had."

"Lucky it was all bought and paid for before he died. They're sitting pretty well. They had good crops last year and it looks good this year, too, Karl told me," said Joe.

"Yah, it turned out well for Karl, didn't it?' remarked George. "He made the right decision to stay in this country, I think."

"And, of course it was lucky for Dorothy that he did!' exclaimed Ron.

The women had been in the kitchen fixing supper all this time. Cheryl passed through and Livvie asked her, "Where's Linda? I haven't seen her for a long time."

"Oh, she's upstairs sleeping in her bed," Cheryl informed her mother.

"Really? She's actually sleeping? I can't believe it. I never could get that girl to nap."

"Do you suppose she isn't feeling well?" asked Min.

"I'll maybe go up and check on her." Livvie left the kitchen and hurried up the stairs. She found her 5-year-old daughter sleeping. She looked flushed, Livvie thought. She felt of her forehead and it was quite hot. She went to the bathroom and got a cool, wet washrag and put it on Linda's forehead.

"Oh, Mommy," Linda stirred. She looked up at her mother and said, "I don't feel very good."

"I can tell that you don't. You're very hot. I'll run down and get you an aspirin and some cold water."

Downstairs again, Livvie stepped out onto the porch and said to her husband, "Stan, Linda isn't feeling well. She's burning up with fever."

"Really? I thought she was out playing."

"No, Cheryl said that she's been sleeping most of the afternoon. I'm going to get some aspirin for her."

"I'll bring it up to her," Stan offered, getting up and following his wife into the kitchen.

Livvie crushed an aspirin between two spoons and filled a glass with cold water. Entering her room, Stan sat carefully on the side of her bed. "Here, honey, swallow this aspirin and drink some water. Maybe it will make you feel better after awhile."

He sat with her a few minutes and then she fell asleep again. He went back downstairs.

"How does she seem to you?" Livvie asked him.

"She took her pill and fell back to sleep again."

Livvie wore a worried frown on her face all the while she served supper to her guests. Rosie and Jeannie, the two nurses in the family, were talking about all the sickness this summer and all the people admitted to their hospitals.

"Polio is on the rise again, too, this summer," remarked Rosie. "About as bad as back in '46."

Livvie gave Stan a concerned look. "Now, Olivia," said Magda, "don't you get all worried that Linda has polio. I'm sure it's just the flu."

"Maybe after we're done eating, Rosie and Jeannie could go up and check her over," suggested Min.

"We can certainly do that," said Jeannie. Rosie agreed.

After the meal was over, Cheryl came and told her mother that Linda was awake and calling for her.

"Why don't you two come up with me," she said to her two sisters-in-law.

"How are you feeling now, dear?" asked Livvie, when the three of them entered Linda's room.

She looked wide-eyed at her two aunts. "Remember that Rosie and Jeannie are nurses," Livvie said soothingly. "They're going to check you out, just as if you were at the doctor's office."

"So, Lindy Lou," Rosie said to her niece. "Tell me exactly how you're feeling. Does it hurt anywhere?"

"My head hurts," Linda said, touching her forehead.

"Anywhere else?" asked Jeannie. "Does your neck hurt, too?"

"No. Just my head."

After a few minutes, Rosie and Jeannie left and headed back downstairs. Livvie stayed for awhile to make sure her daughter was resting comfortably.

"I'll come back in a little while. Do you want anything?"

"Maybe some orange juice."

"OK. I'll come back with some in a few minutes, dear."

Livvie joined the rest of the women in the kitchen. "So, what do you think?" she looked first at Rosie and then at Jeannie.

"I think it's just the flu," said Rosie.

"It probably is, but you can see how she is tomorrow," said Jeannie. "If she develops any more symptoms, you should maybe call the doctor and get his advice."

"Like what symptoms?" asked Livvie, still rather worried.

"Well, like vomiting, stiffness and pain in the back and neck."

"I'll watch for that," said Livvie. "Thanks for going up and checking her out. Maybe she'll be much better by tomorrow."

"She probably will," agreed Rosie.

Ron came into the kitchen. "Marty is practically falling asleep in his chair out there. We maybe better head back home." Ron had driven and they had picked up Marty and Jeannie.

"OK. We're ready," Jeannie said of her and Rosie.

Marty came into view just then. "Hey, big guy! Are you all tired out after last night?" asked Ron.

"What did he do last night?" asked Min.

"We were all at the Vet's Club," replied Ron. "You should have seen your oldest son!"

"Why? What was he doing?" she asked sharply.

"He and Jeannie were dancing up a storm!"

"You should have seen them jitterbugging!" exclaimed Rosie. "They're really good!"

"Where did you learn to dance like that?" asked Min.

"I first learned when I was in the army. We danced a lot at the USO's."

"We go to the Vet's Club almost every Saturday night so we've been dancing quite a bit lately," said Jeannie. "My feet sure hurt today."

"Well, if you'd wear some sensible shoes, maybe they wouldn't hurt," teased Marty.

"Let's be going, then, gang," said Ron. The two couples thanked Livvie and Stan for the nice afternoon and congratulated them again on their fine son.

After they had left, Magda said, "It sounds like those four are having some good times together. I remember when Art and I used to go dancing so much. Art is a great dancer."

"Yes, I remember that he was. Maybe still is!" said Min.

We just don't seem to have the desire to go out much anymore," Magda said.

"Well, Stan and I sure don't get out much anymore, either," laughed Livvie.

"You're too busy raising kids!" said Carrie.

"Speaking of kids, Linda said she wanted some orange juice." She went to fix some for her daughter.

"I'll just run up with this and be right back," she told the women.

Linda was sleeping again so she just left the juice on the nightstand and came back down.

A car came into the yard and it was Karl and his new family. "More company," Livvie called to Stan.

"I didn't know if we should come this late," apologized Dorothy, "but we had a gift for the new baby and our kids are anxious to see him."

"Oh, it's not late yet," Livvie assured her. "He's been sleeping for quite awhile now so he should be waking up soon. He's been such a good baby today."

"Have you had supper?" Min asked them.

"Oh, yes, we ate at the doings over at the church. They had such a big lunch!" replied Dorothy.

Karl joined the men, who were now gathered in the living room, and the talk naturally turned to farming. Harvest time would soon be upon them again.

"Did I tell you that we're taking a trip to Norway this fall?" Karl asked the group.

"Well, you said you might, but is it for sure that you're going?" asked Art.

"Yah, I bought tickets the other day when I was in Fargo. We'll take the train to Chicago and then on to New York and then get on the boat there."

"I bet Dorothy is excited," Joe remarked.

"Oh, yah, for sure. I want Dorothy to meet my mother. She's getting up in years, you know. We wish that we could take all the kids but that would cost way too much. Maybe someday," he told them.

In the kitchen, Dorothy was telling the women the same thing and they were excited for her.

"It sure would be fun to go over there," mused Magda.

"Well, get Art to take you there. You should go before you get too old, you know!" said Dorothy.

"I know, but Art isn't much for travelling. He hasn't been very far from here his whole life."

"Well, Joe hasn't either, but I think that maybe someday he may want to do some travelling. After we retire from farming," said Min.

"And when might that ever be?" asked Magda. "Joe and Art are the same. They'll never quit until they're too old to get up on a tractor!"

"Well, Joe has some sons to take over so maybe he'll quit sooner than that," ventured Carrie.

"Only one son is farming full time right now," said Min. "And I don't know for sure about Allan. He seems to really like school and who knows what he'll find to do after he graduates."

"If he graduates," corrected Magda. "Didn't you say yourself that you don't know if he'll stick it out till the end?"

"Well, I don't know anything for sure," laughed Min. "Time will tell."

Karl and Dorothy and their kids didn't stay very late as it had been a long day for them already. After seeing the baby and giving him a cute little romper set as a welcome gift, they said their goodbyes.

"It was good you stopped by," Livvie told them, as they made their way out onto the porch.

"It was fun to see your new little one," said Dorothy.

"He isn't so little! By the looks of him, he'll soon be helping you with the farming there, Stan," joked Karl.

Stan just beamed with pride as he stood there holding the baby.

Joe and Minerva were the next to leave. "I think we might have a field that's ready to swath tomorrow or the next day," Joe told Stan.

When everyone else had left, Livvie hurried on up to check on Linda again. She was still sleeping but seemed awfully hot when her mother felt her forehead.

"I'm going to bring the aspirin bottle upstairs and some water and when she wakes up again, I'll have her take another one," she told Stan.

Livvie didn't get much sleep that night. The baby was awake quite a bit, as he had slept most of the day. Linda was restless and actually vomited twice before morning.

"I'm going to call the doctor in the morning, as soon as the clinic opens," Livvie told Stan, when she crawled back into bed to try and get a few minutes of sleep.

Stan lay there, thinking and worrying until dawn. *What if my little girl actually has polio? It's too awful to imagine.*

Linda looked and felt worse in the morning, so Livvie got on the phone and called the clinic. She had to wait for Dr. Pray to call her back. They waited almost an hour before the phone rang. She ran for it.

After telling the doctor how Linda was feeling, he suggested that they bring her in so he could have a look at her. "Just in case," he said.

"Just in case of what?" Stan wanted to know.

"I don't know. Do you suppose that he, too, thinks that it could be polio?"

"Well, he probably doesn't want to take any chances, especially with so much of it this summer."

"I'll call Mom and see if she can come and stay with Cheryl and the baby," said Livvie. She headed right for the phone. She had to think a minute about what her folks' new number was. They all had just gotten new phones, ones with rotary dialing, as Kindred had just switched to that system. There was no longer a need for an operator for local calls.

When she hung up, she said, "Mom will be right over. We better get ready to go."

They made a comfortable bed in the back seat of their car for Linda. They had to carry her, as she was too weak and sick to walk. They brought a small bucket along in case she had to vomit again.

When they got her to the clinic, they were able to get right into the doctor's office. Dr. Pray carefully checked the sick little girl. When he finished his examination, he took a chair opposite her worried parents. He looked very tired, Livvie thought.

"Mr. and Mrs. Murphy, I know that you are worried that Linda here has polio. I don't think that she does, but I want her to stay in the hospital for a day or two so we can keep an eye on her."

"Oh, no!" exclaimed Livvie.

"Right now, I think that it's just the flu, but if she should develop some other symptoms, it would be beneficial if she was here so we could take the proper measures if need be," he explained to them kindly.

"Like what other symptoms are you worried about?" asked Stan.

"If she should experience stiffness in her neck or back, and also difficulty in swallowing and hoarseness, that would give us some concern."

Stan and Livvie didn't know what to say. Dr. Pray stood up and said, "Well, then, we'll find a room for your little girl and I'm sure everything will be all right. We just want to take precautions."

Stan stood, too. "Yes, doctor, I understand."

Stan and Livvie stayed at the hospital all day until late evening. They thought they should go home and come back in the morning. They needed to take care of some things at home. This turn of events had been so unexpected.

Carrie said she would come back the next morning and stay with the kids again. Stan called his dad and told him that he wouldn't be able to help him the next day, either.

"That's OK, Stan. Art and I will get the swathing done when the time comes. You just stay there as long as you need to."

Carrie was so worried. She prayed most of the day, every time that her thoughts turned to her little granddaughter. The baby was good and took his bottle just fine for her. She tried to divert Cheryl's attention to positive things as she was worried, too. They baked together and even tried sewing some doll clothes for the girls' dolls.

Livvie called late in the afternoon. Linda wasn't any worse. She still hadn't developed any of the dreaded symptoms. Livvie and Stan planned to stay overnight with Ron and Rosie and would call again the next day.

They sat up at the hospital all the next day, close to Linda. Livvie took the Bible that was on the nightstand next to the bed. She turned to the Psalms and looked up some of her favorite passages. She found Psalm 9, verse 10: "Those who know thy name put their trust in thee, for thou, O Lord, hast not forsaken those who seek thee."

Psaalm 46, verse 1, was another favorite of hers: "God is our refuge and strength, a very present help in trouble. Therefore we will not fear though the earth should change...." *Or that our little girl should die.* Livvie quickly banished such thoughts from her mind.

She put the book away and recited the twenty-third Psalm from memory. "Even though I walk through the valley of the shadow of death, I fear no evil; thou art with me; thy rod and thy staff, they comfort me."

Is this my "valley of the shadow of death?" she wondered.

Stan worked out his nervousness by pacing the halls. He felt so helpless, with his little girl lying there so sick and he, unable to do anything about it.

Late in the afternoon, Dr. Pray finally came in to see Linda again. He examined her and then turned to her parents.

"There's no change that I can see, and maybe this is good. I'll be perfectly frank with you," he went on. "There are several things to worry about here. There's encephalitis and there's polioencephalitis, or poliomyelitis. In the first two, the patient may have convulsions and sometimes go into a coma."

Livvie started crying, and Stan put his hand on her shoulder.

"Linda isn't showing any signs of this, at least not yet, but her fever is still a little high. Then there's also a mild form of polio, which is often mistaken for the flu but it does not cause paralysis. Maybe by tomorrow we'll know more, one way or another."

When Dr. Pray had left, Livvie and Stan got up and stood close by Linda's bed. She looked up at them and said, "Mommy and Daddy, I don't feel very good. I'm so hot."

"I know you are, dear, but the nurses are doing everything they can to make you comfortable," said Livvie.

Just then a nurse appeared and said it was time for Linda's medication. "Then we'll put some cold packs on her head and chest again. We need to get that fever down."

Late that night, Livvie and Stan went over to Ron's and tried to sleep for awhile. They were up at the crack of dawn, gulped down some coffee and toast and were back at the hospital early the next day.

"The doctor is on the floor," said one of the nurses, "so he'll be in here in just a few minutes."

"What kind of a night did Linda have last night?" Livvie asked the nurse.

"Well, I just got on duty but I'll look here in her chart." Reading the notes, she said, "It says here that the patient rested comfortably most of the night." Looking up at Livvie, she said, "That sounds good, doesn't it?"

Livvie didn't know what sounded good anymore. She just wanted her little girl well and home again, running around.

Dr. Pray stuck his head in the door. "Good morning," he said. "Let's have a look at our little girl here." He examined her carefully, checking her neck and limbs for soreness or rigidity. Linda didn't wince or seem to feel any pain there. "Does it hurt when you swallow, Linda?"

"No, but I don't like those big pills," she said weakly.

The doctor just laughed. "No one likes those pills!" He sat in the chair by her bed. "Linda, can you tell me about your pets at home? Do you have any?"

"I have a dog. His name is Barney. I have many kittens, too, but they don't all have names."

The doctor stood. "I wanted her to talk so I could tell if there was any hoarseness to her voice. I don't detect any. So far, so good." He patted Linda's legs under the blankets and said, "You just get better now, so you can get home to Barney."

Stan followed him out into the hall. "What do you think, doctor?"

"I'm thinking that it's not polio or encephalitis. That it's just a bad case of the flu. By tomorrow we should know for sure."

Stan related this to Livvie and they looked at each other. Tears welled in Livvie's eyes. "I've been praying so much for her. I'm trusting in the Lord that she will get better very soon."

"I've been praying, too. And I know that our parents and family have been, also."

"I miss little Bobbie," said Livvie. "My arms feel such an emptiness."

"Maybe we'll be able to go home tomorrow for a little while, if Linda is better."

"Let's go and call home and see how everything is going," suggested Livvie.

CHAPTER 24

As it turned out, Linda was released from the hospital a couple of days later. She was progressing nicely and was feeling much better. Her fever was normal.

"So, what do you think it was?" Stan had asked Dr. Pray before they left the hospital.

"I think it was a bad case of the flu," he replied.

"Are you sure it wasn't a mild case of polio, then?" asked Livvie.

"No, I don't think it was. And your daughter would have recovered just as quickly at home, but I just wanted her here in case it turned out to be something different."

"Yes, I understand, and I'm glad she was here, too," said Stan.

"Linda will need plenty of rest when she is home recuperating," warned the doctor.

"We'll see that she gets it," said Livvie.

Cheryl was so happy to have her sister home again that she waited on her, hand and foot. "Watch out or you'll spoil her," laughed Stan.

Carrie and George came by that first evening to see her. "We won't stay long. We don't want to tire her out," said Carrie.

"Oh, it's so good to be home again!" exclaimed Livvie. "I missed the kids so much. And thank you for the good care you took of them."

That night, when all of her children were in their beds, sleeping for the night, Livvie stole into their separate rooms and stood looking down at each one.

"How precious they are to me," she said in a soft voice. She knelt down by each of their beds and thanked God for them. The baby started to squirm, so she picked him up, not that he needed anything, but just to feel the comfort of his solid little body against her breast.

She sat down in the rocker in his room and rocked slowly back and forth. She thought back to the time right after her miscarriage and how distraught she had been. *Little did I know then that God would bring me joy once again.*

Another homecoming occurred about a month later. This time it was Kenny who was released from the State Hospital in Jamestown and was allowed to come home. He was doing quite well, and, if he took his medication regularly, he would do all right at home.

One Sunday, when Ron was home for the weekend, he stopped by to see his old pal. Kenny seemed genuinely happy to see him and they had a good visit.

"Ron," Kenny said, "I need to apologize to you and to your family. I gave you all quite a scare, with that gun and all." Here he shook his head slowly back and forth. "I don't know what came over me, but it was something that I felt coming, over a long period of time. The doctors call it depression. Thank goodness for this medicine. I almost feel normal now."

"I'm glad to have my old friend back again," said Ron. "And Kenny? You don't still think that I stole Rosie away from you, do you?" Ron asked, hesitantly.

"No, I guess not. I'm happy for you two. Bring her over sometime and maybe we can go out, just like old times."

"I wish things could be like they used to be, Kenny. I mean, I wish you hadn't lost most of your sight."

"Yah, that damn war!" said Kenny. He was silent for awhile. "At the hospital, they suggested that I learn to read by Braille. Just in case I lose my sight entirely."

"Are you going to do that?" asked Ron, hopefully.

"I might," replied Kenny. "There's a place in Fargo that I could take lessons. I may go there this winter."

"That's wonderful, Kenny. I'm glad to see you're pulling yourself together."

"Well, I'll give it a try."

Carrie stopped in at the new Ulness Drug one afternoon and had a good visit with Beatrice. Only a few customers interrupted them from time to time. Beatrice was excited about her new business venture. She had ordered uniforms for herself and her hired help. They were green, short-sleeved dresses with white aprons.

The soda fountain was a popular spot, especially now that school had started. It was a hangout for the students after school. There was a back room with a tiled floor in which stood about four or five ice-cream tables with matching chairs.

"Carl got them from the Sons of Norway," Beatrice told Carrie. "They used to have them in their little place out at their park, over by Norman Church."

"Yes, I remember seeing them there."

"Well, anyway, they wanted to sell them so we were lucky enough to buy them. I painted the table tops green and put a covering on the chair seats."

"It looks very nice," commented Carrie, looking around.

"The interesting thing about these sets is that they originally came from this store when Ben Anderson had this as his jewelry store. He had a soda fountain, too."

"Well, you know, I think I remember seeing them in here, a long time ago, when I worked on the Daud farm by Davenport. We came in here once in awhile for ice cream."

Carrie made some small purchases and left her friend when the high school kids started coming in after school.

"I think Beatrice and Carl are going to do very well in their store," Carrie told George later that evening. "She has it fixed up real nice there."

"We'll have to stop in some evening for a sundae or a malt when we go to town."

"Yah, that would be fun. Beatrice said they'd been real busy on Saturday nights."

"Allan's got a girlfriend now," announced Stan one morning, arriving at his folks' place.

"He does?" said Min. "And who might that be?"

"Her name is Kathy Walter and her dad is the new depot agent in Kindred. She's working at the drug store. Allan met her at a dance in town a few weeks back."

"I always thought he'd find someone in Fargo at the college there," Min commented.

"Well, I guess he's really fallen for her. She's a real looker, I hear!" exclaimed Stan.

"And how do you know all this?" asked his mother.

"I was in town to the bank yesterday and I ran into one of his classmates,

Eddie, and he told me all about it."

"Well, I'll have to ask Allan about it when he comes home this weekend."

"I'm sure he'll be coming home every weekend now," laughed Stan.

The nation was a little stunned to find themselves involved in another war the following summer, the summer of 1950. It was in a little place called Korea this time. North Korea had invaded South Korea and the newly-formed United Nations demanded that they withdraw immediately. North Korea didn't comply, so the UN sent troops there to force them back north. There were 41 countries involved, but the US. provided the bulk of the manpower.

"I can't believe we're at war again!" cried Min. "I thought the war we just went through was supposed to be our last."

"Yah, I did, too," agreed Joe. "The war to end all wars."

"I hope Allan doesn't have to get involved."

Allan was still dating this girl named Kathy and had brought her around to his folks' on several occasions.

"My little brother seems head-over-heels in love," Stan commented to his mother one day.

"Oh, I'm sure it isn't anything serious yet," she scoffed.

"Don't be too sure of that," laughed Stan.

There were some changes on the main street of Kindred that summer. The Ulness family moved into the upstairs apartments above their store. Also, next door, a new building was coming up. Someone was putting up a brick building which would house a movie theater. The town was excited about this addition to their community.

"Won't it be fun to have a real theater in our own little town!" exclaimed Livvie to Stan.

"Yes, that will be something, all right."

"Who's building it?" she asked.

"A man named Mindemann. I guess he's making living quarters on the second floor for his family."

"Where did they come from?" asked Livvie.

"Down by Barney, I guess. He's actually a farmer down there."

"Really? How can he farm and manage a theater, I wonder?"

"Beats me," said Stan.

Marty came out to the farm one Saturday and kind of hung around all day. Min could tell that something was bothering him. Finally, late in the afternoon, she cornered him and asked him if everything was all right.

He hung his head and was silent for sometime. Min waited patiently for her son to speak.

"Well, it's this way," he started. "Jeannie and I aren't getting along too well."

"What seems to be the matter?" Min asked, alarmed.

"Well, a number of things. For one thing, she's very jealous of me. She thinks I'm paying too much attention to other women when we're out. Then she flies into a rage when we get home."

"So, are you paying too much attention to the other women?" his mother asked, pointedly.

"No, Mom. You know how I like to talk to people, and be friendly to everyone, and that includes other women. I don't mean anything by it."

"I know, son. It's just your nature. But doesn't she know this?"

"Well, most of the time, she does, but sometimes she just gets in these funny moods and then I'm in trouble. It's like I'm walking on eggs. I never know where I stand. She wants to go out on Saturday nights, but then she gets mad if I look at someone else. So then, I suggest that we just stay home and then she accuses me of being an old fuddy-duddy. I can't win!" Marty sat down and put his head in his hands.

Min felt sorry for her son. He didn't deserve all this. He was a good person. "You said there were other things, too?" she asked.

"Jeannie wants to have kids so bad, but it's not happening. So this gets her down, too. Maybe if we could just have a baby, she'd be different."

"Have you considered adopting?"

"We've talked about it and maybe we might do that," he said, "but then, if we're not exactly getting along so good, it's not fair to try and adopt a baby."

"Oh, Marty, you have a problem there," said Min, feeling great sympathy for him. "I don't know what to tell you. You'll just have to make the best of the situation."

"But there's times when I don't think I can take it anymore." Marty was almost sobbing. "She gives me the silent treatment for days on end sometimes."

"You'd never think of a divorce, would you?" Min asked, worried now.

When he didn't answer right away, she grew horrified. "You wouldn't do that, would you? We sure don't want a divorce in the family!" she stated, emphatically.

"No, Mom, I'll try not to go that far. We'll work things out somehow."

He stood now, as if to leave. "I better be going. I just needed to come out here today and get out of the house for awhile. When she gets over these moods, then things are just fine for a few weeks, so I don't know." He ran his hand through his hair in a worried gesture.

Min gave her son a hug and told him that she would be praying extra hard for them.

"Thanks, Mom. Say goodbye to Dad for me. I've gotta go."

In December of that year, Cheryl came home from school one day all excited. "There's a new girl in our grade who started school today. Her name is Kay and her dad is building the theater in town."

"Why, that's nice," said Livvie, almost absently. "Did you wash your hands? You can have a piece of cake and a glass of milk," she told her two girls.

Cheryl was in the fourth grade now and Linda was in second.

"Maybe if we get to be real good friends," Cheryl chattered on, "I'll get to go to the movies free!"

"Oh, don't expect that," admonished her mother. "Did she say when the theater will be opening?"

"Oh, not for a few months yet, I guess."

That Christmas, there were two exciting announcements in the Murphy household. Ron and Rosie and Marty and Jeannie all came out for Christmas Eve, and unknown to each other, they both announced that they were going to have babies.

"Oh, how exciting!" exclaimed Min, standing and clapping her hands together in delight. Rosie and Jeannie were hugging each other, surprised at each other's news.

"Why didn't you tell me?" squealed Rosie.

"And why didn't you tell me?" laughed Jeannie.

"Well, we wanted to tell the folks first so we waited until tonight," said Ron.

"Same with us," said Marty.

“It was hard to keep our news a secret because you all know how long we have waited for me to get PG,” said Jeannie. She was beaming with pleasure. Min silently hoped that things would work out for the couple. *Thank you, Lord*, she prayed silently.

“So, when are these babies due?” asked Livvie, also excited with the good news.

“I’m due in June,” said Rosie. She looked at Jeannie.

“I’m due in May!” exclaimed Jeannie.

“Oh, so much excitement,” said Min. “Let’s have a little celebration. Joe, go get that wine you’ve been saving for a special occasion. If this isn’t special, I don’t know what is. I’ll get some little glasses.”

That next spring, the war in Korea was still going on. Several local boys had been drafted. Min was worried about Allan but tried not to think about it too much.

“I couldn’t bear to have another son go off to war,” she’d told Joe time after time.

President Truman had removed the popular General MacArthur from his command and that had stirred quite a controversy across the country.

“I think that Truman should have let him do what he wanted to do—attack the Chinese mainland,” said Joe to George one evening, when the two couples were together. The Chinese Communists had entered the war on the side of North Korea.

“Well, I guess his superiors felt that this would increase the risk of a world war,” commented George.

“And we surely don’t want another world war!” exclaimed Carrie, hotly.

“Well, I think MacArthur was a darn good man,” said Joe, defending his earlier comment.

“That he was, and still is. Maybe he’ll get into politics,” ventured George.

“Speaking of politics,” said Joe, “I wonder if they’ll get Eisenhower to run for president next year.”

“Oh, I don’t think so,” replied George. “He’s pretty set against it.”

“Well, don’t count him out.”

One Friday evening in April, the “K” Theater opened its doors to the public. The first movie showing was “Wabash Avenue.” Cheryl had been invited to a birthday party for one of her classmates, one of the two Sharons, and they were all going to the movie after their cake and ice cream.

"Cheryl has been so excited for the last week that she can hardly stand it," Livvie told her mother on the phone the day of the grand opening.

"Well, this is pretty exciting for those young girls," replied Carrie. "George and I are planning to go to the movie Sunday evening. If you and Stan want to go one night, just let us know, and we'll come out and watch the kids for you."

"Thanks, Mom. We may take you up on that more than once!"

On the very last day of May, Marty called out to the farm with the long-awaited news. Jeannie gave birth to a baby boy and Marty was so excited that he could hardly talk.

"Oh, Marty, I'm so happy for you," said Min. "Give Jeannie our love and congratulations. We'll be in as soon as we can get away here to see that new baby."

They named the baby Joseph Martin and they would be calling him Joey. Grandpa Joe was very proud that the baby was named after him.

"He even looks a little like you, Dad," Marty told his father when he got on the phone.

"Oh, the poor kid," said Joe, smiling from ear to ear.

The 10th of June brought another baby into the Murphy clan. Rosie and Ron had a baby girl and they named her Barbara Rose. "We'll be calling her Barbie," Ron told his parents.

"I'm just so happy and excited over all these babies!" exclaimed Min. She had called over to Carrie and George's to tell them the latest news.

"Well, you sure have a bunch of grandchildren all of a sudden. Two new babies and then there's little Bobbie, who's not very old yet either. You're going to be a busy grandmother," Carrie told her, chuckling.

"Oh, I know. And I'm going to love every minute of it."

The "K" Theater ran many great movies and the townspeople loved having a real theater in their town. George and Carrie went quite often. Before each main feature, there was always a newsreel of the world happenings. They saw the Korean War played out before their eyes. It was said that this war was the bloodiest war so far for the US. Several more local boys were headed for Korea and the town held its breath, hoping that they would all return. The memory of World War II was still too fresh in everyone's mind.

The post-war economy continued on into the early fifties. The same went for the farm economy. Things were quite good for the farmers. The grain prices were up, so they were buying new machinery and expanding their farms.

Allan Murphy started his last year of college in the fall of '52. He'd graduate the following spring. He was in the ROTC program—the Reserved Officers Training Corps— and would, upon graduation, be going into the service. His mother was not happy at all about this turn of events.

"I've already gone through having two sons in uniform. I don't want to have to worry about another one overseas," she stated emphatically.

Allan tried to console her, but she didn't want to hear it. "I think," she said to Joe one day, "that Allan has always wanted to be a soldier, ever since his two older brothers were in the service, and that's why he's doing this."

"That could be," agreed Joe.

"I just hope that the war in Korea is over before he has to go in. I sure don't want him to go over there."

"Well, time will tell, Min. Don't worry so about it yet."

In the winter of '53, the community's attention was taken up by their high school basketball team. The Kindred Vikings, after a slow start, were having a pretty good year and they were looking forward to a trip to the state tournament.

George had gone to most of the games so far. He had just returned home from an exciting game between Kindred and one of their long-time rivals, Walcott, a town just to the south of them.

"It's so much fun to watch those guys play. Jack, and Earle, and that Erickson boy, and all of them. They're all good."

One evening in January, George and Carrie went to a game that had been talked about as the "game of the year." The high school team, now somewhat cocky, had challenged a group of the alumni basketball players to an exhibition game.

"So who will be some of the older players, then?" Carrie asked George, as they drove into town.

"Well, there's Don Ulness, Don Driscoll, Ossie Twedt, Jerry Bjelde, Keith Trom, and let me think now, who else would there be."

"The older Erickson boy?"

"Oh, yes. Curt. Then there's Lee Thompson, Paul Vangerud, and Buddy Lykken. I think that's the ones that Clem mentioned in the Tribune."

"I'm sure Beatrice and Carl will be there, then, if Don is playing," commented Carrie.

"Oh, you can be sure that they'll be there," said George. "Well, here we are. Look at all the cars!"

Once inside the gym, George and Carrie were able to find seats near Carl and Beatrice.

The younger players were sure that the alumni fellows would be really out of shape and unable to keep up with the present Kindred Vikings team. It turned out to be a fast-paced game and very close scoring. The alums pulled it off, winning 39-38.

"That sure was a real squeaker, wasn't it?" commented Carl.

"Why don't you stop over for a cup of coffee?" suggested Beatrice to the Johnsons.

"Well, I guess we can do that," said Carrie. "It will be fun to see your place."

They hadn't been in the upstairs apartment yet, where the Ulness family now lived.

During coffee, Carl and George were talking about the new '53 cars which were going to be unveiled the next day.

"I'm going to Rich's Garage to see the new Chevy," Carl told George. "The paper said that it's so 'startlingly new' that we will be amazed."

"Yah, I'm looking forward to seeing the new Chryslers at Rustad's, too. That New Yorker DeLuxe is supposed to be really some car, they say."

The next day, George suggested that Carrie come with him to town in the afternoon. "We'll make a day of it. We'll look at all the new cars and then we can have supper at the Hotel, and then take in the Will Rogers movie."

"Oh, that sounds fun. We'll get to see how the Backstrands have remodeled the café, then I need to get some groceries, too."

The next evening, after eating at the hotel cafe, Carrie went to the Elstad's Grocery Store to get a few things. As she came out, she noticed Joe and Min's car parked right out front. She stopped to talk to Min and Magda, who were sitting in the back seat.

"The men are over at Rustad's, looking at the new cars," Min said.

"We saw them this afternoon," Carrie told them. "Very nice. I have to go put these groceries in our car and then hurry over to Larsen's to pick up those cake mixes that are three for a dollar."

"I still make all my cakes from scratch," sniffed Magda.

"Well, I like to have these on hand for emergencies," Carrie retorted.

"Yah, I do, too. They aren't too bad, as far as mixes go," agreed Min.

"We do all our shopping at Evingson's Store," Magda told them.

"We started shopping mostly at Elstad's now, because of the S & H Green Stamps," Carrie answered. "I've got almost three books filled already. Well, I better hurry along. George is going to meet me in ten minutes. He went over to Petry's Hardware to get some paint. Then we're going to the early movie."

"Have fun!" Min called after her.

By the middle of March, basketball fever had spread over the community. There was a good possibility that the team would make it to State. First, of course, they had to make it through the Class "C" district tournaments, which were to be held in their own gym in Kindred.

"That's a definite advantage for our boys," George told Carrie. It turned out that Kindred won the tournament easily and then they were headed to Lisbon for the regionals the following week.

"I think we should drive down there for the game tonight," George suggested. "Maybe Carl and Beatrice want to go along with us."

"Should I give them a call?" asked Carrie.

"Yah, tell them we'll pick them up."

Carrie came back from the phone and told her husband that Beatrice said that they had plans to drive with the Ted Ericksons. "Maybe another night," she'd said.

Carrie went the first night, but stayed home the next. "Enough is enough," she'd told George.

The Kindred fans were overjoyed when their team won the regionals, too, and now they were on their way to the state tournament, which was to be in Valley City this time.

"There's going to be a bus going there," George told Carrie a few days later. "I'd sure like to go see the games."

"Well, why don't you go if you want to," she told him. "I don't mind."

"I'll see. I'll talk to some of the guys tomorrow and see if they're going."

Joe Murphy called the next morning and said that he'd like to go and it was decided that they'd both go on the bus.

Allan called home late one night during the tournaments and talked with his mother. "I heard on the radio that Kindred won their first game in Valley City tonight," he said excitedly. "Did Dad go?"

"Yes, he went on the bus. It was full, I guess."

"Well, tomorrow afternoon some of us guys are going to drive over there and stay overnight.

"Won't you be missing some classes?" she asked.

"No, I'm done early on Fridays. I asked Marty if he wanted to go and he did, but Jeannie put up a fuss so now he can't."

"Oh, dear," said Min.

"We'll be back Sunday. Just thought I'd let you know. I have to run now. I've got some other calls to make."

The second night's game was a real thriller. Kindred played Bowden, a team from the western part of the state. Hilding Ronning and Jack Stenhjem led the team in scoring and they beat Bowden 51-49.

The Ericksons had ridden along with George and Carrie and there was a lively discussion about the game all the way home.

George and Carrie went back the last night for the championship game. This time the Vikings played Willow City. Kindred was behind most of the game, but Allan Erickson's long shots put the team to within five points of a tie. His daring shots gave the fans a thrill and Willow City a scare. The final score was 57-48, with Willow City taking the title. Allan was high point man and Hilding came in second.

"Well, second place is pretty darn good, I think," George commented to Ted, who had ridden with them again.

"Yah, this is the furthest that Kindred has gone in the state tournaments," he agreed.

The team and fans were welcomed back late Saturday night, with a police escort down the Kindred Highway to the school. There, some of the ladies had stayed back and fixed a smorgasbord lunch for everyone. There was a lot of excitement and speeches and back slapping.

"Well, now that basketball season is over, what are we going to do for entertainment?" laughed George on their way home.

"Maybe we can get something done at home!" exclaimed Carrie. "I think I've had enough of ball games to last me a long time. Until next year anyway!"

CHAPTER 25

The community soon found other things than basketball to occupy their time. Carrie loved to sing so she decided to take part in the community chorus. They were planning to put on an Easter Cantata. It would be under the direction of the much-loved high school music teacher, Victor Hehn. He had done a marvelous job with the school choral groups and they had taken many awards for outstanding excellence in high school competition.

This meant that Carrie had to go to choir practice every Sunday afternoon, but she enjoyed it and George said he didn't mind her going.

"Why don't you come and sing, too?" she had asked him after the first practice. "They need a few more tenors."

"Oh, I can't sing that good," he'd answered.

"Well, I think you can. I listen to you in church every Sunday and I think you sing very well."

"Oh, no, I couldn't do that," he protested again.

"Well, you think about it this week," she told him.

By the next Saturday evening, she had him convinced that he should give it a try the next afternoon. It turned out that he just loved singing with a group. "As long as I can follow the guy next to me, I'll be all right," he told Carrie, after the practice.

Their daughter-in-law, Lenora, was singing in the group, too, so she invited them to come home with her and join them for supper.

"Freddie is cooking tonight," she laughed, "so don't expect much."

Sandra and Larry were excited to have their grandparents stop by and join them for supper. Sandra was now a very grown-up looking 14-year-old. Larry would be twelve, come summer.

Freddie had indeed cooked supper and had it already to serve. He had fried hamburgers and potatoes and there was ice cream for dessert.

"This is our usual Sunday-night supper," explained Lenora.

"Well, it's very good, Freddie," said his mother. "But I sure didn't know you had become such a cook!"

"Actually, this is the only thing I know how to make," he laughed.

"But the kids love it," said Lenora.

"So, Dad, are you going to buy one of those new television sets soon?" Freddie asked his father over coffee.

"I haven't really looked into them yet, but I suppose it is the coming thing."

"How about you, Freddie?" asked Carrie.

"I've been looking at some of them, but there are so many different brands and different prices. I looked at the ones at the Electric Shop, and then Gambles is selling the Coronado."

"Kindred Plumbing and Heating sells Admiral, I noticed yesterday when I was in there," said George.

"Minerva said that they were looking at one over at Fredrikson's in Davenport," mentioned Carrie.

"They sell the RCA sets over there," George said.

"Yah, it's confusing all right," said Freddie. "The sets are priced all the way from $179 up to $324. I guess we'll wait a little while. Save up our money for one."

"I had to laugh the other day," Carrie chuckled, "when Livvie told me that Cheryl had been invited to stay overnight at Elaine Ulness' and they had walked over to the Gambles Store and were watching the test patterns on the TV sets. They thought that was pretty exciting!"

"Well, I think it's a trend that is here to stay," Freddie said, as they all helped clear up the dishes. "It will replace radio as the popular thing to listen to."

"Why don't you stay and we'll play a game with the kids for awhile," suggested Lenora.

"Oh, please stay, Grandma and Grandpa," cried Larry.

"Well, I guess there's nothing we have to hurry home for," said Carrie, looking at George.

After a few games of Chinese Checkers and one of Old Maid, the grownups had had enough so they sat and visited for awhile.

"Did you hear that Clem is selling the Tribune to someone?" asked George.

"Yah, I met the man. His name is Lawrence Knutson. He was in the bank the other day with Clem."

"So, won't we have 'Klem's Komments' anymore?" asked Carrie.

"Oh, Clem said he'd stay around for awhile. Kind of ease out of the business and break the new guy in," replied Freddie.

"Did Livvie tell you the news, Lenora?" asked Carrie, turning to her daughter-in-law.

"No. What?"

"Ron and Rosie are going to have another baby."

"Oh, how wonderful! Let's see, how old is their little girl now?"

"She'll be just two in June. The new baby isn't due until September."

"How about Marty and his wife, then?"

"I haven't heard anything about them lately."

Shortly before ten, George suggested that it was time for them to head for home.

"I'm glad that you're singing in the chorus now, George," said Lenora.

"Well, I got talked into it," he laughed, "but I think I'm going to enjoy it."

"It should be a wonderful cantata. I just love the songs," said Carrie.

Allan Murphy graduated from college in June and he went into the service a week later. He was sent to Fort Riley, Kansas. His girlfriend, Kathy, was very upset about him having to go into the service. She carried on something awful the day he left.

"I don't know how that girl is going to stand having him gone for three years," said Magda, as she witnessed the scene at the bus depot.

"I don't either," said Joe, shaking his head.

"Well, I don't know how I'm going to stand it either," said Min, "but at least I didn't create a big scene, like she did."

In July, the nation was happy to hear that the Korean War had ended. "At least he won't be sent over there," Min consoled herself.

"Maybe he'll get to just stay in this country and serve," said Joe, hopefully.

But that was not to be. In September, Allan called and told them that he was being sent to Germany."

"Germany!" shouted Min. "I thought we were all done with that country."

"Well, Mom, we have several bases over there. To keep the peace, you know. Don't worry about me."

"I'll be praying for you, Allan," she told him before he hung up.

"I'll be counting on that!"

In September, Ron and Rosie had their second baby, a boy this time. They named him Mark Ronald.

"He has a little shock of red hair," Min told Carrie over the phone. "No red hair in our family, but I guess Rosie's mother had reddish hair."

"Too bad Rosie's mother had to die so young, isn't it?' said Carrie. "She's missing out on her grandchildren."

"Yes, Rosie said the same thing the other night. She misses her an awful lot now. She was only twelve when her mother died, you know. She and her dad and sister were determined to make it so they didn't let themselves mourn for her too much at the time. Now Rosie says that she thinks about her a lot."

"Well, it's probably because she's a mother herself now."

"I told her the same thing," said Min.

"How is Marty's little boy? Getting big?"

"Oh, my yes! He's a regular chunk!" chuckled Min.

"Do you get to see him much?"

"Marty brings him out quite often on Saturdays. He said he wants him to know what it was like to grow up on the farm."

"What do you hear from Allan?" asked Carrie.

"He'll be leaving for Germany next week."

"Well, at least there's no war going on over there," said Carrie.

"No, but I'll be happy when the next three years are over and he's home safe and sound."

"Three years is a long time, isn't it? Is his girl going to wait that long for him, I wonder?"

"Well, she better! He's very much in love with her," answered Min.

Just before Christmas that year, Livvie went into the Drug Store and Kathy, Allan's girlfriend, was in there working.

"Hi, Kathy!" she greeted the young woman. "Have you heard from Allan lately?" she asked, conversationally.

Kathy got a funny look on her face. "Oh, ah...haven't you heard from him for awhile?"

"No, we haven't. Why?" asked Livvie, concerned now.

"Well, we....ah....aren't....ah....going together anymore," she stammered.

"Oh, my!" gasped Livvie. "I didn't know that. Sometimes those letters take awhile, you know." Not knowing what more to say, Livvie started looking at some merchandise at the make-up counter.

Kathy didn't volunteer any more information and, as she seemed a bit self- conscious, Livvie hurried up and made her purchase and left the store.

When she got home, Livvie hurried up and called over to the Murphy farm. Min answered.

"Min, have you heard from Allan in the last few days?" She tried to keep her voice casual.

"No, we haven't. It's been over a month now. Why do you ask?"

Livvie told her mother-in-law about her encounter with Kathy in the store awhile earlier.

"Oh, dear!" remarked Min with worry in her voice. "I wonder how Allan feels about that."

"I suppose Kathy just felt that she didn't want to wait for him anymore," Livvie surmised. "Well, maybe you'll be hearing from him soon."

It was another whole month before the Murphys finally heard from their son. He told them that he'd gotten a "Dear John" letter from Kathy and that he was pretty broken up about it. That's why he hadn't written sooner, he'd said. He didn't feel like doing anything, not even write to his family.

Min felt bad for her son, just imagining what it would be like to be far from home and then get a letter like that.

"Well, Allan will get over it eventually," Stan told his mother. "Maybe he'll find a little German girl," he joked.

"Don't even say that!" admonished Min.

"Just kidding!" he said, as he hurried out of the house, cookie in hand.

In the summer of '55, Kindred was gearing up to celebrate their Diamond Jubilee. The three-day celebration would take place over the Fourth of July. The community was stunned, however, when the news reached them that a deadly tornado had struck near the neighboring town of Walcott on Saturday evening, July 2.

George had been watching the weather late in the afternoon as the skies grew very dark to the south of him. "With this heat and humidity, anything could happen tonight," he commented to Carrie.

While they were eating supper, it started to rain and it kept on for some time, even hailing a little and it got quite windy and very dark.

Shortly after supper, there came a news bulletin over the radio that a tornado had been sighted near Walcott. A little later, a program was interrupted to say that the storm had done great damage on the ground and that possibly some lives had been taken.

"Oh, dear!" exclaimed Carrie. "I wonder who that was!" She called Beatrice to see if she had heard anything from her folks, who lived in Walcott.

"No," Beatrice said, "I've been trying to call them but no answer. I'll keep trying and get back to you if I hear something."

Freddie came driving into the yard and jumped out of the car and ran up to the house. "Did you hear about the tornado?"

"Yes! Do you know anything more than they've been saying on the radio?" asked George.

"My neighbor has family living in Walcott and he talked to them and they think that two people were killed. A baby and an older man."

"Oh, no!" exclaimed Carrie. "How terrible!"

"They're going to need some help down there. Shall we take a drive and have a look?" George asked his son.

"Yah, I'll go with you. Let's take my car."

"Wait!" called Carrie. "I want to go along." She grabbed her sweater from the hook and ran to join them.

"It sure rained a lot in a short while, didn't it?" commented Freddie.

"I just was checking my gauge when you came into the yard and it showed about two inches."

There were many cars going down the Gol Road towards Walcott. After a few miles, they started to see damaged trees and then as they reached the Walcott Road, there was some devastating sights. Huge trees, completely pulled up by the roots, missing buildings, roofs torn off.

"Oh, this is just awful," Carrie cried.

They met a car on the road and it was someone Freddie knew. He stopped and rolled down his window. "Have you heard yet who was killed?" asked Freddie.

"Well, it was the little Fjelstad baby and a 79-year-old man. A Bakko."

"Oh, dear, we know many of the Bakkos," said Carrie. "This is awful. This is awful," she kept on repeating.

"Well, maybe they don't want all these spectators driving around here," Freddie said, after they had viewed all the damage. "We better go back home."

"We'll hear more about it on the late news tonight," said George.

When they got home, they turned on the radio and the news came on shortly. "Thirteen-month-old Cecelia Fjelstad and 79-year-old H.N. Bakko were killed tonight in a deadly tornado," the announcer said. He went on to tell of all the damage and destruction. The storm had raged through ten or more farms in the area.

Carrie and George sat glued to the radio in horror. They could hardly believe what they were hearing. They knew both the families who had suffered fatalities.

The news was on for an extra half-hour, updating the listeners with more information as it came in.

"Maybe Freddie and I should take my truck down there in the morning and see if we can help in the clean-up," said George.

"This will surely put a damper on the celebration in Kindred, won't it?" said Carrie.

As it turned out, some of the Jubilee doings were rescheduled as many of the townspeople wanted to help out at Walcott.

The pagaent, however, was presented Sunday and Monday evenings. It was titled "Kith and Kindred" and both George and Carrie took part in the "human flag" presentation at the end of each performance.

This made for a very impressive finale. The women choir members were dressed in red and white, and the men were in blue and white and held white stars. They stood on risers, built especially for the occasion. There were five rows, each 30 inches high, with a stairway on each side.

From a distance, the choir, all standing in place, looked like the flag of the United States. As the members were finding their places on the risers, an organ was playing "America the Beautiful." The pagaent cast members came out on stage, followed by servicemen wearing their uniforms and carrying the flag. When everyone was in place, the national anthem was sung.

Marty and Ron were two of the servicemen who took part. Carrie could see Marty's face from where she stood on the risers and she could see that he had tears rolling down his cheeks.

"I don't think I saw a dry eye in the audience," Livvie remarked afterwards. "It was so moving!"

A huge fireworks display followed and then a dance was held in the school gym. This facility was packed with people. There was hardly room to dance at first. Whole families were there, including Stan and Livvie and their three children, even little Bobbie.

"There were no babysitters available for tonight," Livvie remarked. "Everyone's here!"

Late in the evening, Freddie told Livvie that he and Lenora had to leave. "I have to get up early tomorrow. We're going to try and clean up the streets before the parade and I volunteered to help."

"What are they going to do?" asked Stan.

"We're going to use road graders and push the mud off the streets."

"Yah, that 2-inch rain didn't help any, did it?" said Stan.

For the past few weeks, a road crew was getting the streets in Kindred ready to be hard-surfaced. They weren't able to get it done in time for the celebration, so when the heavy rain came, it really made a mess.

"See you tomorrow," Livvie called to Freddie and his family as they left the dance.

The streets were cleaned off early in the morning so, by parade time, they were in passable shape. The parade had 90 units in all and it was "the best parade ever," claimed the townspeople.

By early September of that year, Kindred's street project was finished. A new "soil cement" was used to the cost of $97,000. The residents were proud of the finished product and a celebration was called for. A Kindred Appreciation Day was held later that month. A large crowd enjoyed a barbeque dinner, a baseball game between the City Slickers and the Sod Busters, and a band concert in the street.

Another treat was a male quartet from Walcott, which was well received. "Those guys can really sing, can't they?" said Freddie.

"Yah, I know those Bakko boys and they're all good singers," said George. "And Heglie and Wigtil are sure good, too."

The evening was topped off by a dance, which was held again in the school gym.

"They should have had the dance out on the new street," remarked Stan.

"That would have been fun," said Livvie.

"So, where's the rest of your family?" Carrie asked Livvie. "Didn't they come to the dance?" Only Bobbie was by his mother's side.

"Well, Linda is over there with her friends and Cheryl is around here somewhere, pouting."

"Why is that?" laughed Carrie.

"She wanted to go to the dance with her friends but I told her she had to go with us. She thinks she's so grown up now, you know. She's starting to get a little boy-crazy, too, so I guess my worries are just beginning!"

Carrie laughed again.. "Yes, I remember going through a little of that with you."

Cheryl came up to her mother just then. "Mom, can't I go with the girls uptown? They're going up to the café for some lunch," she pleaded.

"No, you stay here now," said Livvie.

"Well, Elaine and Gloria and Kay and all the other girls are going. Why can't I? And Linda Swenson is having a slumber party tonight after the dance."

"Cheryl, we've been over this before. You're too young to be running all over town. Those girls are older than you, even if you are in the same grade."

"I wish I lived in town," huffed Cheryl, folding her arms across her chest in a defiant manner.

Carrie could see tears forming in her eyes. She went over and put an arm around her granddaughter's shoulders.

"It isn't easy being your age, dear," Carrie said kindly. "Your mother and I went through the same thing." Cheryl looked up at her grandma.

"You'll grow up soon enough," Carrie told her. "How is school going for you this year?"

"Fine," Cheryl answered.

Cheryl had just turned thirteen that spring and was now starting her freshman year in high school.

"I can't believe you're already in high school!" exclaimed Carrie.

"I wish I were older," wailed Cheryl.

Livvie gave her daughter a warning look and the girl went back to talk to her friends.

"I saw Allan's old girlfriend, Kathy, a while ago," remarked Livvie. "She was with Eddie."

"Have they been going together?" asked Carrie.

"I don't know. I haven't heard anything about her lately."

Changing the subject, Livvie said, "Did you know that they're going to be giving those new polio shots in school next week?"

"I read that in the Tribune. I'm sure glad someone came up with that vaccine."

"Me, too. Now we parents don't have to worry so much every summer about our kids getting polio. I'm going to bring Bobbie in, too, for a shot."

At Christmas time that year, the Murphy house was filled with grandchildren. Little Joey and Barbie were rambunctious 4-year-olds now and the newest member, Ron and Rosie's Mark, was two. With Stan and Livvie's three, that made six grandchildren.

"I think we're going to have to get a bigger table," laughed Min, as she tried to get everyone seated around it."

"I'll get the card table and put up in the living room," volunteered Joe. "The older kids can sit there."

As Joe led the table prayer, he prayed for their son, Allan, who was not with the family this day, but was still in Germany.

"So what do you hear from Allan?" asked Marty, helping himself to the mashed potatoes. "Did you get a Christmas letter from him?"

"We got one day before yesterday," answered Joe. He looked at his wife before saying more. "It seems that he's found himself a girl over there."

"I told you Mom," laughed Stan. "He'll be bringing home a German girl next summer."

"And I told you not to say things like that!" she replied hotly. Everyone laughed.

A month later, they received another letter from Allan, telling more about this girl he'd met. "Her name is Eva and she is blonde and very pretty," he'd written. "I like her a lot."

These last five words struck fear into Min's heart. "Oh, no!" she said. "I certainly hope he doesn't get serious about a foreign girl!"

"When's he coming home?" asked Carrie one Sunday when they were over visiting the Murphys.

"Not soon enough to suit me!" huffed Min.

"He will be getting out in June," said Joe. "Another five months."

"A lot can happen in that time," said Min.

Carrie thought that Min seemed genuinely worried about her son. "Oh, I'm sure he'll soon forget all about her and come home and marry some girl from here," said Carrie, trying to console her friend.

As it turned out, Allan did not forget about this German girl named Eva. In March, he sent a letter to his folks, telling them that he was in love with the girl and that they planned to get married.

This news put Min to bed for the rest of the afternoon. Magda came over after she heard the news.

"For heaven's sake, Minerva, get a hold of yourself. It's not the end of the world!"

"Well, that's easy for you to say, Magda. It's not your son who will be bringing home a foreign wife," wailed Min.

"No, he's not my son, but I've always loved him like he was. I care about him very much. All your kids are like my own." Magda took out a hanky and started wiping the tears that were starting to form.

Min sighed deeply and sat up in bed. "Oh, Magda, I'm sorry. I know you've always cared deeply for our family."

"Maybe this won't be so bad. She's probably a very nice girl," said Magda, after composing herself.

"Well, I don't know about that, but I guess I better get up before Joe gets in."

"He won't take very kindly to the way you're acting, you know," Magda told her sister-in-law.

"I know." Min straightened herself up and then the two women went downstairs. "I'll make some coffee."

"No, I've got to get home and start supper," said Magda.

Later, when Joe came in for supper, he eyed Min with caution. "So, Min, are you going to be all right with the news that came today, then?"

Min sat down hard on a chair by the kitchen table and burst into tears. Joe let her cry for a while before saying what he had to say.

"Min, pull yourself together. We're not going to let this get us down. We'll make the best of it. Put a smile on your face and announce to your friends that, yes, Allan is bringing home a very nice girl and we're certainly happy about it."

Min looked at her husband with horror. "But that would be lying!" she said.

"Not exactly," said Joe. "It's a matter of standing behind our son's decision and supporting him. It won't be easy for him, either, at first, and it certainly won't be easy for her."

"I guess you're right," Min sighed. "As always," she added with a hint of a smile. "Here I am, acting like a silly fool again."

He got up and patted her on the arm tenderly. "Well, it was a little bit of a shock, that's for sure. But we're going to make the best of it from now on. You will try, won't you?" he asked.

"Yah, I'll be all right, I guess. But it may take a little getting used to."

In early May, Allan wrote and told them that he and Eva were wading through a lot of red tape and would get married over there as soon as they received the needed papers.

"He's going to get married over there, then!" said Min. "Couldn't he at least wait until he gets home and get married here, with all of his family?"

He'd included a picture of himself and Eva together in this last letter. "She is a pretty girl, isn't she?" commented Joe, looking at the picture closely.

"Yah, I guess she is," admitted Min, reluctantly.

Another letter came a week later. "Get the honeymoon cottage ready," Allan had written. They weren't married yet but they thought it would be soon, he'd said.

"They want to live in that little house?" Min said to Joe, surprised.

"Well, I'm sure it will only be for a short while. We don't even know what he plans to do when he gets home."

"I wonder if he'll want to stay here and farm."

"He sure hasn't given us much information in his letters, has he?" huffed Min.

"Well, he's in love and busy trying to get married," laughed Joe.

A telegram arrived the first of June from Germany. Allan stated that they'd gotten married that morning and they'd be home June 10.

"Well, we better finish getting the house ready for them, then," said Min. "We better get that table from Magda and Art's moved over there. I'll finish cleaning and get some new curtains up."

Joe had to chuckle at his wife. She was actually getting a little excited about the situation.

She'll come around yet.

By the morning of the tenth, everything was ready. The little cottage was spotless and Min had even put a bouquet of flowers on the table and a pretty cloth. The windows shone under new, crisp curtains.

Allan had called the day before from Boston and he and Eva would be taking a bus later that day and would arrive in Fargo the next evening. He asked that just Marty or Ron meet them and drive them out to the farm. He didn't want the whole family there at the bus station.

"That's maybe for the best," said Joe. "It might be too much for her, meeting all of us at once, in a public place."

"Yah, I think we should tell Stan's and Art and Magda to wait until tomorrow to come over, don't you think?" wondered Min.

"That's probably a good idea. Let her meet just a few of us at a time."

Min was so nervous the whole afternoon that she hardly knew what to do with herself. "I wonder what time they'll be getting here?" she asked Joe several times.

Joe kept busy out in the barn and in the yard. Min finally decided to busy herself with some mending that needed doing. She was sitting in the rocker after supper when she heard a car drive into the yard. She jumped up and hurried to the kitchen window. It was Ron's car. She held her breath.

Allan stepped out first. He was still in uniform. He helped a young woman out next and then reached in for some luggage. She looked up at him and smiled. She was pretty, thought Min. Then she saw the woman look towards the house. Min stepped back from the window quickly. She braced herself and went outside to meet her new daughter-in-law.

CHAPTER 26

The newlyweds were getting along just fine and seemed very happy together. Friends of the Murphys decided that there should be a reception for the couple. It was held in the church basement a few weeks after their arrival.

"It will give everyone a chance to meet your new wife," Min had told Allan, "and to offer their congratulations to the both of you."

"Oh, all right," said Allan. "I was just thinking that maybe Eva would be a bit overwhelmed by it all."

"She will do just fine," Min had assured her son.

"Mom, I've been wanting to tell you how grateful I am for the way you and Dad have accepted her. I know how it must have caught you by surprise."

"Well, I can't say that I was very happy when we got your letter saying you were going to marry a German girl," Min admitted. "But, it's going much better than I expected and you seem very happy, and that's what's important."

Allan got up and gave his mother a hug. "I've got to go now, but thanks again. Eva's probably got supper ready and waiting."

During the first few days after Allan and Eva's arrival on the farm, the new bride stayed pretty much to herself, in their little cottage. But then, she started to come over to the big house each day on her own. Min thought that perhaps she was lonely over there with Allan busy helping the men with the farming all day.

She'd follow Min around and watch her do everything from gardening to cooking to ironing to sewing. "I want to see how you do everything so I'll know how to do things the American way," she'd told her new mother-in-law. It wasn't long before she was pitching in wholeheartedly.

"That girl knows how to work, that's for sure!" Min told Magda one day.

"She sure handles the language well, doesn't she?" remarked Magda.

"Yes, she does. She said that she had taken English in school and then after the war, she had worked in the homes of American officers."

"Does she say much about her family or childhood or how it was to live there during the war?" asked Magda.

"No, whenever I ask her those kinds of questions, she clams up. The only one she'll talk about is her grandmother. I think they were very close. Of course, she's dead now, I guess."

"Well, I like her," announced Magda firmly. "And Minerva, I'm proud of the way you have handled the situation. I didn't know about you there for awhile, before they arrived."

Min laughed. "Well, I didn't know how I was going to do, either. But she's so nice and easy to like that it has been going quite well."

"Well, I can see why Allan fell in love with her," said Magda. "I never did like that Kathy very well, the one he used to go with. There was just something about her."

"I never got to really know her myself," confided Min. "All I know is that Allan had been pretty crazy about her."

"Puppy love!" huffed Magda. "That's what that was."

"Allan was telling me that last weekend they went to a dance at Horace and who do you suppose was the first person they ran into when they came in the door, but Kathy!" said Min.

"Oh, no! How did that go, then?"

"Well, after he got over his surprise, he just introduced the two women, saying that Kathy was an old friend. Kathy was with some guy that Allan didn't know. I guess she's engaged to him."

"Well, all's well that ends well," said Magda.

A couple months later, after the harvest was over with, Joe dropped a bombshell. "Min," he said, "I think that Allan and Eva should move into this house and we should move out."

"Wh....what!" she stammered. "What do you mean by moving out? Where would we go? Into town?"

"Oh, no, not into town!" he exclaimed, emphatically. "I've been thinking that this house is too big for the two of us and that little cottage over there is way too small for them to live in much longer. It's going to be hard to heat it this winter, and...."

"But where will we live?" asked Min, impatiently. "That's what I'm waiting for you to tell me."

"I was thinking...."

"You sure have been doing a lot of thinking lately," Min interrupted her husband.

"Well," he laughed, "when you're sitting on the combine all day, you have a lot of time to think. Anyway, I was thinking that we could build a new house, a smaller one than this."

"And just where did you have in mind?" she asked, her eyebrows raised and her hands on her hips.

"There's a nice spot on the east side of the trees here, over by the coulee. I've always thought that it would be a nice place for a house."

Min was trying to visualize this spot in her mind.

"C'mon, let's get in the pickup and I'll take you over there," he said, excited by the prospect of showing her his choice spot.

"Well, all right," she said reluctantly. She removed her apron and followed him out of the house.

Later that evening, Joe and Min had popped over to Allan and Eva's and the four of them were sitting around the little kitchen table. Eva had put on the coffeepot and she set out pieces of fresh chocolate cake that she had made that afternoon.

"Your cake is delicious," remarked Joe, after taking several bites.

"Oh, do you think so?" she asked. "It's your wife's recipe but I know that I can never make anything as good as she can."

"You certainly can, Eva!" exclaimed Min. "This is very good indeed."

Allan gave his mother a grateful smile. "Eva has a little inferiority complex," he chuckled. "She doesn't give herself much credit, but I think she's a marvelous cook." He reached for his wife's hand and gave it an affectionate squeeze.

"The reason we stopped over this evening," Joe began, "is that we have something important to discuss with you both."

The young couple's eyes focused on Joe intently. "What is it, Dad?"

"How would you like to move into the big house?" he asked, getting right to the point.

"And live with you?" Allan asked.

"No," laughed Joe. "Not with us. We'd move out, maybe build a new house and let you two have ours."

"Build a house? Where would you build? In town?"

"No!" he answered firmly. "Like I told your mother, I'd never live in town."

"Where then?"

"We've picked out a site just east of the trees, back by the coulee. A nice little spot for a new home."

"Well, this is really a surprise," said Allan. He looked at his wife, who had been silent, watching the exchange between father and son. He took her hand again.

"You indicated that you want to stay on the farm and you certainly can't keep living in these cramped quarters much longer."

"No, I guess it would be a cold house to spend the winter in," agreed Allan. "When were you thinking of moving? Would you start your house this fall?"

"Yah. I was in town today and talked with Johnny Skarie about building us a house out here and he said that he could start in about two weeks. We could get the basement dug and the house pretty well along before winter sets in."

"Whew!" said Allan, getting up to get more coffee for everyone. "What do you think, hon, would you like to live in that big house over there?"

Eva's eyes sparkled and she nodded her head. "That would be very nice, but it is a big house for us, too."

"Well, maybe you'll be starting a family soon and then you'll need all those bedrooms," said Joe. Eva just blushed and looked at her husband.

"I guess this is as good a time as any to tell you the news," Allan said to his parents. "Eva is going to have a baby."

"Oh, how wonderful!" exclaimed Min. She came around and gave her daughter-in-law a hug. "That is great news."

"Yes, we are so happy about it," Eva said. "I didn't know if I would be able to have children." She didn't go into details and Min didn't ask any questions.

"This is great timing, then," said Joe, getting up. "It's getting late, we better get going. We'll talk about this more tomorrow." Min followed him out of the little house.

"Thanks for coffee," Min called back to the young couple standing in their doorway.

"We probably won't be able to sleep tonight," laughed Allan. "All this excitement!"

It wasn't more than a week later when Eva came to Min's door one afternoon, her eyes red-rimmed from crying.

"What's the matter, child?" Min asked.

"I think I've lost the baby," Eva started weeping again.

"Oh, no!" exclaimed Min. "Come in, my dear, and sit down. Are you sure?"

Eva nodded her head in the affirmative. "I've had bleeding and cramping all day and a short while ago....well, I think that is when I lost it for sure."

"Oh, I'm so sorry, Eva. I know how you and Allan were looking forward to having this baby."

"Yes, he will be so disappointed. I wasn't sure if I would ever be able to have children, after....after some things that happened to me when I was younger. And then when I found out that I was pregnant, I was so happy."

"Had you been to the doctor yet?" asked Min.

"No, we were going to make an appointment soon."

"Perhaps you should go to one anyway, now, and be checked over."

"Yes, I guess I should do that."

"Livvie has a doctor in Fargo that she really likes. Maybe she would give you his name and the telephone number and you can call him."

"Yes, that would be nice to go to her doctor."

"Livvie experienced a miscarriage, too, some years ago, and it was very hard on her. Maybe she'll come and visit with you soon."

Later that week, digging began on the basement for the new house.

"My, things sure are moving fast, aren't they?" remarked Magda to Min, as they both stood and watched the proceedings. "I was so surprised when Art came home one day and said that you and Joe were moving!"

"Well, we're not moving far, are we?" laughed Min.

"No, and I'm glad of it," said Magda. "It sure wouldn't seem right if the two of you weren't living right across the road from us."

"Well, people have to make some changes as the years go by, you know."

"Yah, well, I'd never get Art off the farm, that I know for sure."

"Don't be too sure about anything," laughed Min.

The two women got back in the car, as the wind was getting a bit chilly, and Min drove over to Magda's to let her off.

"Don't you want to come in for a cup of coffee?"

"Well, maybe I will," said Min. "A hot cup of coffee would feel good right now."

"How is Eva doing, now, after her miscarriage?" Magda asked.

"Oh, she's feeling all right but she still gets pretty weepy when we talk about it. She went to the doctor yesterday. Livvie called for her and was able to get her right in."

Grandpa Ivar stepped into the kitchen. "Oh, it's you, Min. I thought Magda was talking to herself again!" he teased.

"Do you want to join us for some coffee?" Magda asked her father-in-law.

"Why, sure. I can always drink more coffee. How is the basement project coming along?"

"Well, the men said that the dirt digs up pretty good. It's been some time since we've had rain."

"Hope it holds off for awhile longer for you," Ivar said, taking a chair by the table.

"Yah, the boys are busy with the plowing, too, now."

"I bet Joe is glad to have Allan back to help with the farming."

"Yes, it's been nice to have him back. He seems to be happy to stay on the farm. We didn't know how it would go, him going off to college, and then being in the service for those three years. Sometimes, then, the young guys want to go off and do other things."

"I always thought that Allan would end up being a farmer," said Ivar. "Now, Martin, I thought he would be, too. He seemed to like it so much growing up, but then, the war came along and things changed for him."

"Yes, many things changed for Marty," sighed Min. She stirred her coffee reflectively.

"How is it going for Martin and Jeannie now?" asked Magda.

"I really don't know," admitted Min. "Things seem to be going pretty good, and then, sometimes, when he comes out here, I think he looks so sad."

"Well, little Joey certainly is a bright spot in his life," said Magda.

"He sure isn't little anymore, is he?" laughed Min. "He's only five but he looks a couple years older."

"He's such a big kid. So tall and husky," contributed Ivar.

"He really likes coming out to the farm here. All he talks about is tractors and combines and trucks."

"Well, it will be easy to know what to get him for Christmas," chuckled Magda.

"I guess I better be going," Min said, getting up. "I told Eva I'd help her make a pie yet this forenoon. She was going over to Livvie's when I left, to pick apples."

"Say, how is Livvie's....real mother, Merrie, doing? I heard she had to have an operation?" asked Magda.

"She's home already, I guess, so she must be doing OK."

"How old are her children now?"

"Oh, they're out of high school by now. The girl is going to nurses school and the boy is working in Wahpeton."

"Do they know that Livvie is really their sister?" asked Magda.

"I don't know if their mother has told them yet or not. I'll have to ask Livvie that sometime." Min headed for the door. "Well, thanks for the coffee."

The conversation at Thanksgiving time at the Murphy's revolved around the new house, of course, but also the November presidential election. Eisenhower and Nixon had won again in another landslide victory.

"That's quite a road project for the country that Ike has initiated, isn't it?" remarked Art. He and Magda had been invited over for Thanksgiving dinner, along with Grandpa Ivar.

"Yah, I guess when Ike was in Germany at the end of World War II, he was impressed with the autobahn highway over there," related Joe.

"Well, it's going to be great for cross-country travel in the years to come, that's for sure," said Art.

"Not that you do any of that cross-country traveling!" Magda teased him.

"No, I don't like to be away from home, I'll admit, but it will be good for the country as a whole," Art defended himself.

"Who wants to take a little drive over to see how the new house is coming?" asked Joe, pushing back from the table.

All the kids started clamoring to go, but their grandpa said only the grownups would be going this trip. "How about if Ron and Rosie and Jeannie and Marty go with me first, and then the rest can go a little later.

The remaining women began to clean up the kitchen after the big meal. Stan took the kids out to the barn to see the new baby kittens.

"The weather sure is nice for it being the end of November, isn't it?" remarked Magda.

"Maybe it will be a nice winter this year, I hope," said Livvie. "Of course, the kids all want lots of snow, though."

"Livvie, how do your folks like their new television set?" asked Min, as she ran the dishwater.

"Oh, they really like it a lot, I guess. Whenever I call over there, they're always watching something."

"Well, Joe wants to get one, but I said we have too much expense now with the new house, so maybe we'll wait for awhile," said Min.

"Art wants to get one, too," chimed in Magda. "Maybe at Christmas time. I think that Grandpa would enjoy it."

"Now that the kids are all out of the house," said Livvie, "I can tell you that Stan is getting us one for Christmas, but it will be a big surprise. The kids have been asking for one for the past year."

The first carload returned to the house and Joe took the rest of those who wanted to take a look at the new house.

"It's coming along pretty good, isn't it?" Rosie remarked to Min. "When do you think you will be able to move in?"

"Well, Mr. Skarie isn't promising anything for sure, but we think that by February it should be ready."

"I bet Allan and Eva are certainly anxious to move in here," said Jeannie.

"Oh, yes, I'm sure they are, but they're being very patient. They seem to kind of like their cozy little place over there," Min told them.

Late in the afternoon, as everyone was seated around the table playing cards or else in the living room, talking, there came a rap on the door. Joe got up to answer it.

"Well, Jake and Kenny! How nice to see you two. Come right in."

Ron got up at the mention of Kenny's name. He gave his old friend a bear hug. "It's good to see you, Kenny. How're you doing?"

"Pretty good," he answered. Ron took his coat and told him to join them at the kitchen table. "We're playing hearts. Wanna play a game with us?"

Kenny hesitated a bit, and Ron realized that he would probably have trouble seeing the cards. "Mom, do we still have those cards with the extra big numbers?"

"Well, I think they're in the bureau. I'll go and take a look." She soon came back with the special deck and it was shuffled and put into play.

"How will that work for you, Kenny?" asked Ron, clearly happy to have his friend join them once again.

"This will be great," he answered. "We'll have to get a deck of these at home. Dad and I like to play Rummy in the evenings sometimes."

After awhile, Kenny told the group, "I have some good news to tell you. I went to the eye doctor in Fargo last week and he said that my good eye had not gotten any worse and he said that he could get me some real strong glasses so that I could see much better out of that eye."

"Why, that's wonderful," said Allan. "Would you be able to drive then?"

"The doctor said that maybe I could do a little driving out in the country here but not in traffic. My side vision is no good, you know. I'd be able to drive the tractor in the field and help Dad more."

Ron was so pleased at the positive change in his old pal. "I'm glad things are working out better for you now, Kenny."

The first day of the new year, 1957, started out with a bang. There was a snowstorm that left many inches on the ground.

"So much for our mild winter," Livvie said dryly.

"Well, the kids will be happy. They can use their sleds now," said Stan.

"If you can get them away from the TV!" laughed Livvie.

Their new television set had been a big surprise on Christmas morning. Stan, with help from his brother, Allan, had carried it into the living room after the kids were asleep. The set was on from morning until night, even when only the test pattern was showing.

In February, the Murphys' new house was indeed ready and they moved in on Valentine's Day, with a lot of help from their family. A couple days later, Min and Eva set about cleaning the big house from top to bottom.

"We'll get our spring housecleaning done a few months early," remarked Min. The following weekend, Allan and Eva moved their few things into the big house.

"It sure didn't take us long, did it?" laughed Allan. "We hardly had anything."

"Just wait until you've lived there for almost forty years, son," warned Min.

Two weeks later, Stan and Livvie and Allan and Eva organized a house-warming party at the new house for Joe and Min. It was on a Sunday afternoon and it was a total surprise to the new inhabitants. Marty's and Ron's came out from Fargo. Also invited were Carrie and George, Freddie and Lenora, Karl and Dorothy, Art and Magda, Grandpa Ivar, Jake and Kenny and a few other neighbors. Every corner of the house was filled with people.

Everyone brought food and the supper table groaned with the weight of it all. Livvie had brought paper plates, to Min's relief.

"I was wondering where I would find enough plates for this bunch when you all started coming in!" she'd exclaimed.

The girls wouldn't let Min do a thing in the kitchen. "You just go out there and enjoy your guests now," they told her. "Take them on a tour of the house."

Before supper, some parlor games were initiated by Magda and Livvie. Everyone laughed uproariously when "airplane rides" were given to unsuspecting volunteers. The person who was chosen for the ride was blindfolded and told to stand on a board, which was actually a leaf from the dining table. He was to put his hands on the shoulders of the two men who were going to raise him up. Instead, these two men kneeled down but the person on the board thought he was going up. He was then told to "jump" but he was too scared to do that as he thought he was near the ceiling. When he finally made the plunge, he found that he was only about a foot off the floor.

After everyone ate the hearty meal, the honored couple was presented with a housewarming gift from the group. Joe and Min were given a beautiful mirror.

"We thought you needed this over your sofa, there," suggested Livvie.

"Oh, its just beautiful and we thank you all so much," said Min, wiping tears from her eyes. Joe thanked everyone, too, and he was also a little choked up and lost for words.

On the way home from the party, Carrie and George talked about what a fun time it had been. "I wonder what Eva thought about all are crazy goings-on," remarked Carrie. "Sometimes I've noticed, the few times I've seen her, a sad expression on her face when she doesn't think anybody's looking. Almost a haunted look about her eyes."

"Well, maybe she had it kind of rough during the war, there, in Germany," said George.

"Perhaps, but it seems like she's been hurt very badly. She has such a....a....fragileness about her. Like she could break at any moment."

“I think she seems very nice. Maybe she tries a little too hard to be liked, though. It can’t be easy for her.”

When they were getting ready for bed, Carrie sighed and said, wistfully, “My, they certainly have a lovely house, don’t they?”

George looked over at his wife. “Would you like to have a nice, new house like that, then?”

“Oh, I guess a new house would be fun but I’m very happy with what we’ve got, aren’t you?”

“I’m happy wherever you are,” he said, and she chuckled.

“You sure know how to say the right thing, don’t you, Mr. Johnson?”

CHAPTER 27

One Saturday, late in March, the Murphy men, Joe, Stan and Allan, decided to go to an auction sale down by Wahpeton. They asked George to go along with them. Livvie had planned a fun day for the women. She invited them over for a lefse-making party. It was Min, Eva, and Carrie, Livvie and the girls.

Livvie had boiled up a large batch of potatoes earlier and by the time the ladies arrived in the early afternoon, they were cooled down enough to use. Min brought her lefse grill and Livvie also had one. Carrie and Min did the rolling and Livvie and Eva did the frying. Eva had helped Min several times to make this Norwegian specialty so she was getting quite good at the task.

"I don't like the rolling out very much, though," she told them. "I like to do the frying best."

Livvie had Cheryl and Linda taking turns, trying both the rolling and the frying so they would learn how to do it. Cheryl, who was now a sophomore in high school, was quite good at it, but Linda, an eighth grader, was having trouble mastering the art.

"I just can't do this!" Linda exclaimed, laying the rolling pin down hard. She took off her apron and left the room in a huff.

"She gets frustrated so easily," Livvie said, explaining her youngest daughter's actions.

"Oh, it will come in time," said Min. "I think it took me an awful long time, too, when I was young, to get the hang of rolling things out. Pie crusts, too, were a real challenge."

"You'd never know it now," Eva said. "You make wonderful crusts."

"That's the result of lots of practice," said Min. "I wonder how many pies I've made in my life! Joe and the boys all love pie. That's their favorite dessert."

When the lefse making was half done, Livvie announced that they would take a little break. "And taste the fruits of our labor!" she exclaimed.

She set out pieces of the "scrap lefse" and put the butter dish in the middle of the table and told the ladies to sit up. She poured coffee and milk.

"C'mon, Bobbie and Linda," she called into the living room. "Have some lefse with us."

"Oh, I'm getting to really like this stuff," said Eva, helping herself to another piece.

"It kind of grows on you, doesn't it?" said Carrie, and the others laughed knowingly.

"The men will surely enjoy this when they get back from their sale," said Min.

"Well, it will go good with the pot roast that's in the oven. I made enough for all of us, so plan to stay for supper when the men get here," Livvie told them.

"Mom, look!" shouted Bobbie, as he looked out the window. "It's snowing like crazy!"

"Well, for goodness sake! It must have just started."

"I hope it doesn't snow too much, so that the men have a hard time getting back."

"OK, let's get back to work, then," announced Livvie. "Linda, do you want to try rolling out some lefse again? You have two grandmas here to help you so this is a good time to learn."

"Oh, I suppose I could try once more," Linda answered, reluctantly.

"I'm going back to watch TV," said Bobby.

"You watch too much TV, I think," said Min.

"Aw, Grandma," he said. "It won't hurt me."

The ladies were so engrossed in their task that they didn't pay much attention to the weather for some time. When they were frying the last pieces of lefse, Livvie looked out the kitchen window.

"Oh, my goodness!" she exclaimed. "Just look at that, will you!"

Everyone rushed to a window. The snow was coming down so thick that they couldn't see across to the barn.

"Oh, dear!" said Min. "What will the men run into, I wonder?"

Livvie looked at the kitchen clock. "It's almost five o'clock. They should be here about six, I figured."

"Well, I don't know if they'll make it by then, now," said Carrie.

"How far is this town, Wahpeton?" asked Eva, concern showing in her voice.

"It's about an hour's drive from here," Min told her.

"Well, let's get this kitchen cleaned up before they come," suggested Livvie. "We may even have to wipe up the floor a little, with all the flour that was flying around here today!" The ladies chuckled and all pitched in with the clean-up.

Six o'clock came and no men yet. "Mom!" Linda called from the other room. "They're talking about the weather on the TV. They're calling it a 'big storm' with many inches of snow. Oh, boy!"

The women hurried into the living room to watch the weather news. It didn't sound good, Livvie thought, but didn't want to express her concern.

When it was almost 7 o'clock, Livvie announced that she thought they shouldn't wait any longer for the men. "We'll start eating, I think."

She finished setting the table and she put the pot roast in the middle. "Come, everyone," she called. "Does anyone want any lefse?" she asked before sitting down herself.

"Oh, I don't think I want to see another piece of that stuff for at least a few days," groaned Cheryl. "I've already eaten too much of it."

"Me, too," agreed Bobbie.

No one had very big appetites, so when Livvie was going to dish up the dessert, she didn't have any takers. "Well, we'll have it later, then," she told them.

The dishes were done up and the pot roast was put in the warming oven. It was now 8 o'clock.

"Well, let's all sit down in the living room and wait. Maybe there's something good on TV now," suggested Livvie.

"The Jack Benny Show is just starting," said Bobby. "I like that."

They all enjoyed the hour-long program, but many times their eyes would wander to the clock on the wall, or someone would go and look out the window during commercials.

"It hasn't let up at all yet," announced Carrie, after coming back from the kitchen. "I still can't see the barn."

"Oh, dear," said Min. "I sure wonder where the men ended up. It would be nice if we'd get a call from them."

"Yah, I hope they aren't sitting in the ditch someplace," said Carrie.

Worry was creeping into every voice now. They had each tried to keep it at bay before but just too much time had passed with no word. Eva kept silent, but she was nervously walking the floor.

The 10 o'clock news came on with more talk of the storm. This did nothing to calm their fears. It sounded like it wouldn't let up until the middle of the night.

"Well, ladies, it's going to be a long night, it looks like," said Livvie. "Maybe we'll have to play some cards or something."

"Anything to get our minds off the storm," said Min.

"Let's play a game that the kids can play, too." suggested Carrie.

"How about Rummy!" yelled Bobbie, jumping up from the floor.

"OK," said Livvie. "You get the cards."

The four women and three children gathered once again around the kitchen table. Livvie took the cards and shuffled them and dealt them out. Eva didn't know how to play this game, but it didn't take long before she was winning a few hands herself.

"Beginner's luck, they say," laughed Carrie.

"Mom, can we make popcorn?" asked Linda. "Please?"

"Well, I suppose we could."

"Oh, boy!" exclaimed Bobby. "Can we have some pop, too?"

"Check and see what we have in the refrigerator, will you?"

It was about midnight when they finished their pop and popcorn and another few hands of cards. Bobby was tired and went and laid down on the sofa. Linda went up to her room and went to bed without being told.

"I guess there probably won't be church tomorrow morning," said Min.

"I'm sure no one will be able to get out. There's bound to be a lot of drifts, with this wind."

Concern and worry were etching everyone's face now. Cheryl expressed a common concern when she said, "What if they don't make it home?"

"They'll make it home sometime, Cheryl, but probably not tonight," Livvie told her daughter. She couldn't possibly think the worst. They had to remain hopeful.

Livvie roused Bobbie and told him to go on upstairs to bed. "You go to bed, too, Cheryl."

The four women tried to get comfortable in the living room. The late night movie was still on so they watched that but no one could really concentrate on it.

"Maybe we should all just go up and go to bed. There's room for everyone," suggested Livvie.

No one moved. "I guess I'd rather just sit here and wait it out," said Min.

The others agreed.

"Shall I make some coffee, then?" asked Livvie.

"No, no, we're fine, I think," said Carrie, looking around. "That root beer filled me up."

"I'm hoping that they've found shelter at some farm place along the way," said Carrie.

"Yah, I'd hate to think of them sitting in the car, freezing all night," agreed Min.

"Oh, what if they freeze to death!" wailed Eva. She slumped onto the sofa and put her head in her hands.

"Now, now, let's try not to think like that, my dear," said Min, trying to comfort her daughter-in-law.

"Well, it could happen," cried Eva. "I've heard of it happening." She started to shake and Min took the afghan from the back of the sofa and put it around Eva's shoulders.

"What if Allan dies out there? What would I do? I don't have anybody but him. I don't even have my baby anymore. I lost my baby!" Eva flung off the afghan and got up and started pacing again.

"Oh, what would I do? I couldn't live without him," she was starting to get hysterical now.

Livvie looked at Min, wondering what they were going to do with the distraught young woman. Min got up and tried to take her by the arm and lead her back to the sofa. Eva just waved her arms around frantically.

"You all have family who love you, but I only have Allan!" she exclaimed loudly.

"Eva, calm down now," said Min. "We all love you and I'm sure you have family back in Germany who love you. Anyhow, you aren't going to lose Allan. He's coming back to you. We just have to wait until tomorrow."

Min finally got Eva to sit back down again. "You're wrong about me having a family back home who loves me, you know," Eva told them. "I have no one there anymore. No one." She began to cry softly. Livvie got up and got a tissue for her.

"I think I need to tell you all some things about me and my past," she sniffled.

"You don't have to tell us anything, Eva," Min said, gently.

"I want to tell you! I need to tell you!" she was talking loudly again now. Livvie worried that she would wake the children.

"All right, dear," soothed Min. "Tell us what you want to tell us."

Eva wiped at her eyes and took a deep breath, and then began her story. "I was born in Danzig, which was in West Prussia at that time. It was a port city. My father was a sailor, but I never knew him. My mother didn't marry him. She didn't want me and never loved me."

Eva was speaking in almost a monotone voice. She had a faraway look in her eyes. "We lived with my grandparents. My mother worked on a streetcar. Later, my mother had another daughter, but still she did not marry."

Eva pulled the afghan tightly around her shoulders now. The others shifted in their places, not knowing where this was leading.

"In 1939, Germany invaded Danzig and turned it into a German city. Then they took Poland, the east half, with Russia taking the west half. Then Hitler wanted all of Poland so he invaded again." Eva paused for quite sometime, as if thinking what to say next.

"It was awful, living under the Nazis," she continued. "We weren't allowed to say anything against them. There were spies everywhere. Neighbors spied on neighbors. Children were supposed to spy on their parents and turn them in if they heard their parents talking against the Fuhrer." She paused again and tears filled her eyes.

"Dear, you don't have to tell us these things if it is too painful, you know," said Min, gently.

Eva squared her shoulders and continued. "They used terrible means to intimidate us! My best friend had two little sisters....ages 2 and 3. The Nazis came into their house one day and took those two little girls and....and....they nailed their tongues....to the table!" Eva started to sob. "They....suffered terribly....and the people....were forced to watch this....this horrible thing. It was done to scare everyone so that they wouldn't say anything against Hitler."

Eva slumped back and held her arms tight across her chest. She was trembling, Livvie noticed. Livvie got up and went to her sister-in-law.

"Eva," she said, kneeling down in front of her. "You don't need to go on if you don't want to."

"Yes!" she almost shouted. "Yes, I must!"

Before long, she continued with her story. "The war lasted six long years. It was very hard for us. My grandfather died. My grandmother....she was the only one who truly loved me. She had a radio that she kept hidden. We weren't allowed to have them. We might hear the truth then. She listened to the BBC. Towards the end of the war, we were living in cellars because of the bombing. We heard on the radio that the Americans were coming, but that Roosevelt had given orders for them to stop and let the Russians advance as far as Berlin." Eva paused here again for awhile. The other women looked at each other in the awkward silence.

"The day before the Russians came, it was my Confirmation day. The next morning....the minister was....found hanged." Her voice faltered here. "We didn't know....if it was suicide or murder, but we suspected that the Nazis did it."

"Oh, Eva," said Min, almost sobbing herself. She shook her head, back and forth, hardly believing all she was hearing.

"It gets worse," Eva told her. "It gets worse." She got up and started pacing again.

"The Russians were going to liberate us. They came down into the cellars where we were living then. They were the ugliest people I had ever seen. They were Mongolians, serving in the Russian army. They were so coarse and backwards. They even drank water from the toilet stool! They had never seen flush toilets before."

Eva was still pacing, with tears streaming down her face. "These men were savages. They raped all the girls and women, even our 82-year-old landlady!

Eva cried tears of anguish and then got control of herself again. "I was just thirteen then. My cousin and I were raped, too. We were forced to drink vodka. When we screamed, those ugly men knocked our teeth out. We were gang-raped. Afterwards, they put manure on our faces."

Eve started to pace wildly. She was sobbing hysterically. The other women were crying, too. Never had they heard such terrible things. Min got up and put her arms around Eva and tried to sooth her. They rocked back and forth, their arms around each other.

"I can't believe it," said Carrie. "How could someone do such awful things to innocent people. Women and children."

"Eva, how have you been able to live with all these terrible memories?" asked Livvie.

"I try to blot them out of my mind, but at night, you know....they sometimes come back to haunt me. Allan has been so good for me. He listens and then I feel better for awhile. That's why I needed to tell you these things tonight." She went to the window and looked out into the night. "Oh, Allan!" she almost screamed. "You must come back to me!"

"Eva, he will come back," said Min. "You'll see, tomorrow sometime, when it is possible for them to travel, they will get home."

"I'm sure that they are stranded at some farm place and maybe they don't have a phone so they can't let us know," Livvie rationalized. She got up and headed for the kitchen. "I'm going to make some coffee. I sure could use a cup."

A short while later, the women were sitting around the kitchen table. Livvie had placed a plate of cookies out for them to eat with their coffee.

After the coffee and cookies were enjoyed, Eva started in again. "I need to finish my story. I need to tell you. I only wish it was the Americans who had liberated us there. The Russians were so terrible. They had us form work brigades and do clean-up work for them. Some citizens were made to go and clean the rivers. Boats and ships had sunk and bodies floated into the river. The people had to take nets and pull up the bodies....and some fell apart."

The women all gasped at this. "Oh, this just makes me sick!" exclaimed Livvie.

"I am sorry to tell you these awful things, but that is the way it was," Eva told them. "The Russians then made us march to Danzig and then they put us on cattle cars. About 80 to a car. We were shoved in there and I was pushed in a corner and I laid in a manure pile. I was already sick with typhus, from the unsanitary conditions that we had been living in. When we got to Danzig, we could see that is was a pile of rubble. Then we went to Berlin, where I was put into the hospital. There the nurses poured kerosene on me to kill the lice. I had open sores so it really hurt!" Eva shivered at the memory and the others winced, just listening to her.

"My condition got worse and I was left for dead. I would have been carried away with the other corpses, but somebody figured out that I was still alive and rescued me. I was put back in a room. The hospital had already sent my death certificate to my mother. When they found out I was still alive, she and my grandmother came to the hospital. They were standing over my bed, and when I opened my eyes, my mother threw my death certificate at me and said, 'Why didn't you stay dead!' "

Livvie's hand flew to her mouth in horror. This was the worst she had heard so far! The others just gasped and couldn't believe that a mother could be so cruel. Eva was sobbing so hard that she couldn't stop for quite sometime. Min took her from the table and sat her down on the sofa once again. The others followed them into the living room.

"Again, I am so sorry that I am telling you such horrible things," said Eva, "but I have to tell someone. Allan tells me that it is good to talk about it."

"Perhaps it is, Eva, but I can see that it is very hard on you," said Min.

Eva continued on with her story. "I got well and went to school in Berlin for awhile. Then some of us were sent to a concentration camp to clean that out. We actually lived there for awhile. We had to take dead bodies out of a cave there. I finally ended up in East Germany, working for a farmer and then for a seed handler. He hired a guide to get me to West Germany, where my mother and sister were. We were trying to go through a barbed-wire fence and then some Russian soldiers appeared and captured us. We had a hearing and the commandant, who had a kind heart, told a soldier to take me across the border. He opened up the barbed-wire and pushed me across. I got a railroad ticket to go to the German province by Denmark, where my mother now lived."

Eva got up again and stood in the middle of the floor. She wrung her hands nervously. "This was not a good move. I was almost raped by my mother's new husband. He told me, 'You did it with the Russians, you'll do it with me!' I threw an iron at him and it went out the window. My mother sent me away after this incident."

"What did you do then?" asked Livvie, aghast.

"I worked at various jobs, I worked on a farm as a maid. I worked in vineyards and even a cigar factory. I went to southern Germany and worked for some French officers. I got various jobs through the labor offices in Augsburg and Stuttgart. My last job was for an American captain and his family in Wurzburg. That was where I met Allan."

"How did the two of you meet?" asked Livvie.

"Well, another maid and I went to a church to see some slides on America. We wanted to hear about that country. Afterwards we went to a gasthouse. We were reading some magazines there and Allan came and sat down beside me. That's how we first met. We dated for awhile and fell in love." Eva's voice softened, and the wild look in her eyes faded.

Livvie glanced up at the clock on the wall. "Why, it's almost two o'clock!" she told the others. "I think we should all go to bed for awhile, don't you think?" No one disagreed. "I'll find places for all of you to sleep upstairs and I'll take the sofa here."

“Eva, you look exhausted,” said Min. “I hope that you can get some sleep after what you’ve just told us.”

“I think it’s going to be difficult for any one of us to sleep, after what we’ve heard,” Carrie said.

“Good night, everyone,” Livvie told them a little later, as she was headed back downstairs to make a bed for herself in the living room. “I hope you sleep well.”

Livvie got comfortable on the sofa and began praying for the safety of the men. She finally fell asleep to the sound of the howling wind outside the living room window.

CHAPTER 28

The telephone rang about mid-morning. Livvie rushed to answer it. It was Stan and he told her that they were all right and that they had spent the night at a farm home.

"Couldn't you have called us from there?" Livvie asked, relieved at the sound of his voice. "We were worried sick about you!"

"There was no phone. I'll tell you all about it when we get home. They're clearing Highway 81 now, so we'll be home in a couple of hours, I figure."

"OK. We'll be waiting for you," Livvie told him.

Carrie and Min were sitting at the kitchen table and heard the one-sided conversation. "So, they're all right?" asked Min.

"Yes, they spent the night at some farm place, Stan said. They'll be home in a couple of hours."

"Thank goodness!" exclaimed Carrie.

The kids were still sleeping, and so was Eva. "It's good that Eva is still sleeping," said Min. "I can imagine how tired out she must have been after telling us all those horrible things."

"She probably didn't get to sleep right away, either," remarked Carrie. "I know it took me awhile before I drifted off."

"Yah, I kept thinking of some of the things that she'd told us."

"Well, I think I'll make some vegetable soup for the guys to eat whenever they get here," Livvie said.

"I'll help you," said Carrie, getting up and putting her coffee cup in the sink. "Where are your potatoes?"

About a half-hour later, the kids started coming down, one by one, and were hungry for breakfast. "You can fix yourselves some cereal," Livvie told them. "We're getting some soup ready for the men." She told them the good news.

It was almost noon before they heard Eva stirring upstairs. When she came into the kitchen, she looked like she'd put in a rough night.

"The men are OK!" Livvie told her right away. Eva's eyes brightened and tears began to form.

"Oh, thank goodness," she said. "I'm so relieved. Did they call?"

Livvie related the little she had been told on the phone. "They'll be home soon now."

Eva sat down by the table and Livvie brought her a cup of coffee. "Did you sleep very well, then, Eva?" asked Carrie.

"It took me quite awhile to fall asleep. I tossed and turned a lot. Good thing I was sleeping alone," she remarked. She stared into her cup for a few long minutes.

"I'm sorry I burdened you all with my life's story last night," Eva confessed.

"Oh, don't be sorry, Eva," said Min. "Perhaps it helps you to talk about it and it helps us to understand you better."

"I'm sure it was awfully difficult for you to tell us everything," said Carrie. "Is it getting easier for you to cope with all of it after all these years?"

"I don't know. It doesn't seem to get any easier, as time goes by. The memories are still so vivid. I know that I'll never forget." She shook her head slowly back and forth.

"Isn't it something how that war still keeps affecting our family and many other families, after this much time has passed," commented Min.

"What is it now, about twelve years since the war ended?" asked Carrie.

"About that." Min looked thoughtful. "In some ways it seems like a long time ago, and then, again, it seems like it was just yesterday that we heard that the war had ended."

"So, Eva, what is your relationship with your mother, now?" asked Livvie.

"We're still not close. I didn't see much of her after the war. I write once in awhile but she rarely answers."

"And you never knew your father?"

"No, she never talked much about him. I want her to tell me his name and maybe someday she will. I'd like to look him up if I ever go back to Germany. Allan said we can go back some time if I want to."

"He may not be very excited to find out he has a daughter that he didn't know about," said Min.

This made Livvie think about her own search for a father who didn't want to meet his daughter. Ever since her futile trip up to Canada some years back, she had never spoken his name to anyone. She rarely thought about him anymore.

"Let's get the table set, then," said Livvie, getting up and heading for the cupboard. "We'll be having guests for dinner!"

It was almost one o'clock before they saw the car coming into the yard. They all crowded around the door to give the men a great welcome. After much hugging and tears, the men got their outer wraps off and were told to wash up and be seated for dinner. Livvie ladled up the soup as Stan related the events of the day before.

"When we left Wahpeton, it was snowing pretty good but we thought we could make it. It wasn't long, though, before we could hardly see a thing and we knew we couldn't make it much further so when I saw this mailbox, I thought we better turn in the driveway. George went up to the house and knocked and knocked but there was no answer. He came back to the car and we figured we'd sit there until the farmer came home."

"Well, he didn't come home," said Joe, taking up the story. "We finally got so cold, we decided that we would go and try to get into the house to keep from freezing to death."

Eva's hand flew to her mouth. "That's what we were so worried about!"

"The door wasn't locked so we just let ourselves in," said George. "Boy, it felt good in there! We were getting so cold."

"Yah, we couldn't have stood it much longer out in that car," said Joe.

"We couldn't find a phone anywhere, so we couldn't let you ladies know that we were safe. That was the hardest part, knowing how worried you'd all be," Stan told them.

"The farmer never came home and before we left his place this morning, we wrote a note and put a few dollars on the table for the use of his house."

"Won't they be surprised when they finally get home!" exclaimed Carrie.

"We think it was a widower, living there alone. The house hadn't had a woman's touch for quite some time, it seemed," commented Joe.

"We read his name on the mailbox," said Stan, "so we know where we were."

"How far had you gotten?" asked Carrie.

"We had just passed Dwight, so it was a little north of there that we stopped."

"Well, all's well that ends well," said Carrie. "It did give us quite a fright, though," she admitted. She looked at Eva.

The young woman turned to look at her husband. "I was so afraid that you were never coming home to me again! It made me tell my life's story to these other ladies, here, and I'm afraid that it upset them quite a bit."

Allan looked at each of the women for their reaction.

"It was quite a story, that's for sure," said Min.

"It's hard to believe that such cruelty exists," agreed Carrie.

"Well, I think we better head for home, Carrie," suggested George, rising from the table.

"Yah, we better be going, too," said Joe. "It seems like a long time since we left home yesterday."

"Remember to take your packages of lefse, everyone," Livvie reminded the women, as they were getting ready to leave.

The storm produced nearly three inches of new snow, but that proved to be the last snow of the season and it started warming up fast by the first of April. The farmers planted their crops pretty much on schedule.

"The crops look really good this year," Stan remarked to Livvie one evening. "I think I'll build a new garage this fall if we have a good harvest."

"Oh, that would be nice, that's for sure."

About two weeks later, shortly before the Fourth of July, a rainstorm produced heavy rains and hail, scattered throughout the area. After the storm, Stan told Livvie he was going to take a drive and check on damages.

"Want to come along?" he asked.

"Maybe I will," she answered. "Cheryl, I'm going with Dad for a little ride," she called to her oldest daughter.

Stan drove slowly by all his fields and even got out to check more closely on some. "I don't see any great damage so far," he told Livvie. "Let's drive up around Dad's and see what's happened there."

When they drove into the Murphy yard, Joe and Allan were standing by their pickup. They both looked glum.

"Did you get much hail up here?" Stan asked, rolling down his window.

"Well, not so much right on the place here, but the north half-section is almost a total loss. The wheat is flattened to the ground."

"Oh, no!" exclaimed Stan. "How about the west eighty?"

"That got a little damage, too, but not nearly as bad."

Stan and Livvie continued on their drive. As they got closer to home again, the fields looked so much better. "I wonder if my folks got any hail down there," said Livvie.

"We could take a drive over there," suggested Stan.

"You know, we sure have been lucky all these years we've been married," said Livvie. "I don't recall that we've had one crop failure."

"No, I guess we've had pretty good crops right along. Some years better than other, of course."

"We've really got a lot to be thankful for," Livvie continued. "We have three healthy, beautiful children, we have our health, our parents are in good health. What more could we ask for?"

"Yah, I'd say that life has been good to us."

"God has been good to us," corrected Livvie. "We need to remember to thank Him for all our blessings more often, I think."

"It doesn't look like there's been any hail to amount to anything on your Dad's place," remarked Stan, as they turned into the Johnson driveway. They stopped in front of the house and Livvie hurried in, dodging some puddles on the sidewalk.

Carrie appeared at the screen door. "Well, what a nice surprise. Are you out for a drive, looking at all the rain?"

"Yah, we drove up to the Murphys'. They got a lot of hail on one of their wheat fields."

Stan joined them and tried to wipe off his shoes before entering the house. He finally decided to just take them off. "How much rain did you get here?" Stan asked Carrie.

"I'm not sure, but it really rained hard for quite awhile there."

"Haven't you been out to check your rain gauge yet?" Stan asked, as he walked into the living room and saw George sitting in his favorite chair.

George turned and waved a greeting to his son-in-law. "No, I haven't gone out there yet. After supper I didn't feel good, so I was just resting for awhile here."

Carrie and Livvie came into the room. "Yah, he said he had some chest pains after we got done eating so I'm a little concerned, but he thinks it's nothing." Carrie looked worried and an alarm went off in Livvie's head at her words.

"Dad, you could be having a heart attack! Why don't you go in to the doctor?"

"Oh, I feel better now. Maybe it was indigestion."

"What did you eat for supper?" asked Livvie.

"I just warmed up some hotdish that we'd had yesterday," Carrie told her. "Nothing spicy or anything."

"Well, if you get this again," Livvie told her father, "you better get to the doctor."

"Oh, all right, I maybe will," laughed George. "Why all this concern over nothing, anyway?"

"Dad! It might be something serious."

"OK, OK," he said. "Why don't you two sit down? How much rain did you get over there?" he asked Stan, trying to change the subject.

"Almost two inches. It was getting a little dry so it was welcome, but I feel bad for those who got heavy hail."

The phone rang and Carrie scurried to answer it. After a few minutes, she came back into the room. "That was Beatrice. She said that their brother-in-law, Tollof Grant, up by Horace, got totally hailed out tonight!"

"Not again this year!" exclaimed George. "That happened to him last year, too."

"My Dad always calls that area the 'hail belt' over there," said Stan. "They seem to have the worst luck."

"Oh, that's too bad," said Livvie, shaking her head. "We were just talking about how lucky we've been all these years with our crops."

"Should I put the coffee pot on?" asked Carrie.

"Oh, no, don't bother. We need to get home. We told the kids we were just going for a little ride."

The harvest was good that fall so Stan started building his new garage. "It will be a two-stall one," he told Livvie. "A place for our car and my pickup both."

Joe and Allan's harvest was marginal but they weren't complaining too much. Their neighbors to the northeast were so much worse off.

Allan and Eva had some great news to share with the rest of the family. Eva was pregnant again and in her third month and feeling great. "I think I will be successful this time," she laughed.

"Oh, I certainly hope so!" said Livvie, giving her sister-in-law a hug. "Eva, you look so good, you're just glowing!"

"Stan, can you drive Cheryl into town tonight for that party?" Livvie asked.

"What party was that again?"

"Don't you remember? I told you about it at dinnertime today. Elaine is having her big sixteenth birthday party tonight."

"Oh, yah, the boy-girl party," he said. "Do you think that Cheryl should be going to these yet?"

"Stan, she's fifteen now, you know, and it's at Elaine's house. It should be all right."

Later that evening, as Stan was taking Cheryl to town, he quizzed her about who was going to be there and what they would be doing.

"All I know is that we're going to have a scavenger hunt. I'll tell you the rest after the party, Dad!" laughed Cheryl.

"Have a good time, then," said Stan, as he dropped her in front of the drug store. Elaine's family lived in the apartment above the store. "I'll be here at twelve o'clock to pick you up."

"OK." Cheryl rolled her eyes. "I think that I could have driven in by myself, you know."

"After you get your license, young lady," chuckled Stan.

Stan ran some errands and then went to the pool hall to kill some time until midnight. He got into a game of cards with some of the fellows there. About eleven o'clock, Stan heard the phone ring and saw the bartender go and answer it. The men were kidding each other about whose wife it might be.

The bartender headed right for Stan. "It your wife, Stan. She sounds awful upset."

Stan hurried for the phone by the bar. "Livvie? What's the matter?"

"Oh, Stan, can you come home quick and get me? It's Dad. He's had a heart attack!"

Stan went to tell the other guys what had happened and hurried out. Then he remembered Cheryl. He went back into the bar and asked one of his neighbors, whose daughter was also at the party, if he would bring Cheryl home, too.

"I sure will, Stan. You better hurry now."

As Stan and Livvie were coming into the Johnson's yard, the ambulance from Fargo was just loading George into the back. Livvie fairly jumped out of the car before it came to a complete stop.

"Dad!" she shouted, running to try and catch him before the doors to the vehicle closed.

The ambulance attendants stepped aside so that Livvie could see her father. "I'll be all right, Livvie," said George, reaching for her hand. "Can you and Stan bring your mother into the hospital?"

"Sure we will, Dad. We'll be right behind you."

Carrie came running out of the house, carrying her purse. "Mom, we'll take you in to Fargo. Jump in!"

They followed the ambulance all the way in. It wasn't speeding too much, so Livvie took that as a good sign. They had to wait in the waiting room for quite awhile until the doctor had finished his examination. Finally, they were let in to see him.

Carrie started to cry when she saw her husband. "Don't cry, dear," George told her. "The doc said that I had a mild heart attack and that I should be just fine."

Carrie stayed by his bedside all night. Livvie and Stan went home around two o'clock.

"Can you bring me some clothes tomorrow when you come back in?" Carrie asked Livvie. She had arranged to stay with her niece, who lived in Fargo, until George was released.

George was doing well over the next few days and it was thought that he could go home soon. The phone rang late one evening, however, at Stan and Livvie's. It was the hospital, telling them that George had had another heart attack and that they better hurry in.

Stan was speeding all the way in and Livvie wrung her hands in her nervousness. They met Livvie's cousin in the hallway.

"How is he?" asked Livvie.

"He's rallying a little but it doesn't look good, Livvie." The two cousins embraced and then Livvie entered her father's room.

Carrie jumped up at the sight of her daughter. Livvie could tell that she had been crying. "Oh, Mom!" she cried. "Is he going to make it?"

"I don't know, Livvie. The doctor just left and he said he'd be back early in the morning. He seemed to think that George would make it through the night and then he'd know more in the morning. They'll take some tests."

"Have you been able to talk to him?'

"No, they have him sedated now. He was so restless."

Carrie and Livvie sat down in the only two chairs in the room. Stan stuck his head in the door. "May I come in?" he asked in a low voice.

"Sure, Stan," Carrie told him. "He's sleeping now."

It was a long night but finally they could see the sun coming up through the east window.

"I think I'll go down for a cup of coffee," Stan said. "Anybody else want some?"

"Yah, you can bring me a cup," Carrie told him. "That would taste good right now."

"I don't care for any," said Livvie.

Shortly before eight, the doctor came in and checked on his patient again.

"He's holding his own, but we're going to take some more tests now. I'll send a nurse in for him after a bit."

George looked like he wanted to say something. Carrie and Livvie both leaned in close. "I'm going to make it," he whispered. "Don't look so afraid, you two."

"Oh, Dad!" Livvie fought to keep back the tears. She squeezed his hand.

"Well, you just better make it, George Johnson!" Carrie tried to sound stern. "You can't go and leave me now."

Later that morning, the test results came back and the doctor returned just before noon. He looked rather grim, Livvie thought.

"I don't like what I see here," he said, indicating the paper he was holding in his hand. "He's had quite a bad attack this time. Only time will tell."

George knew that it was bad this time. He wanted to say so many things to his family. That afternoon, after a good rest, he reached for Carrie's hand. She grasped it and held it firmly.

"Carrie, my dear wife," he said, looking at her. "I want to tell you some things, just in case I don't have much time left."

"Oh, George," she sobbed. "Don't talk like that. You're going to get well."

He ignored that remark. He chose his words carefully. "I need to tell you how much I love you. You have been the light of my life all these years. I'm so glad I found you. You've made me so happy." He rested here, plainly out of breath.

"I love you, too, George, and you've also made me very happy. We've had a good life together, haven't we?"

"Yes, we have," he answered. "If I don't get well, I want you to go on with your life and be happy."

"Oh, George..."

"Please, let me go on," he told her. "I'm not afraid to die. I know where I'm going. I'm going to be with my Savior. And you'll join me someday, I know."

"Yes, George, we'll be together for all eternity." She started crying softly. Her tears fell onto his hand.

Livvie came back into the room just then. She had been down the hall. She looked at her parents, sitting there, holding on to each other. These two dear people, she thought to herself, who mean the world to me. A lump formed in her throat and tears pricked her eyes once more. She just stood quietly and watched the scene.

Her parents held on to each other silently, neither wanting to let go of the other. Carrie caressed George's big, rough hand lovingly. She brought it to her mouth and kissed it gently.

George glanced up and saw Livvie in the doorway. "Livvie," he called to her in a barely audible voice. She came immediately to his bedside.

"Yes, Dad?" She took his other hand, which he held out to her.

"You've made our life so happy. I'm so glad you came to us."

"I'm glad about that, too," she told him.

"Are you?" he asked. "Any regrets, the way things turned out for you?"

"No regrets," she said, and meant it.

"Your real father....I hope that you find him someday, if that would make you happy."

"I am happy, Dad," she sobbed. "You're my 'real father' and always have been. I don't know why I was always hoping to find someone else. Someone who didn't want me."

"Livvie, Livvie," he said gently, "it was only natural that you would wonder about him."

"Well, I don't need him anymore!" she exclaimed.

George closed his eyes and said, "I'm....so....tired...."

"We'll let you rest now, dear," Carrie said, standing up and pulling the blanket up over his chest. She and Livvie took the two chairs again and talked quietly.

"Where's Stan?"

"He went down to the lounge to read the paper."

Presently, a nurse came into the room and, after checking on her patient, she said, "Mr. Johnson is very low. I don't think he'll last much longer."

Carrie and Livvie both jumped up and went to the bed, one on each side.

Stan came in just then and saw the looks on their faces.

"What's happened?"

"The nurse just told us that he doesn't have long left," Livvie told her husband.

"I just saw Freddie come off the elevator so he'll be here shortly. He said he was going to try and talk to the doctor."

"Can you go out in the hall and see if you can find him? He needs to come in here right away!" exclaimed Livvie.

No sooner had she said that then her brother hurried in the room. "I got here as soon as I could," he explained, throwing off his coat and hat. He came close to the bed. Livvie moved over so he could get close. He took George's hand. There was no reaction.

"I think he's slipped into a semi-coma. The nurse said this may happen at the end," Carrie said. She started sobbing and so did Freddie. Stan put his arm around Livvie and drew her close.

They all stood, watching the beloved face of their husband and father. "Oh, I can't believe this is happening!" cried Carrie. "He was always so healthy until just lately."

"I know!" exclaimed Livvie. "I just thought he'd live forever, he was so strong and....and he was....my dad." She was crying, too, now.

The nurse came back in and stood at a respectful distance. "The doctor is coming in a few minutes," she announced.

A short while later, he came bursting into the room. After one look at George, he quickly read over his chart and then looked at the family. "I'm sorry. I think the end is near now."

Just then they heard a little gasp from the bed. George was taking his last breath. A little blood trickled from out of his mouth. Livvie gasped and looked on horrified. So this is what it was like to die, she thought.

Carrie moved close and took her husband's hand once more. She held it awhile and then tucked it by his side. She leaned over and kissed his cheek.

"Goodbye, my dear," she said as calmly as she could. "I'll be seeing you later. Only God knows when."

Livvie marveled at how calm her mother seemed. She's in shock, Livvie thought.

"He's with his Maker now," Carrie said.

CHAPTER 29

George Johnson was buried in the Gol Cemetery on the last day of September, 1957. The church had overflowed with friends and neighbors. So many people mourned the passing of such a good and fine man.

Both Carrie and Livvie held up well through the afternoon. They had done their crying the last several days. "My tears are all dried up, I think," Livvie had said.

She found, though, that in the next weeks to come, tears would come at unexpected times. She called her mother several times a day to see how she was doing. Carrie assured her that she was doing all right.

"God is certainly helping me through this. So many people have told me they are praying for me. I can feel it."

Livvie prayed fervently for that peace, too. One thing that she did finally have peace about was her long-standing desire to find her birth father. She no longer cared if she found him. This was a relief to be rid of this consuming passion. George had been her real father and she needed no other.

Freddie and Livvie were worried about having their mother live alone on the farm during the winter so they were trying to convince her to move to town.

"Ma, the house next to Lenora's folks' is vacant. Maybe you would want to move in there for the winter," Freddie said to her one evening when he had gone out to the farm.

"Well, I'll think about it. I really don't want to be stuck out here when we start getting a lot of snow." Freddie was relieved to hear that she felt the same way that he and Livvie did.

By mid-October, Carrie had made up her mind to move. Livvie and Lenora spent a couple days cleaning up the little house that had stood empty for over a year. Only what Carrie really needed was moved. She planned to move out to the farm again, come spring, she'd told her kids. That was OK with them, for now.

Carrie found that she rather liked living in town. She had company every day. Her friends would come over for coffee and her kids and grandkids came by often. It was Freddie and Livvie's secret wish, however, that she would like it so well, that she wouldn't move back to the farm in the spring. They thought the yard and garden were getting too much for their mother.

One afternoon in early November, Livvie was working out in the yard. It was an unusually warm day for that time of year. She was cleaning up the last of the dead vines in her garden where she had grown squash and pumpkins. She heard a car drive into the yard. She didn't recognize the vehicle and thought with some irritation that maybe it was a salesman of some sort. It stopped at the end of the sidewalk. Livvie started walking towards it.

A young man stepped out and straightened himself up before heading up the walk. Carrie hurried to intercept him before he reached the back door. "Hello," she called, getting his attention.

"Good afternoon," the young man said politely, removing his hat and waiting for her to catch up with him. He hesitated a bit before asking, "Are you Olivia Murphy?"

"Yes, I am," she answered, waiting for more.

"There's someone out in the car who would like to meet you." He said nothing further but motioned for her to follow him. Her curiosity was piqued by the time they reached the car. She saw an older man open the door and raise himself slowly and deliberately to a standing position.

He turned to her and stared for a few moments. "I'm Alphonse Kastet," he said simply. Livvie felt as if a fist had been slammed into her stomach. She became weak in the knees. Here, before her, stood the man whom she had been waiting to meet all these years and now she didn't know what to do or say.

"I....I....don't know what to say!" she exclaimed. She leaned on the car for support.

"I know this is a great shock to you and I must apologize for not letting you know we were coming."

Father and daughter merely stood and looked at each other. When Livvie finally remembered her manners, she said, "Well....ah....why don't we go into the house?"

"This is my son, Leo," said Alphonse, awkwardly.

The young man held out his hand to Livvie. They shook hands and then she led the way to the house. She was shaking so badly, she could hardly control her movements.

She offered them chairs by the kitchen table. "Here, I'll put the coffee on," she told them.

"Oh, don't go to any trouble for us," said Alphonse.

"It's no trouble," she replied, but, still shaking, she had trouble putting the coffee grounds into the basket. She spilled some on the counter and hoped they hadn't seen that.

With that task done, she joined them by the table. Alphonse said, "I can see, Olivia, that I have upset you terribly."

Her emotions flooded to the surface, and she found herself unable to hold back the tears. Tears of frustration, relief, uncertainty and many other feelings combined. She couldn't answer him. She didn't trust herself to speak.

"I will tell you about myself," he said kindly. "First, let me say that I am not proud of the way I treated you when you came up to Canada many years ago to see me. I want to explain." He was silent for a few moments. "My wife, Claudine, lay dying at the very time that you were there. She had cancer and she lasted only another month. I didn't want to upset her with....things from my past. And, to be truthful, I was so taken by surprise when I received your phone call that morning, that I didn't know what to do about it. But I did save the note that you had handed to my son that morning. I've had it hidden in the bottom of a drawer since then."

Livvie got up and got cups and put them on the table in front of her guests and then put the coffeepot and some cookies on the table. Again she sat down opposite the man who claimed to be her father.

"Some....things....have developed now that have prompted me to own up to my past," he continued. He paused to pour some coffee into his cup.

Livvie could see that his hands were shaking, too. *This cannot be easy for him, either.*

"You see, I was rather a....a wild, young man. I came from a large family and there wasn't enough work for all us boys so I came down to the States to find work on farms there. I worked on many throughout the state for several years." Looking at his son rather apologetically, he said, "I liked girls and gambling. There were always young, hired girls on these farms, and I guess I took advantage of many of them." He looked away, embarrassed.

"You mentioned Merrie Munseth. Your....real mother," he continued.

"Of course, I remember her. She had a real bad crush on me and I liked her, too. I had received word that my father was very ill so I took off for home without saying goodbye to her. I never saw her or heard from her again."

"Would you have....done things differently if you had known....about....me?" Livvie asked the question that had plagued her all these years. She was almost afraid to hear the answer.

He was silent for a long time. Finally he said, "Olivia, I can't lie to you. I would still have taken off and I wouldn't have come back. I wasn't the type of young man to own up to my responsibilities at that time. I'm not proud of that, but it is the truth of the matter."

Livvie didn't know what to say to this. Tears pricked her eyes once again.

"I'm sorry," he said, softly. He took out a handkerchief and blew his nose.

Leo rose and said that he was going out to have a look around the farm. When he had left, Livvie said, "You know, I've waited all these years to meet you and ask that question, and I guess I was hoping for an entirely different answer."

"I'm sorry to disappoint you....again." He looked down at his hands and they were both silent for awhile.

"Are you planning to go and see Merrie?" Livvie asked.

"I would like to talk to her, yes. I'd like to apologize to her. You see," he said, shifting in his chair, "I've just found out that I, too, have cancer. I don't have a lot of time left, so I want to make things right with as many people as I can."

"Oh!" exclaimed Livvie. "I'm sorry to hear that."

"Well, I just found out a couple months ago and I told my family about....you....and I said that I had to make this trip down here."

"This means a lot to me, to finally meet you. I had wanted this for so many years, and then when my....Dad....died a few months ago, I had decided that I didn't need you in my life. He had been my real father. And now you appear out of nowhere!" Livvie shook her head in disbelief.

"I maybe should have warned you that I was coming," he told her.

"Well, I didn't warn you, either, when I came up there to find you," said Livvie. "How long are you going to stay....around here?"

"Just a few days, perhaps."

"Where are you staying?"

"We thought we'd stay in a hotel in Fargo."

"Maybe you'd like to stay here," Livvie suggested before even thinking it through.

"Oh, no, I couldn't do that to your family," he protested.

"Well, maybe you should. I could call Merrie and have her come over here. That maybe would be easier for her."

Livvie finally convinced him that they should stay the night. She went to the phone and called Merrie, and told her to come over later. "You might want to come alone, though."

"Oh, no!" exclaimed Merrie when told the reason for the visit. "I don't know if I want to see him."

Livvie explained the circumstances and finally Merrie agreed to come over. Livvie wondered what Stan would think when he came home and found this particular stranger in their house.

She didn't have long to find out. Stan came in the yard to see a strange car and a young man walking around by the barn. It must be that John Deere salesman again, he thought at first. Then he noticed the Canadian license plates on the car. His heart skipped a beat. He went first to the young man and introduced himself.

"I'm Leo Kastet from Canada," the young man told him. That was all Stan needed to know. He headed for the house, Leo following behind.

He came barging in the back door, a little too noisily. He saw father and daughter sitting by the table. In that first instant, he was struck by how much they looked alike. *It's the eyes.*

Livvie and Alphonse both stood. "Stan, this is Alphonse Kastet. My father."

Stan extended his hand out to the older man. His grasp was firm but weak.

"How do you do?" said Stan, somewhat formally. He looked at Livvie to see how she was taking this unexpected meeting. She smiled lamely. He went to her side and put his arm around her shoulder.

Livvie started fixing supper as Stan went to pick up the kids from school.

"What will your children think of my being here?" asked Alphonse. "Do they know about me?"

"The two girls know the situation, but I haven't explained it yet to Bobbie. I thought he was too young yet. Maybe Stan will prepare him on the way home."

A short while later, the children came in the back door somewhat hesitantly. The girls were eyeing the stranger closely. Bobbie ducked around everyone and dashed up to his room.

"Bobbie, come back here!" commanded Stan.

"That's all right, Stan," said Livvie, "he can come down later. It will be hard for him to understand this."

"I guess you're right."

Livvie turned to her daughters, who were still standing near the kitchen door. "Girls, I want you to meet someone. This is Alphonse Kastet from Canada and his son Leo. He is my....father. And your grandfather."

Livvie had told the girls about the situation some years ago, never thinking that they'd be faced with meeting the man.

"How do you do?" said Cheryl, rather stiffly.

Linda just nodded her head in his direction.

"Well, let's all go into the living room," suggested Livvie. "Supper won't be ready for awhile yet."

They all filed into the next room and sat down on the sofa and chairs. Livvie knew this was going to be awkward and was wondering what to say when Alphonse took over and addressed the girls.

"I've been telling your mother about my past and I came here to apologize to her for not being a part of her life all these years. I, of course, didn't even know of her existence until she and your father made that trip up to Canada some years back."

Livvie could hear the stairs creaking and knew that Bobbie was sneaking down to listen. She went to the bottom of the stairway and motioned for him to come down. He ran to her and she pulled him close as they sat down on the sofa.

"Hello, young man," said Alphonse, looking toward the six-year-old. Bobbie looked up at his mother for direction.

"Bobbie, this is my....real father. I was adopted when I was a baby by the grandparents you know, George and Carrie, but my birth mother and father were this man and Merrie Munseth. You know her, of course, but I never explained to you why she was also your grandmother."

Bobbie looked confused and Livvie said, "You won't quite understand all this right now, Bobbie, but I'll try and explain it more later."

He seemed satisfied with this and leaned back and just watched the grownups.

"Tell us about your family up in Canada," said Stan.

"Well, I married a wonderful woman named Claudine and we had six children. Five boys and one girl. They're all married except Leo, here. He's the youngest. I have twelve grandchildren so far."

"And what did your family think when you told them about....me?" asked Livvie.

"They were surprised, of course, but accepted it pretty well. I haven't told my daughter yet. She lives in Toronto and I haven't seen her in awhile. She's planning to come for Christmas, though. She knows of my illness."

Shortly after they had eaten supper, Merrie came over. She came quietly in the back door and only Livvie was in the kitchen at the time. Merrie looked very hesitant.

"Maybe I should have Alphonse come in here and the two of you can talk alone for awhile. Would that be better?" she asked her mother, who nodded her head.

Livvie could tell that she was very nervous. She reached out and squeezed her hand. "It'll be all right. He's very nice."

The rest of the family stayed in the living room and gave Alphonse and Merrie time to come to terms with the situation in private. After awhile, Livvie went to join them.

Alphonse stood looking at his daughter and the woman who gave birth to her. Tears came to his eyes. He took both their hands in his. "All I can say is that I'm sorry for any pain that I caused either of you. Especially you, Merrie. I took advantage of you and then left you in a terrible situation. I knew your father and I'm sure it was very hard for you."

Merrie was too overcome with emotion to speak so she could only nod. Livvie held tightly onto her hand, fighting back tears herself.

"I only hope that my coming here will bring some peace to you as it will to me. I felt that I needed to do this before I....before I die."

Livvie broke down and sobbed. "I just lost my....my Dad.... And now I'm going to lose my father so soon after I find him!" Merrie put her arms around her daughter.

Alphonse looked at Merrie. "There's one good thing that came out of all this," he said, looking now at Livvie. "This wonderful young woman here. Olivia." He opened up his arms and Livvie fell into them. They stood there, father and daughter, for quite some time. Livvie got control of herself and stepped back.

"I....I'm glad you came," she told him simply.

Early the next morning, Livvie called Carrie. "Mom, I want you to come over this morning. I have something to....show you." She knew that if she told her who was there, she wouldn't come.

Stan took the kids to school and she made breakfast for her two Canadian guests, who had slept late.

"I'd like to do one more thing before I leave here," said Alphonse. "I'd like to take a drive over to the old Daud farm."

"Well, there isn't much left over there now." She told him how she and Stan had lived on that farm when they were first married and that the girls were born there.

"Is the big barn still standing?"

"No, that burned down some years ago. We sold the land when we moved here," she explained. "No one lives on the place. Many of the buildings were torn down. The big house is still standing, I believe. We actually lived in the foreman's house."

"Maybe we could go over there this morning," said Alphonse, "and then we will head back home after that."

"Do you have to leave this area so soon?" Livvie asked her father.

Leo spoke up. "Father is getting very tired, from the trip and all. I think it's best if we go back home soon. He doesn't feel well most of the time, you know."

"No, I suppose not. I'm sorry I didn't think of that." She looked at her father with concern.

"I called my....adopted mother this morning and asked her to come over here. I guess you knew her back when you worked on the Daud farm. Carrie Amundson was her name."

Livvie could see Alphonse stiffen up at the mention of her mother's name. "Carrie. Carrie Amundson. That's the woman who adopted you?"

"Yes, and I think I had told you that before, didn't I?"

"Well, if you did, it didn't register. Yes, I knew a Carrie Amundson at the farm and she had a brother who worked there. Amund was his name, I believe."

"Yes, that's my uncle. He lives over in Davenport now. He used to have the garage there."

"Oh, yes, I remember how he was always repairing things on the farm.

Quite a handy fellow. I won a few dollars off him in poker, too," laughed Alphonse.

Livvie cleared up the breakfast table while the men packed up their things. Carrie came driving into the yard and hurried up the porch steps.

"My goodness, what is it you have to show me, Livvie?" she asked as she let herself in.

"Well, Mom, prepare yourself. You better sit down. My real father, Alphonse Kastet has come to see me."

"What!" Carrie exclaimed in surprise. "Did he come here?"

"Yes, and he's still here. He and his son are upstairs. They stayed here last night."

"Oh, my!" She took a chair by the table. "How did that go, then?" Carrie looked around nervously. She wasn't excited to meet the man again, after all these years. She had never told Livvie about their relationship.

"It went fine," declared Livvie. "Merrie came over last night, too. He came down here to make amends and to meet me. He hasn't long left. He has cancer, he told us."

"Oh, no. That's too bad, Livvie."

Just then, the two men came back into the kitchen. Carrie stood and Livvie introduced them.

"Oh yes, I remember you very well, Carrie," said Alphonse, almost sheepishly.

Livvie told her mother that the two men wanted to go and take a look at the old farm. "Why don't you ride along with us?"

"Yes, do that," said Alphonse.

"Well, I guess I could."

They took two vehicles. Livvie and Carrie in one and the two men in their own car. Livvie led the way. Carrie was rather quiet during the short drive. Her thoughts went back so many years. It had rather rattled her to see this man after all these years. She hadn't seen him since the day when he had taken her out for a buggy ride and then had tried to 'compromise her'. He was fired the very next day and had left in a hurry.

"What are you thinking so hard about, Mom?" asked Livvie as they turned onto the road that would lead them to the farm.

"Oh, just about those days, so long ago, when I worked there," she told her daughter, evasively. Carrie didn't think that the episode between her and "Alphie," as he was called then, was something that her daughter needed to know.

The two cars pulled to a stop in the old farmyard. Everyone got out and surveyed the place in silence.

"So this is the big, bonanza farm of many years back, is it?" said Alphonse, finally. "It sure looks different now." He went on to tell his son about what a busy, bustling place it used to be. They began walking slowly in the direction of the site where the huge barn used to stand.

"There was even a railroad spur that brought in cars to pick up the grain that we harvested here."

"Imagine that!" said Leo, impressed.

Alphonse pointed out many things and he and Carrie began walking off on their own, reminiscing about this building or that. They stopped at the spot of the old garage where Amund used to do his repair work.

"Look, you can still see the foundation," said Carrie.

Alphonse turned and looked at her. "Carrie, while we have these few moments alone, I need to apologize for that afternoon, so long ago, when I tried to....to....take advantage of you. I'm sorry, and I'm glad that you put me off."

When Carrie didn't say anything, he went on. "I was a wild one in my youth. Sowing my wild oats here and there, and I'm not one bit proud of it. Will you forgive me?"

Carrie looked closely at the man standing across from her. She could see the handsome man that he used to be.

And those eyes! Those special eyes. Livvie's eyes.

"Yes, I'll forgive you, Alphie," she said, softly.

"Isn't it funny how it all turned out," he said. "I left a child back here that I didn't even know about and then she becomes your daughter." He shook his head back and forth. "If she hadn't come looking for me awhile back, I'd never have known about her, I suppose."

"She always had that on her mind. She was determined to find her real father."

"Well, I can see that she had very good parents in you and your husband. And I'm sorry to hear that he just passed away. I would liked to have met him."

"Yes, he was a wonderful man. He raised my son, Freddie, as if he was his own and then was a very good father to Livvie. He was a good husband, a very good husband," said Carrie, tears forming in her eyes. She told

Alphonse about her first marriage to Fred Shutz and how he had died and so had their youngest son, Joey.

"You've had a hard life, too, haven't you, Carrie?" he said gently.

"It's been a good life altogether, thanks be to God. But, yes, those first years were hard for awhile there. Until I met George."

"We've both been through a lot since we walked these paths here," he spread his arms to include the whole farm.

Livvie and Leo caught up with the pair and the four walked slowly back to their cars. They walked past the foreman's house, where Livvie and Stan had lived for a few years. Then they stood in front of the big house. It looked very dilapidated and forlorn now.

"Well, we must go now," Alphonse said. He opened his arms to Livvie once again and they held each other for a long time. Tears again pricked Carrie's eyes. She looked at Leo and he was brushing back some that had escaped and were running down his cheek.

Livvie was crying softly and was not ashamed of it. Alphonse, too, had tears in his old eyes. He took Carrie's hand and clasped it tightly. "Thank you for taking such good care of Olivia."

Carrie and Livvie stood and watched the car leave the yard, waving all the while. Tears flowed freely down Livvie's cheeks.

"I'll probably never see him again," she said.

"Are you glad that he came or would it have been better if he had stayed out of your life?"

"Well, I'll admit that his coming has been a bit upsetting, but I guess it's good to have finally met him. Now I can truly lay my search to rest."

After a pause, Livvie continued. "You know, it took a lot of courage for him to come here. That speaks well of him...." Her voice trailed off.

The two women got slowly into their car. As they were driving out of the driveway, Carrie turned and looked again at the big house. The porch was almost falling off the rest of the building. *I spent a lot of time on that porch. We had some good times out there. That's where Alphie came a courtin' a few times and the same with Fred.* She let out a sigh and seemed to slump down in her seat.

Livvie looked over at her mother. "What's the matter, Mom?"

"Oh, I was just thinking. That place back there is where my life in North Dakota got its start. I'm also wondering what the future holds for this old woman now."

"Mom, you aren't an old woman yet!" exclaimed Livvie. "You're still so young at heart."

Carrie laughed. "Yes, and I guess that's what counts."

Livvie saw her mother sit a little straighter in her seat.

"And I'll just trust in the Lord. He'll take care of me. He always has and He always will."

To order additional copies of
HOME FRONT
please complete the following.

$15.95 EACH
(plus $3.95 shipping & handling for first book,
add $2.00 for each additional book ordered.

Shipping and Handling costs for larger quantites
available upon request.

Please send me ______ additional books at $15.95 + shipping & handling

Bill my: ❏ VISA ❏ MasterCard Expires __________

Card # ____

Signature ____

Daytime Phone Number ________________________________

For credit card orders call 1-888-568-6329
TO ORDER ON-LINE VISIT: www.jmcompanies.com
OR SEND THIS ORDER FORM TO:
McCleery & Sons Publishing
PO Box 248
Gwinner, ND 58040-0248

I am enclosing $_____________ ❏ Check ❏ Money Order
Payable in US funds. No cash accepted.

SHIP TO:

Name ____

Mailing Address ____

City ____

State/Zip ____

Orders by check allow longer delivery time.
Money order and credit card orders will be shipped within 48 hours.
This offer is subject to change without notice.

New Releases

Home Front

Read the continuing story of Carrie Amundson, whose life in North Dakota began in *Bonanza Belle*. This is the story of her family, faced with the challenges, sacrifices and hardships of World War II. Everything changed after the Pearl Harbor attack, and ordinary folk all across America, on the home front, pitched in to help in the war effort. Even years after the war's end, the effects of it are still evident in many of the men and women who were called to serve their country.

Written by Elaine Ulness Swenson. (304 pgs.)
$15.95 each in a 6x8-1/4" paperback.

Seasons With Our Lord

Original seasonal and special event poems written from the heart. Feel the mood with the tranquil color photos facing each poem. A great coffee table book or gift idea.

Written by Cheryl Lebahn Hegvik. (68 pgs.)
$24.95 each in a 11x8-1/2 paperback.

Whispers in the Darkness

In this fast paced, well thought out mystery with a twist of romance, Betty Pearson comes to a slow paced, small town. Little did she know she was following a missing link - what the dilapidated former Beardsley Manor she was drawn to, held for her. With twists and turns, the Manor's secrets are unraveled.

Written by Shirlee Taylor. (88 pgs.)
$14.95 each in a 6x9" paperback.

Outward Anxiety - Inner Calm

Steve Crociata is known to many as the Optician to the Stars. He was diagnosed with a baffling form of cancer. The author has processed experiences in ways which uniquely benefit today's readers. We learn valuable lessons on how to cope with distress, how to marvel at God, and how to win at the game of life.

Written by Steve Crociata. (334 pgs.)
$19.95 each in a 6 x 9 paperback

Pycnogenol®

Pycnogenol® for Superior Health presents exciting new evidence about nature's most powerful antioxidant. Pycnogenol® improves your total health, reduces risk of many diseases, safeguards your arteries, veins and entire circulation system. It protects your skin - giving it a healthier, smoother younger glow. Pycnogenol® also boosts your immune system. Read about it's many other beneficial effects.

Written by Richard A. Passwater, Ph.D. (122 pgs.)
$5.95 each in a 4-1/8 x 6-7/8" paperback.

Remembering Louis L'Amour

Reese Hawkins was a close friend of Louis L'Amour, one of the fastest selling writers of all time. Now Hawkins shares this friendship with L'Amour's legion of fans. Sit with Reese in L'Amour's study where characters were born and stories came to life. Travel with Louis and Reese in the 16 photo pages in this memoir. Learn about L'Amour's lifelong quest for knowledge and his philosophy of life.
Written by Reese Hawkins and his daughter Meredith Hawkins Wallin. (178 pgs.) $16.95 each in a 5-1/2x8" paperback.

Pay Dirt

An absorbing story reveals how a man with the courage to follow his dream found both gold and unexpected adventure and adversity in Interior Alaska, while learning that human nature can be the most unpredictable of all.
Written by Otis Hahn & Alice Vollmar. (168 pgs.)
$15.95 each in a 6x9" paperback.

Spirits of Canyon Creek *Sequel to "Pay Dirt"*

Hahn has a rich stash of true stories about his gold mining experiences. This is a continued successful collaboration of battles on floodwaters, facing bears and the discovery of gold in the Yukon.
Written by Otis Hahn & Alice Vollmar. (138 pgs.)
$15.95 each in a 6x9" paperback.

First The Dream

This story spans ninety years of Anna's life. She finds love, loses it, and finds it once again. A secret that Anna has kept is fully revealed at the end of her life.
Written by Elaine Ulness Swenson.
(326 pgs.)
$15.95 each in a 6x8-1/4" paperback

Bonanza Belle

In 1908, Carrie Amundson left her home to become employed on a bonanza farm. One tragedy after the other befell her and altered her life considerably and she found herself back on the farm.
Written by Elaine Ulness Swenson.
(344 pgs.)
$15.95 each in a 6x8-1/4" paperback.

Dr. Val Farmer's **Honey, I Shrunk The Farm**
The first volume in a three part series of Rural Stress Survival Guides discusses the following in seven chapters: Farm Economics; Understanding The Farm Crisis; How To Cope With Hard Times; Families Going Through It Together; Dealing With Debt; Going For Help, Helping Others and Transitions Out of Farming.
Written by Val Farmer. (208 pgs.)
$16.95 each in a 6x9" paperback.

Country-fied
Stories with a sense of humor and love for country and small town people who, like the author, grew up country-fied . . . Country-fied people grow up with a unique awareness of their dependence on the land. They live their lives with dignity, hard work, determination and the ability to laugh at themselves.
Written by Elaine Babcock. (184 pgs.)
$14.95 each in a 6x9" paperback.

Charlie's Gold and Other Frontier Tales
Kamron's first collection of short stories gives you adventure tales about men and women of the west, made up of cowboys, Indians, and settlers.
Written by Kent Kamron. (174 pgs.)
$15.95 each in a 6x9" paperback.

A Time For Justice
This second collection of Kamron's short stories takes off where the first volume left off, satisfying the reader's hunger for more tales of the wide prairie.
Written by Kent Kamron. (182 pgs.)
$16.95 each in a 6x9" paperback.

It Really Happened Here!
Relive the days of farm-to-farm salesmen and hucksters, of ghost ships and locust plagues when you read Ethelyn Pearson's collection of strange but true tales. It captures the spirit of our ancestors in short, easy to read, colorful accounts that will have you yearning for more.
Written by Ethelyn Pearson. (168 pgs.)
$24.95 each in an 8-1/2x11" paperback.

(Add $3.95 shipping & handling for first book, add $2.00 for each additional book ordered.)

Prayers For Parker Cookbook
Parker Sebens is a 3 year old boy from Milnor, ND, who lost both of his arms in a tragic farm accident on September 18, 2000. He has undergone many surgeries to reattach his arms, but because his arms were damaged so extensively and the infection so fierce, they were unable to save his hands. Parker will face many more surgeries in his future, plus be fitted for protheses.
This 112 pg. cookbook is a project of the Country Friends Homemakers Club from Parker's community. All profits from the sale of this book will go to the Parker Sebens' Benefit Fund, a fund set up to help with medical-related expenses due to Parker's accident. $8.00 ea. in a 5-1/4"x8-1'4" spiral bound book.

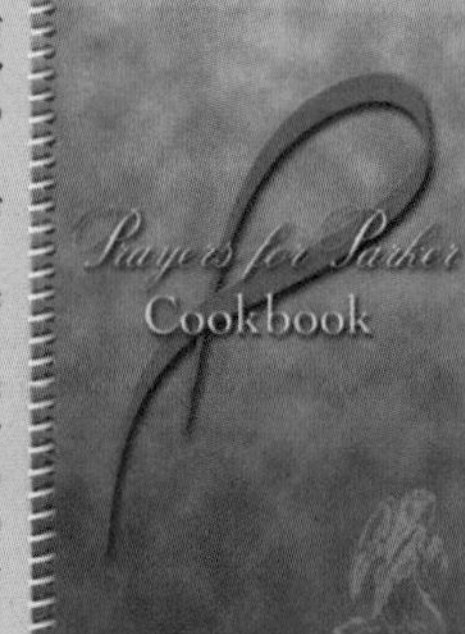